THE MAN WITHOUT QUALITIES

VOLUME II

THE LIKE OF IT NOW HAPPENS (II)

ROBERT MUSIL

*Translated from the German
by Eithne Wilkins and Ernst Kaiser*

Minerva

A Minerva Paperback
THE MAN WITHOUT QUALITIES VOLUME II

First published in Great Britain 1954
by Secker & Warburg Limited
This Minerva edition published 1995
by Mandarin Paperbacks
an imprint of Reed Books Ltd
Michelin House, 81 Fulham Road, London SW3 6RB
and Auckland, Melbourne, Singapore and Toronto

Copyright
All rights reserved

A CIP catalogue record for this title
is available from the British Library
ISBN 0 7493 9583 4

Printed and bound in Great Britain
by Cox & Wyman, Reading

CONTENTS

PAGE

SECOND BOOK

THE LIKE OF IT NOW HAPPENS (II)

73 Leo Fischel's daughter Gerda.   3

74 The fourth century B.C. versus the year 1797. Ulrich once again receives a letter from his father.   13

75 General Stumm von Bordwehr regards visiting Diotima as a pleasant change from the usual run of his official duties.   18

76 Count Leinsdorf shows some reserve.   21

77 Arnheim as the darling of the journalists.   24

78 Diotima's transformation.   28

79 Soliman in love.   37

80 Closer acquaintance with General Stumm, who surprisingly appears at a meeting of the Council.   43

81 Count Leinsdorf makes some comments on practical politics. Ulrich founds Associations.   51

82 Clarisse demands an Ulrich Year.   57

83 The like of it happens, or, Why does one not invent history?   65

84 The assertion that even ordinary life is of a Utopian nature.   72

85 General Stumm's endeavour to get the civilian mind into proper order.   80

86 The King of Commerce and the fusion of interests between Soul and Business, also : All roads to the mind start from the soul, but none leads back again.   93

87 Moosbrugger dances.   110

88 On association with Great Things.   115

89 One must move with the times.   118

90 The dethroning of the ideocracy.   126

91 Bulls and bears on the market of the mind.   130

PAGE

92 Excerpts from rich people's code of living.   141

93 Even by way of physical culture the civilian mind is hard to tackle.   144

94 Diotima's nights.   146

95 The Superman of Letters : Back View.   153

96 The Superman of Letters : Front View.   158

97 Clarisse's mysterious powers and missions.   161

98 Concerning a State that perished for want of a name.   174

99 Of demi-intelligence and its fruitful complement. Also of the likeness between two epochs, of Aunt Jane's lovable nature, and the pernicious nonsense known as the New Age.   184

100 General Stumm invades the State Library and gathers some experience with regard to librarians, library attendants, and intellectual order.   191

101 The hostile relatives.   198

102 Love and strife in the Fischel family.   214

103 The temptation.   226

104 Rachel and Soliman on the war-path.   237

105 Being sublime lovers is no joke.   244

106 Does modern man believe in God or in the head of the world concern ? Arnheim's lack of resolution.   249

107 Count Leinsdorf achieves an unexpected political success.   257

108 The 'unredeemed' nationalities and General Stumm's thoughts about the semantic complex 'redemption'.   264

109 Bonadea, Kakania, systems of happiness and equipoise.   270

110 Moosbrugger's dissolution and preservation.   280

111 So far as jurists are concerned, there are no semi-insane people.   285

112 Arnheim sets his father Samuel among the gods and forms the resolution to secure Ulrich for himself. Soliman wants to learn more about his royal father.   292

113 Ulrich converses with Hans Sepp and Gerda in the pidgin-language of the frontier district between the super-rational and the sub-rational.   305

PAGE

114 The state of affairs gradually becomes critical. Arnheim
    is very gracious to General Stumm. Diotima prepares
    to sally forth into the Illimitable. Ulrich indulges in
    fanciful talk about the possibility of living in the same
    way as one reads.   323

115 The tip of your breast is like a poppy-leaf.   339

116 The two trees of life and the demand for a General
    Secretariat for Precision and the Spirit.   348

117 Rachel's fateful day.   371

118 Well then, go and kill him !   377

119 A counter-mine and a seduction.   391

120 The Collateral Campaign causes uproar.   403

121 Talking man to man.   415

122 The way home.   432

123 The turning-point.   441

SECOND BOOK

THE LIKE OF IT NOW HAPPENS (II)

73 *Leo Fischel's daughter Gerda.*

IN all this hustle and bustle it was long before Ulrich found time
to keep the promise he had given Director Fischel and visit him
and his family. Indeed, to put it precisely, he did not find the
time at all until something unexpected happened : this was a visit
from Fischel's wife Klementine.

She had announced her coming by telephone, and Ulrich was
looking forward to the event not without uneasiness. He had last
frequented her house three years ago while spending some months
in this city. Since his return however he had been there only
once, because he did not want to revive a past flirtation and was
afraid of Frau Klementine's maternal disappointment. But
Klementine Fischel was a woman with ' a great heart ', and in her
daily skirmishes with her husband Leo she had so little opportunity
of making use of it that she had at her disposal a positively heroic
pitch of emotion for special occasions, which unfortunately seldom occurred. All the same, this thin woman with the severe,
somewhat care-worn face was a little embarrassed when she found
herself face to face with Ulrich and asked if she might speak to
him alone, although indeed they were alone already. The fact
was, she said, he was the only person to whose opinion Gerda
would still pay any attention, and—she added—she hoped he
would not misunderstand her request.

Ulrich knew how things stood in the Fischel family. Not only
were the father and mother constantly at war with each other but,
to make matters worse, Gerda, their twenty-three-year-old
daughter, had surrounded herself with a swarm of peculiar young
men who made Papa Leo, very much against his will and gritting
his teeth, the Maecenas and patron of their ' new spirit ', since
there was nowhere where one could meet so conveniently as at his
house.

3

Gerda was so irritable and anæmic and got so frightfully worked up the moment one tried to cut down these social gatherings (Frau Klementine recounted), and of course they were only silly boys without any manners, but still, the mystical antisemitism they studiously displayed was not merely tactless, it also indicated a lack of all decent feeling. No, no (she added), she had not come to complain about antisemitism. It was a sign of the times, and one simply had to resign oneself to it. One might even admit that in some ways there might be something in it. Klementine paused and would have wiped away a tear with her handkerchief had she not been wearing a veil; but as it was, she refrained from shedding the tear and contented herself with having taken her little white handkerchief out of her little bag.

" You know what Gerda is like," she said. " A pretty girl, and so gifted, but—"

" A bit vehement," Ulrich helped her out.

" Ah dear, yes, heaven knows—always extreme."

" And so she's still as Germanically inclined as ever ? "

Klementine now spoke of parents' feelings. ' A mother's pilgrimage ' was what she rather melodramatically called her visit, which had the incidental object of persuading Ulrich to take an interest in her family, since he had, as everyone said, been such a success in the Collateral Campaign. " I can't blame myself enough," she went on, " for having encouraged these goings-on in recent years against Leo's wishes. I didn't see anything wrong in it. These young men are idealists according to their lights. And if one is broad-minded, one must be able to put up with a remark now and then that hurts one's feelings. But Leo—well, you know what he is like—he gets worked up about antisemitism, no matter whether it's merely mystical and symbolic or not."

" And in her free, fair-haired Germanic way Gerda refuses to see the problem ? " Ulrich supplied what was missing.

" About such things she's just the way I was myself when I was a girl. By the way, do you think Hans Sepp has a future ahead of him ? "

" Is Gerda engaged to him ? " Ulrich asked warily.

" The boy hasn't the slightest prospect of being able to keep a wife ! " Klementine sighed. " So how can there be any thought of an engagement ? But when Leo forbade him the house, for three weeks Gerda ate so little that she was nothing but skin and bone." And suddenly she said angrily : " You know, it seems to me like a sort of hypnotism, like a mental infection ! Really, sometimes I almost think Gerda's hypnotised ! The boy is always expounding his views in our house, and Gerda doesn't notice the continual insult to her parents in it all, though otherwise she's always been a good, affectionate child. But if I say anything to her, the answer she gives me is : ' You're old-fashioned, Mamma.' So I thought—you're the only person she thinks anything of, and Leo thinks so highly of you !—couldn't you come and see us some time soon and open Gerda's eyes a little to how callow Hans and his cronies are ? "

As Klementine was generally very correct and this was a *coup d'état*, it was obvious that she must be very gravely worried. In spite of all their quarrels, in this matter she felt herself placed in something like a position of solidarity and joint responsibility with her husband.

Ulrich raised his eyebrows with an expression of concern. " I'm afraid Gerda will say that I'm old-fashioned too. These young people nowadays don't pay any attention to us older ones, and these are questions of principle."

" I did think," Klementine hinted, " perhaps the best way of distracting Gerda would be if you could find something for her to do in this great Campaign there's so much talk about."

Ulrich hastily thought it best to agree to pay a visit, assuring her, however, that it would be a long time before the Collateral Campaign was ripe for any such purpose.

When Gerda saw him come in a few days later, round red patches appeared on her cheeks ; but she gave him a hearty hand-shake. She was one of those modern girls, so delightfully sure of what they wanted, who would become bus conductors on the spot if some cause required it.

Ulrich had not been mistaken in his assumption that he would find her alone. Mamma was out shopping at this hour, and Papa was still at the office. And Ulrich had scarcely taken the first steps into the room when everything came back to him exactly as it had been one day when they had been together before. True, the year had then been some weeks further advanced : it had been spring, but one of those scorchingly hot days that sometimes come floating on ahead of summer, like flakes of fire, and are so difficult for people's not yet hardened bodies to endure. Gerda's face had looked thin and drawn. She had been dressed in white and smelt white like linen laid out to dry on the grass. The blinds had been let down in all the rooms, and the whole apartment had been full of wayward half-light and arrows of heat that slid, broken-tipped, between the sack-grey slats. Ulrich had had the feeling that Gerda consisted through and through of freshly washed linen covers the same as her dress. It had been an entirely objective feeling, and he could have lifted one after the other of these covers off her, calmly, without the least need of any amorous impulse. And this was exactly the feeling that came to him again now. It was an apparently quite natural but pointless intimacy, and they were both afraid of it.

" Why haven't you been to see us for so long ? " Gerda asked. Ulrich told her frankly he had had the impression that her parents did not wish them to be on such intimate terms without marriage in view.

" Oh, Mamma ! " Gerda said. " Mamma is ridiculous. Can't we be friends without people going and thinking of *that* ! But Papa would like you to come more often. So you have become quite important in this big affair ? "

She came out with all this quite openly, exposing the old people's silliness, convinced as she was of the natural alliance uniting the two of them against it.

" I shall come," Ulrich answered. " But now tell me, Gerda, where is it going to lead us ? "

The fact was that they did not love each other. In the old days they had often played tennis together or met at parties, had gone about together, had taken an interest in each other, and in this way had imperceptibly crossed the border-line that exists between oneself and all the people in front of whom one keeps up appearances, and had entered the territory of intimacy where one reveals oneself to the other person in all one's emotional disorder. All at once they found they had become as intimate as two people who have been in love for a long time, who are indeed almost out of love with each other again, only with the difference that *they* had saved themselves the trouble of being in love at all. They wrangled so much that it might have been thought they thoroughly disliked each other ; but that was at once an obstacle and a bond. They knew that there was only a little spark needed to set the whole thing ablaze. If there had been less difference in age between them, or if Gerda had been a married woman, opportunity would (as the saying goes) probably have made the thief, and the theft would, at any rate retrospectively, have produced a real passion ; for people talk themselves into love as they do into anger, by going through the motions. But just because they knew this, they refrained. Gerda remained an innocent girl and was furiously annoyed about it.

Instead of answering Ulrich's question she busied herself with various little jobs about the room, and suddenly there he was standing beside her. It was extremely rash, for one cannot stand next to a girl at such a moment and simply begin talking about something or other. They took the path of least resistance, like a brook that, avoiding obstacles, flows on down a meadow. Ulrich put his arm round Gerda's hips, his fingers just reaching to the line that dips down, following the inner suspender. He turned her face towards him ; it looked bewildered and sweaty. He kissed her on the lips. There they stood then, unable to let each other go or to come closer together. His finger-tips came up against the broad elastic band of her stocking-suspender and flicked it softly once or twice against her thigh. Then he suddenly let go of her and, with a shrug of his shoulders, repeated his question : " Where is this going to lead us, Gerda ? "

Gerda fought down her agitation and said : " Has it got to be like this ? "

She rang and gave orders for something to drink to be brought in ; she set the house in motion.

" Tell me something about Hans," Ulrich begged her gently, when they were sitting down and had to begin to talk about something else.

Gerda, who had not quite regained her composure, did not answer at once. But after a while she said : " You're so conceited. You'll never understand us younger ones ! "

" You can't put me off like that," Ulrich retorted. " You know, Gerda, I think I'm going to give up science. So I shall be going over to the younger generation. Will it satisfy you if I solemnly declare that knowledge is akin to avarice, is only the expression of a sordid collecting instinct, is an overweening capitalism of the inner life ? There is more feeling in me than you think. But I should like to save you from all the phrase-making that is nothing but words ! "

" You must get to know Hans better," Gerda answered limply. But then she suddenly added with vehemence : " All the same, you'll never understand that a person can merge into a community with others, entirely without selfishness ! "

" Does Hans still come to see you as often as he used to ? " Ulrich persisted, though warily.

Gerda shrugged her shoulders.

Her parents had been shrewd enough not to forbid Hans Sepp the house, but to grant him several days each month. In return Hans Sepp, the student, who was nothing and as yet had no prospects of becoming anything, had to give them his word that he would in future not tempt Gerda into anything wrong and would cease his propaganda for German mystical ' action '. In this way they hoped to deprive him of the magical aura of something forbidden. And Hans Sepp in his chastity (for only sensuality craves possession, and is of course a Jewish-capitalistic characteristic) had quietly given his word as required, whereby however he meant that he would refrain not from often coming to the house secretly, or from glowing speeches, ecstatic pressing of hands, or even kisses, all of which was part of the natural life of souls bound together in friendship, but merely from the theoretical propaganda that he hitherto carried on for a union not sanctified by any priest nor legalised by the State. He had given his word all the more readily since he did not consider that either he or Gerda had reached the spiritual maturity necessary for the realisation of his principles, and a safeguard against the promptings of lower nature suited him very well.

But the two young people naturally suffered under this compulsion, which imposed a limitation from outside even before they had found their own inner limit. Gerda in particular would not have put up with this intervention on her parents' part had she not been unsure of herself ; but she felt it all the more bitterly for that. She was actually not very much in love with her young friend ; it was rather that she transformed her opposition to her parents into attachment to him. If Gerda had been born some

years later, her papa would by then have been one of the richest
men in town, even if for that very reason not a particularly
respected one, and her mother would again have admired him
before Gerda had been able to reach the stage of feeling the feuds
between her parents as a conflict in herself. She would then
probably have been proud to think of herself as being of mixed
descent. But in the situation as it was in reality she rebelled
against her parents and their problems in life, refused to knuckle
under to such a heredity, and was as fair, free, Germanic, and
vigorous as if she had nothing to do with them. This was all very
well, but it had the disadvantage that she had never managed to
get the worm that consumed her out into the light. In her
domestic environment the fact that there were such things as
nationalism and an ideology of ' race ' was completely ignored,
although these things actually held half Europe entangled in
hysterical ideas and nowhere did everything revolve around them
more intensely than under the Fischel roof. All that Gerda knew
about them had come to her from outside, in the obscure form of
rumour, hints and exaggerations. The contradiction embodied in
the fact that her parents, although they were generally strongly
impressed by everything that was said by many people, in this
case made a peculiar exception, had early imprinted itself on her
mind ; and because she could not discover any definite and sober
meaning in this spectral problem she connected it, particularly in
her early adolescence, with everything she felt to be disagreeable
and sinister in her parents' house.

One day she got to know the Christiano-Germanic circle of
young people to which Hans Sepp belonged, and all at once felt
she had found her true home. It would be hard to say what these
young people believed in ; they formed one of those countless
little undefined free spiritual sects with which German youth has
swarmed since the decay of the humanist ideal. They were not
racial antisemites, but opponents of ' the Jewish outlook ', by
which they meant capitalism and socialism, science, rationalism,
parental authority and parental overbearingness, and all forms of
calculation, psychology, and scepticism. Their fundamental
axiom was the ' symbol '. So far as Ulrich could follow—and he
had, after all, some understanding of such things—what they
meant by symbols was the great manifestations of the grace by

which all that was tangled and dwarfish in life, as Hans Sepp put it, became clear and grand, overcoming the uproar of the senses and bathing the brow in the rivers of Other-Worldliness. In this way they spoke of the Isenheim Altar-piece, the Egyptian Pyramids, and the poet Novalis. Beethoven and Stefan George they tolerated as intimations. And what a symbol was, expressed in sober words, they did not say, first because symbols cannot be expressed in sober words, secondly because Aryans must not be sober, which is why in the last hundred years they have succeeded only in producing intimations of symbols, and thirdly because there are centuries that only sparsely produce the ineffable and solitary moment of grace in the man who dwells in inner solitude.

Gerda, who was a sensible girl, secretly felt no little mistrust of these wild views ; but she also mistrusted this mistrust, in which she thought she recognised an inheritance of her parents' common-sense attitude. However independent she pretended to be, she had to make frantic efforts not to obey her parents, and suffered from anxiety lest her origin might prevent her from following Hans's ideas. In her heart of hearts she revolted against the taboos set up by the morality of the so-called respectable family, the overbearing and suffocating way that parental authority extended to her own personality, whereas Hans, who came of ' no family at all ', as her mother was accustomed to put it, suffered far less. He had emerged from the circle of his cronies as Gerda's ' spiritual guide ', talked fervently with this girl who was the same age as himself, and tried to transport her into the ' realm of the unconditional ' by means of grandiose expositions accompanied by kisses ; but in practice he adapted himself quite skilfully to the conditions of the Fischel household, so long as he was allowed to reject it all ' as a matter of principle ', which did, of course, lead to continual rows with Papa Fischel.

"Darling Gerda," Ulrich said after a while, "your friends torment you because of your father. They're the most frightful blackmailers I know ! "

Gerda turned pale and then flushed. " You aren't a young man any more yourself," she retorted. " You think differently from the way we do ! " She knew that she had pricked Ulrich's vanity, and added conciliatingly : " I don't think love is anything so very marvellous. I may be wasting my time with Hans, as you say.

Perhaps I shall just have to go without altogether and never be so fond of anyone that I can open my whole soul to him in thinking and feeling, working and dreaming. And I don't even think that would be anything so very terrible, either ! "

" You sound so awfully grown-up, Gerda, when you talk like your friends ! " Ulrich interrupted her.

Gerda became vehement. " When I talk *to* my friends," she exclaimed, " the thoughts go from one to the other, and we know that we live and talk among our own people—do you understand that in the least ? We stand among countless kindred spirits and feel their presence. That is psycho-physical in a way that you definitely—oh, in a way you *definitely* can't even imagine. Because you have always only desired *one* human being. You think like a beast of prey ! "

Why like a beast of prey ? The phrase hung in mid-air, giving her away ; she herself realised how senseless it was, and she was ashamed of her eyes, which were fixed on Ulrich, wide with distress.

" I won't answer that," Ulrich said mildly. " To change the subject, I'll tell you a story instead. Do you know "—and with his hand, in which her wrist disappeared like a child among mountain-crags, he drew her nearer to him—" the exciting story of how the moon was captured ? You know, I suppose, that the earth once had several moons ? And there is a theory, which has many adherents, according to which such moons are not what we think they are—celestial bodies that have cooled down, like the earth itself—but large balls of ice rushing through space, which have come too close to the earth and are held fast by it. Our moon is supposed to be the last of them. Just come and have a look at it ! "

Gerda followed him and searched the sunny sky for the pallid moon.

" Doesn't it look like a disc of ice ? " Ulrich asked. " That isn't what we mean by light ! Have you ever wondered how it comes about that the man in the moon always turns the same way towards us ? The fact is, this last moon of ours doesn't turn any more, it's firmly captured ! You see, once the moon has got into the earth's power, it doesn't only revolve around the earth, but is drawn steadily closer and closer to it. The only reason we don't notice this is that this drawing closer is spread over hundreds of thousands of years or even longer. But there's no getting away from it, and in the history of the earth there must have been epochs, lasting thousands of years, when the moons before this one had been drawn quite close to the earth and went tearing round it at an incredible speed. And just as in our own time the moon pulls after itself a tide varying from three to six feet in height, so then it dragged after it a mountain of water and mud as high as a mountain-range, racing and staggering round the earth. One can't really quite imagine the terror in which generation after generation must have lived on the lunatic earth in those ages. . . ."

" So there were human beings on earth then ? " Gerda asked.

" Yes, indeed. You see, in the end an ice-moon like that breaks up and comes pattering down. And the tide that it has piled up as high as a mountain in its course collapses and closes over the whole globe in one immense wave before it settles down again. And that is nothing more or less than what we call the Flood, a great universal inundation ! How could all the traditional stories agree so exactly if mankind hadn't really experienced it ? And since we still have a moon, such an age will come again some time. It's a queer thought . . ."

Gerda was gazing through the window at the moon, breathless. Her hand still lay in his, and the moon lay in the sky, a pale, ugly patch, and it was precisely this unobtrusiveness that lent a plain, everyday truthfulness to the fantastic cosmic adventure, of which she saw herself, through some association of feeling, as the victim.

" But this whole story simply isn't true," Ulrich said. " The experts say it is a crank theory, and in reality the moon isn't coming closer to the earth at all, but is actually thirty-two kilometres further away from it than it ought to be according to calculations—if I remember rightly."

" Then why did you tell me the story at all ? " Gerda asked, trying to pull her hand out of his. But all the force had gone out of her resentment. It was always the same with her when she talked to a man who was certainly not less intelligent than Hans, but who did not hold wild views and who had well-kept fingernails and tidy hair.

Ulrich gazed at the delicate black down that grew out of Gerda's fair skin as though in a spirit of contradiction. The manifold composite nature of poor modern man seemed to sprout out of this body with these little hairs.

" I don't know," he replied. " Shall I come again ? "

Gerda let her liberated hand work off its excitement on various small objects, shifting them to and fro, and did not answer.

" Well then, so I'll come again soon," Ulrich promised, although that had not been his intention before this reunion.

74 *The fourth century B.C. versus the year 1797. Ulrich once again receives a letter from his father.*

THE rumour had very soon got about that the gatherings at Diotima's were an extraordinary success. During this time Ulrich received an unusually long letter from his father, enclosing a thick file of pamphlets and off-prints. The gist of the letter was :

" My dear son, your lengthy silence . . . It was nevertheless a pleasure to me to hear, from a third party, that my efforts on your behalf . . . my well-intentioned friend Count Stallburg . . . His Highness Count Leinsdorf . . . Our relative, the wife of Permanent Secretary Tuzzi . . . The matter for which I must now ask you to exert all your influence in your new circle is the following.

" The world would fly to pieces if everything that is taken to be true were allowed to pass as such, and if every intention that to itself seems permissible were indeed permitted. It is therefore the duty of us all to establish the one truth and the right intention and, in so far as we succeed in this, with an unflinching sense of duty to keep vigil and see that it be recorded in the clear form of scientific statement. From this you may gather what it indicates when I inform you that in lay circles, but unfortunately to a considerable extent also in learned circles, which have fallen a prey to the promptings of a confused age, there has for some time been an extremely dangerous movement on foot to bring about certain supposed reforms and alleviations on the occasion of the revision of our penal code. I must say by way of preliminary that for some years now a committee convoked by the Minister and composed of experts of repute has been in existence for the purpose of drawing up this revised code. Of this committee I have the honour to be a member, as likewise has my university colleague Professor Schwung, whom you may remember from earlier times when I had not yet fathomed his character, so that for many years he managed to pass as my best friend. Now regarding the alleviations of which I have spoken, I have meanwhile learned by way of rumour—what is, however, I regret to say, in fact only too probable—that in the approaching jubilee year in honour of our revered and benevolent Sovereign, that is to say, as it were by means of exploiting all the feelings of magnanimity that will prevail, particular exertions must be expected to be made in the hope of paving the way for this ill-omened enfeeblement of our juridical system. It goes without saying that Professor Schwung and I are equally firmly resolved to forestall this.

" Bearing in mind as I do that you are not versed in juristic matters, I nevertheless assume that you will be aware that what constitutes the most favoured point of infiltration for this tendency towards a state of juridical insecurity, falsely calling itself humanitarianism, is the endeavour to extend the concept of unsoundness of mind disqualifying a person for punishment, by adding an ill-defined concept of diminished responsibility, so making it cover those numerous individuals who are neither insane nor morally normal and who constitute the army of those inferior persons, moral imbeciles, that unfortunately pollutes our civilisation to an ever-increasing degree. You will see for yourself that this concept of diminished responsibility—if it can be called a concept at all, which I personally deny !—must be very closely connected with the interpretation we put upon notions of complete responsibility, or irresponsibility as the case may be, and I herewith come to the real object of my communication.

" Proceeding from already existing formulations of the law, and in view of the circumstances to which I have alluded, I have proposed, in the committee of investigation mentioned above, that the relevant paragraph 318 of the future penal code should be given the following form :

" ' No criminal act has been committed if the offender was at the time of committing the act in a state of unconsciousness or of morbid disturbance of mental activity such that '—and Professor Schwung put forward a proposal that began with precisely the same words. His, however, then continued with the words : ' he was deprived of his free will ', while mine was to be formulated as follows : ' he did not possess the capacity to recognise the wrongness of his action '. I must confess that at first I myself did not notice the malicious intention in his disagreement with me. I personally have always held the view that with progressive development of intellect and reason the will subjects the desires, or the instincts, to itself, doing so in the form of considered thought and the decision resulting from it. An act that is willed is therefore always one that is associated with thinking, and not an instinctive act. Man is free in so far as he has the power of choice in the exercise of his will ; if he has human cravings, that is to say, cravings that correspond to the sensual side of his nature, in other words, if his thinking is interfered with, he is unfree. Volition is in fact not something accidental, but an act of self-determination necessarily arising out of our ego. Hence the will is determined in the process of thinking, and when thinking is interfered with, the will is then no longer will, but man acts only according to the nature of his cravings ! I am, however, of course aware that in the literature of the subject the opposite view is also upheld, according to which thinking is supposed to be determined in the process of volition. This is a school of thought that admittedly has found adherents among modern jurists only since 1797, whereas that adopted by me has stood up to all attacks since the fourth century B.C. However, I wished to show my readiness to be conciliatory and therefore put forward a formulation uniting both proposals, which would then have read as follows :

" ' No criminal act has been committed if the offender was at the time of committing the act in a state of unconsciousness or of morbid disturbance of mental activity such that he did not possess the capacity to recognise the wrongness of his act and was deprived of his free will.'

" But now Professor Schwung revealed himself in his true colours ! Disregarding my conciliatory attitude, he made the preposterous assertion that the ' and ' in this sentence must be replaced by an ' or '. You perceive the intention. For it is this that differentiates the thinker from the layman, namely, that he distinguishes an ' or ' where the layman simply puts an ' and ', and Schwung was attempting to convict me of superficial thinking, by exposing my readiness to arrive at a compromise, expressed in the ' and ', which was intended to unite both formulations in one, to the suspicion that I had failed to apprehend, in all its implications, the full magnitude of the difference to be bridged !

" It goes without saying that from this moment on I was his unswerving opponent.

" I withdrew my mediatory proposal, feeling compelled to insist on my first formulation's being accepted, without amendment. Since then, however, Schwung has been striving, with perfidious subtlety, to make difficulties for me. He objects, for instance, that according to my proposal, which is based on the capacity to recognise the wrongness of an act, a person who suffers, as does occur, from delusions of a particular nature, and who is otherwise sane, could be acquitted on grounds of mental defect only if it could be proved that in consequence of his particular delusions he assumed the existence of circumstances that would justify his act or cancel out the punishable nature of it, so that he had after all behaved correctly in an imagined, even though wrongly imagined, world. This is however an utterly futile objection, for even though empirical logic recognises the existence of persons who are partly insane and partly sane, the logic of the law must never admit a combination of two juridical states ; in the logic of the law persons are either responsible for their actions or they are not so, and we may assume that even in persons who suffer from delusions of a particular nature the capacity to distinguish right from wrong is in general maintained. If it is blurred in a particular case as a result of delusions, all that is necessary is a particular exertion of the intelligence in order to bring it into harmony with the rest of the personality, and there is not the slightest reason to see any particular difficulty in this.

" Hence I immediately replied to Professor Schwung's argument by saying that if the state of being responsible for the actions and the state of not being responsible for the actions cannot logically exist at one and the same time, it must be assumed of such individuals that these states follow upon each other in rapid alternation, from which—and precisely for his theory—there results the difficulty of answering, with regard to the particular act, the question from which of these alternating conditions it has resulted ; for to this end it would be necessary to bring forward all the causes that had exerted an influence on the delinquent since his birth, and all the causes that had exerted an influence upon his ancestors, from whom he inherited his good and bad qualities. Now, you will find it difficult to credit this, but Schwung in fact had the effrontery to reply by saying that this was indeed the case, for the logic of the law must never admit a mixture of two juridical states with respect to one and the same act, and therefore it must be decided, with reference also to each particular act of volition, whether it was possible for the accused, in the light of his psychological history, to control his volition, or not. He took it upon himself to assert that we have a much more clear awareness of the fact that our will is free than of the fact that everything that happens has a cause, and so long as we are fundamentally free, we are free also in relation to particular causes, whence it must be assumed that in such a case all that is required is a particular exertion of the will-power in order to resist the causally conditioned criminal impulses."

At this point Ulrich abandoned further exploration of his father's intentions, thoughtfully weighing in his hand the many enclosures to which there were references in the margin of the letter. He then cast a hasty glance at the end of the letter, from which he discovered that his father expected from him an ' objective influencing of ' the Counts Leinsdorf and Stallburg and impressed it upon him that he should, in the appropriate committees of the Collateral Campaign and when the right time came, point to the threats to the spirit of the State as a whole that might arise if in the Jubilee Year so important a problem were to be given a wrong formulation and a wrong solution.

75

General Stumm von Bordwehr regards visiting Diotima as a pleasant change from the usual run of his official duties.

THE tubby little general had paid another call on Diotima. Although the role allotted to the soldier in the council-chamber was a modest one—he had begun—he would yet take it upon himself to prophesy that the State was the power of self-assertion in the struggle of the nations and that the military strength displayed in time of peace warded off war. But Diotima had instantly pulled him up short.

" General ! " she said, quivering with anger, " all life rests upon forces that are of peace. Even the life of commerce, if one is capable of regarding it aright, is sheer poetry."

The little general gazed at her for a moment, nonplussed, but soon got into his stride again.

" Your Excellency," he hastened to agree—and in order to understand this mode of address and what it implied one must remember that Diotima's husband was a permanent secretary, that in Kakania a permanent secretary ranked equal with the commander of a division, but that only commanders of divisions were entitled to be addressed as ' Excellency ' and that even they had this right only when on duty ; but since the soldier's profession is a knightly one nobody could have got on in it if he had not addressed them as ' Excellency ' even when off duty, and in the spirit of knightly emulation their wives too were then also addressed as ' Excellency ', without much thought being wasted on the question as to when they were on duty. Such intricate considerations the little general had run through and settled in a flash, in order to assure Diotima instantly, with his very first words, of his unqualified agreement and humble respect. And so he said : " Your Excellency takes the very words out of my mouth. It goes without saying that for political reasons the War Ministry could not be taken into account when committees were being set up, but we have heard that this great movement is to be given a pacifist aim—an international peace-campaign, if I am rightly informed, or the donation to the Palace at The Hague of mural paintings from our own country—and I can assure Your Excellency that we are in heartfelt sympathy with this. People usually have such wrong ideas about the military. Of course, I won't go so far as to say that a young lieutenant does not wish for war, but all responsible quarters are most profoundly convinced that the sphere of force, which we do, alas, after all represent, must be linked with the blessings of the mind, precisely as you yourself, Your Excellency, have just put it."

He dug a little brush out of his trouser-pocket and went over his little moustache with it several times ; this was a bad habit dating back to his cadet days, when the moustache still con-stituted life's impatiently awaited great hope, and he did not know that he did it. His big brown eyes were fixed on Diotima's face, trying to read the effect of his words.

Diotima showed herself mollified, even if she never was com-pletely so in his presence, and deigned to give the General some information about what had been going on since the great com-mittee-meeting.

The General displayed special enthusiasm for the great council, expressed his admiration for Arnheim, and declared his conviction that such a gathering must turn out to be tremendously fruitful in its influence.

" There are after all many people who have no notion how little order there is in things of the mind ! " he expounded. " I am indeed convinced, if Your Excellency will permit me to say so, that most people believe that every day they witness some progress in the general order of things. They see order everywhere—in the factories, offices, railway time-tables and educational institutions, and here I may, I hope, also mention with pride our barracks, which in their modest way positively recall the discipline of a good orchestra—and one may look wherever one likes, everywhere one sees order of some kind, rules and regulations for pedestrians, transport, rates and taxes, ecclesiastical affairs, and commerce, and codes of precedence, etiquette, morality, and so on. In fact I am convinced that almost everybody nowadays considers our era the best-ordered one there has ever been. Have you not the same feeling yourself, in your inmost heart, Your Excellency ? I must say : I have. In fact, so far as I am concerned, if I don't keep a very sharp look-out, I at once get the feeling that the spirit of modern times actually lies in this greater order and that it must have been some sort of muddle or other that brought the empires of Nineveh and Rome to a bad end. I believe most people feel this way about it and quietly go on the assumption that the past is past and gone as a punishment for something that wasn't quite in order. But of course, I admit this notion is a delusion that educated people should not give way to. And there, alas, lies the necessity for power and the soldier's vocation ! "

The General felt profound satisfaction at chatting like this with this high-minded young woman ; it was a pleasant change from the usual run of his official duties.

Diotima, however, did not know how to answer him. For lack of anything better to say she returned to her favourite theme : " We do of course hope to gather around us the most distinguished men we have, but even then the task before us remains a hard one. You simply cannot imagine how many and how diverse are the suggestions that come in, and of course one wants to choose the best. But you were speaking of order, General. The goal will never be achieved by means of order, by means of sober-minded weighing of pros and cons, comparisons and probings. The solution to the problem must be a flash of lightning, a fire, an intuition, a synthesis. Looking at the history of mankind, one sees it is not a logical process of development, but rather something—with its sudden inspirations, the meaning of which only later becomes apparent—that reminds one of a poetic work ! "

" With all due respect to Your Excellency," the General responded, " a soldier-man doesn't know much about poetry. But if anyone can put lightning and fire into a movement, it is Your Excellency—that's something an old officer does understand ! "

76   *Count Leinsdorf shows some reserve.*

SO far the tubby little General had really been quite tame and
civilised, even if he did pay his calls without having been invited
to do so, and Diotima had confided in him more than she had
meant to. What nevertheless surrounded him with an aura of
terror, and always afterwards made her regret her amiability, was
actually not he himself, but, as Diotima explained it to herself, her
old friend Count Leinsdorf. Was His Highness jealous? And if
so, of whom ? Although each time the Council met he did it the
honour of putting in a brief appearance, he showed himself not as
favourably inclined to it as Diotima had expected. His Highness
had a very definite dislike of something that he called Merely
Literature. This was a conception that for him was bound up
with Jews, newspapers, sensation-seeking booksellers, and the
liberalistic spirit of the impotently wordy, commercial-minded
third estate ; the expression Merely Literature had positively
become a new standing phrase of his. Every time that Ulrich
prepared to read him the suggestions that had come in by post,
among which were all those proposals for moving the world
forwards or backwards, he now waved it all aside with the words
that everyone uses when in addition to his own intentions he finds
himself expected to cope with the intentions that everyone else
has, saying : " No, no, I've important things to do today, and all
that, after all, is merely literature ! " Then he would think of
fields, peasants, little country churches, and that order of things
which God had bound together as firmly as the sheaves on a
mown field, the order that was so beautiful, healthy and rewarding
even if it did sometimes tolerate distilleries on country estates in
order to keep pace with progress. But if one has this tranquil
breadth of vision, then rifle-clubs and co-operative dairies, however incongruous they may be, will appear part and parcel of
that solid order and coherence ; and supposing such institutions
should see themselves compelled to make a demand based on
philosophic principles, this demand will have, as one might say,

precedence, due to the demands of spiritual property registered in the Domesday Book of the mind, over any demands made by the mind and spirit of some mere unimportant private person. So it came about that whenever Diotima tried to have a serious talk with him about what she had learnt from her consultations with the Great Minds, Count Leinsdorf would usually be holding in his hand, or would pull out of his pocket, an application from some association consisting of five blockheads and would declare that this piece of paper was of more weight in the world of real cares and concerns than the bright ideas of this or that genius.

This was a spirit akin to that which Permanent Secretary Tuzzi extolled in connection with his Ministry's archives, the nature of which made it impossible to have any official cognisance of the Council's existence, while at the same time they noted with the utmost seriousness every slightest gibe or jeer emanating from the most pettifogging provincial newspaper. And in these troubles Diotima had no one in whom she could confide except Arnheim. But it was Arnheim, of all people, who took His Highness's part. It was he who expounded to her the tranquil breadth of vision that this grand seigneur possessed, when she complained about the preference Count Leinsdorf displayed for rifle-clubs and co-operative dairies. " His Highness believes in the guiding power of time and the land," he interpreted gravely. " Believe me, that is a result of land-owning. The earth simplifies, just as it purifies water. Even I, on my very modest estate, feel this effect every time I stay there. The reality of such a life makes for simplicity." And after some hesitation he added : " His Highness's attitude to life, on a grand scale as it is, makes him also most extremely tolerant, not to say indulgent to the point of recklessness. . . ."

As this side of her very noble patron was new to Diotima, she looked up eagerly.

" I should not like to say with certainty," Arnheim went on with vague emphasis, " that Count Leinsdorf notices how much your cousin, in his position as secretary, abuses his confidence, naturally only in matters of attitude, I should hasten to add, by his scepticism towards lofty plans and by the sabotage resulting from his mockery. I should be inclined to fear that his influence on Count Leinsdorf was not a fortunate one, were it not that this true nobleman is so securely enshrined in the great traditional feelings and ideas upon which real life is based that he can probably well afford to bestow this confidence."

These were strong words, and Ulrich had deserved them. But Diotima did not take so much notice of them as she might have, because it was the other part of Arnheim's pronouncement that made an impression on her—his way of regarding estates not as something to be owned in an estate-owning spirit, but as a form of spiritual massage. She thought this magnificent, and let her thoughts wander after the idea, imagining herself as the lady of the manor in such a setting.

" I sometimes admire," she said, " the broad-mindedness of your criticism where His Highness is concerned. All that is, after all, a vanishing period of history, isn't it ? "

" Yes, to be sure," Arnheim replied. " But the simple virtues, courage, chivalry, and self-discipline, which that caste developed in such an exemplary way, will always keep their value. In short, the noble lord and master ! It is a type to which I have learnt to attach more and more importance even in my business activities."

" This would mean, then, surely, that the noble lord and master is in the last resort almost synonymous with the essence of poetry ? " Diotima asked reflectively.

" You have put it quite wonderfully ! " her friend said in confirmation. " It is the secret of vigorous life. With intellect alone one cannot either be moral or conduct the business of politics. The intellect does not suffice. The things that are decisive take their course above and beyond its reach. Men who have achieved great things have always loved music, poetry, form, discipline, religion, and the knightly virtues. Indeed, I should even go so far as to say that only men who do so turn out to be fortunate ! For these are the so-called imponderables, which go to make up the leader, the true man, and there is even an undertone of it, an uncomprehended residue of it, in the common people's admiration for the actor. But to return to your cousin. It is of course not simply that one begins to be conservative when one has grown too lazy to do anything wild, but it is rather that even though we are all born revolutionaries a day comes when we notice that a person who is simply good, regardless of how one may rate his intelligence—in other words, a person who is reliable, cheerful, brave and loyal—not only gives one incomparable delight, but is also of the real humus in which life is bedded. This is age-old wisdom, of course, but it indicates a decisive change in taste—from the taste of youth, which is naturally focused on the exotic, to that of the mature man. I admire your cousin in many ways, or if that should be going too far—for there is little of what he says that one could stand up for—I should almost be inclined to say that my heart goes out to him, for there is something extraordinarily free and independent about him, together with much that is inwardly inflexible and eccentric. Incidentally, it may be this very mixture of freedom and inner inflexibility that lends him his special charm. But he is a dangerous person, with his infantile moral exoticism, and his highly trained intellect that is always in search of an adventure, without his knowing what it is that drives him to it."

77   *Arnheim as the darling of the journalists.*

DIOTIMA repeatedly had the opportunity of observing the imponderables of outlook and attitude in Arnheim.

It was for instance on his advice that sometimes the representatives of leading newspapers were also included among those invited to the meetings of the ' Council ' (it was Permanent Secretary Tuzzi who had somewhat mockingly given this appellation to the ' Committee for the drafting of a Guiding Resolution with reference to the Jubilee Celebrations of the Seventieth Anniversary of His Majesty's Accession to the Throne '), and Arnheim, although he was present only as a guest, without holding any office, enjoyed a degree of attention from them that put all other celebrities in the shade. Now, the thing is that newspapers, for some intangible reason, are not laboratories and experimental stations of the mind, which they might be to the common good, but generally storehouses and stock exchanges. Plato—to take him as an example, because he, among a dozen others, is commonly referred to as one of the greatest thinkers—

would, if he were still alive, quite definitely be enchanted with that world of ' news ' in which every day a new idea can be created, exchanged for another, or refined, in which a mass of reports comes pouring in from all the ends of the earth, at a speed he never dreamt of, and where a staff of demiurges waits in readiness to test it all immediately for the quantity of reason and reality it contains. He would take a newspaper office to be that *topos uranios*, that heavenly realm of Ideas, of whose existence he wrote in such detail and so impressively that even nowadays all the better sort of people are idealists when talking to their children or employees. And of course, if Plato were today suddenly to walk into an editor's office and prove he was really that great author who died more than two thousand years ago, he would cause a tremendous sensation and be offered the most enviable contracts. Supposing he were then capable of writing a volume of philo-sophic travel-impressions inside three weeks, as well as a few thousand of his well-known short stories, and even perhaps sell the film-rights of one or the other of his older works, he would certainly do pretty well for quite a time. As soon, however, as his return ceased to be topical and Mr. (as he would now be) Plato tried to put into practice yet another of his well-known ideas, which never really came into their own, the editor would merely urge him to write a nice little feature-article on the subject now and then for the woman's or the book page, of course not in that difficult style of his, but as light and readable as possible, with the paper's readers in mind, and the feature-editor would add that he was sorry he could not use such a contribution more than once a month at the most, because there were, after all, so many other good men to be considered. And after that both these gentlemen would have the feeling that they had done a great deal for a man who, although he was the father of European publicists, was nevertheless a little out of date and as regards topicality simply not in the same class as, for instance, Paul Arnheim.

Now, so far as Arnheim himself was concerned, he would of course never have fallen in with such a view, because it would have affronted his feelings of reverence towards all that was great, yet in many respects he would have considered it, after all, very understandable. Today, when everything under the sun is talked about in the same breath with everything else, when prophets and charlatans make use of the same phrases, except for shades of difference that no busy person has time to track down, when newspaper offices are continually being pestered with some genius or other that has turned up, it is very difficult to assess the value of a man or an idea correctly. What it comes to is that one has to rely on one's sense of hearing in order to notice when the muttering, whispering, and shuffling outside the door of the editorial office is loud enough to deserve admittance as the voice of the public. Admittedly, from this moment on genius enters into a different state : it is no longer merely a dubious matter of book-reviewing or dramatic criticism, the inherent contradictions in which the kind of reader every newspaper caters for takes no more seriously than the prattle of children ; it is now accorded the rank of a fact, with all the consequences involved.

Foolish enthusiasts fail to see the desperate craving for idealism that underlies this. The world of those who write and those who have to write is full of big words and ideas that have lost the objects to which they refer. The epithets applied to great men and great enthusiasms outlive the causes to which they were originally ascribed, and as a result a great many epithets are left over. They were coined at some time or other by some distinguished man to be applied to some other distinguished man ; but these men are long dead and gone, and the surviving concepts must be put to use. That is why there is a constant search for the man to fit the epithets. Shakespeare's ' tremendous wealth of imagination ', Goethe's ' universality ', Dostoievsky's ' psychological depth ', and all the other notions that are the heritage of a long literary evolution hang about in their hundreds in the heads of those who write, and simply because business is slack and the goods are piling up these people have now descended to referring to a lawn-tennis player as ' profound in his approach ' and to every fashionable writer as ' great '. Obviously they will always be thankful when they can work their stock of words off on to someone without loss. But it must be someone whose importance is already an established fact, so that the words *can* intelligibly be pinned on to him, though it does not in the least matter where. And such a man was Arnheim. For Arnheim was Arnheim ; what they saw in Arnheim was Arnheim, who as his father's heir had constituted an event even in being born, and there could be no doubt as to the news value of anything he said. All he needed to do was to make the little exertion of giving utterance to something that with good will could be considered important. And Arnheim himself summed this up in a very sound axiom. " A great deal of a man's real importance," he was in the habit of saying, " lies in his capacity to make himself intelligible to his contemporaries."

So this time, as always, he got on splendidly with the newspapers, which ' took him over ', as it were. He merely smiled at ambitious financiers and politicians who would have liked nothing better than to buy up all the newspapers they could lay hands on : such attempts to influence public opinion seemed to him as uncouth and faint-hearted as a man's offering a woman money for her love, when he could have it much cheaper by stimulating her imagination. In answer to the journalists' questions about the Council he had said that the very fact of this assembly proved the profound need for it, for in the history of the world nothing irrational happened. And with this he had struck the keynote of their own professional attitude so splendidly that this statement was quoted in several newspapers. It was, as becomes apparent on closer scrutiny, in fact a good dictum. For people who attach importance to everything that happens would inevitably feel thoroughly uncomfortable unless they had the conviction that nothing irrational can happen ; on the other hand, however, they would, as is well known, rather bite their tongues out than attach *too* much importance to anything, even if it should be distinction itself. The slight pinch of pessimism in Arnheim's pronouncement did much to lend solid dignity to the enterprise, and now even the circumstance that he was a foreigner could be interpreted as indicating the sympathy felt everywhere abroad for these enormously interesting spiritual developments in Austria.

The other celebrities who were concerned in the work of the Council had not the same unconscious gift of appealing to the press, but they noticed the effect ; and since celebrities in general know little about each other and, on their common journey towards immortality, usually set eyes on each other only in the dining-car, the special public reputation that Arnheim enjoyed was accepted by them without further examination, and although he kept away from meetings of all appointed committees, as he had done all along, in the Council itself the role of a central figure automatically devolved upon him. The further this assembly progressed, the clearer it became that he was the really sensational element in it, although at bottom he did nothing to create that effect except perhaps that in conversation with the other celebrities who were members of it he again expressed views that could be interpreted as a luxurious pessimism, the drift of which was that doubtless little was to be expected from the Council, although, of course, so noble an undertaking in itself required of one all the confidence and devotion one could muster. Such delicate pessimism inspires confidence even in great minds. The fact is that for some reason or other the notion that things of the mind nowadays never can have any real success whatsoever is more appealing than the notion of some colleague or other being successful with the products of *his* mind ; and Arnheim's restrained verdict on the Council could be taken as being in conformity with the former possibility.

78   *Diotima's transformation.*

DIOTIMA'S feelings did not follow quite the same straight ascending line of development as Arnheim's success.

It sometimes happened in the midst of a social gathering, in her transformed apartment, with all its rooms stripped of their furniture, that she felt as though she were awakening in a land of dream. Then she would stand, with the room and the people all round her, the light of the chandelier flowing over her hair and on down over her shoulders and hips, so that she could almost feel the luminous flood of it, and was then utterly a statue, was, as it seemed to herself, some figure on a fountain at the very centre of the centre of a world and drenched in sublime spiritual grace. She considered this position a unique opportunity to give reality to everything that one had in the course of one's life believed to be greatest and most important, and was no longer much troubled by the fact that she could not think of anything definite in this connection. The whole apartment, the presence of the people in it, the whole evening, all this enwrapped her like a robe lined with yellow silk ; she could feel it on her skin, though she could not see it. From time to time she turned her gaze to Arnheim, who was usually standing somewhere else in a group of men, talking. But then she would become aware that her gaze had been resting on him all the time, and it was only her awakening that now turned in the same direction. Even without her looking that way, the outermost wing-tips of her soul, as it were, rested always on his face and told her what was going on there.

And, since we speak of plumes, it should be added that there was something dream-like in his appearance too—a merchant, say, with golden angelic wings, who had descended into the midst of this gathering. The rattle of express trains and *trains de luxe*, the humming of motor-cars, the remote peace of hunting-lodges, the flapping of a yacht's sails, were in these invisible folded wings with which her feelings had furnished him, wings that rustled softly with every explanatory wave of his arm. Now, as ever, Arnheim was often away on his travels, and this always gave his presence some quality of reaching away beyond the present moment and local events, which in any case were so important to Diotima. She knew that a secret coming and going of telegrams, visitors and envoys of his own enterprises went on while he was in this city. She had gradually gained a picture, perhaps even an exaggerated one, of the importance of a firm with world-wide interests and of the extent to which it was involved in the affairs of the great world. Arnheim sometimes talked, in a breath-takingly interesting way, about the ramifications of international capital, about oversea trade, and about the political background. Entirely new horizons —in fact, the first horizons of any kind—opened out before Diotima. One needed only to have heard him speak once about, say, Franco-German antagonism, of which Diotima did not know much more than that almost everyone of her acquaintance combined a faint dislike of Germany with some measure of a tiresome fraternal obligation : in his exposition it became a Gallo-Celto-Alpino-thyreological problem interlinked with that of the Lorraine coal-mines and further with that of the Mexican oil-fields and the antagonism between Anglo-Saxon and Latin America.

Of such ramifications Permanent Secretary Tuzzi had no inkling, or at least did not show he had any. He confined himself to
pointing out to Diotima at intervals that in his view Arnheim's
presence in and marked taste for her house could definitely not be
accounted for without assuming the existence of ulterior motives ;
but he remained silent as to their possible nature, not knowing
anything about them himself.

So his wife received a deep impression of up-to-date people's
superiority over the methods of obsolete diplomacy. She had not
forgotten the moment when she formed the resolve to set Arnheim at the head of the Collateral Campaign. It had been the
first great idea of her life, and in arriving at it she had been in a
strange and wonderful state ; she had found herself in a condition
midway between dreaming and dissolving, the idea had floated out
wondrously far and wide, and everything that up to then had
constituted Diotima's world had dissolved, flowing towards the
idea. When it was formulated in words, in so far as this was
possible at all, it amounted, candidly, to precious little : it was a
glitter, a flickering, a peculiar emptiness and a flight of ideas. It
could even be calmly admitted—Diotima thought to herself—
that the core of it, namely the thought of setting Arnheim at the
head of the brand-new patriotic Campaign, was simply an impossible one. Arnheim was a foreigner ; there was no getting
past that. And so this inspiration could not be turned into reality
as quickly and simply as she had represented it to Count Leinsdorf and her husband. But nevertheless everything had come
about just as she had conceived it in that state. For all the other
endeavours to give the Campaign a really sublime content had also
been in vain hitherto. The great inaugural meeting, the work of
the committees, even this private congress—against which, incidentally, Arnheim, by some strange ironic whim of fate, had
uttered a warning—had hitherto produced nothing but Arnheim,
round whom people flocked and who had to keep on talking all the
time and to form the secret focus of all hopes. This was the new
type of man whose vocation it was to take over the helm of destiny
from the old powers. She could flatter herself that it had been
she who had instantly discovered him, talked to him about the
entry of new men into the sphere of power, and helped him to go
his own way here against the opposition of all the others. And so,

should it turn out that Arnheim had really also had some hidden intentions up his sleeve, as Permanent Secretary Tuzzi conjectured, even then Diotima would have been determined, almost as a matter of course, to support him with all the means at her disposal ; for an hour of greatness allows of no petty probings, and she distinctly felt that this was a pinnacle in her life.

Apart from the proverbial lucky dog and his counterpart, the person who is hounded by ill-luck, all men are equally badly off in life, but their lives are, as it were, on different storeys. For people today, who after all in general have only a restricted view of the meaning of their life, the confidence that comes from knowing one's own storey is an extremely desirable substitute. In exceptional cases this confidence may be intensified into the sort of dizzy intoxication one gets from being at a great height or having great power, just as there are people who become giddy on a high storey of a building, even when they know quite well they are standing in the middle of the room and the windows are shut. When Diotima reflected that one of the most influential men in Europe was working together with her on the task of bringing ideas—the *mind*—into the domains of power, and how they had both been brought together by what was surely nothing less than the hand of fate, and what was going on, even if on this day in the high storey of a universal Austrian work of humanitarianism there was actually nothing in particular going on—when she reflected on all this, the tangles of her knotted thoughts soon loosened into loops, the speed of thinking accelerated, its course became simplified, a peculiar sensation of happiness and success accompanied the thoughts that occurred to her, and a state of influx brought her flashes of understanding that were a surprise even to her. Her self-confidence was heightened. Successes that she would formerly not have dared to believe in lay now in tangible proximity. She felt more cheerful than she was accustomed to feel ; sometimes indeed daring jokes occurred to her, and something that she had never before in her life observed in herself—waves of gaiety, even of exuberance—passed through her. She felt as though she were in a turret room with many windows. But this had its uncanny side too. She was tormented by a vague, general, unutterable sense of well-being, which created an urge towards some form of action, some universal, all-embracing action of which she could not form any definite picture. It might almost be said that she suddenly became conscious of the turning of the globe under her feet, and she could not get rid of this awareness. At other times these violent processes without tangible content were as frustrating as a dog jumping about almost under one's feet, without one's knowing how it had got there. And so Diotima was at times frightened by the alteration that had taken place in her without her express permission, and all in all what her condition most resembled was that pallid nerve-racking grey that is the colour of the faint, gossamer sky in that despondent hour when the heat is at its greatest.

In all this Diotima's striving towards the ideal underwent an important change. This striving had never been quite clearly distinguishable from a decorous admiration for great things ; it was a genteel idealism, a restrained state of exaltation, and since in these more robust modern times it has almost been forgotten what this means, it may be useful to give yet another brief description of it. There was nothing concrete about this idealism, for concreteness suggests craftsmanship, and getting down to craftsmanship means dirtying one's hands ; on the contrary, it was reminiscent of the flower-paintings done by archduchesses, for whom models other than flowers are not suitable on grounds of propriety. And what was especially characteristic of this idealism was the concept of ' culture ' : it felt itself to be cultured through and through. It could also, however, be called harmonious, because it detested all that was uneven and unbalanced, and saw it as the function of education to bring into harmony with each other all the crude antagonisms that unfortunately exist in the world ; in short, it was perhaps by no means so different from what is even nowadays—though admittedly only in quarters where the great bourgeois tradition is upheld—understood by a sound, solid and dignified idealism, which is one that discriminates very precisely between objects that are worthy of it and such as are not, and for reasons of higher humanity is far from sharing the conviction held by the saint (and also by doctors and engineers) that even moral waste-matter is a source, all unexploited, of heavenly calorific power. If in earlier days Diotima had been wakened from her sleep and asked what she wanted, she would have answered, without having to stop and think, that the power of love in a living soul yearned to communicate itself to the whole world ; but after being awake for a while she would have qualified this with the remark that in the modern world, such as it had become as a result of the superabundance of civilisation and intellect, it would, of course, be safer, even in the case of the noblest natures, to speak only of a striving analogous to the power of love. And she would really have meant it. There are still thousands of people nowadays who are something like scent-sprays diffusing the power of love. When Diotima sat down to read her books, she pushed her beautiful hair back from her forehead, which gave her appearance a touch of the logical, and she read with a sense of responsibility and in the endeavour to mould for herself, out of what she called culture, an instrument to aid her in the far-from-easy social situation in which she found herself. And it was so too that she lived ; she distributed herself in tiny droplets of rarefied love among all the things that deserved it, condensing as a cloudy breath upon them at some distance from herself ; and all that she was actually left with was the empty bottle of the body that was one of Permanent Secretary Tuzzi's domestic chattels. Before the arrival of Arnheim this had finally led to attacks of profound melancholy, at a time when Diotima was still alone between her husband and that greatest source of radiance in her life, the Collateral Campaign ; since then, however, her condition had reformed itself in a very natural manner. The power of love had contracted vigorously and had, as it were, returned into the body ; and the ' analogous ' striving had become one that was very egotistical and unequivocal. The notion, first evoked by her cousin, that she was in a state preliminary to performing an act of some kind, and that something she could not yet bring herself to imagine was on the point of happening between herself and Arnheim, had a degree of concentration so much higher than all the notions that had occupied her hitherto that she felt exactly as though she had made the transition from dreaming to waking. And as a result a void, such as is peculiar to the first instant of this transition, had opened up in Diotima, and from remembered descriptions she had reason to think that this was a sign of the beginning of a great passion. She believed she could put such an interpretation on much that Arnheim had said recently. His accounts of his position, and of the virtues and duties necessary in his life, were preparations for something that was inexorably approaching, and Diotima, sensing the spiritual pessimism inherent in every act, surveyed everything that had hitherto been her ideal, just as a person whose trunks are packed casts a last glance round the rooms that have been his home for years and from which the life has now almost gone. The unexpected result was that Diotima's soul, temporarily unsupervised by the higher faculties, behaved like a schoolboy set free from school who careers around until the moment when he is overwhelmed by the mournfulness of his senseless liberty ; and as a result of this remarkable circumstance there for a short time entered into her relations with her husband, and in spite of increasing alienation, something that strangely resembled, if not love's late springtide, at least then a blend of all the seasons of love.

The Permanent Secretary—that slightly built man with his pleasant aroma of tanned dry skin—could not understand what was going on. It had several times struck him that while guests were present his wife gave an impression of being oddly dreamy, withdrawn, remote, and strung up, at once in a really nervous state and somehow aloofly absent. But when they were alone, and he approached her, somewhat timidly and disconcertedly, in order to find out about it, she would suddenly fall on his neck in unreasoned gaiety and press extraordinarily hot lips on his brow, reminding him of the barber's curling-tongs when they came too near his skin during the curling of his moustache. This sort of unexpected tenderness was disagreeable, and he would stealthily wipe the traces of it away when Diotima was not looking. But if it should happen that he tried to clasp her in his arms, or, even more annoyingly, if he had already clasped her, she would reproach him agitatedly with having never loved her, but only flinging himself upon her like a wild beast. Now, the thing was that a certain measure of sensibility and capriciousness was a definite part of the picture that he had had from his youth of a desirable woman who was the complement to masculine nature, and the intellectually illumined grace with which Diotima handed one a cup of tea, or took up a new book, or passed judgment on any problem about which, as her husband was convinced, she could not possibly know anything, had always enchanted him by its formal perfection. The effect it had on him was that of unobtrusive dinnertime music, something that he was exceedingly fond of; but of course Tuzzi was also entirely of the opinion that the detachment of music from meal-times (or from church services), and the endeavour to cultivate it for its own sake, was in itself an inflated piece of middle-class self-importance, although he knew that this could not be said openly and it was in any case not the sort of thing that he ever spent any time thinking out in detail. What then was he to do when Diotima at one moment embraced him, at another irritably declared that, living with him, a person with a soul had no freedom to rise to her true essential self? What could the answer be to demands of the kind that he should think more of the deep ocean of inner beauty instead of concentrating on her body? All of a sudden he was expected to discriminate clearly between that Eros in whom the spirit of love floats free, unhampered by base desires, and downright sexuality. Such things were, of course, the sort of mere bookish cleverness one could laugh at. But if they were propounded by a woman who was at the same time undressing—with such doctrine on her lips! Tuzzi thought to himself—then they positively became insult and injury. For he could not fail to notice that Diotima's underclothing had progressed some distance in the direction of a certain worldly frivolity. True, she had always given care and deliberation to matters of dress, since her social position made it necessary both that she should be smart and that she should not seem to enter into competition with ladies in high society. But as regards the gradations possible in underclothing, which extend from hard-wearing respectability to the filmy frilliness of lechery, she was now making concessions to the beautiful that she would formerly have stigmatised as unworthy of an intelligent woman. If, however, this was commented on by Giovanni (Tuzzi's name was Hans, but for stylistic reasons he was re-christened in keeping with his surname), she would blush right down to her shoulders and talk about Frau von Stein, who had not made any concessions even to a man like Goethe! And so Permanent Secretary Tuzzi was no longer supposed to detach himself, when he thought the time had come, from his concern with important affairs of state, which lay beyond the limits of private life, and find relaxation in the bosom of his household. On the contrary, he now found himself at Diotima's mercy; and whereas there had hitherto been a clear line of demarcation between exertion of the mind and recreational indulgence of the body, it seemed now to be expected of him that there should be a return to the strenuous and slightly ridiculous unity of mind and body appropriate to days of courtship and reminiscent of the caperings of a cock-pheasant or the versifying of a love-sick youth.

It is scarcely too much to say that at times it made him feel, in his inmost being, something amounting to disgust, and because of this the public success that his wife was having at this period was almost physically painful to him. Diotima had public opinion on her side, and that was something that Permanent Secretary Tuzzi in all circumstances respected so much that he was afraid of showing a lack of understanding if he countered Diotima's incomprehensible caprices with a show of authority or too sharp a mockery. It gradually became clear to him that being the husband of a distinguished woman was a tormenting affliction, one to be carefully concealed, indeed, rather similar to emasculation caused by an accident. He took great pains to keep it dark. Soundlessly and inconspicuously he came and went, wrapped in a cloud of amiable official impenetrability, whenever Diotima was having a reception or a conference, and now and then would offer his advice in a politely helpful way or utter an ironical and yet comforting remark. He seemed to pass his existence in a separate, though friendly disposed, neighbouring world, apparently always in agreement with Diotima, even now and then when they were alone still entrusting her with a little mission, openly showing approval of Arnheim's frequenting the house and, in the hours left over from the weighty cares of his office, studying Arnheim's writings and hating men who wrote books, for being the cause of his troubles.

For here was a question to which the main question—why Arnheim frequented his house—now sometimes reduced itself : Why did Arnheim write ? Writing was a special form of prating, and prating men were something Tuzzi could not stand. It always aroused in him the urgent need to clench his jaws and spit through his teeth, like a sailor. There were of course some exceptions, which he tolerated. He knew some senior officials who after their retirement had written their memoirs, and also some who occasionally wrote for the newspapers. Tuzzi's explanation was that an official writes only if he is discontented or if he is a Jew, because according to his firm conviction Jews were ambitious and discontented. Furthermore, men who had achieved great things in practical life had written books about their experiences, but this only in the evening of their life and in America or, at the outside, in England. It goes without saying that Tuzzi was versed in literature and, like all diplomats, had a preference for memoirs, from which one could pick up witty sayings and knowledge of mankind. But it must after all mean something that such things were no longer written nowadays, and his taste was probably an old-fashioned one, not in keeping with an age of functionalism. Finally, people also wrote because it was a profession. This was something to which Tuzzi accorded full recognition, so long as it brought in enough money or the person concerned came under the heading, which did after all somehow exist, of ' poet '. He even felt moderately honoured to be giving hospitality to the leading men in this profession, to which he had hitherto reckoned the writers who were secretly in the Foreign Ministry's pay ; but without thinking about it much he would also have counted the *Iliad* and the Sermon on the Mount, both of which he very much revered, among those achievements whose origin was to be explained by the existence of a profession practised either independently or under patronage. But how on earth a man like Arnheim, who had not the slightest need to do so, came to write so much was a problem behind which Tuzzi, and now with a vengeance, suspected something—something to which, however, he had not come an inch nearer.

79 *Soliman in love.*

SOLIMAN, the little Negro slave, or as the case might be, Negro prince, had during this time managed to convince Rachel, Diotima's little maid, or as the case might be, confidante, that it was their duty to keep an eye on what went on in the house, in order to forestall some sinister plan of Arnheim's when the moment came. More precisely, he had not really convinced her ; but still, the two of them kept watch like conspirators and listened at the door every time there were visitors. Soliman told a tremendous number of stories about couriers travelling to and fro and mysterious personages coming and going in the hotel where his master was staying. He said he was prepared to swear the oath of an African prince that he would discover the secret meaning of it. The oath of an African prince was to consist in Rachel's putting her hand between the buttons of his jacket and his shirt and laying it on his bare chest, while he would speak the formula and with his own hand do the same to Rachel as she to him. But Rachel refused. All the same, little Rachel, who had the privilege of dressing and undressing her mistress and telephoning on her behalf, and through whose hands Diotima's black hair flowed every morning and evening, while golden speeches flowed through her ears—this ambitious little thing who had been living as though on the top of a pillar ever since the Collateral Campaign existed, and from whose eyes, day after day, tremulous floods of adoration rose towards the woman who was so like a goddess, for some time now had delighted in plainly and simply spying on that woman.

Through open doors of neighbouring rooms or through the lingeringly diminishing gap of a closing door or simply while she was slowly doing some small job nearby, she would try to overhear all that was said by Diotima and Arnehim, Tuzzi and Ulrich, salvaging glances, sighs, hand-kissings, words, laughter, and gestures, like scraps of a torn document that she could not fit together again. But it was above all the little aperture of the key-hole that revealed a wealth of sensations, curiously reminding Rachel of the long-forgotten time when she had lost her honour. Through it the gaze penetrated deep into the inmost recesses of the rooms. Broken up, in pieces as flat as cardboard, the people floated about in there, and the voices were no longer held fast within a narrow framework of words, but grew vegetatively, spreading as meaningless sound. The awe, reverence, and admiration that held Rachel bound to these persons then gave way and came undone in a state of wild dissolution ; and this was as exciting as when a lover suddenly with his whole being penetrates so deep into the beloved that all grows dark before the eyes, and behind the drawn curtain of the skin the lights flare up.

Little Rachel crouched before the key-hole, her black dress tightened over knees, throat and shoulders. Soliman in his livery, crouching beside her, was like hot chocolate in a dark green cup ; at times, when he lost his balance, he would steady himself against Rachel's shoulder, knee, or skirt, with a quick movement of his hand, which would rest there for an instant and then hesitantly, caressingly let go, until only the finger-tips still touched her, and finally these also withdrew. He could not help giggling, and then Rachel would lay her small, soft fingers on the swelling bolsters of his lips.

Soliman, incidentally, in contrast with Rachel, did not find the Council interesting and, whenever he could, dodged the task of helping her to wait on the guests. He preferred to come along when Arnheim made a visit alone. Then, of course, he had to sit in the kitchen and wait until Rachel was free again, and the cook, who had got on so well with him on the first day, became cross because since then he had grown almost dumb. But Rachel never had time to sit in the kitchen for long, and when she went out again, the cook, who was a woman in her thirties, paid motherly little attentions to Soliman. He would tolerate them for a while, with the haughtiest expression his chocolate face could assume, but then would get up and, pretending he had forgotten something or was looking for something, turn his gaze thoughtfully to the ceiling, take up a position with his back to the door, and begin to walk backwards, exactly as if this enabled him to see the ceiling better. The cook by now knew this clumsy performance was coming the moment he got up and rolled his eyes, showing the whites ; but out of annoyance and jealousy she behaved as though she made nothing of it. And Soliman finally ceased to give himself any trouble with the act, which had already become something like an abbreviated formula, down to the moment when he stood on the threshold of the brightly lit kitchen, hesitating a short while longer with the most innocent expression he could adopt. And then the cook made a point of not looking. Soliman slid away backwards into the shadowy hall like a dark reflection into dark water, listened a second longer, quite superfluously, and then suddenly began, in fantastic leaps and bounds, to track Rachel through the strange house.

Permanent Secretary Tuzzi was never at home, and Soliman was not afraid of Arnheim and Diotima, because he knew they had ears only for each other. He had even several times made the experiment of knocking something over, and had not drawn attention to himself. He lorded it in all the rooms like a stag in the forest. His blood thrust upwards through his head like antlers with eighteen poignard-sharp points. The tips of these antlers brushed along the walls and ceilings. It was the custom in the house to keep the curtains drawn in all the rooms at times when they were not being used, so that the colours of the upholstery should not fade in the sunlight, and Soliman stole through the gloaming with wide movements of his arms as through leafy undergrowth. He enjoyed doing this with exaggerated stealthiness. He was intent on violence. This boy, coddled and corrupted by women's curiosity, had in fact never yet had intercourse with a woman, but had only picked up the vices of European boys, and his cravings were as yet so unstilled by experience, so unbridled, burning in all directions, that his desire did not know whether to quench itself in Rachel's blood or in her kisses, or in a freezing up of all the veins of his body, the moment he set eyes on the girl who was the object of his love.

Wherever Rachel might hide, he would suddenly loom up, smiling with delight over his success in tracking her down. He would bar her way, and neither the master's study nor Diotima's bedroom was sacred to him. He would pop out from behind the curtains, from under the writing-desk, from behind wardrobes, and from under beds, and Rachel's heart almost stood still every time with horror at such impudence and the danger to which he exposed them, the moment the half-darkness somewhere condensed into the darkness of a face with two rows of white teeth gleaming in it. But as soon as Soliman stood face to face with Rachel, the girl of flesh and blood, he was once more in the trammels of convention. This girl was so much older than he, and as beautiful as a fine shirt that one simply cannot bring oneself to crumple and dirty in the very first moment when it has come back all fresh from the laundry, and altogether she was simply so real that all his imaginings paled away in her presence. She reproached him for his bad behaviour and lauded Diotima, Arnheim, and the honour of being allowed to do one's share in the Collateral Campaign. But Soliman always had little presents with him for her, bringing her now a flower that he had pulled out of the bunch his master had sent to Diotima, now a cigarette that he had stolen at home, or a handful of sweets that he had scooped out of a bowl in passing. Then he would just press Rachel's fingers and, as he conveyed the present to her, lay her hand upon his heart, which burnt inside his black body like a red torch in a dark night.

And once Soliman penetrated even into Rachel's own room, whither she had had to withdraw with some sewing on strict instructions from Diotima, who the previous day had been disturbed by some scuffling in the hall while Arnheim was there. Before beginning her period of house-arrest, Rachel had hastily looked round for him, without, however, finding him. But when, sadly, she entered her little room, there he was sitting on her bed, dark and grinning, gazing at her. Rachel hesitated to shut the door, but Soliman jumped up and did it. Then he rummaged in his pockets, pulled something out, blew some fluff off it, and drew near to her, dangerous as a hot smoothing-iron.

" Hold out your hand ! " he commanded.

Rachel held it out to him.

He had some twinkling shirt-studs in his hand, and tried to fix them into the cuffs of Rachel's dress.

Rachel supposed they were glass.

" Jewels ! " he explained proudly.

The girl, who at this word had a foreboding of evil, quickly drew her arm back. It was not that she suspected anything definite. The son of an African prince, even if he had been kidnapped, might still have jewels secretly sewn into his shirt. One could never know for certain. But she was instinctively afraid of these studs, as though it were poison that Soliman was holding out towards her, and suddenly all the flowers and sweets that he had been giving her all along began to seem queer to her. She pressed her hands to her body and looked at Soliman, aghast. She felt she ought to speak to him very seriously ; she was older than he and worked for a good mistress. But at this moment all she could think of was such sayings as ' Honesty is the best policy '

and ' Do as you would be done by '. She turned pale. These
words seemed too ordinary. She had learnt her everyday wisdom
in her parents' house, and it was a stern wisdom, as plain and
beautiful as old pots and pans handed down from generation to
generation ; but one could not do much with it, for such old saws
were always only one sentence long and then that was the end of it.
And at this moment she was ashamed of such childish wisdom, as
one is ashamed of old threadbare clothes. That the old chest that
has been kept in some poor people's attic a century later becomes
an ornamental addition to some rich people's drawing-room was
something she did not know ; and like all respectable simple
people she admired a new wickerwork chair. And this was why
she searched her memory for something she had learned in her
new life. But however many wonderful scenes of love and terror
she remembered from the books Diotima had given her, none of
them was just what she needed here ; all the fine words and feelings had their own situation and as little fitted to hers as a key
fits the wrong lock. It was the same with the magnificent pronouncements and admonitions she had received from Diotima.
She felt a glowing mist swirl around her and was on the brink of
tears. At last she said vehemently :

" I don't steal from my master and mistress ! "

" Why not ? " Soliman bared his teeth.

" I won't do it ! "

" I didn't steal. It belongs to me ! " Soliman exclaimed.

' A good master or mistress provides for us poor people ',
Rachel felt. Love for Diotima was what she felt, and boundless
respect for Arnheim, and profound horror of those mutinous and
mischievous people that the brave police called subversive elements. But she had no words for all this. Like a gigantic waggon
overladen with hay and fruit, its brakes no longer working, this
whole load of emotion within her began to rumble downhill.

" It's mine ! Take it ! " Soliman insisted, reaching out again
for Rachel's hand. She snatched her arm away. He tried to hold
it, gradually lashing himself into a frenzy, and when he was near
to having to let go, because his boyish strength was not a match for
Rachel's resistance and she was pulling herself out of his grip with
the whole of her body, he bent forward, no longer knowing what
he was doing, and bit into the girl's arm, like an animal.

Rachel gave a scream, which she had to stifle, and hit Soliman in the face.

But in this moment his eyes were already full of tears, he threw himself on his knees, pressed his lips to Rachel's dress and wept with such passion that Rachel could feel the hot tears coming through on to her thighs.

She remained standing helplessly before the kneeling boy, who clutched at her skirt and dug his head into her body. She had never before in her life encountered an emotion like this, and gently she moved her fingers through the yielding wiry mop of Soliman's hair.

80 *Closer acquaintance with General Stumm, who surprisingly appears at a meeting of the Council.*

MEANWHILE the Council had been enriched by a remarkable addition. In spite of the very strict sifting of those asked to attend, one evening the General had put in an appearance and made a particular point of thanking Diotima for the honour done him by her invitation. The soldier's role in the council-chamber was a modest one, he declared, but to be allowed to be present, even though only as a mute onlooker, at such an eminent gathering had been his inmost longing ever since his youth. In silence Diotima let her eyes roam over his head, in search of the culprit. Arnheim was talking to His Highness like one statesman to another. Ulrich, with an air of unspeakable boredom, was gazing at the *buffet*, apparently counting the cakes. The accustomed scene presented a solid front, without the smallest gap through which such an unusual suspicion could penetrate. On the other hand, however, there was nothing Diotima was so sure of as that she herself had not invited the General, unless she was to assume that she walked in her sleep or suffered from attacks of amnesia. It was an uncanny moment. There the little general stood, indubitably with an invitation in the breast-pocket of his forget-me-not-blue tunic ; for it was impossible to suspect a man in his position of such outrageous impertinence as to put in an appearance without it. On the other hand, over there in the library stood Diotima's elegant writing-desk, and locked up in the drawer of it were all the printed invitation-cards that were left over, scarcely anyone but Diotima herself having access to them. Could it have been Tuzzi ? she wondered briefly. But that too seemed hardly probable. It remained something like a spiritualistic enigma how the invitation and the General had come together; and since Diotima was in her private affairs rather given to believing in supernatural powers, she felt a shiver go through her from head to foot. However, she had no choice but to bid the General welcome.

Incidentally, he himself had marvelled a little at the invitation. The fact that it had come after all had surprised him, since on his two visits Diotima had regrettably shown not the slightest sign of any such intention. It had struck him too that the envelope, obviously addressed by a menial hand, bore inaccuracies in the formulation of his rank and style such as were not to be expected of a lady in Diotima's social position. But the General was an easy-going man, and it was not his way to suspect anything unusual, not to speak at all of anything supernatural. He assumed that there had been some little slip, which, however, was not going to stop him from enjoying his success.

For Major-General Stumm von Bordwehr, chief of the War Ministry's department for army education and cultural improvement, was sincerely pleased with the official mission that had come his way. At the time when the great inaugural meeting of the Collateral Campaign was imminent, the chief of Administration had sent for him and said to him : " I say, Stumm, old man, look here, you're one of these chaps that read books, aren't you ? We'll write you a letter of introduction, and along you go. Take a bit of a look at it, and tell us what they're up to." And afterwards, however much he had protested, the fact that he had not managed to get a foothold in the Collateral Campaign was a blot on his escutcheon, one that he had vainly tried to wipe out by his visits to Diotima. And so he had gone hot-foot to Administration when the invitation had come after all, and, daintily and with a certain nonchalant impudence setting one foot before the other, his paunch protruding, had reported, still a little out of breath, that the event at which he had aimed and which he had been expecting had now, of course, occurred after all.

" Well, there you are," Lieutenant-General Frost von Aufbruch remarked. " I always thought you'd pull it off." He waved to a chair and offered Stumm a cigarette, switched on the electric sign over the door that said ' No admittance, important conference ' and then briefed Stumm for his mission, which consisted for the most part in reconnoitring and reporting back. " The point is, we don't want anything special, don't you know. Just you go along as often as you can and show them we're still on the map. Not being on any of the committees is all right as far as it goes, I dare say. But there's no earthly reason why we should be kept out of it altogether when plans are being made about a presentation, of what you might call a spiritual nature, for the birthday of our Supreme Commander and Sovereign. None at all. And that's why I picked on you and mentioned you to His Excellency the Minister for the job. Nobody can have anything against *your* being there. Well, good luck, old man—make a good show of it." Lieutenant-General Frost von Aufbruch nodded pleasantly.

And General Stumm von Bordwehr, forgetting that a soldier is not supposed to show any sign of emotion, clicked his heels, as it were from the bottom of his heart, his spurs jingling, and said : " Very good, sir ! Thanks awfully, old man."

If there are civilians who are belligerent by nature, why then should there not be officers who love the arts of peace ? Kakania had a great many of that kind. They painted, collected beetles, went in for stamp-collecting, or studied the history of the world. The many small garrisons, and the fact that regulations did not permit officers to come before the public with intellectual achievements except with the approval of their superior officers, usually lent their endeavours a peculiarly personal touch. General Stumm, too, had gone in for such hobbies in earlier years. He had originally served with the cavalry, but he was not much of a horseman ; his small hands and short legs were not suited to holding on to and controlling an animal as unreasonable as the horse, and he also lacked the qualities needed for the giving of military orders to such a degree that his superiors in those days used to say of him that if a squadron were to parade on the barrack-square with the horses' heads, instead of, as was usual, their tails, towards the stable wall, that would be enough to make him incapable of getting them out through the gates. In revenge little Stumm for a time grew a beard, very dark brown and rounded at the edges ; he was the only officer in the Emperor's cavalry who wore a beard, but regulations did not specifically forbid it. And he began to collect pocket-knives, scientifically. On his pay he could not afford a collection of weapons ; but of knives, classified according to their construction, with or without corkscrew and nail-file, and also according to the brand of the steel, the place of origin, the material of the case, and so on, he soon possessed large numbers, and in his room there stood tall cabinets with many shallow drawers, all neatly labelled. This brought him a reputation for scholarship. He could also write poetry, and even as a cadet at the military academy had always got top marks in Religious Instruction and in Composition ; and so one day the colonel called him into the office. " You're never going to make a useful cavalry officer," he said to him. " If I put a six-months' infant on a horse and sent him out in front of the squadron, he'd put up about as much of a show as you do. But it's a long time since the regiment had anyone at Staff College. Why don't you send your name up, Stumm ? "

So for two glorious years Stumm attended the staff college in the capital. There too he showed himself lacking in the intellectual acuteness essential to horsemanship, but he never missed a military concert, he frequented the museums, and he collected theatre programmes. He contemplated going into civil life, but he did not know how to set about it. The final result was that he was put down as neither suitable or definitely unfitted for service on the general staff ; he was regarded as clumsy and lacking in keenness, but on the other hand as a philosopher. So he was transferred to a staff job, being attached to the headquarters of an infantry division for another two years, to see how he would shape, and at the end of this period he belonged, as a cavalry captain, to the large number of those who, constituting the general staff's auxiliary reserve, never get away from the line, unless something quite out of the ordinary happens. Captain Stumm now served with another regiment, here too passing for an expert in military

theory. But his new superior officers also soon had pretty much
the same idea about the six-months' infant where practical soldier-
ing was concerned. His career was that of a martyr, all the way
up to the rank of lieutenant-colonel; but even as a major he no
longer dreamt of anything but a long furlough on half-pay, until
the time when he would be put on the retired list as an acting
colonel, that is to say, with the formal rank and the distinctions of
a colonel, even though without a colonel's pension. He no longer
cared in the least about promotion, which in line regiments went
according to seniority, slow and steady as the ticking of some incredibly slow clockwork. He wanted no more of those mornings
when, as the sun is only just rising, one comes in from the barrack-
square, having been cursed up hill and down dale, with dusty
boots, and goes into the mess to add the emptiness of several
wine-bottles to the emptiness of the long day still lying ahead.
He wanted no more of regular-army sociability, regimental anecdotes, and those regimental amazons who spent their lives at their
husbands' side, echoing their progress up the scale of rank on a
silvery scale of social notes, accurately pitched and so inexorably
refined as to be only just within the range of human hearing. And
he wanted no more of those nights when dust, wine, boredom,
the expanses of fields that had been galloped over, and the tyranny
of the horse, that everlasting subject of conversation, drove the
comrades-in-arms, married and unmarried alike, into that revelry
behind heavily curtained windows where wenches were stood on
their heads to have champagne poured into their petticoats—girls
that they had had hauled along, trembling with awe, fear, and
curiosity, by the universal Jew of those god-forsaken little Galician garrison-townships, who was like some cock-eyed, poky little
general store where one could get everything from love to saddle-
soap on credit, at interest. His only consolation in those times
was the studious enlarging of his collection of knives and cork-
screws, and many of these too were brought along for the crack-
brained lieutenant-colonel by the unfailing Jew, who rubbed
them up on his sleeve before he laid them on the table, with a
reverential expression on his face as though they were relics from
prehistoric graves.

The unexpected turn came when a comrade who had been
at the staff college with Stumm raised him from oblivion and

proposed his transfer to the War Ministry, where the department of army education was looking out for an assistant chief with outstanding civilian qualities of mind. Two years later Stumm, who had meanwhile advanced to the rank of colonel, was already in charge of the department. He was a different man since what he was mounted on was no longer the sacred animal of the cavalry, but an office chair. He became a major-general and could feel fairly certain that in time he would become a lieutenant-general. He had of course long ago shaved off his beard, but now, with advancing age, he was growing a forehead, and his tendency to tubbiness lent his appearance a look of something like all-round cultivation. Now too he was happy, and happiness is the very thing that enhances efficiency. He had been cut out for a position at the top, and this became apparent in everything. There was happiness for him in everything, in the dress worn by a strikingly got-up woman, in the audaciously bad taste of the then modern style of Viennese architecture, in the spread of variegated colour in a large vegetable-market, in the grey-brown asphalty air of the streets, that soft asphalt-atmosphere full of miasmas, scents and odours, in the din of the streets that would split apart for seconds, releasing one single sound, in the innumerable variety of civilians, and even in the small white-covered tables of the restaurants that were so incredibly individual, even if, undeniably, they all looked alike—in all this there was a happiness that echoed in his head like the jingling of spurs. It was a happiness such as civilian persons find only in a railway excursion into the countryside : one does not know how, but one is going to spend a day that will be green, gay, and somehow over-arching, dome-like, overhead. Encased within this feeling was that of his own importance, the importance of the War Ministry, of education and culture, and of every other human being ; and all of it was so intense that since he had been here Stumm had not even once thought of visiting the museums again or going to the theatre. All this was in fact something that seldom rose to the surface of consciousness, but it permeated everything, from the general's gold and scarlet braid to the carilloning of the church bells, and was itself rather like a music without which the dance of life would instantly come to a standstill.

Dash it all, he had made headway ! That was what Stumm

thought about himself as now, to fill the cup to overflowing, here he was standing in these rooms, in the midst of this celebrated assembly of great minds ! Here now he was ! His was the one and only uniform in these mind-permeated surroundings ! And there was something else, into the bargain, to make him marvel. If one imagines the sky-blue globe of the world slightly heightened in tone to the forget-me-not blue of Stumm's military tunic and consisting wholly and solely of happiness, fraught with meaning, filled with the mysterious brain-phosphorus of inner illumination, and then right at the centre of this globe the general's heart, and upon this heart, like the Virgin Mary standing on the serpent's head, a divine woman whose smile was interwoven with all things and was itself the secret gravity of all things : then one has approximately the impression that Diotima had made on Stumm von Bordwehr from the first hour when her image had filled his slowly moving eyes. General Stumm was really as little fond of women as of horses. His rather short plump legs had never been at home on horseback, and when, to make matters worse, he had had to talk horses even off duty, he used to dream at night that he had ridden himself sore, down to the very bone, and could not dismount ; in the same way, too, his natural disinclination for exertion had always made him disapprove of amorous excesses, and since his duties were quite fatiguing enough for him in them-selves he did not need to let off steam through any nocturnal safety-valves. True, in his day he had been no spoil-sport ; but whenever he spent his evening not among his knives but among his brother-officers, he generally took refuge in a wise remedy, his sense of physical harmony having soon taught him that one could rapidly drink one's way from riotous *joie-de-vivre* to a state of somnolence, and that had been much more in his line than the perils and disappointments of love. Only later, when he married and before long had to support two children as well as their ambitious mother, did he become fully conscious of how sensible his former habits of life had been, before he had succumbed to the temptation of matrimony, into which he had undoubtedly been lured solely by a certain unmilitariness attaching to the idea of a married warrior. Since that time he had developed a vivid extra-matrimonial ideal of womanhood, of which he obviously must have had the unconscious seeds in him before, and it consisted in a mild infatuation with women who intimidated him and thus relieved him from any obligation to exert himself gallantly. When he gazed at the female portraits that he had been in the habit of cutting out of illustrated magazines in his bachelor days—though this had always been merely a sideline to his main activities as a collector—he saw they all had this characteristic ; but he had not realised it at the time, and it had developed into overwhelming adoration only since his encounter with Diotima. Quite apart from the impression made by her beauty, he had right at the start, when he had heard that she was a second Diotima, had to resort to the encyclopædia to see what on earth a Diotima was, and then he did not completely grasp the allusion and could not see more than that it was connected with the great circle of civilian culture of which he, in spite of his position, unfortunately still knew far too little ; and so the intellectual superiority of the world merged with the physical charms of this woman. Nowadays, when the relations between the sexes have become so simplified, it cannot be too strongly emphasised that this is the most sublime experience a man can have. General Stumm's arms felt intellectually much too short to encompass Diotima's lofty voluptuousness, while his mind at the same moment experienced the same thing where the world and its culture were concerned, so that a gentle infatuation infiltrated into all that happened, and the General's roundish body was pervaded by something like the floating roundness of the globe itself.

It was this adoration that, a short time after Diotima had dismissed him from her immediate company, again led Stumm von Bordwehr back to her. He took up a position close to this admired woman, which he did all the more readily since he knew nobody else, and listened carefully to her conversations. He would have liked nothing better than to take notes, for, had he not been an ear-witness of the words with which Diotima welcomed the most various celebrities, he would not have thought it possible for anyone so to toy smilingly with such intellectual riches as with a string of pearls. Not until after she had several times ungraciously turned away from him did her gaze recall him to a sense of how ill it befitted a general to play the listener-in, and so force him to retreat. He strolled a few times solitarily through the overcrowded apartment, drank a glass of wine, and was just about to select a decorative point of vantage against a wall, when he discovered Ulrich, whom he had already seen at the first meeting. At this moment his memory lit up : Ulrich had been an inventive and restless lieutenant in one of the two squadrons over which General Stumm, then a lieutenant-colonel, had held gentle sway. ' One of my own sort,' Stumm thought, ' and even at his age he's got to this high position ! ' He made a bee-line for Ulrich, and after they had shaken hands on their re-union and chatted for a while about all the changes that had come about, Stumm indicated the gathering all around them and remarked : " Splendid opportunity for me to get acquainted with the world's main civilian problems ! "

" Well, General, you're in for plenty of surprises," Ulrich replied.

The General, who was in search of an ally, shook him warmly by the hand. " You were a lieutenant in the ninth Uhlans," he said in a tone of great significance, " and some day it'll turn out to have been a great honour for us, even if the others don't yet quite realise it as I do ! "

81 *Count Leinsdorf makes some comments on practical politics. Ulrich founds Associations.*

WHILE in the Council there had not yet been the slightest sign of anything like a result, the Collateral Campaign had been making tremendous progress at the Palais Leinsdorf. It was there that the threads of reality converged, and there Ulrich went twice a week.

Nothing astonished him so much as the number of associations and clubs that there were in existence. There came forward associations for field-sports and associations for water-sports, temperance associations and drinking-clubs, in short, associations and counter-associations. These associations existed to promote the interests of their members and to hamper those of the others. It gave one the feeling that everybody must belong to at least one association.

"You know, sir," Ulrich said in amazement, "this can no longer be called mere busybodiness, as one is innocently used to thinking it is. What we have here is a revelation of the monstrous fact that in the kind of highly organised State we have invented, with all its law and order, everyone still belongs to some band of highwaymen . . . ! "

But Count Leinsdorf had a weakness for Associations. "You must bear in mind," he replied, "that no good has ever yet come of ideological politics. What we must go in for is *practical* politics. I don't mind going as far even as to say that the all too intellectual endeavours going on around your cousin do harbour a certain danger ! "

"Will you let me have directives, sir ? " Ulrich asked.

Count Leinsdorf looked at him. He was wondering whether what he was about to reveal was not after all too audacious for the inexperienced younger man. But then he made up his mind.

"Well, you see," he began cautiously, "what I'm going to tell you now is something you may perhaps not know, because you are young. Practical politics means not doing the very thing one would like to do. On the other hand, one can win people over by granting some of their minor wishes."

His listener gazed at him, evidently awe-struck. And Count Leinsdorf smiled, a little flattered.

"Very well then," he began to expound. "What I was just saying is this—practical politics must on no account be based on the power of ideas, they must be determined by practical needs. Everybody, of course, would like to make all the beautiful ideas come true. That goes without saying. And so one must not do the very thing one would like to do ! Kant himself said so."

"So he did ! " Ulrich exclaimed in surprise at this piece of information. "But one must have a goal, all the same, mustn't one ? "

"A goal ? Bismarck wanted to see the King of Prussia great. That was his goal. He didn't know at the start that he would have to make war on Austria and France in order to achieve it, and that he would found the German Empire."

" I gather you mean to say, sir, that we should wish to see Austria great and mighty, and leave it at that ? "

" We have four years ahead of us yet. All sorts of things may happen in these four years. One can put a nation on its feet, but it must walk by itself. You see what I mean ? Put it on its feet—that's what we must do ! And a nation's feet are its established institutions, its parties, its associations and so forth, and not just the talk that goes on ! "

" Your Highness ! Even though it may not sound exactly so, that is a truly democratic thought ! "

" Well, well, it may be aristocratic too, though my fellow-peers don't see what I mean. What old Hennenstein and Türckheim said about it was that the whole thing would just turn out to be a mess. So let us set to work with caution. We must work on a small scale to begin with. Be as nice as you can to the people who come to us."

And so in the period immediately following Ulrich did not turn anyone away. For instance, a man came to see him and talked at great length about stamp-collecting. To begin with, he said, it made for friendship between the nations. Secondly, it satisfied the urge for property and position, which, as could not be denied, was the basis of society. Thirdly, it required something more than knowledge—one had to make decisions of a downright artistic nature. Ulrich took a good look at the man. His outward appearance was careworn and shabby. But the man seemed to sense the question in this gaze, for he asserted that stamps were also of great commercial value, which must not be under-estimated, the turnover amounting to millions ; the great stamp-auctions brought dealers and collectors from all over the world. It was a way of becoming rich. But speaking for himself, he was an idealist. He was completing a special collection, in which nobody showed any interest at present. All he wanted was that a great stamp-exhibition should be held in the Jubilee Year, and he would see to it all right that people began to take notice of his special field !

After him came another one, with the following story. When walking through the streets—but it was still more exciting if one took a tram—he had for years been in the habit of counting the number of strokes in the block letters of the names of shops (A for instance had three, M four) and dividing the sum by the number of letters. The average quotient had so far consistently remained two and a half. But obviously this could not be considered invariable, for it might alter with the very next street. This meant that variations caused great distress, whereas correct results caused great satisfaction, all of which resembled the cathartic effect ascribed to tragedy. If on the other hand one counted the letters themselves, what became apparent—and it was something that the gentleman he was addressing could convince himself of by experiment—was that divisibility by three remained a rare and wonderful exception to the ordinary rule, so that the majority of shop-signs positively brought about a sensation of disharmony that could be clearly observed—apart, that was, from those multiple letters, namely those made up of four strokes, such as for instance those in the word MEW, which caused a sensation of quite particular happiness. And what did this indicate ?— Ulrich's visitor asked. Simply that the Ministry of Health must issue a regulation encouraging the choice of four-stroke letter series in shop-signs and as far as possible suppressing the use of one-stroke letters such as O, S, I and C, the unproductiveness of which was the cause of mental depression.

Ulrich looked at the man and kept some distance away from him. Yet his visitor did not really give the impression of being a lunatic ; he was a ' better-class ' man in his thirties, with an intelligent and pleasant expression. He went on to explain calmly that the ability to do mental arithmetic was indispensable in all walks of life, that it was in keeping with the principles of modern educational methods to give lessons the form of a game, that statistics had often revealed profound relations between things long before their explanation was known, that the grave damage caused by an excessively bookish education was well known, and in conclusion that the great excitement that his findings had hitherto aroused in everyone who had decided to repeat his experiments spoke for itself. If the Ministry of Health could be induced to take over his discovery and make full use of it, other nations would soon follow suit, and the Jubilee Year would thus turn out to be a blessing for all humanity.

Ulrich gave all these people the following advice : " What you must do is found an Association. You have almost four years still

ahead of you, and if you succeed, I am sure His Highness will
exert all his influence on your behalf."

Most of them, however, already had an Association, and then
matters stood differently. It was relatively easy when a football
club agitated for its outside right to be given an honorary pro-
fessorship in order to demonstrate the importance of present-day
physical culture ; for in such a case one could always give them
to understand that the matter was under consideration. But it was
difficult in such cases as that of the approximately fifty-year-old
man who announced himself to be a senior executive officer in a
government department. His forehead shone with the nimbus
appropriate to a martyr's brow, and he declared himself the
founder and president of the Öhl Shorthand System Association,
who was taking the liberty of drawing the attention of the Secretary of the great patriotic Campaign to Öhl's system of shorthand.

Öhl's system of shorthand, he expounded, was an Austrian
invention, which was doubtless sufficient explanation of the fact
that it failed to be brought into general use or even to meet with
encouragement. He would make bold to ask whether the Secretary himself was a practising stenographer. And when Ulrich
answered in the negative, the intellectual advantages of shorthand
were explained to him. There was a saving of time, and also a
saving in mental energy. Had he ever considered the tremendous
waste of intellectual productivity that went on, day in, day out,
in the formation of these curlicues with all their prolixity, inexactitude, bewildering repetitions of similar elements and the
confusion between genuinely expressive, significant graphical com-
ponents and merely arbitrary personal flourishes ?

Ulrich became acquainted, to his amazement, with a man who
pursued ordinary handwriting, harmless as it had always seemed,
with inexorable hatred. From the point of view of a saving in
mental labour shorthand constituted a vital problem for the progress of humanity in this age of increasing haste. But from the
moral point of view, too, the question of Short or Long was of
decisive importance. The long-eared or asinine script, as it
might be called in conformity with the senior executive officer's
bitter strictures on its senseless loops, led people into inexactitude,
arbitrariness, extravagance, and a slovenly misuse of time, in

contrast with which shorthand educated one to precision, concentration of will-power, and manliness. Shorthand, he said, was in itself an education in doing what was necessary and refraining from the unnecessary and irrelevant. Did the Secretary not agree with him that inherent in this was a piece of practical morality that was of the greatest importance above all to Austrians? But the question could also be approached from the æsthetic point of view. Was prolixity not rightly considered ugly? Had not the great classical writers themselves laid it down that a high degree of appropriateness to the purpose was in itself an essential component of the Beautiful? But from the point of view of public health too (the senior executive officer continued) it was of the first importance to shorten the time spent in sitting humped over desks. Only after the shorthand problem had been expounded in this manner, and, to the listener's amazement, from other scientific points of view as well, did the visitor begin on the infinite superiority of Öhl's system over all other systems. He showed that from all the points of view hitherto considered every other system was nothing but a betrayal of the idea of shorthand. And then he proceeded to an account of his sufferings. There were the older, more powerful systems, which had had plenty of time to form alliances with all thinkable sorts of material interests. The commercial colleges taught the Vogelbauch system and were opposed to any kind of change, an attitude that—in accordance with the law of inertia—was of course also adopted by the world of commerce. Newspapers, which, as anyone could see, made a great deal of money out of advertisements by commercial colleges, set their face against all proposals for reform. And the Ministry of Education? That was the bitter irony of it all! said Herr Öhl. Five years ago, when it had been decided to make shorthand compulsory in secondary schools, the Ministry of Education had set up a committee of enquiry to investigate proposals as to the system to be chosen, and it went without saying that this commission was made up of representatives of the commercial colleges, the world of commerce, parliamentary stenographers who were of course hand in glove with the newspaper reporters, and no one else. It was as clear as daylight that the aim was to get the Vogelbauch system accepted. The Öhl Shorthand Association had uttered a warning and a protest, exposing this crime against the nation's precious inheritance. But the Ministry's doors were shut in the faces of its representatives, and still were !

Cases like this Ulrich reported to His Highness.

" Öhl ? " Count Leinsdorf asked. " And so he's an official ? " His Highness rubbed his nose for a long time, but came to no decision. " Perhaps you ought to see his departmental chief, and see if there's anything in him ? " he wondered after a while. But he was in a creative mood and withdrew his suggestion again. " No, I tell you what we'll do, we'll draw up a memorandum. Let them do the talking ! " And he added some confidential remarks that were intended to give Ulrich deeper insight into such matters. " You see, with all these things you never can tell whether they're nonsense or not. But the point is, my dear fellow, something important regularly results from the sheer fact that one attaches importance to something. I notice this, for instance, in the case of this Herr Doktor Arnheim, who is so thoroughly run after by the newspapers. The newspapers could just as easily do something else, after all. But when they do this, well, then Dr. Arnheim becomes important. You said, I think, this man Öhl has an Association ? That, of course, doesn't prove anything either. But on the other hand, we agree that one must be up-to-date, don't we ? And when a great many people are in favour of something, one can be pretty sure that something will come of it."

82 *Clarisse demands an Ulrich Year.*

IT was certainly for no other reason that Ulrich came to see her than that he had yet to give her a stern talking-to about the letter she had written to Count Leinsdorf; when she had come to see him recently, he had forgotten all about it. Still, it occurred to him on the way out that Walter was undoubtedly jealous of him and would be upset about this visit as soon as he heard of it. Yet Walter simply could not do anything to stop it. This situation, in which the majority of men find themselves, was really, if one came to think of it, rather a comical one : it is only after office-hours that men have time, if they happen to be jealous, to keep an eye on their women-folk.

The time of day that Ulrich had chosen for his trip out to see Clarisse made it unlikely that he would find Walter at home. It was very early in the afternoon. He had rung up to say he was coming. The windows looked as though they had no curtains, so intensely did the reflected whiteness of the snowy landscape gleam through the panes. In this inexorable light, which had closed in round the furniture and everything else, there Clarisse stood, and from the centre of the room looked, laughing, towards her friend. Where the slight curves of her slim body rounded out towards the window she flashed in vivid colours, while the shadow-side of her was a blue-brown mist, from which forehead, nose and chin jutted out like snowy ridges, their sharpness blurred by wind and sun-shine. It was less a human being that she reminded him of than the meeting of ice and light in the spectral solitude of an Alpine winter. Ulrich got a glimpse of the spell that she must at times cast on Walter, and his mixed feelings for his boyhood friend gave way for a brief moment to some insight into the spectacle pre-sented to each other by two human beings whose life he perhaps, after all, hardly knew.

" I don't know if you told Walter about the letter you wrote to Count Leinsdorf," he began, " but I've come to have a private talk with you and warn you to keep off such schemes in future."

Clarisse pushed two chairs along and made him sit down.

" Don't talk to Walter about it," she pleaded. " But tell me what you have against it. I suppose it *is* the Nietzsche Year you mean. What did this Count of yours say about it ? "

" What on earth do you expect him to have said about it ? It was positively crazy, you know, the way you connected it up with Moosbrugger ! And he'd probably have thrown the letter away anyway, even without that."

" Oh, would he ? " Clarisse was very disappointed. Then she declared : " So then it's lucky you have a say in these things too ! "

" I've told you already, you're simply mad ! "

Clarisse smiled, taking this as a piece of flattery. She laid her hand on her friend's arm and asked : " But you do think the Austrian Year is all nonsense, don't you ? "

" Naturally."

" But a Nietzsche Year would be a good thing. And why shouldn't it be all right to want something just because we happen to think, ourselves, it would be a good thing ? "

" And what exactly is your idea of a Nietzsche Year ? " he asked.

" That's your business ! "

" Don't make silly jokes."

" I'm not ! Tell me why it seems a silly joke to you to want to put into practice the things you think spiritually important ? "

" I'll tell you with pleasure," Ulrich answered, freeing his arm from the touch of her hand. " It doesn't have to be Nietzsche, after all. It might just as well be Christ or Buddha."

" Or you. Go on, work out an Ulrich Year ! " She said this just as calmly as she had on a previous occasion urged him to liberate Moosbrugger. This time, however, he was not absent-minded, but was looking her straight in the face while he listened to her words. On Clarisse's face there was only her usual smile, that involuntary smile that always broke forth like a merry little grimace squeezed out by the effort she was making.

' Oh, all right,' he thought to himself, ' she doesn't mean any harm.'

But Clarisse drew nearer to him again. " Why don't you make a Yourself Year ? You would have the power to do it now, I think, wouldn't you ? You mustn't tell Walter anything about it, I've told you that already, nor about the Moosbrugger letter either. Simply not mention I've been talking to you about it. But I assure you, this murderer is musical. Only he can't compose, that's all. Haven't you ever noticed that every human being is at the centre of a celestial globe ? When he moves from his place, it goes with him. That's the way to make music. Without any conscience, simply like the celestial globe all around one . . . ! "

" And so you want me to work out something of that sort for a year of my own, do you ? "

" No," Clarisse answered, just to be on the safe side. Her narrow lips were about to open in speech, but they tightened again, and the flame shot soundlessly out of her eyes. It was hard to say what radiated from her at such moments. One felt scorched as though one had come too near to something red-hot. Now she smiled ; but it was a smile that curled on her lips like ashes left after the flaring in her eyes had burnt itself out.

" That's just the sort of thing I could think out, though only in the last resort," Ulrich went on. " But I'm afraid what you want me to do is to make a *coup d'état* ! "

Clarisse reflected. " Well, then let's say a Buddha Year," she suggested, without taking any notice of his objection. " I don't know what Buddha insisted on. Well, only more or less. But let's just accept it, and once one regards it as important, then one jolly well ought to carry it out ! For either a thing deserves to be believed in, or it doesn't ! "

" All right, steady on. Nietzsche Year was what you said. But what actually was it that Nietzsche demanded ? "

Clarisse meditated. " Well, of course, I don't mean a Nietzsche monument or a Nietzsche street," she said in some embarrassment. " But people ought to be got to the point of living the way—"

" The way he demanded ? " Ulrich interrupted her. " But what *did* he demand ? "

Clarisse tried to find an answer, hesitated, and finally replied : " Oh, well, you know that yourself . . ."

" I know nothing at all ! " he teased her. " But I can tell you one thing—one can realise demands for an Emperor-Francis-Joseph-Jubilee-Year-Soup-Kitchen, or fulfil those of the Society for the Care and Protection of Domestic Cats, but one can no more give solid and enduring form to great thoughts than to music ! And what does that mean ? I don't know. But there it is."

He had now finally retreated to the little sofa, behind the small table ; this position was easier to defend than that on the little chair. In the clear space in the middle of the room, as it were on the far bank of a deceptive reflection prolonging the shining table-top, Clarisse was still standing and talking. And her slender body was quietly talking and thinking too. She actually felt everything she wanted to say first of all with her whole body, experiencing a ceaseless urge to do something with it. Ulrich had always thought her body hard and boyish, but now, softly swaying on feet close together, Clarisse all at once seemed to him like a Javanese

dancer. And he thought suddenly that it would not surprise him
if she fell into a trance. Or was he in a trance himself? He was
making a long speech.

" You would like to live according to your own ideas," he heard
himself say, " and you would like to know how that can be done.
But an idea is the most paradoxical thing in the world. The flesh
combines with ideas like a fetish. It becomes magical when there's
an idea in it. An ordinary box on the ears may, by association
with the ideas of honour, punishment, and the like, become a
matter of life and death. And yet ideas can never conserve themselves in the state in which they are strongest. They are like those
substances that when exposed to the air instantly transform
themselves into another, more permanent, but corrupted form of
existence. You have been through it often. For you are an idea
yourself, one in a particular state. You are touched by a breath
of something, and it's like when the quivering of strings suddenly
produces a note. And then there's something there in front of you
like a mirage, and the tangle of your soul takes on shape, becoming
an unending cavalcade, and all the beauties of the world seem to
stand along its road. Such things are often brought about by one
single idea. But after a while it comes to resemble all the other
ideas that you have had before, subordinating itself to them and
becoming part of your outlook and your character, your principles
and your moods. By then it has lost its wings and taken on an
unmysterious solidity."

Clarisse's only reply was : " Walter's jealous of you. Not about
me, or anything like that. But because you look as though you
could do the things he would like to do. See what I mean?
There's something about you that deprives him of himself. I
don't quite know how to express it."

She looked at him searchingly.

Their speeches seemed to interlace.

Walter had always been life's favourite spoilt child, sitting, as
it were, upon its lap. No matter what happened to him, he transformed it, imbuing whatever it was with a tender and affectionate
vitality. Walter had always been the one who experienced more
than others did. ' But this capacity to experience more is one of
the earliest and subtlest signs by which mediocrity can be recognised,' Ulrich thought to himself. ' The relations between things

rid experience of its personal poison or sweetness.' That was more or less it. And this very assurance that it was so was itself a connection, one for which one received neither a kiss nor a goodbye for ever. And yet Walter was jealous of him, was he? He was pleased to hear it.

" I told him to kill you," Clarisse reported.

" What ? "

" Kill you, that's what I said. After all, if you didn't amount to as much as you think you do, or if he were better than you and could only get peace of mind that way, it would be the logical conclusion, wouldn't it? And anyway, you can defend yourself."

" I must say, you don't go in for half-measures," Ulrich said, somewhat taken aback.

" Well, after all, we only talked about it. By the way, what do you think about it yourself? Walter says one mustn't even think such things."

" Oh yes, thinking about it's all right," he replied hesitantly, taking a careful look at her. Clarisse had her peculiar charm. Might it be said that it was as though she were standing somehow beside herself? She was both absent and present, and both very close together.

" Oh, *thinking* ! " she interrupted scornfully. She spoke towards the wall against which he was sitting, as though her eyes were fixed on a point somewhere in the air between them. " You're every bit as passive as Walter ! " These words, too, fell midway between them ; they kept their distance like an insult, and yet at the same time made it up to him by a confidential intimacy without which they could not have been uttered. " But what *I* say is : if you can think something, then you ought to be able to do it too," she insisted drily.

Then she moved away, walked to the window, and stood there with her hands clasped behind her back.

Ulrich stood up quickly, went over to her, and laid an arm round her shoulders. " Dear little Clarisse," he said, " you've just now been behaving a bit queerly. But I must put in a good word for myself. After all, I don't really matter to you, I should say."

Clarisse was staring out of the window. But now her gaze sharpened ; she was focusing on something out there in order to have something to hold on to. She felt as though her thoughts had been outside somewhere and were only just returning to her now. This sensation of being like a room, with the feeling still in it of a faint vibration from the shutting of the door, was not new to her. On and off she had days, even weeks, when everything round about her was lighter and brighter than usual, as though it would not need much effort to slip right off into that and go walking about the world without oneself. And then, again, there came difficult times in which she felt as though imprisoned; these generally lasted only a short while, but she was afraid of them as of a punishment, because then everything became narrow and sad. And in the present instant, which was distinguished by its clear, sober calm, she felt unsure; she no longer quite knew what she had wanted only a moment earlier, and this kind of leaden clarity and seemingly tranquil control was often the preliminary to the time of punishment. She tensed herself up, with the feeling that if she could keep the conversation going in a convincing way she would get herself back on to safe ground.

" Don't call me ' dear little '," she said sullenly, " or else it'll turn out to be me who kills you ! " Even as she said it, she heard it sound like pure fun. So she had succeeded. She turned her head cautiously to take a look at him. " Of course, that was only a way of putting it," she went on, " but you must realise that I mean something. Where did we leave off ? You said one can't live according to an idea. You haven't got the right sort of energy, neither you nor Walter ! "

" You called me—most horrifyingly—a passivist. But there are two kinds. There's a passive passivism, which is Walter's kind. And there's an active one."

" What is active passivism ? " Clarisse asked curiously.

" A prisoner's waiting for the chance to break out."

" Bah ! " said Clarisse. " Excuses ! "

" Well, yes," he conceded. " Perhaps."

Clarisse still held her hands clasped behind her back and stood with her legs wide apart, as though in riding-boots. " You know what Nietzsche says ? To want to know for sure is like wanting to walk on solid ground, it's cowardice. One must start at some point to do what one is out to do, and not just talk about it ! And it's you above all that I expected to do something special some day ! "

She had suddenly got hold of one of his waistcoat buttons and was twisting it, her face lifted to his. He involuntarily laid his hand on hers in order to protect the button.

"There's something I've been thinking about for a long time," she continued hesitatingly. "The whole rotten beastliness of things today doesn't come about because people do it, but because everyone lets it happen. It goes on growing out into the void." After this achievement she looked into his eyes. Then she went on vehemently: "Letting things happen is ten times more dangerous than doing things! Do you see what I mean?" She struggled inwardly, not sure whether to describe this more exactly. Then she added: "You do understand just what I mean, don't you, darling? Even though you do always say one should let things go their own way. But I know very well how you mean it! I've even sometimes thought to myself that you're the Devil."

These again were words that slipped out of Clarisse's mouth like a lizard. She was startled. After all, at the beginning she had only been thinking about Walter's begging for a child.

Ulrich noticed a flicker in her eyes, which were gazing up at him with a yearning expression. Her upturned face seemed to be flooded with something—not with anything beautiful, but rather with something at once ugly and pathetic. It was like a violent outbreak of sweat, behind which the face became blurred. But it was non-physical, purely imaginary. He felt himself infected with it against his will, and a slight absent-mindedness overcame him. He could no longer put up any real resistance to the madness in this way of talking, and finally he grabbed her hand, made her sit down on the sofa, and sat down beside her.

"And now I will tell you all about why I don't do anything," he began, and then fell silent.

Clarisse, who, in the instant of feeling his touch, had returned to her normal state of being, urged him on.

"One can't do anything, because—but you won't understand this anyway—" he began, going right to the beginning, but then he took out a cigarette and devoted himself to lighting it.

"Come on!" Clarisse prompted. "What were you going to say?"

But he remained silent.

So she pushed her arm behind his back and shook him, like a boy wanting to show off his strength. That was the nice thing about her, one did not need to say anything at all ; the mere gesture or suggestion of the extraordinary was quite enough to set her off in the world of imagination.

" You great big criminal ! " she cried out, and tried in vain to hurt him.

At this moment, however, they were disagreeably interrupted by Walter's return.

83 *The like of it happens,*
or,
Why does one not invent history ?

WHAT could Ulrich have said to Clarisse, anyway ?

He had kept silence because she had aroused in him a queer desire to utter the word ' God '. What he had wanted to say was something like this : ' God is far from meaning the world literally. The world is an image, an analogy, a figure of speech, that He must make use of for some reason or other, and it is of course always inadequate. We must not take Him at His word ; we ourselves must work out the sum that He sets us.' He wondered whether Clarisse would have agreed to regard it as a game of Indians and Cowboys or Bobbies and Thieves. He was sure she would. If someone took the first step, she would press close to his side, like a she-wolf, and keep a sharp look-out.

But there was something else that he had also had on the tip of his tongue, something about mathematical problems that did not admit of any general solution, though they did admit of particular solutions, the combining of which brought one nearer to the general solution. He might have added that he regarded the problem set by every human life as one of these. What one calls an age—without knowing whether one should by that understand centuries, millennia, or the span of time between schooldays and grandparenthood—this broad, unregulated flux of conditions would then amount to approximately as much as a chaotic succession of unsatisfactory and (when taken singly) false attempts at a solution, attempts that might produce the correct and total solution, but only when humanity had learnt to combine them all.

In the tram, going home, he remembered this. There were some other passengers travelling townwards, and the presence of these other people made him a little ashamed of such thoughts. One could tell by looking at them that they were on their way home from definite occupations or setting out towards definite entertainments, indeed one could tell even by their clothes what lay behind them or what their plans were. He studied the woman sitting next to him. She was without doubt a wife and mother, getting on for forty, very probably married to a professional man in the academic sphere, and she held a little opera-glass on her lap. Sitting beside her, thinking his thoughts, he felt like a small boy playing at something, and, what was more, like a small boy playing at something rather naughty.

For thinking a thought that does not have a practical purpose is surely a not quite decent, a furtive occupation ; and it is particularly the sort of thoughts that take tremendous strides as on stilts, touching experience only with tiny soles, that are open to the suspicion that they may be of disreputable origin. True, in earlier times, people talked of winged thoughts and flights of fancy, and in Schiller's day a man with such noble and exalted questions in his breast would have been greatly looked up to ; nowadays, on the other hand, the prevailing feeling is that there is something not right with such a person, unless it happens to be his profession and his source of income. Obviously, values have been shifted round. Certain questions have been taken out of man's heart. What has been set up for the breeding of high-flying thoughts is a kind of poultry-farm known as philosophy, theology or literature, where in their own way they multiply and increase beyond counting ; and that is quite convenient, for faced with such expansion nobody any longer needs to reproach himself with not being able to look after them personally. Respecting expert skills and specialisation as he did, Ulrich was at bottom determined not to raise any objection to such a division of activities. All the same, he still granted himself permission to think, in spite of being no professional philosopher. And at this moment he was picturing to himself that here was the road leading to the State organised on the beehive pattern. The queen would lay her eggs, the drones would lead a life devoted to the pleasures of the flesh and of the mind, and the workers would work. It was quite possible to imagine mankind so organised ; the total achievement might even be increased. At present every man has, so to speak, the whole of mankind within himself, but by this time that has quite obviously become too much and no longer works at all efficiently ; the result is that the humanities and humanitarianism have practically become sheer swindle. For the success of this State it would perhaps be necessary to make new arrangements in the division of labour, in order that an intellectual synthesis might be effected in one special group of these groups of workers. For without intellect . . . ? What Ulrich meant was that he would not much care for it. But this was of course a prejudice. After all, one does not really know what are the things that matter.

He shifted in his seat and considered the reflection of his face in the window-pane opposite, in order to distract his thoughts. But what happened after a while was that his head, floating there in the fluid glass, became wonderfully insistent somewhere half-way between the interior and the exterior of things, demanding some kind of completion.

Was there really a war going on in the Balkans, or not ? Some sort of intervention was undoubtedly going on, but whether that was war or not he did not exactly know. There were so many things stirring humanity. The record for high-altitude flying had again been broken—something to be proud of. If he was not mistaken, it was now 3,700 metres, and the man's name was Jouhoux. A Negro boxer had beaten the white champion, so winning the world championship ; Johnson his name was. The President of France had gone to Russia ; there was talk of world peace being in danger. A newly discovered tenor was earning sums in South America that had never been equalled even in North America. There had been a terrible earthquake in Japan—the poor Japanese. In short, there was a great deal going on. These were stirring times, round about the end of 1913 and the beginning of 1914. But two years, or five years, earlier the times had also been stirring times : every day had had its excitements. And yet one had only a faint memory, or no memory at all, of what had actually been happening then. One could put it all more briefly. The new cure for syphilis was making . . . Research into plant-metabolism was becoming . . . The conquest of the South Pole seemed . . . Professor Steinach's experiments were arousing . . . In this way quite half the definiteness of things could be left out, and it did not make much difference. What a strange affair history was, come to think of it! It could safely be asserted of this and that event that it had by this time found its proper place in the annals of history, or certainly would find it; but whether this or that event had ever occurred at all was not by any means certain. For what is essential to the occurrence of anything is that it should occur in a particular year and not in another or perhaps not at all; and it is also essential that the occurrence should itself occur, and not merely something similar or the like of it. But that is precisely what nobody can assert of history, unless he happens to have written it down at the time, as the newspapers do, or unless it is a matter of professional or pecuniary affairs, for it is naturally important to know in how many years one will be entitled to a pension or when one will possess a certain sum of money or have spent it; and in such a context even wars can become memorable affairs. This history of ours looks pretty unsafe and messy, when looked at from close at hand, something like a half-solidified swamp, and then in the end, strangely enough, it turns out there is after all a track running across it, that very 'road of history' of which nobody knows whence it comes.

This *being the material of history* was something that made Ulrich indignant. The luminous, swaying box in which he was travelling seemed to him like a machine in which several hundred-weight of humanity were shaken to and fro in the process of being made into something called 'the future'. A hundred years earlier they had sat in a mail-coach with just the same look on their faces, and in a hundred years from now heaven only knew what would be happening to them, but they would be up-to-date people sitting just the same way in the up-to-date machines of the future. Feeling this, he revolted against this impotent putting-up-with changes and conditions, against this helpless contemporaneity, the unsystematic, submissive, indeed humanly undignified stringing-along with the centuries—and it was just as though he had suddenly rebelled against the hat, curious enough in shape, that he wore upon his head.

Involuntarily he got up and finished his journey on foot. In the city, that larger receptacle for humanity in which he now found himself, his sense of discomfort gave way to good humour again.

It was a crazy notion of little Clarisse's to want to have a Year of the Mind. He concentrated his attention on this point. What made it so senseless ? But one might just as well ask why Diotima's patriotic Campaign was senseless.

Answer number one : because world history was a story that undoubtedly came into existence just the same way as all other stories. Nothing new ever occurred to authors, and one copied from the other. That was the reason why all politicians studied history instead of biology or the like. So much for authors.

Answer number two : history, however, came into existence for the most part without any authors. It evolved not from a centre, but from the periphery, from minor causes. It probably did not take as much as one was given to thinking it did to turn Gothic man or the ancient Greek into modern civilised man. For human nature was equally capable of cannibalism and of the *Critique of Pure Reason*. It could produce either with the same convictions and qualities according to what the prevailing conditions were, and, in either case, the inner differences that corresponded to the large-scale differences in the external world were on a very small scale indeed.

Digression number one : Ulrich recalled a similar experience dating from his military period. The squadron rode in double file and ' Passing on of orders ' was practised, an order spoken in a low voice being passed on from man to man. Now, if the order given in front was : ' Sergeant-major to move to the head of the column ', what came out at the rear was : ' Eight troopers to be shot immediately ' or something of that sort. And it was in a similar manner that world history came about.

Answer number three : if one were therefore to transplant a whole generation of present-day Europeans, while still in their infancy, into the Egypt of the year five thousand B.C. and leave them there, world history would begin all over again at the year five thousand, at first repeating itself for a while and then, for reasons that no man can guess, gradually beginning to deviate.

Digression number two : the law of world history, it now occurred to him, was nothing but the fundamental principle of government in old Kakania, namely that of ' muddling through '. Kakania was an immensely shrewd State.

Digression number three—or answer number four ? The course of history was therefore not that of a billiard-ball, which, once it had been hit, ran along a definite course ; on the contrary, it was like the passage of the clouds, like the way of a man sauntering through the streets—diverted here by a shadow, there by a little crowd of people, or by an unusual way one building jutted out and the next stood back from the street—finally arriving at a place that he had neither known of nor meant to reach. There was inherent in the course of history a certain element of going off the course. The present moment was always like the last house of a town, which somehow no longer quite counts among the townhouses. Each generation asks in amazement : Who am I and what were my predecessors ? There would be more sense in asking : Where am I ? and in assuming that one's predecessors were not of a different kind, but merely in a different place. That would get us a little further, he thought.

It was he himself who had all the way along been giving his answers and digressions these numbers, and while doing so he had glanced now into a passing face, now into a shop-window, in order not to let his thoughts run away with him entirely. But now, in spite of this, he had gone slightly off his course, and he had to stop for a moment to make sure where he was and find the best way home. Before taking this route, he made an effort to re-state his question once again and exactly. What it came to was that crazy little Clarisse was quite right : one ought to make history, one ought to invent it, even if he had denied it while they were arguing. But why did one not do so ?

At this moment all that occurred to him by way of answer was Director Fischel of Lloyd's Bank, his friend Leo Fischel, with whom in years past he had now and then sat outside a café in the summer. For Fischel—if Ulrich had been having this conversation with him instead of conducting it as a monologue—would now have answered in his characteristic way : ' I wish I had your worries ! '

Ulrich was grateful to him for this refreshing answer that he would have given. ' My dear Fischel,' he immediately replied in his thoughts, ' it's not as simple as all that. I say history, but what I mean, you will remember, is our life. And after all I admitted from the very start that there is something very improper about my question : why does man not make history ? That is, why does he only attack history like an animal, when he is hurt, when things are on fire close behind him ? Why, in short, does he make history only in an emergency ? Well now, tell me, why does that sound improper ? What have we against it, although what it amounts to, after all, is only that man shouldn't let human life drift the way things will always drift if you let them ? '

' But everybody knows how that happens,' Director Fischel would retort. ' One must be thankful if the politicians and the clergy and the big-wigs who haven't anything else to do, and all the other people who trot around with their fixed ideas, don't make a mess of everyday life. And apart from that, there's modern knowledge. If only every second person nowadays wasn't an ignoramus ! '

And of course Director Fischel was right. One must be thankful if one knew enough about stocks and shares, and if other people didn't do too much in the history line just because they claimed they knew something about it. One couldn't get along without ideas—heaven forbid !—but the right thing was a certain equilibrium between them, a balance of power, an armed peace in the realm of ideas, so that no side could set too much happening. Modern knowledge was in fact Fischel's sedative.

All this was a feeling fundamental to civilisation. And yet there was no getting past the fact that the contrary feeling also existed and was becoming more and more marked, that the times of heroical-political history, which was made by hazard and its knights, were to a large extent obsolete and must be replaced by a planned answer to the problems, an answer in which all those whom it concerned would play their part.

But here the Ulrich Year came to an end with Ulrich's arrival on his own doorstep.

84

The assertion that even ordinary life is of a Utopian nature.

HERE at home he found the customary stack of letters and papers sent on to him by Count Leinsdorf. An industrialist had offered a prize, of an unusually large sum of money, to be awarded for the best achievement in the military training of civilian youth. The archiepiscopal diocesan court had stated its views on the project for the founding of a large orphanage, declaring that it must point out the difficulties that would result from indiscriminate inter-denominationalism. The Committee for Culture and Education reported on the success of the provisionally announced definitive suggestion for a great Emperor-of-Peace-and-Nations-of-Austria Monument in the vicinity of the Palace ; after appropriate con-sultation with the Imperial-Royal Ministry of Culture and Educa-tion, and enquiry among the leading art associations and engineers' and architects' societies, the resulting divergences of opinion had been so considerable that the Committee found itself in the posi-tion of being able to announce, without prejudice to requirements such as might later eventuate and subject to obtaining the assent of the Central Executive Committee, a competition for the best idea for a competition with regard to a monument, pending a decision as to whether such a monument was to be erected at all. The Chamberlain's Office, after due perusal, returned to the Central Executive Committee the proposals that had been sub-mitted for perusal three weeks earlier and stated that although it was unable at present to inform the Committee of any Most Gracious expression of opinion, it considered it desirable that for the time being public opinion should be allowed to take shape on these points as on others. The Imperial-Royal Ministry of Culture and Education regretted, re the Committee's communica-tion reference number such-and-such, that it was not in a position to recommend any action in support for the Öhl Shorthand Association. The Block-Letter Association for the Improvement of National Health announced its foundation and applied for a financial grant.

And in such a manner it went on. Ulrich pushed aside this batch of gleanings from the real world and meditated for a while. Suddenly he got up, called for his hat and coat, and announced that he would not be at home for the next hour or hour-and-a-half. He hailed a cab and returned to Clarisse.

Darkness had fallen. Only through one window in the house did a little light shine on to the road. The footprints in the snow had frozen hard, forming holes that one stumbled in. The outside door was shut and the visitor was not expected, so that shouts, knocking, and clapping of hands remained unanswered for quite a while. When at last Ulrich stood inside the room, it seemed to be no longer the room that he had left only a short time ago, but an estranged, astonished world containing a table laid for the simple meal that two people were to share in solitude, chairs on each of which lay something that had made itself at home there, and walls that seemed only reluctantly to give way before the intruder.

Clarisse, who was wearing a plain woollen dressing-gown, laughed. Walter, who had let the late-comer in, blinked in the light as he put the big door-key away in a table-drawer.

" I have come back," Ulrich said without beating around the bush, " because I still owe Clarisse an answer."

Then he resumed at the point where his conversation with Clarisse had been interrupted by Walter's arrival. After a while the room, the house, all sense of time, had vanished, and the words hung somewhere high over the blueness of space, in the meshes of the stars. Ulrich elaborated the programme of living the history of ideas instead of the history of the world. The difference—he began by saying—would lie, first of all, less in what happened than in the significance attached to it, in the intention associated with it, in the system embracing each individual happening. The system at present prevailing was that of reality, and it was like a bad play. It was not for nothing that one talked of ' the theatre of world events ', for in life the same roles, complications, and plots kept on arising. People loved because there was love, and in the same way that love was always made ; people were proud on the pattern of the Noble Savage, or proud as a Spaniard, as a virgin, or as a lion ; indeed, in ninety out of a hundred cases even murder was committed only because it was regarded as tragic and magnificent.

Moreover, the successful political moulders of reality, apart from the very great exceptions, have much in common with the scribblers of box-office successes ; the lively events that they create, boring as they are in their lack of intellectual content and novelty, nevertheless, precisely for this reason, reduce us to that condition of drowsy lowered resistance in which we will put up with anything if only it is a change. So regarded, history is seen to arise out of routine ideas and all that is indifferent in the realm of ideas, and reality arises primarily out of the fact that nothing is done for the sake of ideas. All this might be briefly summed up, he asserted, by saying that we cared too little about what happened and too much about to whom, where, and when it happened, so that what mattered to us was not the spirit of events but their plot, not the making accessible of some new content of life but only distributing what was already in existence, in a way exactly corresponding to the difference between good plays and merely successful plays. The conclusion to be drawn from this was, however, that one must do the very opposite, namely first of all abandon the attitude of personal greed towards one's experiences. So one would have to look upon these experiences less as upon something personal and real and more as upon something general and abstract, or rather, one would have to regard them with as much detachment as if they were something painted or as if one were listening to a song. They must not be given that turn towards oneself ; they must be turned upward and outward. And if that was to be valid for the personal attitude, something must be done, furthermore, on a collective scale, which Ulrich could not quite describe but referred to as something like the pressing of the grapes, the cellaring of the wine, and something he called the thickening of the intellectual juices, without which the individual, of course, could not feel anything but helpless and abandoned to his own resources. And while he was talking thus, he remembered the moment when he had said to Diotima that reality ought to be abolished.

It was almost a matter of course that Walter began by declaring all this to be a perfectly commonplace assertion. As if the whole world, literature, art, science, and religion were not a ' pressing and cellaring ' anyway ! As if any educated person denied the value of ideas or did not pay homage to the spirit, to beauty and goodness ! As if all education were anything but an initiation into an intellectual and spiritual system !

Ulrich made his case clearer by pointing out that education signified no more than an initiation into whatever happened to be the contemporary and prevailing thing, which had arisen out of haphazard arrangements, from which it followed that in order to acquire intellectuality and spirituality one must first of all be convinced that as yet one had none. This he called an entirely open attitude, poetically creative and morally experimental on a large scale.

Now Walter declared the assertion was an impossible one. " You have a charming way of putting it," he said. " As though we had any choice at all between the living of ideas and the living of one's own life ! But perhaps you will recall the quotation : ' I am no subtly reasoned book, I am a man, of contradictions made.' Why don't you go still a step further ? Why not demand that we should abolish the belly for the sake of pure ideas, and be done with it ? But my answer to that is : ' Of common substance man is made.' The fact that we stretch out our arm and withdraw it, that we don't know whether to turn right or left, that we are made up of habits, prejudices, and earth, and yet go our way according to our strength—*that* is the thing that makes man human ! And so all one needs to do is to measure up what you say against reality, even approximately, and it will turn out to be, at the most, literature ! "

" If you will permit me," Ulrich conceded, " to include all the other arts under that heading too, all doctrines of the art of living, all religions and so on, then, certainly, I will make a similar assertion, namely that our existence ought to consist wholly and solely of literature."

" Oho, so you call the mercifulness of the Saviour or the life of Napoleon *literature* ? " Walter exclaimed. But then something better occurred to him. He turned towards his friend with the calm air of one who holds a trump card in his hand and declared : " You are the kind of person who declares that the meaning of fresh vegetables is tinned vegetables."

" I dare say you're right. You might also say I'm the sort of person who will only cook with salt," Ulrich admitted calmly. He did not want to talk about it any more.

But here Clarisse joined in, turning to Walter. " I don't know why you argue with him. Haven't you always said, whenever there was something special happening to us : ' Now this is something one ought to be able to perform on a stage, in front of everybody, so that they would all have to see it and understand it.' Really one ought to sing ! " she said, and turned to Ulrich in agreement. " One ought to *sing* oneself ! "

She had got up and walked forward into the little circle of the chairs. Her bearing was a slightly awkward embodiment of her wishes, as though she were about to dance before them.

Ulrich, who was sensitive about the bad taste of such exhibitions of feeling, at this instant remembered that most people—or, to be quite frank about it, the average person, whose mind is stimulated without being able to create—do cherish this wish to act out the role of themselves. They are after all the same people in whom ' something unutterable ' happens so easily : truly, this is their favourite expression and the foggy hinterland against which the thing they utter appears vaguely magnified, so that they never recognise its proper value. To put a stop to it, he said : " That's not what I meant, but Clarisse is right. The theatre proves that violent states of personal experience may serve an impersonal purpose, a complex of meaning and metaphor, that just about half separates them from the person."

" I know exactly what Ulrich means ! " Clarisse chimed in again. " I can't remember anything ever having been a special pleasure to me because it happened to me personally. The main thing was that it happened ! Take music, for instance," she said, turning to her husband. " You surely don't want to ' have ' it, do you ? It gives no other happiness than that of being there. We draw the experiences towards our self and spread them out again in the same movement. We want ourselves, certainly, but we don't want to own ourselves as pedlars own their wares ! "

Walter clutched at his temples. But for Clarisse's sake he went on to a new refutation. He exerted himself to make his words come out with the force of a steady, cold jet. " If you place the value of an attitude only in the radiation of intellectual energy," he said to Ulrich, " then I should like to ask you—surely that would only be possible in a life that had no other purpose than the generating of intellectual energy and power ? "

" It is the life that all existing States and governments claim they are striving towards," Ulrich retorted.

" And so you mean to say, in such a State people would live according to great feelings and ideas, according to systems of philosophy and what they read in novels ? " Walter continued. " Well then, I ask you further : would they live in such a way that great philosophy and poetry would *arise*, or in such a way that the very lives they lived would, so to say, be philosophy and poetry in terms of flesh and blood ? I have no doubt as to which you mean, for the first alternative would be in no way different from what is anyway understood by a civilised State nowadays. But since it is the second you mean, you overlook the fact that there philosophy and poetry would be pretty superfluous. And so, apart from the fact that nobody can even begin to imagine this life of yours, this life lived according to the nature of art, or whatever you like to call it, it would mean nothing more or less than the end of art ! " So he concluded, producing this trump with special emphasis for Clarisse's benefit.

It had its effect. It took even Ulrich a little while to recover. But then he laughed, asking : " But don't you know that every perfect life would be the end of art ? It seems to me you yourself are on the way to giving up art for the sake of perfecting your life, aren't you ? "

He did not mean it maliciously, but Clarisse pricked up her ears.

" Every great book," he went on, " breathes this spirit, which loves the destinies of individuals because they are at loggerheads with the conventional forms that the community tries to impose upon them. It leads towards decisions that evade decision. All one can do is reproduce their lives. Extract the meaning from all poetic works, and what you will have is a denial, not complete of course, but an endless series of individual examples that are based on experience, negating all valid rules, principles, and prescriptions on which society is based, the very society that is so fond of these poetic works. Ultimately a poem, and the mystery of it, cuts the meaning of the world clear, where it is bound fast to thousands of ordinary words, cuts it loose, and so makes it into a balloon that goes floating up and away. If we call that beauty, as it is usual to call it, then we ought to see that beauty is an unspeakably ruthless upheaval, far more cruel than any political revolution ever was."

Walter had grown pale to the lips. This view of art as a negation of life, as something in antagonism to life, was one that he hated. In his eyes it meant bohemianism, the last vestige of an outgrown desire to *épater le bourgeois*. He noticed the irony in the inevitable fact that beauty could not exist in a perfect world because it would have become superfluous ; but what he failed to hear was his friend's unuttered question.

For Ulrich himself was perfectly aware of the one-sidedness of what he had asserted. He might just as well have said the opposite of what he had said, and, instead of asserting that art was a denial, have called it love. For it beautifies what it loves ; and there is perhaps in the whole wide world no other means of making an object or a being beautiful than that of loving it. And it is only because even our love is a thing of bits and pieces that beauty is something like intensification and contrast. And it is only in the sea of love that a concept of perfection beyond all possibility of intensification merges into one with the concept of beauty, which is based on intensification. Once again Ulrich's thoughts had touched the very borders of the ' kingdom ', and he stopped short in irritation.

Meanwhile Walter had collected his thoughts, and after having first declared his friend's suggestion that people should live more or less as they read to be a commonplace one, and a moment later declaring it to be an impossible one, he now set out to prove that it was both vicious and beastly.

" If a man," he began in the same tone of artificial restraint as before, " were to make your proposal the basis of his life, he would have—to say nothing of other impossibilities—to approve of practically everything that stimulated a fine idea in him, indeed of everything that had this possibility inherent in itself. That would of course mean universal decadence. But since that side of things is presumably a matter of indifference to you—or perhaps you are thinking of those vague general arrangements of which you didn't give any details—I should merely like some information about the personal consequences. It seems to me that inevitably such a man, in all cases when he did not happen to be the poetic creator of his own life, would be worse off than an animal. If no idea occurred to him, no decision would occur to him either, and so for a large part of his life he would simply be at the mercy of his urges, his moods, and the usual banal passions of humanity, in a word, he would be at the mercy of the most utterly impersonal element in the make-up of a human being, and for as long as the obstruction in the upper system persisted, he would just have to carry on sturdily letting happen to himself, so to speak, whatever happened to occur to him ! "

" He ought then to refuse to do anything ! " Clarisse answered in Ulrich's place. " That is the active passivism of which one must be capable in certain circumstances ! "

Walter could not bring himself to look at her. The capacity for refusal, after all, played a large part in their life together. This was Clarisse who had jumped up and stood there on the bed, looking like a small angel in her long nightdress falling to her feet, and, with teeth flashing, had declaimed in the Nietzschean manner : " Like a plummet I cast my question into your soul ! A child and the wedded state are your desire, but I shall ask you : Are you the man to whom it is permitted to desire a child ? Are you the conqueror, the master of your virtues ? Or is it the beast, and natural need, that speaks out of you ? " In the half-darkness of the bedroom it had been gruesome enough to watch, and in vain he had tried to lure her back under the bed-clothes. And so now in future she would have a new slogan at her disposal : active passivism, of which one must be capable if need be. This was entirely the voice of a Man Without Qualities. Did she confide in him ? Was it then he who was encouraging her in her oddities ? These questions wriggled like worms in Walter's breast, and he felt almost sick. He became pale as ashes, and all the tension went out of his face, so that it shrivelled up in helpless wrinkles.

Ulrich noticed this and asked in concern whether anything was the matter.

With an effort Walter said there was nothing the matter, and added, with a valiant smile, that Ulrich should just go on to the end of his nonsensical talk.

" Oh, lord, yes," Ulrich admitted indulgently, " you're not so far wrong. But out of a spirit of sportsmanship we are often tolerant of actions that are injurious to ourselves, if only our enemy performs them in an elegant manner. The value of the execution then rivals the value of the damage. Very often, too, we have an idea that we act on for a bit, but after a while its place is taken over by habit, inertia, selfishness, and the promptings of our urges, because that is the way things work. And so what I have described is perhaps a condition that cannot by any means be carried to its conclusion. But one thing must be said for it : it's nothing more or less than the prevailing condition in which we live."

Walter had pulled himself together again. " If one turns truth upside down, one can always say something that is just as true as it is topsy-turvy," he murmured mildly, without hiding the fact that he was not interested in any further argument. " It's just like you to maintain that something is impossible but real."

Clarisse, however, rubbed her nose very vigorously. " Oh, but I think it's very important that there's something impossible in all of us," she said. " It explains so much. While I was listening I got the feeling : if someone cut us open our whole life might look like a ring, just something round about something." She had already a moment earlier pulled off her wedding-ring and now peeped through it at the lamp-lit wall. " I mean, after all there's nothing in the middle of it, and yet it looks just as if that were the very thing that is important to it. And that's something even Ulrich can't express perfectly just in a flash ! "

And so this discussion unfortunately ended hurtfully for Walter after all.

85 General Stumm's endeavour to get the civilian mind into proper order.

ULRICH had probably been out an hour longer than he had said he would be when he left the house, and when he returned he was told that an officer had been waiting for him for some length of time. To his surprise the visitor waiting for him upstairs was General von Stumm, who hailed him in the comradely spirit of bygone regimental days.

" My dear fellow," the General exclaimed as Ulrich came in, " you must forgive me for butting in on you so late, but I couldn't get away from duty any earlier, and anyway I've been sitting here surrounded by your books for a good two hours—upon my word, a collection fit to frighten one stiff ! "

After some exchange of courtesies it appeared that what had brought Stumm along was an urgent problem very near to his heart. Sitting with one leg perkily crossed over the other, which was a little difficult for a man of his embonpoint, and stretching out his arm and his little hand, he declared :

" Urgent ? What I always tell the fellows on my staff when they come along with an urgent file is : there's nothing urgent on earth except going to the privy. But seriously, what brings me to you is something of terrific importance. I've already told you that I regard your cousin's house as a special opportunity for me to become acquainted with the most important civilian problems in the world. After all, it *is* something non-military for once, and I can assure you I'm frightfully impressed. But on the other hand, although we brass-hats may have our weaknesses, we're not nearly as stupid as most people think. I hope you'll agree with me that when we do get down to doing something we make a thorough job of it. You do agree ? Well, that's what I expected of you. So I can put things quite frankly and confess, in spite of what I've just said, that I'm ashamed for this military mind of ours. Yes, ashamed—that's what I said ! I dare say, apart from the Chaplain-General I'm the man in the army these days who has the most to do with things of the mind and spirit. But I don't mind telling you, if one takes a good look at our military mind, outstanding as it is, it looks like a morning roll-call. I sincerely hope you haven't forgotten what a roll-call is ? Well, there it is, the orderly officer puts down so many men and horses present, so many men and horses absent, sick or otherwise, Uhlan Leitomischl absent without leave, and so forth. But what he doesn't report is *why* so many men and horses are present or sick and so on. And precisely that's the sort of thing one always needs to know when one has anything to do with the civil administration. The soldier's way of putting things is short, simple, and to the point, but I very often have to palaver with these chaps from the civilian Ministries, and they always ask, at every turn, why what I propose should be done, and keep on referring to considerations and complications of a higher order. Well then—I take it I can rely on you that what I am going to say now is between you and me and the gatepost—I've put a suggestion to my chief, His Excellency Frost von Aufbruch, or rather, I mean it to be more in the way of a surprise for him, that I am using this opportunity at your cousin's to have a thorough go at really getting the hang of these considerations and complications of a higher nature, and, if I may say so without seeming to boast, to graft them on to the military mind. After all, we have in the forces doctors, vets, dispensers, chaplains, auditors, commissariat officers, engineers, and bandmasters. But what is still lacking is a department of co-ordination with the civilian mind."

Ulrich noticed only now that Stumm von Bordwehr had brought a courier's satchel up with him : it was propped against a leg of the writing-desk, one of those large hide bags, to be carried by a strong strap slung over the shoulder, used for transporting documents through the far-flung buildings of government offices and through the streets from one department to another. Obviously the General had arrived accompanied by an orderly, who must be waiting downstairs, though Ulrich had not noticed anyone ; for it seemed to be a great effort for Stumm to manage the heavy satchel, which he pulled on to his knees in order to get the little steel lock, which looked monstrously like a piece of war-machinery, to open.

" I've not been wasting my time since I've been taking part in your enterprise," the General said, smiling, while his pale blue tunic grew tight around the gold buttons as he stooped. " But you see, there are things I can't quite find my way about in."

He fished out of the satchel a whole handful of loose sheets of paper covered with weird inscriptions and diagrams.

" Your cousin," he began to explain, " well, I once had a thorough talk with your cousin about this—what she wants, naturally enough, is that her endeavours to set up a spiritual monument to Our Most Gracious Sovereign should bring forth an idea that would, as it were, be paramount to all the ideas that people have nowadays. But I've already noticed, much as I can't help admiring all these people she invites for this purpose, that it's a devilish difficult thing to do. If one of them says one thing, the other one goes and says the opposite—I dare say you've noticed it too ?—but what strikes *me* at least as far worse is that the civilian mind seems to be the same as what, if it's a horse, you call a poor doer. I dare say it comes back to you ? You can feed double rations to a beast of that sort, and it won't grow any fatter ! Or let's say," he said in qualification, since his host had raised a slight objection, " all right then, you can also say it grows fatter every day, but it doesn't develop any bone and its coat doesn't shine. All it gets is a grass-belly. Well now, that fascinates me, you know, and I've made up my mind to look into this question of why the whole thing can't be got into proper order."

Smiling, Stumm handed his former lieutenant the first of the sheets of paper. " People can say what they like about us," he expatiated, " but order is something we military have always been good at. Here, that's the consignment of the main ideas I got out of these people at your cousin's meetings. You'll see, when you get each one of them by himself, it turns out that what he thinks most important is something different from what each of the others thinks."

Ulrich looked at the paper in astonishment. It was drawn up in the manner of a registration form, or indeed of a military list, with horizontal and perpendicular lines dividing it into fields, in which there were entries in words, and words that somehow seemed not quite to fit into such a framework. There in the copy-book penmanship of army administration were the names : Jesus Christ ; Buddha, Gautama, otherwise Siddharta ; Laotse ; Luther, Martin ; Goethe, Wolfgang ; Ganghofer, Ludwig ; Chamberlain . . . ; and many others, and it was obvious that this list was continued on another page. Then, in a second column, came the words Christianity, Imperialism, Century of Communications, and so on, with yet other columns of words adjoining them.

" I might also call it pages from the Domesday Book of Modern Culture," Stumm explained. " For we have elaborated it further, and it now contains the names and the originators of the ideas by which we have been moved in the last twenty-five years. I had no idea what a job it would be ! "

And when Ulrich asked how he had got this inventory together, he happily explained the procedure according to his system.

" I had to get a captain, two lieutenants and five N.C.O.s working on it, to get it done in such a short time. If it had been permissible for us to use completely modern methods, we would have sent a questionnaire round to all regiments, asking : ' Who do you think is the greatest man ? ' the way they do it nowadays in the newspapers and the like, you know, together with the order to send in a report of the results. But of course you can't do that sort of thing in the army, because naturally no unit can be allowed to report any answer but ' His Majesty The Emperor '. So then I thought of investigating what books are most widely read and have gone into the biggest editions. But there we pretty soon discovered that apart from the Bible it's the Post Office New Year's booklet with the postage rates and the old jokes in it, which every householder gets from his postman in return for his annual tip. And that again made us realise how difficult the civilian mind is, for generally the books that pass for the best are of course those that are suitable for every reader, or at least, as I've been told, in Germany an author has to have a great many like-minded readers before he can pass as having an unusual mind. Well then, so we couldn't take that road either. And how it was done in the end I can't tell you at the moment—it was an idea Corporal Hirsch had, in co-operation with Lieutenant Melichar—but we managed it."

General Stumm put the sheet of paper aside and, with an expression heralding considerable disappointments, produced another. After completing a survey of the Central European stock of ideas he had not only discovered to his regret that it consisted of nothing but contradictions, but he had also been amazed to find that these contradictions, when more closely investigated, began to merge into each other.

" By now I've got used to being told something different by each of the famous people at your cousin's, when I ask them to enlighten me," he said. " But what I simply can't get the hang of is why, after I've been talking to them for some time, it strikes me that they've all somehow been saying the same thing. Perhaps it's just that my regular-army brain can't cope with it."

What was in this manner bothering General Stumm's mind was no small matter, and was really something that ought not to have been left merely to the War Ministry, although it might be demonstrated that it was all intimately connected with war itself.

The present age has had a number of great ideas bestowed on it ; and, by a special benevolence on the part of destiny, each idea has been accompanied by its counter-idea, so that individualism and collectivism, nationalism and internationalism, socialism and capitalism, imperialism and pacifism, rationalism and superstition are all equally at home in it, and in addition to these there come flocking the remnants of countless other pairs of opposites of a similar or a lesser contemporary value. By now this seems as natural as day and night, hot and cold, love and hatred, and the fact that each tensor-muscle in the human body has its contrary-minded extensor to go with it, and General Stumm would not, any more than anyone else, have had the notion of regarding this as anything unusual if his ambition had not been plunged into this adventure as a result of his infatuation with Diotima. For love will not content itself with the fact that the unity of Nature is based upon opposites ; but in its yearning for a tender atmosphere it demands a unity without contradictions. And that was why the General was trying in every possible way to establish that unity.

" I have here," he told Ulrich, at the same time showing him the relevant pages, " a catalogue, which I have had prepared, of the ideas-in-chief, that is to say, it contains all the names that have as it were led larger army-units of ideas to victory in modern times. This other page here is an *ordre de bataille*. This one is a strategical plan. This an attempt to establish depots or ordnance bases, from which to move supplies of ideas up to the line. But I dare say you will notice—you see I have had it clearly emphasised in the draft—if you look at one of the idea-units in action at present, that it receives its supplies of fighting-troops and intellectual war-material not only from its own bases but also from those of its enemy. You will see that it is continually shifting positions and suddenly, without any cause, it turns its front and fights against its own lines of communication. And then again you will see that the ideas are ceaselessly going over to the enemy, and then back again, so that you will find them now in one, now in another line of battle. In short, one can't draw up a decent plan of communications or a line of demarcation or anything else, either, and the whole thing, if I may say so without offence, looks —not that I can really bring myself to believe it !—like what every commanding-officer would call a hell of a mess ! "

Stumm slipped several dozen pages at once into Ulrich's hand. They were covered with strategical plans, railway-lines, networks of roads, charts of range and firing-power, symbols denoting different units, brigade headquarters, circles, squares, and areas of cross-hatching. Just as in a thorough-going general-staff plan of campaign, there were red, green, yellow and blue lines running this way and that, and there were little flags of various kinds, with various meanings (such as were to become so popular a year later), painted in all over the place.

" All this doesn't get us anywhere ! " Stumm sighed. " I've tried changing the method of representation and tackling the matter from the military-geographical point of view, instead of from the strategical, in the hope that in this way I would at least get a clearly defined field of operations. But that wasn't any good either. And there you have the experiments in orographic and hydrographic representation."

Ulrich saw mountain-peaks marked, which branched out in all directions and in other places formed into masses again, and springs, networks of rivers, and lakes.

" I have tried a lot more experiments of various kinds," the General said, and in his gay and lively eyes there was now a faint gleam of irritation or even panic, " trying to get the whole thing reduced to unity. But d'you know what it's like ? Just like travelling second-class in Galicia and picking up crabs ! It's the lousiest feeling of helplessness I ever knew. When you've been spending a lot of time among ideas, you get an itching all over your body, and you can't get any peace even if you scratch till you bleed ! "

Ulrich could not help laughing over this vivid description.

But the General implored : " No, no, don't laugh ! Look here, this is what I thought : you have become an outstanding civilian and in your position you will understand these things, but you will understand me too. So I've come to get you to help me. I have much too much respect for everything to do with the mind to believe that I can be right."

" You take thinking much too seriously, Colonel," Ulrich said consolingly. The ' colonel ' just slipped out, and he apologised, saying : " You wafted me back into the past so pleasantly, General Stumm, to the time when you sometimes used to order me to join you in a philosophic discussion in a corner of the mess. I can only repeat, one mustn't take thinking as seriously as you are doing at the moment."

"Mustn't take it seriously!" Stumm groaned. "But I can't go on living without a higher order in my head! Don't you understand that? I simply shudder when I remember how long I lived without it on the parade ground and in barracks, surrounded by my mess-mates' dirty jokes and all that talk about sex!"

They sat down to supper. Ulrich was touched by the childlike inspirations on which the General acted with such manly courage, and by the inexhaustible youthfulness that came from having spent the right period of one's life in small garrisons. He had invited the companion of vanished years to stay and share his evening meal with him, and the General was so much under the influence of his wish to enter into Ulrich's mysteries that even the spearing of each little slice of sausage with his fork was something to which he devoted a quite special attention.

"Your cousin," he said, raising his wine-glass, "is the most admirable woman I know. It is quite rightly said that she is a second Diotima. I have never seen anything like her before. You know, my wife—you haven't met her—well, I really can't complain—and then there are the children. . . . But a woman like Diotima—ah, now, that's quite a different matter! At receptions I sometimes take up a position at her rear—what a presence! what imposing curves!—and at the same time in front she talks away to some outstanding civilian or other in such a learned way that, upon my word, I wish I could take notes! And this Permanent Secretary she's married to has no idea what he's got there. I apologise if you happen to be particularly fond of this fellow Tuzzi, but I can't stand him myself! He just creeps around and smiles as if he knew what time of day it was and wasn't going to let anyone else into the secret. But he can't pull the wool over my eyes, for, with all my regard for everything civilian, government officials take the back seat. They're nothing but a kind of civilian soldiery that try to get the better of us at every opportunity, and always with the brazen politeness of a cat sitting on a tree and looking down at a dog. Take Herr Doktor Arnheim, for instance —he's of a different calibre," Stumm went on chattily. "Conceited too, perhaps, but there's no getting away from it, one must acknowledge such superiority." He had obviously drunk a little hastily after talking so much, for he was warming up and becoming confidential. " I don't know what it is," he continued, " perhaps the reason I don't understand it is that nowadays even a chap's own mind is so complicated, but although I myself admire your cousin as if—well, to make no bones about it, just as if I had had a great lump of something sticking in my throat—I must say it's a relief to me all the same that she's in love with Arnheim."

" What ? You mean to say you're sure there's something going on between them ? " Ulrich asked rather eagerly, although it should not really have affected him much.

Stumm goggled at him distrustfully with his short-sighted eyes, which were now misty with excitement, and then put on his *pince-nez*. " I didn't say he'd had her," he retorted in the rough-and-ready terminology of the mess, took his *pince-nez* off again, and added in a quite unsoldierly manner : " Not that I'd have anything against it. Damme, I've told you one gets a complicated intellect in that company. I'm certainly no nancy, but when I imagine the embraces that Diotima could bestow on this man, I feel almost like embracing him myself, and vice versa, I feel as if it were my kisses that he gives Diotima."

" He gives her kisses, does he ? "

" Oh, how am I to know—after all, I don't go round spying on them ! I only mean, if he did. What it comes to is, I don't even understand myself. But anyway I once saw him holding her hand, when they thought nobody was looking, and there they stood for a while, as quiet as it is when the order's been given ' Shakos off, kneel for prayers ', and then she said something to him in a soft imploring voice, and he said something in answer, and I made a point of remembering the exact words of both of them, because it's so difficult to make sense of it. What she said was : ' Ah, if one could only find the redeeming idea, the idea that would be salvation ! ' and what he said was : ' Only a pure, unbroken idea of love can bring us salvation ! ' It was obvious he had taken it too personally, for she certainly meant the redeeming idea she needs for her great enterprise. What are you laughing at ? Oh well, laugh if you like, I've always had my little oddities, and now I've made up my mind to help her. It must be possible. There are so many ideas, and one of them, after all, must be the redeeming one. Only you must bear a hand."

"My dear General," Ulrich said, "I can only repeat that you take thinking too seriously. But since you attach importance to it, I'll try to explain to you, as well as I can, how a civilian thinks."

They had reached the cigar stage. And Ulrich began : "First of all, General, you're on the wrong road. It is not, as you think, that the mind is to be found in civilian life, and the body in the army. It is precisely the other way round. For the mind means order—and where is more order to be found than in the army ? There every collar is exactly four centimetres high, the number of buttons is laid down in regulations, and even in nights over-flowing with dreams the beds still stand in a straight line along the walls. The deployment of a squadron in battle formation, the lining up of a regiment, the proper position of bridle and bit—all these, you see, are intellectual values of high significance. Or else there are no intellectual values at all ! "

"Don't try to bamboozle me ! " the General grumbled, but somewhat warily, in doubt whether to mistrust his ears or the wine that he had drunk.

"You are too hasty," Ulrich insisted. "Science is possible only where events can be made to repeat themselves, or at least can be checked—and where is there more repetition and checking of everything than in the army ? A cube would not be a cube if it weren't just as cubical at nine o'clock as at seven. The laws of the orbits of the planets are a sort of ballistics. And we wouldn't be able to arrive at any notion of anything, or any sort of judgment at all, if everything only flitted past once. If something is to be valid and have a name, it must be repeatable, many specimens of it must exist—if you had never seen the moon before, you would think it was an electric torch. Incidentally, the great embarrass-ment that God causes to science consists in His having been seen only once, and that at the creation of the world, before there were any trained observers on the spot."

Here it becomes necessary to put oneself in Stumm von Bord-wehr's place. Since his days at the military academy everything had been prescribed for him by regulations, from the shape of his cap to the conditions under which he could marry, and he felt little inclination to open his mind to such doctrines as these.

" My dear fellow," he retorted cannily, " that's all very well, but it doesn't really concern me. I must say, it's quite a good joke to say that it's we in the army who invented science. Only I'm not talking about science, but, as your cousin puts it, about the soul, and when she speaks of the soul, what I really feel like doing is stripping to the skin, it's so little in keeping with a uniform ! "

" My dear Stumm," Ulrich went on doggedly, " a great many people accuse science of being soulless and mechanical and of making everything it touches the same. But oddly enough they don't notice that there is a much worse regularity in matters of sentiment than in those of reason. For when is a feeling really natural and simple ? When it can be automatically expected to manifest itself in everybody when the circumstances are the same ! How could one demand virtue from everyone if a virtuous act were not one that could be repeated as often as one likes ? I could give you a great many more examples of the same sort. And if you flee from this bleak regularity into the darkest depths of your being, where the uncontrolled impulses are at home, into those moist animal depths that save us from evaporating in the light of our intellect—what do you find ? Stimuli and reflex-tracts, the grooves of habits and skills, repetition, fixation, imposed patterns, series, monotony ! *There's* uniform, barracks, regulations for you, my dear Stumm. And the civilian soul has a remarkable kinship with the military. One might say that wherever it can it emulates this model, which it can never quite equal. And where that is not possible, it is like a child that has been left alone. Just take, for instance, a woman's beauty. What surprises and overwhelms you as beauty, the thing that makes you believe you are seeing it for the first time in your life, is something you have inwardly long known and been in search of, and there was always an antici-patory glimmer of it in your eyes, a glimmer that has now merely been intensified into full daylight. On the other hand, if it is really a matter of love at first sight, or beauty that you have never perceived before, you simply don't know what to do about it. Nothing like it has gone before, you have no name for it, you have no emotion as a response to it, you are simply boundlessly bewil-dered, dazzled, reduced to a state of blind astonishment and idiotic stupor that hardly seems to have anything in common with happiness . . ."

Here the General vigorously interrupted his friend. He had up to now been listening with that practised air which one acquires on the barrack-square, when being subjected to disapproval and criticism from one's superior officers, having to listen to words that one must be able to repeat if necessary and yet must not really take in, because otherwise one might just as well ride home on an unsaddled hedgehog. But now Ulrich had touched him to the quick and he exclaimed fervently :

" 'Pon my word, that's an outstandingly correct description you give ! When I become really absorbed in admiration for your cousin, everything in me dissolves into nothing. And when I make a real effort to pull myself together so as to have an idea at long last which might be of use to her, the same thing happens— what I get is an extremely disagreeable feeling of emptiness. I'd be going too far to call it imbecility, but I must say it's pretty like it. And so, if I understand you rightly, what you mean to say is that we military are quite respectable thinkers. As for the civilian mind—well, your idea that we're the model it's based on is something I must reject—I suppose it's just one of your jokes— but I do sometimes think myself that we have pretty much the same sort of mind. And what there is above and beyond that, you mean to say, I mean, all these things that strike us soldiers as so downright civilian-like, such as the soul, virtue, devoutness, and sentiment—this chap Arnheim can make great play with it, with incredible ease—well, so although you take the view that that's mind all right, of course—you do even say *there* are precisely those —what d'you call 'em—' considerations of a higher nature', but then you go on and say it all simply drives one silly. And that's all perfectly true, but in the end, of course, the civilian mind *is* the one that's superior. I'm sure you won't deny that, now, will you ? And now I ask you—how does it all make sense ? "

" What I said just now was first of all—and here's something you've forgotten—first of all, I said, the mind is at home in the army, and now I say, secondly, the body is at home in civilian life . . ."

" But I say, that's nonsense, isn't it ? " Stumm objected suspiciously. The physical superiority of the military was a dogma, precisely like the conviction that the officer-caste stands nearest to the Throne ; and even though Stumm had never thought of himself as an athlete, the moment doubt seemed to be cast on the possibility, the certainty sprang up in him that a civilian paunch of equal dimensions to his must nevertheless be considerably softer.

" No more and no less nonsense than everything else," Ulrich said in self-defence. " But you must let me finish. It's like this : round about a hundred years ago the leading brains in German civilian life believed that the thinking citizen would deduce the laws of the world out of his own head while sitting at his desk, just as one can prove those theorems about triangles. And the thinker in those days was a man in nanking trousers who flung his hair back from his forehead and did not know even the paraffin-lamp, much less electricity or the phonograph. That over-weeningness has since been driven out of us with a vengeance. In these hundred years we have got to know ourselves and Nature and everything very much better, but the result is, so to speak, that whatever one gains in the way of order in matters of detail one loses again where the totality is concerned, so that what we get is more and more systems of order and less and less of order itself."

" That fits in with the result of my investigations," Stumm confirmed.

" Only most people aren't as keen as you are on trying to find a summarising order," Ulrich continued. " After our past exertions we have landed up in a period of regression. Just picture to yourself how these things work these days. . . . When an important man brings an idea into the world, it is immediately seized by a process of division consisting of sympathy and anti-pathy. First of all the admirers tear great chunks out of it, just as it suits them, and rend their master to pieces as foxes rend a carcase. Then the opponents destroy the weak spots. And in a short time there is nothing left of any achievement but a stock of aphorisms from which friend and foe can help themselves when-ever they feel like it. The result is general ambiguity. There is no Yes without a No attached to it. You can do whatever you like, you'll find twenty of the finest ideas in favour of it and, if you like, another twenty against it. One practically comes to believe that it's the same as with love and hatred and hunger, where tastes must differ if everyone is to come into his own."

" Splendid ! " Stumm exclaimed, quite won over again. " I

said something of the kind to Diotima myself ! But don't you think one ought to see this confusion as the justification for the army's existence ?—and yet I'm ashamed to believe it even for an instant ! "

" I would advise you," Ulrich remarked, " to give Diotima a hint that God—for reasons that are as yet unknown to us—seems to be about to introduce an age of physical culture. For the only thing that gives ideas some sort of foothold is the body to which they belong—and there you, as an officer, would of course have a certain advantage."

The tubby little General started back. " As far as physical culture goes, I'm no more of a beauty than a peach with its skin off," he said after a momentary pause, with bitter satisfaction. " And I must also tell you," he added, " that I only think of Diotima in an honourable way and only wish to pass muster in her eyes in the same way."

" What a pity," Ulrich said. " Your intentions are really worthy of a Napoleon, but you won't find this a suitable century for them ! "

The General took the mockery in good part, with the dignity lent him by the thought of suffering for the lady of his heart. After some meditation he said : " Anyway, thank you very much for all the interesting advice you've given me."

86

The King of Commerce and the fusion of interests between Soul and Business, also : All roads to the mind start from the soul, but none leads back again.

AT this time, when the General's love yielded to his admiration for Diotima and Arnheim, Arnheim ought already long ago to have made the resolve to return no more. Instead, however, he was making arrangements for a prolonged stay ; the rooms he occupied in the hotel were permanently reserved for him, and it seemed that the bustle of his life had come to a complete standstill.

The world was at that time being shaken by all sorts of happenings, and anyone who was well informed, towards the end of the year nineteen hundred and thirteen, had a picture of a seething volcano, even though there was a universal, as it were hypnotic, belief, originating in the peacefulness of production, that this volcano could never again erupt. This belief was not equally strong everywhere. Through the windows of the beautiful old palace on the Ballhausplatz, where Permanent Secretary Tuzzi held sway, light often fell on the bare trees in the gardens opposite until late at night, and cultured persons sauntering past in the darkness would feel a thrill of awe. For just as the figure of the ordinary carpenter Joseph is permeated with that of Saint Joseph, so the name ' the Ballhausplatz ' permeated that noble building there with the aura of being one of those half-dozen mysterious kitchens where, behind drawn curtains, the fate of mankind was concocted. Herr Dr. Arnheim was kept tolerably well informed as to these processes. He received telegrams in code and, from time to time, a visit from one of his employees, coming from the firm's headquarters with items of confidential information ; the windows of his apartment at the front of the hotel were also often lit till late at night ; and an imaginative observer might have been excused for believing that here a second, a counter-government was keeping vigil, a modern, apocryphal battle-station of economic diplomacy.

Nor did Arnheim ever fail to do his own part towards producing such an impression ; for without the power of suggestion provided by external things man is only a sweet, watery fruit without a husk. Even at breakfast, which for this reason he did not take alone, but in the public breakfast-room of the hotel, he gave his secretary, who took it all down in shorthand, the directives for the day, with the administrative skill of an experienced ruler and the politely quiet attitude of a man who knows he is being watched from all sides. None of these directives would by itself have been enough to cause Arnheim pleasure, but as they not only shared their place in his consciousness with each other, but were, besides, restricted by the presence of the stimuli of breakfast itself, they necessarily rose into the heights. Probably—and this was one of his favourite thoughts—human talent in general needs to be limited to some extent if it is to unfold ; the really fruitful strip of territory between overbearing freedom of thought and a disheartened vanishing of all thoughts is, as every connoisseur of life knows, exceedingly narrow. Besides, however, he was also convinced that it was very important *who* had any particular thought ; for it is known that new and important thoughts seldom have only a single finder, and on the other hand the brain of a man who is accustomed to thinking ceaselessly produces thoughts of varying value : hence inspirations always have to receive their finality, their effective, successful form, from outside, not only out of the process of thinking, but out of the whole complex of the individual's circumstances of life. A question from the secretary, a glance at a neighbouring table, a greeting from someone entering the room, anything of that sort would always, and at the right moment, remind Arnheim of the necessity of making himself an imposing figure ; and this consolidation of appearance then instantly became transferred to his thinking also. He had summed up this aspect of his experience of life in the conviction, well suited to his needs, that the thinking man must always at the same time be a man of action.

Yet in spite of this conviction he did not attach over-much importance to his present activity. Even although with it he was pursuing an aim that under certain circumstances might be surprisingly rewarding, he was afraid that by his stay he was sacrificing time in a way that could not be justified. He repeatedly reminded himself of that cold ancient dictum *divide et impera*. It is one that applies to all intercourse with human beings and things and demands a certain devaluation of every individual relationship by the totality of them, for the secret of the state of mind in which one bends one's will to acting successfully is the same as that of the man who is loved by many women, while he himself does not favour any one to the exclusion of the others. Yet that availed Arnheim nothing. His memory presented him with the demands that the world imposes on a man born to a life of great activity ; in spite of that, however, after much repeated investigation into his own inner being, he could not close his eyes to the fact that he was in love. And that was a queer state of affairs, for a heart that is getting on for fifty years of age is a tough muscle that refuses to expand as easily as does that of a twenty-year-old in the flowering season of love ; and it caused him considerable discomfort.

He first of all observed with concern that his widespread international interests were withering like a flower cut off at the root, and insignificant impressions of everyday life, down to a sparrow on the window-sill or the friendly smile of a waiter, were positively bursting into bloom. In surveying his moral concepts, which otherwise amounted to a large system of how to be always right, a system through which nothing slipped, he became aware that they were growing poorer in relevance, at the same time, however, taking on a certain physical quality. This might be called devotion ; but there at once was one of those words that usually have a much wider and, for that matter, a different meaning. For without devotion one cannot get on at all : devotion to a duty, to someone higher in rank, or to a leader, devotion to life itself in its richness and variety, had at other times, when understood as a masculine virtue, for him been the quintessence of an upright attitude that, for all the ' openness ' that went with it, consisted more in reserve than in expenditure of feeling. And the same could be said of fidelity, which, when confined to one woman, takes on a nuance of narrowness ; the same could be said likewise of chivalry and gentleness, unselfishness and delicacy, all of them virtues that are generally imagined in association with women, but which thereby lose their richest quality, so that it is difficult to say whether the experience of love only flows towards a woman as water concentrates in the deepest and generally not most unobjectionable spot, or whether the experience of love for women is the volcanic centre in the warmth of which all things live that flourish upon the surface of the earth. A very high degree of male vanity therefore feels more comfortable in the company of men than in that of women ; and when Arnheim compared his wealth of ideas, which he had borne into the spheres of power, with the state of bliss brought about by Diotima, he could not shake off the impression that a retrogressive movement had taken place in his life.

At times he felt a need for embraces and kisses, like a youth who, when his desire is not granted, flings himself passionately at the feet of her who refuses him ; or he surprised himself longing to burst into sobs or to utter words that would be a challenge to the whole world, and finally even to carry off the beloved in his own arms. Now, we all know that on that irresponsible margin of the conscious personality whence fairy-tales and poems come, all sorts of childish memories are also at home, becoming visible when, on exceptional occasions, the faint intoxication of fatigue, the disinhibiting influence of alcohol, or some other disturbance, casts light into these realms. Nor had Arnheim's fits of rapture any more body than such phantoms have, so that he would not have had any cause to become agitated about them (and as a result of such agitation greatly to intensify the original emotion), if these infantile regressions had not been so insistent as to convince him that his psychic life was full of faded moral ' specimens '. The general validity that he always strove to give to his actions, as a man with the eyes of all Europe upon him, suddenly showed itself to him as something not of the inner life at all. Perhaps that is only natural if something is meant to be valid for everyone ; but what was startling was the inversion of this conclusion, which likewise thrust itself upon Arnheim's attention : for if what is generally valid is non-internal, then it follows that the inner man is the non-valid. And so Arnheim was now haunted, at every step, not only by the urge to produce something like a wrong and blaring trumpet-note, to do something unreasonably illegitimate, but also by the burden of his awareness that, on the level of something above and beyond reason, this would be the right thing to do. Since he had come to know again the fire that was making his tongue dry, he was overwhelmed with the feeling that he had forgotten some path he had originally been following, and that the whole of the ideology of the great man (with which he had been filled) was only the emergency substitute for something he had lost.

Thus nothing was more natural than that he should now begin to recall his childhood. In his childhood portraits he had big dark round eyes, such as painters give the Child Jesus disputing with the doctors in the Temple ; and he saw all his governesses and tutors standing round him in a circle, marvelling at his intellectual gifts, for he had been a clever child and had always had clever teachers. He had however also proved himself to be a warm-hearted, sensitive child that would not endure any injustice.

Since he himself had been much too carefully sheltered for any injustice to have happened to him, he made strangers' wrongs his own when he encountered such things in the street and threw himself into battles on their account. That was a very considerable achievement, as becomes clear if one bears in mind how much was done to prevent him from doing this and that never more than a minute passed without somebody rushing up to separate him from his opponent. And because in this way such battles lasted just long enough for him to have had this or that painful experience, but because they were always interrupted just in time to leave him with the sensation of his unflinching courage, to this day Arnheim still thought of them with approval; and this lordly quality of a courage that would shrink from nothing later passed over into his books and his convictions, in the way this is necessary to a man who has to tell his contemporaries how they must behave if they want to be self-respecting and happy.

So this childhood condition had remained comparatively intact and alive in him; but another, which had appeared somewhat later and to some extent as the transformatory continuation of the first, now appeared to be dormant or, to put it more correctly, petrified—the stoniness here alluded to being, however, of no ordinary stones, but of diamonds. It was the condition of love that now, in contact with Diotima, had been startled up into new life, and the characteristic thing about it was that in his youthful days Arnheim had first come to know it entirely without its being associated with women, indeed, without any definite persons being involved at all; and there was something perplexing about this, which he had never come to terms with all his life, although in the course of time he had become acquainted with the most modern explanations for it.

' What he meant was perhaps only the incomprehensible manifestation of something still absent, like those rare expressions that appear on faces without having any relation to those faces, being related, in fact, to some other faces suddenly surmised beyond the horizons of visible things; what he meant was little melodies in the midst of noise, feelings in human beings; and indeed, there were feelings in him that, when his words groped for them, were not yet even feelings, but only as if something had extended in him, its tips already dipping in, moistening, as things sometimes do extend on fever-bright spring days when their shadows creep out beyond them and lie as quietly, all flowing in one direction, as reflections lie in a stream.'

This was how it was expressed, though admittedly much later and with a different nuance, by a poet whom Arnheim held in high regard (not that he himself understood him), because it was accounted a sign of initiation to know of this evasive man living withdrawn from the public gaze. As for Arnheim, he associated ـuch allusions with the kind of talk about the awakening of a new soul that had been current in his youth, or with those elongated, thin girls whose portrayal was then so popular and whose lips looked like the fleshy chalice of a flower.

At that time, round about the year 1887—' good heavens, almost a generation ago ! ' Arnheim thought—photographs of himself showed him to be a modern ' new ' man, as it was called then : that is to say, in these pictures he was wearing a high-cut black satin waistcoat and a wide cravat made of heavy silk, reminiscent of the Biedermeier fashion, but at the same time intended to give a suggestion of the Baudelairean, a tendency stressed by an orchid (a new fad then) that would protrude from a buttonhole with magical malevolence whenever Arnheim junior went out to dine and had to assert his youthful personality in a company of robust business men, his father's friends. On working-days, on the other hand, what the photographs were inclined to show by way of adornment was a ruler peeping out of a pocket of the soft English tweed suit, to which—comically enough, and yet heightening the significance of the head—a much too high stiff collar was worn. That was what Arnheim had looked like, and even now he could not refrain from regarding this image of himself with a certain measure of benevolence. He had played lawn tennis—a game still played, in those early days, on lawns—well and with all the keenness appropriate to a passion that had not yet become the common thing. To his father's amazement, and quite publicly, he went to workers' meetings, for during a year as a student in Zurich he had made noxious acquaintance with socialist ideas ; on the other hand, he had no qualms, another day, about recklessly galloping on horseback through a workers' settlement. In short, it had all been a whirl of contradictory but new intellectual elements that created in him the enchanting illusion that he had been born at the right time, an illusion that is always very important, even though later on, of course, one realises that its value does not lie precisely in its rarity. Yes, Arnheim, later yielding more and more room to conservative thought, was even in doubt whether this constantly recurring feeling of being the latest on the scene was not an expression of Nature's wastefulness ; however, he did not part with it, for he was extremely disinclined ever to part with anything that he had once possessed, and his collector's nature carefully preserved within him everything that existed at that time. Only it seemed to him today, however rounded and various his life might present itself to him as being, that what had had quite a different and last-ing influence on him was something that had then seemed to be among all things the most unreal : namely that romantically expectant state of mind which had whispered to him that he should belong not only to the bright and bustling world, but also to another world, one that hung suspended within it like a holding of the breath.

These states of vaporous reverie, which through Diotima's influence were now recurring in all their original intensity, had then called a halt to every sort of activity and stir ; the tumult of youthful contradictions and the hopeful ever-changing vistas had given way to a soundless day-dream in which all words, happen-ings, and demands became one and the same in their depths, which were so deeply different and remote from the surface of things. At such moments even ambition was hushed, the events of reality were as far off as the roar of traffic beyond a garden wall, and it seemed to him the soul had overflowed its banks and was only now truly present. It cannot be too strongly emphasised that this was not a philosophy, but an experience as physical as seeing the moon, outshone by the light of morning, hovering pale and mute in the sky of day.

In such a state of mind the young Paul Arnheim, even in those days, would lunch or dine at a smart restaurant, perfectly self-controlled, would appear in every kind of society, carefully and appropriately dressed, and everywhere would do what was to be done. But it might be said that in all this from himself to him-self was no nearer and no further than to the nearest human being or object, that the external world did not leave off at his skin and the internal world did not only shine out through the window of reflection, but that both united into an individed state of absence and presence at once, which was as mild, calm and lofty as a dreamless sleep. What manifested itself then was a truly great indifference to moral values and a sense of their all being equal ; there was nothing small and nothing big ; a poem, or the kissing of a woman's hand, was equal in weight to a work in several volumes or some great act of statesmanship, and everything evil was meaningless, just as, at bottom, everything good also became superfluous in this state of immersion in the tender primal kinship of all created things.

And so Arnheim behaved quite normally. Only he seemed to do so in an intangible atmosphere of significance, behind the flickering flame of which the inner man stood motionless, watching the outer man, who was eating an apple, perhaps, or being measured for a suit by his tailor.

Was that, after all, an illusion or the shadow of some reality that one would never entirely understand ? To this the only answer that can be given is that all religions have at certain stages of their development asserted it to be reality, and so have all lovers, all romantics, and all those people who have a hankering for the moon, for spring, and for the blissful dying of the days in early autumn. In the course of time, however, it fades out ; it evaporates or dries up—it is impossible to say which—till a day comes when one realises that something else is there in its place, and it is forgotten as rapidly as only unreal experiences, dreams, and illusions can be forgotten. Since this primal and cosmic love-experience generally makes its appearance simultaneously with the first personal falling in love, one later generally manages to believe, into the bargain, that·one knows what value to attach to it, reckoning it among the follies to which one is entitled only before one is old enough to vote. That, then, was the nature of it ; but since in Arnheim's case it had never been associated with a woman, it could of course not vanish from his heart in the natural way together with her. Instead, it was overlaid by the impressions that were imprinted on his personality when, at the end of his studies and his year of travel, he entered his father's business. Since he did nothing by halves, there he soon discovered that the productive and healthily active life was a more magnificent poem by far than all those that the poets thought out in their garrets. And this was an entirely different matter.

Here now for the first time his gift for being a paragon became apparent. For the poem of life has the advantage over all other poems that it is, as it were, set up in capital letters, irrespective of its content. Even the smallest articled pupil employed in a firm of world-wide dimensions has the whole world circling round him and the continents peeping over his shoulder, so that nothing he does is without significance. But all that circles round the solitary author in his room is, at most, the flies, no matter how much he may exert himself. This is so obvious that many people, from the moment when they begin to create in the medium of life itself, regard everything that used to move them before as ' mere literature '; that is to say, the effect it has is at best weak and muddled, but generally one that is contradictory, cancelling itself out, and is in no relation to the fuss made about it. This was naturally not quite the way it was with Arnheim, who neither denied the noble feelings inspired by art nor was capable of regarding anything that had once strongly moved him as being folly or delusion ; as soon as he recognised the superiority of his mature manly outlook over the dreamy attitudes of his youth, guided by the new wisdom of his manhood he set about accomplishing a fusion of both groups of experience. What he did there was in fact exactly what is done by all the many people who make up the majority of the educated classes and who, after entering on their career, do not wish to turn their backs entirely on their former interests, indeed, on the contrary, only now arrive at a calm, mature relationship to the enthusiastic impulses of their younger years. Discovering the great poem of life, in which they know they too are doing their share, restores to them the dilettante's courage that they had lost at the time when they burnt their own poems. Writing their part of life's poem, they are now at liberty to regard themselves indeed as *born* experts and set about permeating their daily round with a sense of intellectual responsibility, feeling themselves faced with a thousand small decisions in making it moral and beautiful, modelling themselves on the notion that Goethe lived thus, and declaring that without music, without Nature, without the sight of children and animals at their innocent play, and without a good book, they would not enjoy life at all. These so spiritually conscious middle classes are, among the Germans, still the main consumers of art and of all not-too-difficult literature ; but its members very understandably look upon art and literature, which once seemed to them the con-summation of their own desires, with condescension in at least one eye, as though looking down upon an earlier stage of develop-ment—even though this may be more perfect in its way than it was ever granted to *them* to be. Alternatively, what they think about it is pretty much what, say, a manufacturer of corrugated iron would inevitably think of a sculptor of ornamental plaster figures if it were his weakness to regard such products as beautiful.

Such were culture's middle classes, and Arnheim resembled them as a superb double carnation of the garden variety resembles a weedy little pink that has sprung up at the roadside. Never was there for him any question of intellectual revolution or of a fundamental innovation ; it was always only a weaving of the new into the already existent, a taking possession, gentle correction, moral re-animation of the faded privileges of the powers now pre-vailing. He was no snob, no worshipper of that section of society that took precedence over him in rank. Being received at Court and being as much in contact with the high nobility as with high government officials, he sought to adjust himself to this environ-ment, yet by no means as an imitator but merely as a connoisseur of the conservative feudal style of life, neither himself forgetting his bourgeois, so to speak Frankfurt-Goethean origins, nor trying to make others forget them. But with this achievement his capacity for antagonism was exhausted, and any greater contrast would have appeared to him untrue to life. He was, indeed, in-wardly convinced that the men of action—and at their head, con-solidating them on the brink of a new era, the business men, those who were at the helm of life—were called at some point in time to relieve the old powers of their sovereignty ; and this gave him a certain quiet arrogance, which had been shown to be justified by the subsequent course of events. But even though one might regard money's claim to power as a fact, the question still remained open how the desired power was to be used rightly. The bank directors' and great industrialists' predecessors had had an easy time of it ; they were knights in armour who merely carved up their enemies, leaving it to the clergy to wield the weapons of mind and soul. On the other hand, although the man of today possesses in money, as Arnheim realised, the surest modern method of managing all relationships, yet in spite of the fact that this method can be as hard and accurate as a guillotine, it can also be as touchily sensitive as a sufferer from rheumatism—one need only think of the aching and limping of the money-market at the slightest cause—and is most delicately bound up with everything over which it rules. Through his understanding of this delicate interlocking of all forms of life, which only the blind arrogance of the ideologist can forget, Arnheim came to see the prince of commerce as the synthesis of revolution and permanence, of armed power and bourgeois civilisation, of reasoned audacity and honest-to-goodness knowledge, but essentially as a symbolic prefiguration of the kind of democracy that was about to come into existence. By unresting, disciplined work at his own personality, by intellectual organisation of the economic and social complexes accessible to him, and by giving thought to the leadership of the whole State, and its structure, he hoped to meet the new age half-way—that new age in which those social energies that fate and Nature had made unequal would be properly and fruitfully organised, and where the ideal, instead of being shattered by contact with the inevitable limitations of reality, would be purified and strengthened. To put it more technically, he had brought about the fusion of interests between Business and the Soul by elaborating the over-all concept of the Prince of Commerce; and the sensation of love that had once caused him to feel everything was fundamentally one thing now formed the nucleus of his conviction as to the unity and harmony of culture and all human interests.

About this time, too, Arnheim began to publish his writings, and in them the word ' soul ' emerged. It may be supposed that he used it as though it were a method, a flying start, as a sovereign term, for it is safe to say that princes and generals have no souls, and among financiers he was the first to have one. It is also certain that in this a part was played by the need to defend himself, in a manner impenetrable to the business mind, against the extreme rationality of his more intimate surroundings, particularly against the qualities of leadership and the superiority in business sense possessed by his father, beside whom he was gradually beginning to assume the role of the ageing crown prince. And it is equally certain that his ambition to master all there was to be known—a taste for polyhistory developed to such a standard that no single man could have lived up to it—found in the soul a means of devaluing everything that his intellect could not master. For in this he was not different from his whole era, which had newly developed a strong religious tendency, not as the result of any religious destiny, but merely, as it seems, out of a feminine and irritable rebellion against money, knowledge, and calculation, to all of which it passionately succumbed. But what was questionable and uncertain was whether Arnheim, when he spoke of the soul, himself believed in it and ascribed to the possession of a soul the same reality as to his own possession of stocks and shares. He used it as a term for something for which he had no other term. Being carried away by his need—he was a talker who did not easily let anyone else get a word in—and later on, after he had become aware of the impression that he could make on others, more and more frequently in his writings too—he would refer to it as though its existence were just as surely established as one assumed that of one's own back to be even though one cannot see it. He was seized by a genuine passion to write in this manner of something vague and yet cloudily significant that is interwoven in the all too definite complex of world commerce as a deep silence is interwoven with eager words. He did not deny the usefulness of knowledge. On the contrary, he himself was impressive as a result of his industrious compilations, as only a man can be who has at his disposal all the means of making such compilations possible. But after he had made his impression he would explain that above and beyond the realm of perspicacity and exactitude there was a realm of wisdom that could be apprehended only in a visionary way. He described the will that founds States and enterprises of world commerce in such a way as to let it be understood that with all his greatness he was nothing but an arm that had to be moved by a heart beating somewhere out of sight. He explained to his listeners the progress that had been made in technique, or the value of the virtues, in the most ordinary everyday manner, just as the man in the street thinks of these things, only to add, however, that such an expenditure of natural and mental energies must, of course, amount to no more than fatal ignorance if one had no inkling of the fact that these things were stirrings of an ocean that heaved far below them, its surface scarcely rippled by their waves. And he uttered such statements in the manner of proclamations made by a regent for an exiled queen, one who had received his instructions directly from her and was ordering the world accordingly.

Perhaps this ordering of the world was his real and most violent passion, a craving for power far surpassing everything that even a man in his position could afford, and one that led directly to the result that this man so mighty in the domains of reality at least once a year felt himself compelled to retire to his castle in the Mark Brandenburg and dictate a whole book to his stenographer. That queer cloudy awareness of significance that had emerged for the first time, and most intensely, in his days of youthful enthusiasm had found this outlet for itself. But at times it still visited him directly too, even though with diminished force. In the bustle of his world-wide enterprises it would overcome him like a sweet enchantment rooting him to the ground, a longing for quiet cloisters, whispering to him that all contradictions, all great ideas, all worldly experience and worldly effect were a unity not only as it is vaguely understood in terms of culture and humanism, but also in a wildly literal and flickeringly idle sense, such as invades one on a morbidly beautiful day when one is inclined to sit gazing out over river and meadows, one's hands crossed in one's lap, and feels no urge ever to detach oneself again. In this sense his writing was a compromise. And because there is only one soul, and that is not tangible, but is in exile, thence making its presence known only in one single way, a way remarkably indistinct or equivocal, whereas on the other hand there are so innumerably many, positively such an infinity of problems in the world to which this its royal message can be applied, so, with the passing of the years, he began to find himself in that serious embarrassment into which all legitimists and prophets get if the whole thing lasts too long. Arnheim only had to sit down in solitude to his writing, and with positively spectral prolificity his pen began to conduct his thoughts from the soul to the problems of the mind, of the virtues, of economics and politics, problems that, irradiated from some invisible source, appeared in clear and magically integral illumination. There was something intoxicating in this urge for expansion ; but to make up for that it was associated with that split in the consciousness which is in many people the precondition of creative writing, inasmuch as the mind excludes and forgets everything that does not fit in with its purpose. Speaking face to face with someone and, through the medium of that person, being linked with the earth in all its complexity, Arnheim would never have let himself go that far ; but bent over a sheet of paper that lay there prepared to mirror his views, he joyfully indulged himself in a metaphorical expression of convictions that were only to a very small degree solid and to a very large degree a mere mist of words, its sole claim to reality, which was however not inconsiderable, being that it arose spontaneously and invariably at the same places.

Anyone who feels inclined to blame him for this should bear in mind that to possess a double mental personality has long ceased to be the sort of trick that only lunatics can bring off. On the contrary, at the speed at which we live today the possibility of political understanding, the ability to write a newspaper article, the vigour required to believe in new movements in art and literature, and countless other things, are wholly founded on a talent for being at certain hours convinced against one's own conviction, for splitting a part off from the whole content of one's consciousness and for spreading it out to form a new state of entire conviction. For this reason it was only a point in Arnheim's favour that he was never quite honestly convinced of what he was saying. By the time he had reached the prime of his life, he had made some utterance concerning all and everything that existed ; he possessed extensive convictions and saw no frontier at which he might have been forced at any point in the future to cease from gaining new convictions, harmoniously evolved out of the old ones, if he kept on in the same manner. A man who thought to such effect, and who in other states of consciousness spent his time checking balance-sheets and estimates of the profit to be made on deals under consideration, could not fail to notice that this was a kind of action without shape or course, though it went on spreading out, as it seemed, inexhaustibly ; its only limitation lay in the unity of his person ; and although Arnheim was very well able to stand large quantities of his own self-awareness, this was nevertheless not a satisfactory state of affairs for his intellect.

Admittedly, he put the blame on the residue of irrationality that life everywhere reveals to the informed observer. He also tried, shrugging his shoulders, to reassure himself with the reflection that in the present era everything tended to overflow its borders. And since nobody can entirely elevate himself above the weaknesses of his century, he even glimpsed in this a valuable opportunity to practise the virtue of modesty—a virtue characteristic of all great men—by setting up above himself, quite unenviously, such figures as Homer or Buddha, because they had lived in more fortunate epochs. Yet with the passing of time, when his literary success reached its peak without any decisive change having taken place in his crown-princely existence, that residue of irrationality grew oppressively, and so too did the lack of tangible results and the uncomfortable sense of having missed his target and having forgotten his original resolve. He surveyed his work, and even though he saw that it was good, he sometimes could not help feeling himself separated by all these ideas from some primal, nostalgically remembered origin, as by a wall of diamonds that grew thicker every day.

Something disagreeable of this kind had happened to him only very recently, upsetting him deeply. He had used the leisure that he now permitted himself more often than usual to dictate to his secretary an essay on the essential accord between State architecture and the conception of the State, and he had broken off a sentence that was to go " We see the silence of the walls when we contemplate this building " after the word ' silence ' in order to linger for a moment over the image of the Cancelleria in Rome, which had just then, of its own accord, risen up before his inner eye. But when he glanced over his secretary's shoulder at the paper in the typewriter, he noticed that his secretary, hastening on ahead as usual, had already written down : " We see the silence of the soul when . . ." On this day Arnheim dictated no more, and on the following day he had the sentence scored out.

What weight was there now, compared with experiences of such extent and depth of background, in the somewhat commonplace experience of physical love for a woman ? Arnheim had to confess to himself, to his regret, that it weighed exactly as much as the recognition, summing up his life, that all roads to the mind start from the soul but that none of them leads back again ! Certainly many women had thought themselves fortunate in having intimate relations with him ; but whenever they were not of the 'kept' type, they were always educated, professional women or artists, for with these two species, the kept woman and the woman who could provide for herself, it was possible to come to an understanding based on a clear-cut relationship. The moral needs of his nature had always guided him into relationships in which his instinctual life and the accompanying inevitable conflicts with women were to some extent backed up by reason. But Diotima was the first woman to reach out into his meta-moral, that is to say, more secret life. For this reason he sometimes eyed her somewhat askance. After all, she was nothing but the wife of a civil servant, socially very presentable, of course, but still, without that highest degree of human culture that only power can bestow ; and after all, his due was a girl from the American financial oligarchy or the English high nobility, if he ever wanted to tie himself down. He had moments when what rose up in him was an entirely primitive nursery antagonism, a naïve and cruel childish arrogance, or the dismay of the sheltered child being taken for the first time to a council school, and then his growing infatuation took on the aspect of a menacing disgrace. And if at such moments he took up his business affairs with the ice-cold superiority of a spirit that had died to the world and returned again, the cool reasonableness of money, which nothing could contaminate, seemed, in comparison with love, an extraordinarily immaculate power.

But this meant no more than that for him the time had come when the prisoner wondered how he could have let himself be robbed of his freedom without fighting to the death for it. For when Diotima said : " What are world events ? *Un peu de bruit autour de notre âme . . .* ! " he felt a tremor go through the edifice of his life.

87   *Moosbrugger dances.*

ALL this time Moosbrugger was still in a cell at the *Landesgericht*, while his case was under consideration. His counsel had got new grist to his mill and was doing his best with the authorities to prevent the case from too quickly reaching a final and irreversible conclusion.

To all this Moosbrugger smiled. He smiled out of boredom.

The boredom of it all rocked his thoughts like a cradle. Generally boredom blots thoughts out. But his it rocked to and fro. This time, anyway. It was a state such as an actor is in, sitting in his dressing-room and waiting for his cue.

If Moosbrugger had had a big sword, he would have taken it now and chopped the head off the chair. He would have chopped the head off the table and the window, the bucket, and the door. And then upon everything that he had chopped the head off he would have set his own head, for in this cell there was nothing but his own head, and that was wonderful. He could imagine it sitting on the things—the broad skull, the hair covering it all over like a fur cap pulled down over the low forehead. He liked the things then.

If only the room had been bigger and the food better !

He was quite glad that he was not allowed to see people. He found people hard to endure. They often had a way of spitting or of hunching up their shoulders that made one feel quite hopeless and want to hit them in the back with one's fist, as though one had to knock a hole through a wall. Moosbrugger did not believe in God, but in his own power of reasoning. The eternal verities he referred to contemptuously as : the beak, the sky-pilot, the cops. He had to settle his whole affair on his own, and anyone who does that sometimes gets the feeling that everyone is putting obstacles in his way. He saw before him what he had often seen : the ink-stands, the green baize, the pencils, then the Emperor's portrait on the wall, and the way they all sat there. In his order of things this was like a gin-trap, only covered over not with grass and leaves but with the feeling : ' That's how it gets you.'   Then he would usually remember the way it was outside, a bush growing at the river-bend, the creaking of a draw-well, fragments of places all jumbled up, an endless store of memories, things he had not known he had liked at the time. And he dreamt : ' I could tell them a thing or two ! ' As a young lad dreams. And that young lad they had locked up so often that he never grew old. ' Next time I'd better take a closer look at it,' Moosbrugger thought, ' else they'll never understand me at all ! ' And then he smiled sternly and talked to the judges about himself like a father saying of his son : ' He's a good-for-nothing, lock him up good and proper, perhaps then he'll pull himself together.'

Naturally now he was sometimes annoyed with the prison regulations. Or something ailed him. But then he could ask to be taken to the prison doctor or for an interview with the governor, and so everything got put right again somehow or other, after all, and settled down like water over the corpse of a dead rat. Not that he imagined it just like that, of course : but now almost all the time he had the feeling of being spread out like a big twinkling pool that nothing could disturb, though he had no words for this.

The words he had were : h'm-h'm, uh-uh.

The table was Moosbrugger.

The chair was Moosbrugger.

The barred window and the bolted door were himself.

He did not mean that in a way that was at all crazy or unusual. It was simply that the elastic had gone. Behind every thing or creature that tries to come quite close up to one there is an elastic band, stretching. Otherwise, of course, in the end the things might go right through each other. And in every movement there is an elastic band that never quite lets one do what one would like to. These pieces of elastic now all at once were gone. Or was it merely the hampering feeling as of elastic ?

Maybe one can't tell the difference all that clearly ? ' For instance, women keep their stockings up with elastic. There it is,' Moosbrugger thought. ' They wear elastic round their legs like amulets. Under their skirts. Like the rings they paint round the fruit-trees to stop the worms crawling up.'

But this is mentioned only in passing, lest anyone believe

Moosbrugger felt the need to be chums with everything. That's not the sort he was at all. It was merely that he was inside and outside.

Now he lorded it over everything, and he bossed it about. He was getting everything straight before they killed him. He could think of whatever he liked : on the instant it was as obedient as a well-trained dog to which one says : ' Down, sir ! ' In spite of being in prison, he had a tremendous feeling of power.

On the dot the soup came. On the dot he was waked and taken out for exercise. Everything in the cell was on the dot, strict and immovable. Sometimes all this seemed to him quite incredible. By some strange inversion he felt that all this orderliness had its origin in him, although he knew it was imposed upon him.

Other people have such experiences lying in the summery shade of a hedge, with the bees buzzing and the sun moving small and hard through the milky sky : the world then revolves around such people like a mechanical toy. In Moosbrugger this was started off simply by the geometrical pattern of his cell.

He noticed, too, that he had a craving for good food that drove him nearly mad. He dreamt of it, and by day the outlines of a good plate of roast pork would rise up before his eyes with almost uncanny persistence, as soon as his spirit returned from other pre-occupations. " Two portions ! " Moosbrugger would then command. " No, three ! " He thought it so hard, enlarging the image so greedily that he instantly became full and felt sick ; he gorged himself in his thoughts. ' Why,' he wondered, wagging his head slowly from side to side, ' do you feel like bursting so quick after you want to eat ? ' Between eating and bursting lie all the pleasures of the world. Hell, what a world ! There were hundreds of examples you could take to show how narrow a space it was ! To take only one : a woman you don't have is like when the moon at night is rising and rising up the sky, sucking and sucking at your heart. But when you've had her, you'd like to stamp in her face with your boots on. Why was it like that ? He remembered that he had often been asked about this. Well, you could tell them : women are women and men. Because men chase after them. But that was another thing that the people who asked him could never manage to understand properly. They wanted to know why he thought that people were plotting against him. As though even his own body weren't in the plot with them! With women it was quite obvious, of course. But even with men his body knew its way about better than he did himself. One word led to another, you knew what was what, the two of you kept going round and round each other all day, and in a flash you were out over the narrow strip where you get on with each other and no harm done. But if his body had brought this on him, then just let it get on with getting him out of it! So far as Moosbrugger remembered, he had been annoyed or frightened, and his chest, with the arms on it, had gone rushing forward like a big dog that had been told to. More than that Moosbrugger himself could not understand, either. The space between friendliness and being fed up was narrow, that's all there was to it, and once it started like that, then it very quickly became horribly tight.

He remembered very well that the people who could talk in long words and who were always sitting in judgment on him had often reproached him, saying: ' But one doesn't go and kill somebody just for *that*, surely! ' Moosbrugger shrugged his shoulders. People have been done in for a few coppers or for nothing, just because someone else happened to feel like it. But *he* respected himself. *He* was not that sort. In time the reproach had made an impression on him. He would have liked to know why from time to time he felt so tight, or whatever you might call it, so that he had to clear a space for himself by force, to let the blood drain out of his head again. He thought hard. But wasn't it just the same with thinking, too ? Whenever a good time for it began, he could just have smiled with pleasure. Then the thoughts stopped itching inside his skull, and suddenly, instead, there was only a single thought there. The difference was as big as between the toddling of a small child and the dancing of a pretty wench. It was like a spell cast on things. There's someone playing the concertina somewhere, there's a lamp alight on the table, moths come flying in out of the summer night. So now all the thoughts that came to him dropped into the light of the one that was like a lamp. Or Moosbrugger grabbed them, as they came closer, and crushed them between his big fingers, and for a moment, there between his fingers, they were as queer to look at as little dragons. A drop of Moosbrugger's blood had fallen into the world. You couldn't see it, because it was dark ; but he could feel what was going on out there in the invisible. What was tangled was straightening out, there outside. What was crumpled was smoothing out. A soundless dance had begun in place of the unendurable humming with which the world at other times often plagued him. Everything that happened was lovely now : just as a plain girl becomes lovely when she no longer stands alone, but the others seize her by the hand and whirl her round in the dance and the face is lifted, looking up a staircase from where others are already looking down. That was queer. And when Moosbrugger opened his eyes and looked at the people that happened to be near him when everything obeyed him, dancing, even they, too, seemed lovely to him. Then they were not plotting against him, and they formed no wall ; and it became clear that it was only the effort to get the better of him that distorted the faces of people and things, like the carrying of a heavy burden. And then Moosbrugger danced before them. Dignified, he danced invisibly, he who in real life danced with no one, and moved by a music that turned more and more into self-communion and sleep, the womb of the Mother of God, and finally into the stillness of God Himself, a wonderfully unbelievable state of deathly undoing— danced for days on end without anyone's seeing it, until it was all outside, all out of him, clinging to the things about him, brittle and fine-spun, like a cobweb stiffened in the frost.

If you haven't been through all that, how are you going to judge about the other thing ? After the light and easy days and weeks when Moosbrugger could almost slip out of his skin, there always came the long stretches of imprisonment. The prisons of the State were nothing compared to that. Then when he tried to think, everything shrivelled up in him, bitter and empty. The working-men's institutes and night-schools where they tried to tell him how to think were something he hated—he who still remembered how the thoughts in him could take long strides as though on stilts ! On leaden soles he then dragged himself through the world, in the hope of finding some place where it would turn different again.

Today he could only send a condescending smile after that hope. He had never managed to find the point, midway between his two states, where he might perhaps have been able to stay. He had had enough of it. He smiled grandly at death approaching.

Anyway, he had seen a lot. Bavaria and Austria, right down into Turkey. And much had happened that he had read about in the papers while he was alive. It had been a stirring time, on the whole. And in secret he was really rather proud of having lived in it. When you came to think of it, taking it bit by bit, it was a pretty muddled and dreary thing, after all, but still, there it was, his own track ran right across it, and looking back you could see it quite clearly, from birth on to death. Moosbrugger was far from having the feeling that he was going to be executed ; he himself was executing himself, with the aid of other people. That was how he saw what was bound to come. And yet everything was somehow summed up into a whole : the highroads, the towns, the gendarmes and the birds, the dead and his own death. He himself did not quite understand it, and the others even less, though they could talk about it a lot more.

He spat and thought of the sky looking like a mouse-trap painted blue. ' They make them in Slovakia, round, high mouse-traps like that,' he thought.

88   *On association with Great Things.*

THERE is a circumstance that really ought to have been mentioned long ago, which has been touched on in various connections, and the formula for it may be expressed roughly like this : there is nothing so dangerous to the mind as its association with great things.

A man wanders through a forest, climbs a mountain, and sees the world outspread beneath him ; he gazes upon his child when it is put into his arms for the first time ; or he enjoys the good fortune of taking up some position that is generally regarded as enviable. And we wonder : what is going on in him the while ? Surely, it seems to him, this is all something very multiform, profound, and important ; only he has not the presence of mind to take it, as it were, at its word. All that is marvellous before him and outside him, enclosing him like a magnetic casing, draws his thoughts out of him. His glances everywhere stick fast in thousands of details ; but he secretly feels as though he had spent all his ammunition. Outside, the soul-lit, sun-lit, deeper hour, or the hour of greatness, overlays the world with a coating as of galvanic silver, right down to the tiniest leaflets and capillaries ; but at the world's other end, the personal end, a certain inner lack of substance begins to be apparent, and what arises there is what might be called a large, round, empty O. This condition is the classic symptom of contact with all that is eternal and great, as of all sojourn upon humanity's and Nature's peaks. Those people who prefer the company of great things—and among them are numbered, above all, those great souls for whom there are absolutely no small things at all—find that their inner being is drawn out, against their will, into an extensive surface, a generalised superficiality.

The danger of association with great things might therefore also be described as a law of the conservation of mental and spiritual matter, and it seems to be fairly generally valid. The utterances of highly placed persons who are influential on a large scale are usually more lacking in content than our own. Thoughts that are particularly closely associated with particularly worthy and dignified objects are usually of such a kind that, if they were not privileged, they would be regarded as very under-developed. The causes dearest to us—those of the nation, of peace, of humanity, of virtue, and other causes similarly dear—bear upon their slopes the commonest flora of the mind and spirit. Seen like this, the world may seem a topsy-turvy one indeed. But if one assumes that it is permissible for the treatment of a subject to be all the more insignificant the more significant the subject itself is, then it is a world of order.

The only thing is that this law, which can be such a great help towards an understanding of the intellectual life of Europe, is not always equally obvious in its workings ; and, in times of transition from one group of great objects to a new one, the mind setting out to take service with the great objects may even wear a revolutionary aspect, though in fact it is only changing its livery. A transition of this kind was noticeable even in those days, when the people of whom some account is here being given were in the midst of their anxieties and triumphs. For instance, although there were already—to begin with a subject of much consequence to Arnheim—books that sold in very large editions, they were not yet accorded the greatest of respect, even though the stage had now been reached when great respect was shown only to books of anything from a certain level of sales upwards. There were influential industries, such as those of football and lawn tennis, but there was still some hesitation about creating chairs for their respective subjects at the technical universities. All in all, whether it was in fact the late lamented freebooter and admiral, Drake, who introduced the potato from America, thereby bringing about the beginning of the end of the regularly recurring European famines, or whether it was the less lamented, very cultivated and similarly freebooterish admiral, Raleigh, who did so, or nameless Spanish soldiers, or even that worthy rascal and slave-trader, Hawkins—it was a long time before it occurred to anyone to consider these men more important on account of the potato than, for instance, the physicist Al Schirazi, of whom one knows only that he gave a correct explanation of the rainbow. But with the bourgeois age a revaluation of such achievements set in, and by Arnheim's time it had progressed far, being hindered merely by some old-fashioned prejudices still surviving. The quantity of effect, and the effect of quantity, as a new, daylight-clear object of veneration, was still fighting with an ageing, blind, aristocratic veneration for great quality; but in the world of concepts the wildest compromises had already arisen out of this antagonism, just as in the case of the concept of the great mind itself, which, in the form in which we have come to know it in the last generation, inevitably was a synthesis of its own significance and its potato-significance. For what one was waiting for was a man who would have the solitariness of genius but at the same time be as universally comprehensible as a nightingale.

It was difficult to predict what would come about along these lines, since the danger of associating with great things is usually recognised only when the greatness of those things is already halfway to being past and gone. Nothing is easier than to smile over the usher who treated the summoned parties condescendingly in His Majesty's name ; but whether the man who treats Today respectfully in the name of Tomorrow is an usher or not is

something one usually does not know until the day after tomorrow.
The danger of associating with great things has the very disagreeable quality that the things change but the danger always
remains the same.

89   *One must move with the times.*

HERR DR. ARNHEIM had received the heralded visit from two
leading executives of his firm and had had a long conference with
them : in the morning the documents and calculations lay about
the sitting-room, still in disorder, waiting for the secretary to
come and clear them up.   Arnheim had to take decisions, the
delegates were to return by an afternoon train, and today, as
always, he was getting enjoyment out of these circumstances, for
they set up a certain tension among all conditions. ' In ten years,'
he reflected, ' technique will have progressed so far that the firm
will have its own aeroplanes for its senior executives' trips. Then
I shall be able to direct affairs even from a summer holiday in the
Himalayas.' Since he reached his decisions overnight and only
had to check them finally and approve them in the light of day, at
this moment he was at leisure. He had had breakfast sent up to
his room and now, over his first cigar of the day, gave himself up
to mental and spiritual relaxation, thinking of the gathering at
Diotima's that he had been compelled to leave rather earlier than
he wished the previous evening.

   This time it had been an extremely entertaining party. Very
many of the guests were under thirty, many no more than thirty-
five, all still with a little of the Bohemian clinging to them, but
also already with some reputation and noticed in the newspapers.
There were not only native Austrians, but guests from abroad,
from far and wide, who had been attracted by the news that in
Kakania a lady who moved in the highest circles was blazing a
trail for the spirit to make its entry into the world. At times there

was almost a suggestion in the air of the literary and artistic café, and Arnheim smiled when he thought of Diotima, who had seemed quite nervous under her own roof ; but on the whole it had been very stimulating and at any rate an extraordinary experiment, or so it seemed to him. His friend Diotima, disappointed by the fruitless assemblies of the very great, had made a determined attempt to let the most modern spirit pour into the Collateral Campaign, and Arnheim's contacts had been of use to her in this. He merely shook his head when he recalled the conversations that he had had to listen to. Crazy enough they seemed to him. But ' one must give way to youth,' he said to himself, ' one becomes impossible if one simply rejects them '. And so he felt what might be called gravely amused by it all ; for it had been a bit too much all at once.

What was it, now, that they said to hell with ? Experiences as such. What they meant was that kind of personal experience, the earthy warmth and immediate reality of which had set the Impressionism of fifteen years earlier in a state of rapture as though over some miraculous plant. ' Effeminate and muddle-headed ' was what they now called Impressionism. What they demanded was a controlled sensuality and intellectual synthesis.

And synthesis, no doubt, meant on the whole the opposite of scepticism, psychology, investigation and analysis, which were the literary tendencies of the previous generation ?

So far as one could gather, they did not mean this very philosophically. What they understood by synthesis was rather more the need in young bones and muscles for unhampered movement, a leaping and dancing, in which one denies oneself and others any right to criticise and so disturb. If it suited them they did not mind consigning the synthesis to hell too, along with analysis and thinking as a whole. And then they would maintain that the mind must be urged upwards by the sap of immediate experience. Usually, of course, it was members of another group who maintained that ; but sometimes, in their excitement, it was the same ones.

What terrific slogans they had ! The intellectual temperament was what they called for. And a rapid style of thinking that leapt at the throat of the world . . . The sharp-pointed brain of cosmic man . . . And what more of the like had he heard ?

The reconstruction of man on the basis of an Americanised world-labour plan, by means of mechanised energy . . .

Lyricism combined with the intensest dramaticism of life . . .

Technicism—a spirit worthy of the age of the machine . . .

Blériot—one of them had exclaimed—was at that moment soaring over the English Channel at a speed of thirty-five miles an hour ! This thirty-five-miles-an-hour poem was what one ought to write, and chuck the whole rotten rest of literature on the dung-heap !

Accelerism was what they demanded, which meant the maximal increase of the speed of experience on the basis of the bio-mechanics of sport and circus-acrobatic precision . . .

Photogenic rejuvenation through the cinema . . .

And then one of them said that man was a mysterious inner space, for which reason he should be brought into relation with the cosmos by means of cones, spheres, cylinders and cubes. But the contrary was also asserted, namely, that the individualist conception of art underlying the aforementioned opinion was already as good as dead : one must give the coming generation a new sense of habitation by means of communal architecture and settlements. And while in this way an individualistic and a social party had formed, a third intervened to say that only religious artists were in the true sense of the word ' social '. Hereupon a group of modern architects demanded the leadership for itself, religion being in fact the aim of architecture, not to speak of the subsidiary function of love of country and a sense of nationhood. The religious group, reinforced by the cube-and-cone men, objected that art was not a dependent, but a central matter, the fulfilment of cosmic laws. In the course of further discussion, however, the religious group was abandoned again by the cubistic one, which now united with the architects in the assertion that a relation to the cosmos was best expressed, after all, by spatial forms that made the individual element valid and typical. The dictum was uttered that one must project oneself into the soul of man and then hold it fast in three-dimensional terms. Then someone angrily and effectively raised the question what on earth people really believed : which was more important—ten thousand starving human beings or a work of art ? Indeed, as they were almost all artists in some way or other they all held the view that the spiritual recovery of mankind could come only through art, and it was only that they could not agree about the nature of this recovery and the demands that ought to be made upon the Collateral Campaign in order to bring it about. Now, however, the original social group regained the lead, with new voices speaking for it. Out of the question which was more important, a work of art or the misery of ten thousand human beings, the question arose whether ten thousand works of art could make up for the misery of one single human being. Some very robust artists demanded that the artist should not take himself so seriously. Away with his self-glorification! Let him be hungry and social! That was their demand. Life was the greatest and the only work of art, someone said. A booming voice threw in : It's not art that unites, but hunger! A voice of compromise uttered a reminder that the best means of combating over-estimation of oneself in art was a sound basis of craftsmanship. And after this utterance of compromise someone made use of the pause that arose from exhaustion or mutual disgust and asked, calmly once more, whether anyone present really thought that anything could be done so long as not even the contact between man and space had been established. And this was the signal for technicism, accelerism, and the rest of them to speak up again, and the discussion fluctuated this way and that for a good while longer. Finally, however, agreement was reached, because everyone wanted to go home, and yet wanted to have arrived at a conclusion. Therefore all fell in with a statement that went more or less like this : the present time was expectant, impatient, turbulent and unhappy, but the Messiah for whom it was hoping and waiting was not yet in sight.

Arnheim reflected for a moment.

There had constantly been a circle around him. Whenever people on the fringe of it, who could not quite hear or could not make themselves heard, slipped away, others immediately took their place. He had most decidedly been the centre of this new gathering too, even if that had not always been quite apparent during the somewhat unmannerly discussion. After all, he had long been well up in the problems that concerned them. He knew about the cube and its relationships. He had built garden-suburbs for his employees. The machine, with its rationality and its speed, was something he knew well. He was versed in speaking of all aspects of spiritual introspection. And he had money in the rising film-industry. Reconstructing the drift of these arguments he recalled, furthermore, that it had all not been by any means so neat and orderly as his memory involuntarily reproduced it. Such discussions have a peculiar course, as though one had assembled the parties, blindfold, in a polyhedron, and arming each with a stick, told them to go straight ahead ; it is always a confused and tiring spectacle, quite without logic. But is it not an image of the course of things in general ? That too does not result from taboos and the laws of logic, which have at the most the effectiveness of a police-force, but from the unorganised dynamic forces of the mind. This was what Arnheim asked himself when he remembered the attention he had had bestowed on him, and he concluded that one might also say the new way of thinking resembled the process of free association, when the control of the conscious mind was loosened, something that was undeniably very stimulating.

By way of exception he lit a second cigar, although he generally did not permit himself that kind of sensual indulgence. And even as he held the match to it, and the muscles of his face were called into play in the movements of sucking in the first smoke, he could not help suddenly smiling, because he remembered the little general who had addressed him during the party. Since the Arnheims owned a cannon and armour-plating factory and were prepared for vast production of munitions if it should come to the worst, he had understood the slightly comical but likeable General very well when he (speaking quite differently, of course, from Prussian generals, more sloppily, but, one could also say, in a way more expressive of an ancient though one might also add declining culture) spoke to him confidentially—and with positively philosophic sighs !—about the conversations that were going on all round them that evening and which at least in part, as one was bound to admit, had a somewhat radically pacifist character.

The General, being the only officer present, obviously did not feel quite at home, and bemoaned the fickleness of public opinion ; for somebody's comments on the sanctity of human life had just met with acclamation.

" I don't understand these people," were the words with which he had turned to Arnheim, and he had asked him, as a man of internationally outstanding intellect, to throw some light on this. " I don't understand why these people with the new ideas talk in this ignorant way about ' blood-soaked generals '. I have the feeling I understand the older men who usually come here quite well, although I'm sure they're entirely unmilitary too. For instance, that famous poet—I don't remember his name—that tall elderly gentleman with the paunch, who's said to have written the poems about the Greek gods, the stars, and the eternal human feelings—our hostess told me he's a real poet in this age which otherwise at best produces intellectuals—well, as I was saying, I haven't read any of his stuff, but I'm certain I would understand him if his importance really lies mainly in the fact that he won't waste his time on little things. After all, that's what we in the army call a strategist. The sergeant-major—if you'll allow me to bring in such a minor example—naturally has to concern himself with the welfare of every single man in his company. The strategist, on the other hand, reckons with a thousand men as his smallest unit of calculation, and must be capable of expending as many as ten such units at once, if a higher purpose demands it. In my view it's not logical in the one case to call that a blood-soaked general and in the other a preoccupation with the eternal. And I should like to ask you to explain this for me, if it's possible at all ! "

Arnheim's peculiar position in this city and society had aroused in him a certain inclination, at other times carefully restrained, to indulge in mockery. He knew whom this little military gentle-man meant, even if he did not let it become apparent ; and in any case that was of no importance, for he himself could have men-tioned several other varieties of that brand of greatness. They had cut a poor figure that evening ; that was something one could not fail to see.

Musing joylessly for a moment, Arnheim held the smoke of his cigar back between parted lips. His own situation in this circle had also been none too easy. In spite of all the weight he carried, he had had to listen to quite a few ill-disposed remarks that seemed as though they were directed against him personally, and what was being damned was as often as not the very things he had loved in his youth, just as these young people now were in love with the ideas of their own generation. It was a very queer sensation for him, one that might almost be called uncanny, to feel himself venerated by young people who in the same breath ruthlessly sneered at a past in which he himself had his secret share : it made Arnheim feel in himself elasticity, adaptability, and a spirit of enterprise, something that could almost be called the bold recklessness of a bad conscience well concealed. He ran his mind swiftly over what separated him from this new generation. These young people contradicted each other in all and everything ; the only thing they had definitely in common was the attack on objectivity, intellectual responsibility, and the balanced personality.

One special circumstance made it possible for Arnheim to feel something almost like malicious satisfaction where all this was concerned. The over-estimation of certain of his own contemporaries, in whom the personal element obtruded on a particularly large scale, had always been something he did not at all care for. Names, of course, were something that as chivalrous an opponent as he was would never mention even in his thoughts, but he knew exactly whom he was thinking of. ' A sober and modest youth, lusting for illustrious delights '—to speak in the words of Heine, whom Arnheim loved in secret and whom he quoted to himself at this moment. ' One cannot but extol his endeavours and his industrious labours in poetry . . . the bitter effort, the untold doggedness, the grim exertions, with which he chisels out his verses . . .' ' The Muses do not smile upon him, but he holds the genius of language in his hand.' ' The anguishing compulsion to which he must subject himself is what he calls a great deed in words.' Arnheim had an excellent memory and could quote page after page by heart. He let his thoughts roam. He admired the way that Heine, attacking a man of his own time, had then described a kind of figure that only now had come fully into its own, and it stimulated him to emulation when now he turned his thoughts towards that other representative of the great German idealistic outlook, the poet of whom the General had spoken. After the lean here now was the fat species of intellect. His solemn idealism corresponded to those great deep wind-instruments in the orchestra that resemble locomotive boilers stood up on end and produce an unwieldy grunting, rumbling, and rolling. With a single one of their notes they outroar a thousand possibilities. They puff out great bales of the eternal emotions. Anyone who is capable of blowing poetry in any of these manners—Arnheim thought not entirely without bitterness—today passes among us for a poet as distinct from a mere man of letters. And so why not for a general too, and be done with it ? Such people, after all, are on the best of terms with death and constantly need a few thousand dead in order to enjoy the moment of life with dignity.

But at this point someone had asserted that even the General's dog, howling at the moon some rose-scented night, if taken to task might answer : ' What do you mean ? It's the moon, isn't it ? And these are the eternal emotions of my race ', just as one of those gentlemen might answer who are celebrated for that kind of thing. And indeed he might go so far as to add that his emotion was undoubtedly an intense experience, his expression rich in feelings and yet so simple that the public could understand him ; and as regards his thoughts, admittedly they remained subsidiary to his emotion, but that was entirely in keeping with the prevailing demands and had never yet in literature been a real obstacle.

Disagreeably taken aback, Arnheim once again held the smoke of his cigar between his lips, which for a moment remained half-open, a half-raised frontier-barrier between the personality and the outer world. He had at every opportunity praised some of these particularly pure poets, because it was the thing to do, and on some occasions had even given them financial support ; but actually, as he now became aware, he could not endure them or their inflated verses. ' These heraldic creatures that aren't even capable of supporting themselves,' he thought, ' really ought to be rounded up in a reserve, together with the last aurochs and the golden eagle.' And since it was, as the previous evening had shown, not in keeping with the times to support them, Arnheim's reflections concluded not without profit to himself.

90   *The dethroning of the ideocracy.*

THERE are probably good reasons for the phenomenon that in epochs whose spirit resembles a market or a fairground the poets that are considered the proper contrast to this are those who have nothing at all to do with their time. They do not besmirch themselves with contemporary ideas ; what they supply is as it were pure poetry ; and they speak in obsolete idioms of greatness to their circle of the faithful, as though they had just that instant returned from eternity, merely for a short stay on earth, just like a man who, after going to America only three years ago, comes home on a visit speaking his native language with an accent and with some difficulty. This phenomenon is more or less the equivalent of trying to compensate for the hollowness of a hole by putting a hollow dome over it ; and since the higher hollowness only enlarges the ordinary one that was there before, finally nothing is more natural than that a time of such a cult of great men should be followed by another that radically rejects all that fuss about responsibility and greatness.

Arnheim tried cautiously, experimentally, and with the comfortable feeling of being personally insured against damage, to feel his way into this—as he conjectured—coming development. And that was no small matter. While doing so he thought of everything he had seen in America and Europe during the last few years : of the new craze for dancing, whether it meant syncopating Beethoven or transposing the new sensualism into rhythmical terms ; of painting, in which a maximum of intellectual relations was supposed to be expressed by a minimum of lines and colours ; of the film, in which a gesture, its significance known to all the world, by the addition of some small novelty in its presentation threw the whole world into raptures ; and in conclusion simply of the ordinary man in the street and how, even at that time being convinced of the value of sport, he believed that with means comparable to those of an infant kicking its legs in the air he could take possession of Nature's great breasts. The striking thing about all these phenomena was a certain tendency towards the allegorical, if what is understood by that is an intellectual relationship in which everything is supposed to mean more than it has any honest claim to mean. For just as a helmet and a couple of crossed swords were, for the society of the Baroque age, a token of all the gods and their stories, and it was not Lord Harry who kissed the Countess Harriet, but a god of war who kissed the goddess of chastity, so too nowadays when Harry and Harriet cuddle, what they experience is ' time marching on ' or something or other similar out of a collection of ten dozen up-to-date ready-made notions, which of course do not in our own day form an Olympus floating over avenues of yew-trees, but are the whole modern hotch-potch itself. In the cinema, at the theatre, on the dance-floor, and at concerts, in motor-car and aeroplane, in water and in sunshine, in tailoring workshops and commercial offices, there is constantly coming into existence a tremendous surface consisting of impressions and expressions, gestures, attitudes, and experiences. This process, the external aspect of which is of very definite shape right down to its details, resembles a swiftly circling body in which everything thrusts towards the surface and there combines with all the rest, while the interior remains heaving, urgent and amorphous. And if Arnheim had been able to peer several years ahead, he would there and then have seen that nineteen hundred and twenty years of Christian morality, an appalling war with its millions of dead, and whole murmuring forests of poetry that had cast their leafy shade over the female sense of modesty, were all not capable of warding off by a single hour the day when women's skirts and women's hair began to get shorter and the girls of all Europe, after so many centuries of taboos, for a while slipped out of their coverings, naked, like peeled bananas. There were other changes, too, that he would have seen, which he would scarcely have believed possible. And it does not matter how much of it will last or how much of it will disappear again. What it is important to bear in mind is what great and probably vain exertions would have been necessary in order to bring about such revolutions in style of living along the road of intellectual development, so rich in responsibility, by way of philosophers, painters, and poets, instead of by way of tailors, fashions, and chance ; for from this one can guess how much creative energy is generated from the surface of things, and by contrast how barren is the wilfulness of the brain.

This is the dethronement of the ideocracy, of the brain, the shifting of the mind to the periphery ; and this, as it seemed to Arnheim, was the ultimate problem. Admittedly, life has always gone this way. Life has always been reconstructing man from outside inwards. But in earlier times it was with the difference that one felt under an obligation also to produce something from within, bringing it out into the external world. Even the General's dog, which Arnheim remembered now with a kindly feeling, would never be capable of understanding any other line of development ; for this loyal friend of man had had its character formed by the stable, docile man of the previous century and in his image. But its cousin, the wild prairie-wolf, or the capercailzie, which dances for hours on end, would understand it all right. When the capercailzie plumes itself and scrapes the ground with its claws, then, probably, more soul is generated than when a learned man sitting at his desk connects one thought with the next. For in the last resort all thoughts come out of the joints, muscles, glands, eyes, ears, and the shadowy generalised impressions that the bag of skin, to which they all belong, has of itself as a whole. Past centuries may have committed a serious error in attaching too much importance to intellect and reason, conviction, concept, and character ; it was as if someone were to consider the registrar's office and the archives the most important part of a Ministry because they are housed at headquarters, although they are only subsidiary departments that receive their instructions from outside.

And suddenly—perhaps under the stimulating influence of some faint symptoms of dissolution brought about in him by love— Arnheim put his finger on the place where the redeeming idea, the idea that would create order in all these complications, was to be sought : it was somehow sympathetically connected with the concept of increased turnover. It could not be denied that there was an increased turnover of thoughts and experiences in this new age, and indeed it was inevitable, if only as the natural consequence of shunning the time-consuming process of assimilating them intellectually. He pictured the brain of the age replaced by the mechanism of supply and demand, and the painstaking thinker replaced by the business man as a regulating factor, and he could not help enjoying the moving spectacle of a vast production of experiences that would freely combine and dissolve again, a sort of nervous blancmange quivering all over at the slightest jolt, a gigantic tom-tom booming with enormous resonance at even the lightest tap. The fact that these pictures did not altogether harmonise with each other was in itself the result of a state of reverie that they had originally caused Arnheim to be in ; for it seemed to him that it was precisely such a life that might be compared to a dream in which one is simultaneously outside in the midst of the weirdest happenings and quietly lying far inside at the centre, one's ego rarefied, a vacuum through which the feelings radiate and glow like the luminous streamers in a vacuum-tube. It is life that thinks around man and dancingly creates for him the connections that he himself, when he makes use of his reasoning power for the same purpose, can only laboriously glean together and never to such kaleidoscopic effect. So it was that Arnheim mused as a business man, yet at the same time quivering with excitement, down to the twenty tips of his fingers and toes, about the unrestricted psycho-physical intertraffic of an age now imminent. It seemed to him far from impossible that there was something collective and pan-logical coming into existence, and that now, abandoning an outworn individualism, there was one, with all the superiority and the inventive ingenuity of the white race, on the road back to Paradise, but with a plan of reform, intending to introduce a varied, up-to-date programme into the rural backwardness of the Garden of Eden.

There was only one disturbing element. Just as in dreams one has the ability to insert into an event an inexplicable emotion cutting clean through the whole personality, so too one has it in one's waking hours—but only so long as one is fifteen or sixteen years old, and still at school. Even at that age there are, as everyone knows, great upheavals of emotion in one's being, urges and impulses and an amorphous capacity for tremendous experiences ; one's feelings are very much alive, but not yet well defined, and love and anger, happiness and scorn, in brief, all moral abstractions, are twitching events that now enfold the whole world, now shrivel into nothingness. Melancholy, tenderness, greatness and nobility, all are over-arching skies, sublime and empty. And what happens ? From outside, out of the ordered world there comes a finished form—some word, some line of poetry, some dæmonic laughter, or it may be some Napoleon, Cæsar or Christ, or else only the tear dropped at a parent's grave-side—and by some lightning-swift association the ' work ' springs into being. This sixth-form ' work ' is something that is far too easily overlooked. Line for line it is the accomplished expression of the emotion, the most precise coincidence of purpose and ful-filment, and it can be the perfect merging of a young man's experiences with the life of the great Napoleon. It seems, how-ever, that for some reason the association leading from the great to the small is not reversible. Something that one experiences both in dreams and in youth, when one has delivered a grand speech and, on waking, unfortunately just catches only the last words of it, is that these words are in fact far from being as un-commonly beautiful as it seemed an instant earlier. And one then no longer seems to oneself quite as imponderably glittering a creature as the dancing cock of the woods, and knows that one has merely been howling, with much emotional intensity, at the moon, just like the General's much-cited fox-terrier.

And so it wouldn't quite work out that way, after all, Arnheim reflected, coming to his sober senses. But—he added vigilantly—of course one must in good earnest move with one's time. For what, after all, lay nearer to his heart than to apply this old and tried industrial maxim also to the manufacture of life itself ?

91   Bulls and bears on the market of the mind.

THE gatherings at the Tuzzi's now resumed their regular, crowded course.

Permanent Secretary Tuzzi, at a meeting of the ' Council ', addressed his ' cousin ' with the words : " I suppose you realise that all this has happened before ? " He glanced fleetingly towards the seething human contents of his apartment, now alienated to him.

" In the early days of Christianity," he elaborated. " In the centuries immediately before and after the birth of Christ. In that Christo-Levantino-Hellenistico-Judæic melting-pot there were all those innumerable sects." And he began to enumerate : " The Adamites, Cainites, Ebionites, Collyridians, Archontics, Euchites, Ophites . . .", reciting, with the queerly slowed-up haste of someone who moderates his pace in order to conceal his fluent familiarity with the subject, a long list of names of pre-Christian and early Christian religious sects. It created the impression that he wished warily to convey to his wife's cousin that he knew more of what was going on in his house than he was, for special reasons, in the habit of showing.

He then went on to comment on the names he had mentioned, recounting that one sect had been opposed to marriage, because it insisted on chastity, while another, which also insisted on chastity, oddly enough wished to arrive at this goal by means of ritual debauchery. The members of one mutilated themselves because they regarded female flesh as an invention of the Devil ; in another men and women assembled together naked at their devotional gatherings. Theological speculation led some to the conclusion that the serpent that tempted Eve in Paradise had been a divine person, as a result of which they went in for sodomy ; and others suffered no virgins to remain as such, because their learned conviction was that the Mother of God had borne other children as well as Jesus, so that virginity was obviously a dangerous error. There were always some doing something of which others did the opposite, and both for approximately the same reasons and in the same beliefs.

Tuzzi spoke of this with the gravity properly accorded to historical facts, however odd they may be, and yet with a faint undertone of what is still called the smoking-room joke. Ulrich and he were standing close to the wall. The Permanent Secretary, with a little vexed smile, dropped the stub of his cigarette into an ash-tray, continued to gaze abstractedly at the seething throng, and concluded, as though he had set out to say exactly as much as would fit into the time needed to smoke a cigarette, and no more, with the words : " It seems to me that the state of affairs prevailing then, with so many different opinions held and so many quite subjective views, more than a little resembles our situation today with the controversies going on among our literati. Tomorrow they will have gone with the wind. If it had not been that as a result of various historical circumstances an ecclesiastical bureaucracy that was also politically effective came into existence at the right moment, there would hardly be any trace of the Christian faith left today. . . ."

Ulrich agreed with him. " A religious bureaucracy, appointed and paid by the congregation, sees to it that official regulations are not taken lightly. I am generally inclined to think we are unfair to our baser qualities. If they were not so dependable there could never have been any history. For intellectual and spiritual exertions are everlastingly controversial, changing with every wind."

The Permanent Secretary glanced up mistrustfully and then at once looked away again. Remarks of this kind were too wild for his liking. Nevertheless, and in spite of the fact that he had known Ulrich only a short time, his attitude to this cousin of his wife's was strikingly friendly and familiar. He himself came and went and had the air, in the midst of all that was going on in his house, of living in some other, closed world, the loftier meaning of which he kept concealed from every gaze ; at times, however, he seemed unable to resist any longer and could not help revealing himself, however indistinctly, to someone for an instant. It was then always this cousin with whom he struck up a conversation. That was a very natural human consequence of being deprived of recognition, in the way he was deprived, in his relations with his wife, and this in spite of occasional fits of tenderness on her part. Diotima would then kiss him like a little girl—a girl of perhaps fourteen, when out of heaven knows what affectation she smothers some still smaller boy in kisses. Involuntarily Tuzzi's upper lip, under the curled moustache, would tighten in shame. The new conditions that had arisen in his household got his wife and him into impossible situations. He had by no means forgotten Diotima's complaint about his snoring. Meanwhile, too, he had read Arnheim's writings and was prepared to discuss them. There was much he could accept, very much more that he disposed of as erroneous, and a certain amount that he did not understand, though in the confident calm of the assumption that this was the author's loss. But he had always been in the habit, in such questions, of simply stating the view of a man of experience who was accustomed to having his judgment respected; and the prospect, now to be reckoned with, of every time being contradicted by Diotima—in other words, the necessity of entering into unmanly argument with her—was something he felt to be such an improper alteration in his private life that he could not bring himself to have it out with her, in half-conscious wish-dreams even preferring duelling-pistols as a means of settling it with Arnheim.

Tuzzi suddenly narrowed his beautiful brown eyes, frowning in annoyance, and told himself that he must keep a sharper watch over his moods. This ' cousin ', standing there beside him—and he was, in Tuzzi's view, not at all the sort of man one should take up with over-intimately !—reminded him of his wife actually only through an association of ideas that scarcely had any real content, namely their kinship. He had also observed for some time that Arnheim, in a somewhat cautious manner, tended to make a favourite of this younger man, who, on his side, did not conceal his marked antipathy. These two observations did not really amount to much, yet they were enough to make Tuzzi uneasily aware of his own inexplicable liking for Ulrich. He opened his brown eyes wide and for a while stared across the room, round-eyed as an owl, without really looking at anything.

His wife's cousin, incidentally, was gazing straight ahead, just like him, with the bored air of someone who does not feel obliged to keep up party manners, and apparently had not even noticed the pause in their conversation. Tuzzi had the feeling that something ought to be said. He felt the insecurity of a man suffering from imaginary troubles, who might give himself away by his silence.

" You like to think the worst of everything," he remarked, smiling, and as though the statement about the officials of the faith had had to wait in the ante-chamber of his ear until that moment. " And I dare say my wife is not so far wrong in being a little afraid of your collaboration, in spite of her cousinly feelings for you. If I may say so, your ideas about your fellow-men have a downward tendency, a somewhat bearish tone."

" That's an excellent way of putting it," Ulrich answered, and seemed pleased, " even if I'm afraid I don't quite live up to it. It's really history that has always had the bearish or the builish tendencies where speculation in mankind is concerned—in the bearish manner by means of cunning and violence, in the bullish more or less the way your wife is trying to do it here, by means of belief in the power of ideas. Herr Doktor Arnheim, too, if one is to believe what he says, is a bull. You, on the other hand, as a bear by profession must, amid this choir of angels, have sensations that I should be interested to learn more of."

He considered the Permanent Secretary with an expression of sympathy.

Tuzzi pulled out his cigarette-case. He shrugged his shoulders. " What makes you believe I think differently about it from my wife ? " he retorted. He wanted to stop the personal turn the conversation had taken, but by this retort only managed to emphasise it.

Ulrich fortunately took no notice of this and went on : " We are a substance that takes on the form of every mould it happens to get into in one way or the other."

" That's over my head," Tuzzi replied evasively.

Ulrich was pleased. This was a contrast to his own approach. He thoroughly enjoyed talking to a man who did not respond to intellectual stimulation and had no other means of defence, or did not wish to use any other, than simply to step in with his whole personality. His original dislike of Tuzzi had long ago reversed itself under the pressure of his far greater dislike of the fuss going on in Tuzzi's house. The only thing he could not understand was why Tuzzi put up with it, and he indulged in all sorts of conjectures about this. He was getting to know him only very slowly and from outside, rather like an animal one has under observation, where one lacks the useful insight that speech gives one into human beings, who talk because they can't help it. What had appealed to him first was the dried-up appearance of this man who was only just of middle height, and the dark, intense eye, betraying much uneasy feeling, which was not in the least a civil servant's eye and at the same time was far from being what one would have expected from the rest of Tuzzi's personality as it was revealed in conversation—unless, indeed, one was to assume that it was, as not infrequently occurs, a boy's eye looking out from among the entirely different features of the grown man, like a window opening into some unused, locked up, and long forgotten part of the interior. The next thing that had struck Ulrich was Tuzzi's personal aroma. There was about Tuzzi an aroma as of something Chinese, or of dry wooden boxes, or a blend of the effects of sun, sea, and exotic plants, of costiveness, and a discreet whiff of the barber's shop. This odour made Ulrich thoughtful. He had come across only two people with a personal odour, this man and Moosbrugger. When he called to mind Tuzzi's delicate, sharp aroma and at the same time thought of Diotima, over whose grand surface lay a thin haze of powdery scent that did not seem to be covering anything, what he arrived at was antagonistic forms of passion to which the slightly comical real-life cohabitation of these two people did not seem in the least related. Ulrich had to call his thoughts back until they were again at the distance from things that is considered permissible. Only then could he reply to Tuzzi's defensive answer.

" It's presumptuous of me," he began again, in that faintly bored but resolute tone of voice that is used socially to express regret at having also to bore the person one is speaking to because the situation in which both find themselves allows of nothing better, " it can't but be presumptuous if in speaking to you I try to define what diplomacy is. But I crave correction. And so I shall venture to put it like this : diplomacy assumes that a dependable order of things can be attained only by making use of mankind's untruthfulness, cowardice, cannibalism, and so forth, in fact of its solid villainies. It is a bearish idealism—to make use again of your admirable expression. And it seems to me that this is an enchantingly melancholy state of things, because it starts out from the assumption, do you see, that the unreliability of our higher faculties makes us equally capable of treading the road to cannibalism and of treading that to the *Critique of Pure Reason*."

" I am sorry to see," the Permanent Secretary protested, " that you have a romantic picture of diplomacy and, like so many people, confuse politics with intrigue. There may have been something in that when politics were still conducted by princely amateurs. But it no longer applies in a time when everything is dependent on social considerations of a sound middle-class kind.

We are not melancholy-minded. We are optimistic. We must believe in a happy future, or else we should be unable to stand up to our own conscience, which is, of course, in no way different in nature from other people's conscience. If you insist on using the word ' cannibalism ', I can only say the merit of diplomacy is that it holds the world back from cannibalism. But if one is to do that one must believe in something higher."

" What do you believe in ? " his ' cousin ' asked him bluntly.

" Oh well, you know . . ." Tuzzi said. " I'm no longer a boy that I could answer such a question point-blank. All I meant was that the more a diplomat can identify himself with the intellectual and spiritual currents of his time, the easier he will find his profession. And vice versa—it has become clear in recent generations that one needs diplomacy all the more the greater the progress that the mind makes in all directions. But of course that's only natural."

" Natural ? But then you're simply saying the same as myself ! " Ulrich exclaimed with as much animation as was possible within the picture they wished to present—that of two gentlemen engaged in languid conversation. " What I wanted to bring out, regretfully, was that what is intellectual, spiritual, and good cannot exist for long without reinforcement from the bad, evil, and material, and what you say is more or less that the more mind there is in existence the more caution is needed. Let's put it like this, then—one can treat man as a low, rotten cad and in this way get him to do almost anything in the world, or one can make him enthusiastic and in *that* way get him to do almost anything in the world. We waver to and fro between the two methods. We mix the two methods. That's the whole story. It seems to me that I may congratulate myself on being in much deeper-going agreement with you than you are inclined to admit."

Permanent Secretary Tuzzi turned towards his inquisitor. A faint smile lifted his little moustache, and his shining eyes took on a mockingly indulgent expression. He wished to put an end to this sort of conversation, for it was as unsafe as a frozen pavement and as senselessly puerile as boys' sliding on the ice of such a pavement. " You know," he answered, " you will probably think this a barbarous thing to say, but I shall explain what I mean by it—philosophising is something only professors ought to be allowed to go in for ! I except, of course, our recognised great philosophers, I esteem them highly and have read them all. But they are, so to speak, something that simply happens to be there. And our professors are appointed for the purpose, in their case it's a profession and needn't involve any further consideration. After all, we have to have the teachers too if the whole thing isn't to die out. But for the rest the good old Austrian maxim that the citizen isn't supposed to rack his brains about everything was right enough. It's seldom that any good comes of it, and it easily takes on a faint touch of presumption." The Permanent Secretary rolled himself a cigarette and fell silent. He felt no compulsion to excuse his ' barbarism ' any further.

Ulrich watched the movements of his slender, brown fingers, enchanted with the brazen semi-stupidity that Tuzzi had just chosen to display.

" You have stated the same very modern principle," he remarked politely, " that the Churches have been applying to their members for nearly two thousand years, and which for some time now has been adopted by Socialism."

Tuzzi glanced up fleetingly, to discover what his ' cousin ' intended by this combination of allusions. Then he expected that Ulrich would again go off into a long exposition, and was annoyed in anticipation about such everlasting intellectual indiscretion.

But Ulrich did nothing of the kind. He merely scrutinised, with a pleased expression, the man with the pre-1848 ideas who was standing at his side.

Ulrich had long assumed that Tuzzi must have his reasons for tolerating his wife's relations with Arnheim within certain limits, and he would greatly have liked to know what Tuzzi was hoping to achieve by this means. It remained obscure. Perhaps Tuzzi adopted this attitude only in somewhat the same way that the banks regarded the Collateral Campaign, from which they had hitherto held aloof as far as was possible, without, however, depriving themselves of a chance to have at least one little finger in the pie ; and it might be, then, that Tuzzi, thus preoccupied, did not notice Diotima's second springtide of love, although it was, frankly, becoming pretty obvious. Yet this was scarcely probable. Ulrich found it interesting to scrutinise the deep furrows and folds in his neighbour's face and watch the hard modelling of the jaw-muscles when the teeth were clenched on the cigarette-holder. This man aroused in him a sense of pure masculinity. He was rather weary of all his long soliloquies, and the pleasure of working out a picture of a taciturn man was considerable. He was sure that even as a boy Tuzzi had not been able to endure other boys who talked a great deal : it is always they who later develop into men of wit and learning, while the boys who are more given to spitting through their teeth than opening their mouths wide turn into men who do not like any sort of thinking that is not profitable and seek in action, in intrigue, in simple endurance or resistance, some compensation for the inescapable state of feeling and thinking that they are somehow so much ashamed of that they prefer, if possible, to use thoughts and feelings only in order to mislead other people. Tuzzi would, of course, if a remark to this effect had been made in his presence, have rejected it just as decisively as he would reject one that was too emotional ; for it was his principle not to permit exaggerations and eccentricities at any cost, either in this direction or in that. In fact it was as much a mistake to talk to him about what he, as a person, so admirably represented as to ask a musician, an actor, or a dancer what he was really *getting at*. And what Ulrich would best have liked to do at this moment was to pat the Permanent Secretary on the back or gently ruffle his hair, by some wordless, pantomimic means letting the agreement between them have its little play.

What Ulrich failed to picture to himself was only one thing : that not only as a boy, but now too, at this very moment, Tuzzi felt the urge to spit between his teeth, as a way of expelling a jet of masculine self-assertion. For he felt something of the vague benevolence at his side, and the situation made him uncomfortable. He himself knew that in the statement he had made about philosophy there were all sorts of things that it was not precisely desirable to say in speaking to someone he did not know well, and he must have been possessed of a devil to have given his ' cousin ' (for some reason or other he never called Ulrich by any other name) this free and easy proof of his trust. He could not endure talkative men, and he wondered, aghast, whether what it came to was that he was, without knowing it, trying to win this man as an ally in the matter of his wife. At the thought his skin darkened in shame, for he rejected such help ; and he involuntarily took several steps away from Ulrich, poorly disguising his feelings under the mask of a random excuse.

But then he changed his mind and came back, asking : " Do you ever happen to have wondered why Herr Doktor Arnheim makes such a long stay in our midst ? " He had suddenly imagined such a question was the best way of showing that he regarded any affair with his wife as an impossibility.

His ' cousin ' looked at him in unseemly amazement. The right answer was so obvious that it was difficult to find another. " Do you think," he asked hesitantly, " that there really is some special reason for it ? In that case, then, surely only some reason of business ? "

" I am not in a position to make any statement," Tuzzi replied, once again feeling himself wholly the diplomat. " But can there be any other reason ? "

" Of course there can't really be any other reason," Ulrich conceded in mere politeness. " It's an excellent observation of yours. I must confess I hadn't really thought anything of it at all. I more or less assumed it had something to do with his literary tastes. And that, by the way, might be possible, too, mightn't it ? "

The Permanent Secretary accorded this no more than an absent smile. " Then you really ought to be able to tell me the reason why a man like Arnheim has literary tastes at all ? " he queried. But he regretted it instantly, for his ' cousin ' thereupon obviously prepared for one of his circumstantial answers.

" Has it never struck you," Ulrich began, " what an extraordinary number of people talk to themselves in the street nowadays ? "

Tuzzi shrugged his shoulders in indifference.

" There's something the matter with them. Obviously they can't quite experience their experiences, or assimilate them, and have to pass on vestiges of them. It's in the same way, I am inclined to think, that there develops an exaggerated urge to write. Perhaps one doesn't see it so clearly in writing, since there something comes about—varying according to the degree of talent and practice—that grows away out beyond its origin. But in reading it's quite unambiguously clear. Hardly anyone still *reads* nowadays. People make use of the writer only in order to work off their own excess energy on him in a perverse manner, in the form of agreement or disagreement."

" And so you think there's something the matter with Arnheim's life ? " Tuzzi asked, now all attention. " I have recently read his books, purely out of curiosity, because a great many people say he has such political prospects. But I must confess I don't see either the necessity for them or their purpose."

" One might put the question in much more general terms," his ' cousin ' said. " If a man is so rich in money and influence that he can really have everything—why does he then write ? I really ought to put it even more naïvely and ask why all professional story-tellers write. They tell us about something that has not happened in such a way as if it had happened. That's obvious. But does this mean they admire life as the perpetually hard-up admire the rich man, never tiring of dwelling on how little he cares about them one way or the other ? Or do they just go on like ruminants ? Or do they commit fraud, stealing a little happiness, setting up in the imagination something they can never attain, or never endure, in reality ? "

" Did you never do any writing yourself ? " Tuzzi interrupted him.

" I must uneasily confess—never. For I am far from being so happy that I need not do it. I have come to the conclusion that if I don't soon feel the urge to do so, I must kill myself off on grounds of having a totally abnormal constitution."

He spoke with such grave friendliness that, without his intending it, the joke stood up out of the stream of the conversation as a drenched stone rises out of the ripples of a brook.

Tuzzi noticed it, and in his tactful way was quick to restore the *status quo*. " So all in all, then," he concluded, " you say the same as what I mean when I say civil servants only begin to write when they are superannuated. But how does it apply to Herr Doktor Arnheim ? "

Ulrich remained silent.

" Do you know," Tuzzi said, suddenly lowering his voice, " that Arnheim thinks out-and-out pessimistically and not at all bullishly about this enterprise here in which he takes such a self-sacrificing part ? " He had remembered all at once how right at the beginning of it all Arnheim had, in conversation with him and his wife, given utterance to very considerable doubts as to the Collateral Campaign's prospects, and the fact that this had flashed into his mind again after such a long time precisely at this moment seemed to him, he did not quite know how, in some way to indicate a success for his diplomacy, although he had as yet been unable to discover anything at all concerning the reasons for Arnheim's stay.

His ' cousin ' did indeed look astonished.

Perhaps he did so only out of obligingness, because he preferred to remain silent. But in any case both gentlemen, when an instant later they were separated by guests coming up to them, did in this manner take away with them the sense of having had a stimulating discussion.

92 *Excerpts from rich people's code of living.*

ALL the attention and admiration that Arnheim met with might well have made another man feel mistrustful and unsure of himself : he might have imagined that he owed it to his money. But Arnheim considered mistrust a sign of an ignoble attitude, one that was permissible to a man of his lofty position only as a consequence of an unequivocal report on someone's financial standing ; besides, he was convinced that wealth was a personal quality. Every rich man regards wealth as a personal attribute. And so does every poor man. Everyone is tacitly convinced of it. Only logic makes some difficulties by asserting that the possession of money may perhaps confer certain qualities, but can never itself be a human quality. Closer inspection gives this the lie. Every human nose instantly and unfailingly smells the delicate breath of independence that goes with the habit of commanding, the habit of everywhere choosing the best for oneself, the whiff of slight misanthropy and the unceasing consciousness of responsibility that goes with power, the scent rising from a large and secure income. The very appearance of such a man reveals that he is nourished and daily renewed by an exquisite selection of all the cosmic forces. Money circulates close to his surface like the sap in a flower. Here is nothing of borrowed qualities, no acquiring of habits, nothing indirect, nothing received at second-hand : destroy bank-account and credit, and not only has the rich man no money left, but on the day when he realises this he is a withered flower. With the same immediacy with which everyone formerly observed the quality of his richness, everyone now observes the indescribable quality of nothingness in him, which smells like a smouldering cloud of insecurity, unreliability, inefficiency and poverty. Wealth, then, is a personal, integral quality that cannot be analysed without being destroyed.

But the effect and the functions of this rare quality are extraordinarily involved, and it requires great spiritual strength to master them. Only people who have no money imagine wealth as being like a dream. People who possess it, on the other hand, on every occasion when they meet people who do not possess it dwell on the trouble that it causes them. Arnheim had, for instance, often reflected that really every head of a technical or commercial department of his firm considerably surpassed him in specialised knowledge, and he had to assure himself each time that, if regarded from a sufficiently lofty point of view, ideas, knowledge, loyalty, talent, prudence, and so on appear to be qualities that can be bought because they exist in abundance, whereas the capacity to make use of them presupposes qualities that are possessed only by the few who happen to have been born and bred on the heights.

Another and by no means lesser trouble that rich people have is that everybody wants money from them. Money is not the important thing—that is true, and a few thousand or tens of thousands are something the presence or absence of which a rich man does not feel. And so rich people like to stress at every opportunity that money makes no difference to the value of a human being ; and by this they mean to say that they too would amount to as much without money as they do now, and they are always hurt if someone misunderstands them. Unfortunately this not infrequently happens to them precisely in their intercourse with the intelligentsia. For members of the intelligentsia curiously enough often have no money, but only projects and talent, yet they feel themselves not in the slightest diminished in value as a result, and nothing seems to them more obvious than to ask a rich friend, to whom money does not matter, to support them, for some good purpose or other, out of his superfluity. They will not realise that the rich man would like to support them with his ideas, with his ability, and his personal attractiveness. By demanding money from him they put him, furthermore, into a position antagonistic to the nature of money ; for the will of this nature is set on increase, just as animal nature is set on procreation. One can put money into bad investments, and then it perishes on the field of money's honour. One can buy a new motor-car with it, although the old one is still as good as new ; one can stay, accompanied by one's polo-ponies, at the most expensive hotels at internationally smart holiday resorts ; one can give prizes for horse-races or for art, or spend on a hundred guests in one evening as much as would keep a hundred families for a year. With all this one throws the money out of the window like a sower casting his seed abroad, and it comes in through the door again much increased. But to give it away quietly for purposes and people that are of no use to it can only be compared to foully murdering one's money. It may be that these purposes are good and these people incomparable ; then one should advance their cause by all possible means, only not by means of money. That was a principle of Arnheim's, and his consistent application of it had gained him the reputation of being creatively and actively a participant in the intellectual developments of the age.

Arnheim could also say of himself that he thought like a socialist. And many rich people think like socialists. They have nothing against its being a natural law of society to which they owe their capital, and are firmly convinced that it is the man who bestows importance on property and not property on the man. They calmly discuss the likelihood that property will cease to exist some time in the future when they are no longer there, and are reinforced in the opinion that they possess a social character by the further fact that not infrequently sturdy and upright socialists, in convinced expectation of the revolution that is in any case inevitable, till then prefer to associate with rich people rather than with poor.

One could go on in this way for a long time, if one were setting out to describe all the functions of money that Arnheim had mastered. What it comes to is that economic activity is not one that can be considered apart from the various other forms of intellectual activity. It was therefore quite natural that when his intellectual and artistic friends urgently begged him for it, he gave them not only advice but money too ; but he did not always give, and he never gave much. They assured him that he was the only person on earth whom they could ask, because only he had the necessary qualities of mind. And he believed them, being convinced that all human functions were permeated with the need for capital and that this was as natural as the need for air to breathe. At the same time he met them half-way in their view that money was a spiritual power, by employing his power only with exquisitely tactful restraint.

And why in any case is anyone admired and loved ? Is this not an almost unfathomable mystery, round and fragile as an egg ? Is one loved the more truly if it is for the sake of a moustache than if it is for the sake of a motor-car ? Is the love that one arouses because one is a sun-bronzed child of the South more personal than that aroused because one is a child of one of the largest industrialists ? At that time, when almost all well-dressed men were clean-shaven, Arnheim continued to wear, just as he had done before, a small, pointed beard and a short clipped moustache : this small, extraneous and yet familiar feeling on his face, whenever he talked all too self-obliviously in the presence of eager listeners, reminded him, for reasons that were not clear even to him, but in a way that was agreeable, of his money.

93
Even by way of physical culture the civilian mind is hard to tackle.

THE General had for a long time been sitting on one of the chairs that had been placed against the wall all round the intellectual jousting-ground, his ' benefactor ', as he liked to call Ulrich, sitting beside him ; and between them there was an unoccupied chair on which stood two chalice-shaped glasses of invigorating drinks that they had got themselves from the buffet. The General's pale blue tunic had worked up as he sat and now formed furrows over his paunch, reminiscent of a worried brow. The two men were silent, listening to a conversation that was going on just in front of them.

" Beaupré's game," someone was saying, " positively must be called a performance of genius. I saw him play here last summer and on the Riviera the winter before. If he makes a mistake, his luck comes to his aid. And he does make mistakes pretty often. . . . The structure of his game is contrary to a really sound conception of tennis. But by the grace of heaven which has been accorded him he stands outside the normal laws of tennis."

" I prefer scientific lawn tennis to the intuitive game," someone objected. " Braddock, for instance. There may be no such thing as perfection, but Braddock comes pretty near to it."

The first speaker retorted : " The genius of Beaupré, with his brilliant, unsystematic chaos, reaches its peak at the point where knowledge fails."

A third man said : " Perhaps ' genius ' is going a shade too far, don't you think ? "

" What would you call it then ? It's genius that gives a man the inspiration how to handle the ball the right way just at the most unlikely moment ! "

" I should go so far as to say," the Braddockian said in support of this, " that personality must make itself felt whether it's a tennis-racket a man holds in his hand or the fate of nations."

" No, no, genius is a bit much ! " the third protested.

The fourth was a musician. He said : " You're quite wrong. You're overlooking the direct, perceptual thinking there is in sport, obviously because you're in the usual habit of overvaluing the logical, systematic kind of thinking. That's just about as out of date as the prejudice that music is an enrichment of the emotions and sport a way of disciplining the will. But any achievement in the sphere of pure movement is so magical that human beings can't stand it without some sort of protection. You can see it in the cinema if there's no music. And music is inner movement. It stimulates the kinetic imagination. Once one has grasped the magical aspect of music one won't for an instant hesitate to allow that there is genius in sport. It's only science that has no genius—it's mere mental acrobatics."

" So then I'm right," Beaupré's disciple said, " in denying there's any genius in Braddock's scientific game."

" What you're overlooking," Braddock's disciple said defensively, " is that here one must start out from a revaluation of the concept ' science '."

" By the way, which of them beats the other ? " somebody asked.

Nobody knew. Each of them had frequently beaten the other, but nobody could recall the exact figures.

" Let's ask Arnheim," someone suggested.

The group dispersed.

The silence over the three chairs continued for some time. At last General Stumm said thoughtfully : " I wonder—fact is, I was listening to all that—and it seems to me one could say just the same about a victorious general, too, couldn't one ?—apart from the bit about music. What I mean is why do they consider it genius in a tennis-player and barbarism in a general ? " Since his benefactor had given him the advice to try the physical-culture line of attack with Diotima, he had several times meditated on how, in spite of his original distaste for it, he might after all be able to make use of this promising approach to the corpus of civilian ideas. But the difficulties were, as to his regret he could not fail to observe every time, in this direction, too, unusually great.

94   *Diotima's nights.*

DIOTIMA wondered at the fact that Arnheim could bear all these people and even with obvious signs of enjoyment, for the state of her feelings corresponded all too much to what she had several times expressed in saying that world-wide business enterprises were no more than *un peu de bruit autour de notre âme*.

At times she felt bewildered when she looked around and saw

her house full of the nobility of the world and of the mind. All that was left of the story of her life was the extreme contrast between depths and heights, between her situation as a girl, full of anxious middle-class constriction, and this success now dazzling her soul. And although she was even now standing on a dizzily narrow ledge, she felt the inner necessity to lift her foot once more, in the expectation that the way led still higher. The uncertainty drew her on. She wrestled with the decision to enter into a life in which activity, mind, soul, and dream were one. Fundamentally she no longer worried about the fact that there was no sign of any crowning idea for the Collateral Campaign ; even Universal Austria had become a matter of indifference to her ; even indeed the experience that for each great concept that the human mind could produce there was a counter-concept no longer had any terrors for her. The course of events, where they become important, is no longer a logical one : it is more reminiscent of lightning and conflagration, and she had got used to not being able to think anything about the greatness by which she felt herself to be surrounded. What she would have liked best would have been to drop her Campaign and marry Arnheim, just the way in which for a little girl all difficulties are at an end when she drops them and flings herself on her father's chest. But the indescribable outward growth of her activities held her fast. She could not find time to reach a decision. The outer chain of events and the inner ran along beside each other in two independent lines, in spite of her vain attempts to connect them. It was the same as in her marriage, which was even running its course in a seemingly happier way than it had been doing for some time, while the spiritual side of it was all in a state of dissolution.

To be in keeping with her character Diotima should have spoken frankly to her husband ; but there was nothing for her to tell him. Was she ' in love ' with Arnheim ? Her relationship to him could be given so many names that this very trivial one also turned up among her thoughts at times, though seldom. They had not even kissed once, and the soul's extreme embraces were something that Tuzzi would not understand even if they were confessed to him. Diotima was herself at times amazed that nothing more recountable went on between herself and Arnheim. But she had never quite discarded the earnest young girl's habit of

gazing up ambitiously at older men, and she would have found it
easier to imagine something if not literally tangible at least nar-
ratively tangible going on between herself and her cousin, who
seemed to her younger than she was herself, and whom she slightly
despised, than with the man whom she loved and who was so well
able to value it when she dissolved her feelings into general
meditations of great intellectual loftiness. Diotima knew that one
must tumble headlong into fundamentally revolutionary changes
in one's conditions of life, and wake up between one's new four
walls without being quite able to remember how one had got
there ; but she felt herself exposed to influences that kept her
wide awake. She was not quite free from the dislike that the
average Austrian of her time felt towards his German brother. In
its classical form, which has now become rare, this dislike corresponded approximately to a notion that innocently set the venerated heads of Goethe and Schiller upon bodies that had been fed
on sticky puddings and sauces and themselves had something of
the inhuman inner nature of those things. And great as Arnheim's success in her circle was, it did not escape her that after
the first period of astonishment certain resistances had begun to
stir, never taking on form or coming out into the open but nevertheless by their whispering presence making her uncertain and
making her conscious of the difference between her own attitude
and the reserved attitude of several persons on whose behaviour
she had formerly been accustomed to model her own. Now,
dislikes on national grounds are usually nothing but a dislike of
oneself, something fetched up out of the dim depths of the inmost
contradictions in oneself and pinned on to some suitable victim :
it has been a tried and traditional way of doing things since the
earliest days of man, when the medicine-man with a little piece of
stick that he declared to be the seat of the demon would draw the
sickness out of the sick man's body. The fact that her beloved
was a Prussian was an additional source of confusion to Diotima's
heart, adding terrors of which she could not form any clear
idea ; and it was doubtless not entirely unjustifiable that this
undecided condition, which was so markedly distinct from the
simple coarse-grainedness of connubial life, by her was called
passion.

Diotima had sleepless nights. In these nights she wavered

between a Prussian industrial magnate and an Austrian permanent secretary. In the ecstatic luminosity of half-dream Arnheim's grand and glorious life passed before her like a cavalcade. At the side of this loved man she went flying through a firmament of new honours ; but the firmament was of a disagreeably Prussian blue. In the black night, meanwhile, the yellow body of Permanent Secretary Tuzzi still lay beside her own. She was only dreamily aware of this, as of a black-and-yellow symbol of good old Kakanian culture, even though it was but little of that he possessed. The Baroque façade of the great town residence of Count Leinsdorf, her noble and exalted friend, was behind it, and the proximity of Beethoven, Mozart, Haydn, and Prince Eugene hovered about like nostalgia, like a yearning to be home again even before the flight was begun. Diotima could not simply and without more ado make up her mind to take the step out of this world of her own, even though she almost hated her husband for this very reason. In her big, beautiful body the soul sat helpless as in a wide, flowery land.

' I must not be unjust,' Diotima said to herself. ' The administrator, the civil servant, may be no longer awake and open and receptive, but I suppose in his youth he must have had some potentiality for being so.' She recalled hours there had been during their engagement period, though even then Permanent Secretary Tuzzi had no longer been a mere youth. ' He has got his position and personality by hard work and devotion to duty,' she thought tolerantly. ' Yet he himself has no glimmer of realisation that this has been at the cost of the very life of his personality.'

Since her social triumph she thought more indulgently of her husband, and so her thoughts made yet another concession. ' No one is purely a rationalist and a utilitarian. Everyone began by living with a living soul,' she mused. ' But ordinary everyday existence silts him up. The usual passions sweep over him like a conflagration. And the cold world evokes such coldness in him that his soul withers away in it.' Perhaps she had been too modest to confront him with this at the right time and with due severity. It was very sad. It seemed to her she would never summon up the courage to involve Permanent Secretary Tuzzi in the scandal of a divorce, a scandal that would inevitably be a shattering blow to anyone as wrapped up in his official existence as he was.

' Then sooner adultery ! ' she said to herself all at once.

Adultery—this was the thought that Diotima had had for some time now.

The concept of doing one's duty in one's appointed place is an unfruitful one. Enormous quantities of energy are expended for nothing. Real duty lies in choosing one's place and consciously moulding the conditions ! If she was to condemn herself to remaining at her husband's side, come what may, there were still two kinds of unhappiness, the useless and the fruitful, and it was her duty to decide. So far she had never been able to get beyond that element of the painfully coquettish, of unlovely frivolity, that clung to all the descriptions of adultery that she knew. She could not quite manage to imagine herself in such a position. To touch the door-handle of a *garçonnière* amounted to the same, for her, as diving into a cess-pit. To go scampering, with rustling skirts, up the stairs of some strange house—no, a certain moral complacency of her body protested against that. Hastily given kisses were in contradiction to her nature in the same way as fleeting, fluttering words of love. Her inclination was more towards the tragic. The last walk together, goodbyes choked off even in the throat, profound conflicts between the duty of a woman beloved and the duty of a mother—all this was much more in tune with her temperament. But owing to her husband's economical attitude she had no children. And besides, tragedy was the very thing that was to be avoided somehow. So she settled—if it was to come to that—for the Renaissance pattern. A love that lived with a poignard in its heart . . . that was the thing. She could not imagine it very precisely, but there was undoubtedly something rampantly honourable in it—with a background of ruined columns and over them a sky of racing clouds. Guilt and the overcoming of a sense of guilt, pleasure expiated through suffering, all this trembled in the picture she had, filling her with unutterable intensity and awe. ' Wherever a human being finds his highest opportunities and the richest development of his strength, that is the place for him,' she thought. ' For there he is at the same time making his contribution to the profoundest intensification of the life of the Whole.'

She contemplated her husband as well as the darkness permitted. Just as the eye does not perceive the ultra-violet ray of the spectrum, so too this man of the intellect could never notice certain spiritual realities !

Permanent Secretary Tuzzi breathed calmly, unsuspectingly, cradled by the thought that during his well-earned eight hours of intellectual absence nothing of importance could occur in Europe. This tranquillity did not fail to make an impression on Diotima also, and more than once did she then weigh the thought : Renunciation ! Farewell to Arnheim ! Great and noble words of grief, heaven-storming resignation, leave-takings in a Beethovenesque mood—her strong cardiac muscle grew tense under such demands. Tremulous, glitteringly autumnal conversations, laden with the mournfulness of far-off blue mountains, filled the future. But renunciation and the connubial double bed ? Diotima started up from her pillows, her black hair flying in wild ringlets. Now Permanent Secretary Tuzzi's sleep was no longer that of innocence but that of a snake that had just swallowed a rabbit. It would not have taken much to bring Diotima to waking him and, confronted with this new problem, to shriek in his face that she must, must, and *would* leave him ! Such flight into an hysterical scene would have been understandable in her equivocal situation ; but her body was too healthy for that, and she could feel that it simply did not react with extreme horror to Tuzzi's proximity. Faced with this missing horror she was overcome by a dry shuddering. In vain then did the tears try to run down her cheeks. But oddly enough what gave her a certain consolation precisely in this state was the thought of Ulrich. Recently she had not otherwise been in the way of thinking about him at all ; but his queer remarks about wanting to abolish reality and about Arnheim's over-estimating reality had an incomprehensible hovering overtone that Diotima had missed at the time, but which now in these nights came back to her. 'But what this comes to is simply that one should not bother too much about whatever is going to happen,' she told herself irritably. 'Really, one could hardly think of anything more commonplace ! ' And even while she interpreted this idea of his so baldly and simply she knew that there was something in it she did not understand ; and it was precisely from this that the soothing influence radiated, like a sleeping-draught paralysing her despair together with her consciousness. Time flitted away like a dark shadow-line. She felt comforted by the thought that even her lack of lasting despair might somehow be regarded as laudable; yet this did not quite manage to become conscious.

At night the thoughts flow now in brightness, now through sleep, like water in high mountains. And when her thoughts reappeared after a while, quietly flowing on, Diotima had the feeling she had merely dreamt all the frothing that had gone before. The bubbling little stream that lay behind the dark mass of the mountain was not the same as the tranquil river into which she slid in the end. Anger, abhorrence, courage, fear, all had drained away. There must not be such feelings. There were none. In the struggles between souls no one is guilty! And then Ulrich too was forgotten again. For now all that was left was the last mysteries and the soul's eternal longing. Their morality does not lie in what one does. It does not lie in the movements of consciousness nor in those of passion. Even the passions are only *un peu de bruit autour de notre âme*. One can win kingdoms or lose them, but the soul does not stir, and one can do nothing to arrive at one's destiny; but at times it grows out of the depths of one's being, serene and quotidian as the chanting of the spheres.

Then Diotima lay wide awake as at no other hour, but full of trust. These thoughts, the concluding point of which lay somewhere out of sight, had the advantage of very quickly putting her to sleep even in her most sleepless nights. Like a velvety vision she felt her love merging with the infinite darkness that reaches out beyond the stars, inseparable from her, inseparable from Paul Arnheim, not to be touched by any plans and intentions. She hardly had time to reach out for the tumbler of sugared water that she kept on her night-table as a remedy for sleeplessness, but which she resorted to only in this last moment because in the moments of agitation she forgot it. The soft sound of drinking purled, like the whispering of lovers behind a wall, alongside the sleep of her husband, who heard nothing of it. Then Diotima lay back reverently on her pillows and sank into the silence of all being.

95 *The Superman of Letters: Back View.*

IT is almost too familiar a phenomenon to bear mentioning : since her celebrated guests had convinced themselves that the serious nature of the enterprise demanded no great exertions from them, they simply behaved like human beings, and Diotima, who saw her rooms filled with the sound of many voices and much high-mindedness, was disappointed. Sublime soul that she was, she knew not the law of prudence according to which as a private person one behaves in a manner directly the contrary to one's professional behaviour. She did not know that politicians, after having called each other crooks and scoundrels in the debating-chamber, amicably partake of a snack at the same table in the refreshment-room. That judges who, as jurists, have imposed a heavy penalty on some unfortunate, after the conclusion of the proceedings press his hand in sympathy, she knew, but she had never found anything to object to in this. That dancers outside their equivocal occupation often lead an irreproachable life as wives and housewives was something she had several times heard, and she even found it touching. It also seemed to her beautifully symbolic that at times princes laid aside their crowns in order to be human beings and nothing else. But when she became aware that princes of the intellect also like to indulge in going about incognito, this dual behaviour struck her as rather odd. What passion is it, what law underlies this general tendency, bringing it about that outside their profession men pretend they have nothing to do with the men they are within their profession ? After they have stopped work and are at leisure, with their professional cares tidied away, they look exactly like an office that has been tidied up, the writing-things and papers put away in a drawer and the chairs tipped up on the tables. They are made up of two men, and one does not know whether it is in the evening or in the morning that they come to their real selves again.

And so, however much it gratified her to see her soul-mate well liked by all the men she had gathered around her, and in particular that he was so full of initiative in associating with the younger ones, it did at times discourage her to see him so involved in all this social activity, and it seemed to her that a prince of the intellect ought not really to let associating with the ordinary aristocracy of the intellect be of such moment to him, and that he should not be accessible to the changeable traffickings of ideas.

The explanation lay in the fact that Arnheim was not a prince of the intellect but a superman of letters.

The superman of letters is the successor to the prince of the intellect, a substitution corresponding in the sphere of the mind to the replacement of princes by rich men that has taken place in the political sphere. Just as the prince of the intellect had his place in the age of princes, so the superman of letters has his place in the age of the Super-Dreadnought and the super-store. He is a particular manifestation of the mind's association with things of super-size. Hence the least that is expected of a superman of letters is that he should own a motor-car. He must travel extensively, be received by cabinet ministers, and give lectures ; he must make on the leaders of public opinion the impression that he represents a force of conscience to be reckoned with. He is *chargé d'affaires* to the spirit of the nation whenever evidence of a humanitarian outlook needs to be shown abroad. When he is at home he receives visits from notabilities, and all the time he has to think also of his business, which he has to perform with the nimbleness of a circus artiste, whose exertions must not be apparent. For the superman of letters is by no means simply the same thing as a man of letters who earns a great deal of money. He need never himself write ' the book of the year ' or ' the book of the month ' ; it is enough that he has no objection to this kind of evaluation. For it is he who sits on all prize-awarding committees, who signs all manifestos, writes all prefaces, delivers all birthday addresses, has an opinion on all important events and is called in wherever there is a need to show what heights of achievement have been scaled. The fact is, in all his activities the superman of letters never represents the whole nation, but only the progressive section of it, that large, select body that is by now almost in the majority ; and this sets up a constant intellectual tension around him. It is of course life at its present stage of development that leads to this large-scale industry of the mind, just as, on the other hand, industry has hankerings in the direction of the mind, politics, and control of the public conscience ; the two phenomena meet half-way. This is why the role of superman of letters does not indicate one definite and rounded personality ; it represents a figure on the social chessboard, subject to rules and capable of moves that have been evolved in the course of time. The earnest and well-meaning people of this time take the view that it is not much use to them if someone or other has a mind (there is so much of it about that a little more or less does not make any difference, and anyway everyone thinks he has enough for his own needs), but that the anti-mind must be combated, which means that the mind must be exhibited and put through its paces before an audience. And because a superman of letters is more suitable for this purpose than a superior man of letters, who might not be understood by so many people, everyone does his utmost to see that this greatness is brought out on the greatest possible scale.

If this is rightly understood, then clearly Arnheim could not be very gravely reproached for being one of the first, still experimental, though already highly perfected embodiments of this state of affairs ; yet admittedly a certain innate talent for the role was necessary. For the fact is that most men of letters would gladly be supermen of letters, if they only could. But it is the same as with mountains : between the Austrian towns of Graz and St. Pölten, for instance, there are many that would manage to look exactly like Monte Rosa if only they were high enough. Hence the only really indispensable qualification for becoming a superman of letters remains this : one must write books or plays that will do equally well for high and low. One must be effective in the world before one can be effective in the cause of good ; this principle is the basis of every super-literary life. And a strange and wonderful principle it is, directed as it is against the temptations of solitude—positively Goethe's principle of ' effective action ' : one must only bestir oneself in the dear good world and then all the rest will follow of its own accord. For when a writer once begins to be effective, a significant change takes place in his life. His publisher stops saying that a business man who goes into publishing is a sort of tragic idealist, because after all he could do very much better for himself dealing in cloth or un-spoilt paper. The critics discover in him a worthy object for their activities. For critics are very often not wicked men at all, but, thanks to the unpropitious nature of the times, ex-poets who have to pin their hearts to something in order to remain articulate ; they are war-poets or love-poets according to the nature of the spiritual harvest that they must turn to account satisfactorily somehow, and it is easy enough to understand that they naturally prefer the book of a superman of letters for this purpose to that of an ordinary man of letters. Now of course every human being has only a limited capacity for work ; and so the best of this out-put spreads smoothly over the annual publications of the super-men of letters. Hence these works become savings-banks in the nation's intellectual economy, each of them bringing in its train critical interpretations that, far from being mere expense of spirit, are actually investments, and there is correspondingly little left over for anything else. But the thing reaches really super-proportions only with the essayists, biographers and snap-shot historians who use a great man for the relief of their natural needs. Be it said without offence, where their natural needs are con-cerned dogs prefer a busy street-corner to a solitary rock : and how then should human beings, who feel the higher need to leave their name publicly behind them, fail to choose a rock that is noticeably solitary ? Before he knows what is happening, the superman of letters is no longer a being to himself, but a sym-biosis, in the most delicate sense the product of national co-operation, and experiences the most exquisite assurance that life can give—namely that his own prospering is most intimately bound up with the prospering of countless other people.

And probably this is the reason why one finds that a general feature of the super-literary character is a very marked sense of ' good form '. Supermen of letters resort to literary combat only when they feel their own position is threatened ; in all other cases they are remarkable for their balanced calm and benevolence. They are perfect in their tolerance of trivialities uttered in their praise. They do not lightly condescend to discuss other authors ; but when they do so they seldom flatter a man of high rank, pre-ferring to encourage one of those unobtrusive talents that consist of forty-nine per cent. ability and fifty-one per cent. lack of it and which are, as a result, so very good at everything that requires a keen man, but which might be damaged by a strong man, that sooner or later every one of them reaches an influential position in literature. But does that not carry this description beyond the limits of what is peculiar to the superman of letters ? There is an excellent saying that nothing succeeds like success. It is difficult to imagine the stir going on round an ordinary man of letters nowadays even long before he has become a superman of letters, that is, while he is still only a reviewer, book-page editor, broadcast talks organiser, film-script writer, or editor of some little literary periodical. Many of them resemble those little rubber donkeys and pigs that have a hole at the back where one blows them up.

When one sees supermen of letters carefully sizing up the situation and endeavouring to turn it all into the picture of a sound, hard-working nation honouring its great men, surely one ought to be grateful to them ? They ennoble life as they find it by the sympathetic interest they take in it.

Let us try to imagine the opposite—a writer who did not do all these things. He would have to refuse cordial invitations, rebuff people, assess praise not as though he himself were the object of it, but like a judge, tear the natural state of things to shreds, and treat splendid opportunities with suspicion merely because they were splendid ; and he would have nothing to offer in return but processes going on inside his own head, difficult to express and difficult to assess, and the work of a man of letters, something that an epoch already possessing supermen of letters need not set much store by. Would not such a man inevitably remain an outsider and have to withdraw from reality, bearing all the consequences of his attitude ?

That at any rate was Arnheim's opinion.

96   *The Superman of Letters : Front View.*

THE real difficulty in the existence of a superman of letters arises mainly from the fact that, although it is customary to take a commercial attitude in intellectual life, long tradition still makes it necessary to talk like an idealist.   It was this combination of commerce and idealism that took such a decisive place in all Arnheim's endeavours in life.

One comes across such anachronistic combinations everywhere nowadays.   For instance, while the dead are now rushed off to the cemetery at a combustion-engine canter, it is still usual that the roof of the elegant motor-hearse should be decorated with a knightly helmet and two crossed swords.   It is the same in all spheres.   Human evolution is a long, trailing procession ; and whereas about two generations ago business letters were still adorned with fair flowers of speech, today a stage has been reached when one could express all sorts of relations—from love to pure logic—in the language of supply and demand, of security and discount, at least as well as one can express them in psychological or religious terms.   However, this is not done, the reason being that the new language is still not quite sure of itself.   Nowadays the ambitious financier is in a difficult position.   If he wants to be on an equal footing with the more ancient powers that be, he must link his activity up with great thoughts.   But nowadays there are no longer any great thoughts that are accepted without question, for this sceptical age believes neither in God nor in Mankind, neither in crowns nor in morality ; or it believes in the whole lot of it all rolled into one, which amounts to the same thing.   So business men, who think they cannot get along without some sort of greatness for a compass, have had to make use of the democratic dodge of replacing the immeasurable influence of greatness by the measurable greatness of influence.   So now whatever counts as great *is* great ; only this means that in the last resort whatever is clamorously advertised as great also *becomes* great. And it is not everyone's luck to be able to swallow this innermost core of our time without difficulty. Arnheim had carried out many experiments as to how it might be done.

In this connection a man of education may call to mind, for instance, the relations between science and the Church in the Middle Ages. In those days the philosopher had to remain on good terms with the Church if he wanted to be successful and to influence the thought of his contemporaries. Hence the vulgar free-thinker may incline to the opinion that those fetters must have hindered the philosopher's ascent to greatness. But the opposite was the case ; in the opinion of learned experts what resulted was simply an incomparable Gothic beauty of thought. And if it was possible for the mind to pay such deference to the Church without harm to itself, why should it not be able to do the same where commercial advertising is concerned ? Can those whose aim is effective action not be equally effective on these terms ? Arnheim was convinced that it was a sign of greatness not to be too critical of one's own age. The best horseman on the best horse, if he is at loggerheads with his mount, is more likely to take a tumble at a fence than is another rider who adjusts himself to the paces of his nag.

Another example—Goethe ! He was a genius such as the earth will not easily bring forth again, but he was also the ennobled son of a German family of the prosperous tradesman class, and if we see him as Arnheim saw him we recognise him to have been the very first superman of letters that the German nation produced. Arnheim modelled himself on him in many ways.

Something he was particularly fond of was the well-known story of how Goethe, although secretly sympathising with poor Johann Gottlieb Fichte, left him in the lurch when as professor of philosophy in Jena he was reprimanded for having spoken of the Divinity and divine things ' grandly but perhaps not quite decorously ' and ' went about ' his defence ' passionately ' instead of extricating himself from the affair ' in the smoothest way possible ', as the worldly-wise poet-sage puts it in his memoirs. Arnheim would not only have taken exactly the same attitude as Goethe, but by appealing to Goethe's example he would even have tried to convince the world that this alone was the Goethean, the significant thing to do. He would hardly have been satisfied with observing that, oddly enough, people are inclined to show more sympathy with a great man who does something wrong than with a lesser man who behaves correctly ; but he would have passed on to reflect that to wage uncompromising war for one's convictions is not only unfruitful, but also an attitude lacking in depth and in a sense of historical irony. As regards this last, he would simply have called it Goethean, in other words, the irony of in all seriousness making the best of circumstances, with realistic humour—which in the perspective of time is always proved to be right.

When one reflects that today, barely two generations later, the wrong done to the worthy, honest, slightly over-enthusiastic Fichte has long since become a domestic affair adding nothing to his importance, while on the other hand Goethe's importance has suffered no damage worth mentioning, although he did behave badly, then one must admit that the wisdom of time does in fact amount to pretty much the same as the wisdom of Arnheim.

A third example (Arnheim was always surrounded with good examples) and one that reveals the profound significance of the first two : Napoleon ! Heine in his *Reisebilder* portrays him in a manner so exactly agreeing with Arnheim's ideas that it is best to quote his words, which Arnheim knew by heart. ' It is such a mind, ' Heine says, speaking of Napoleon—but he might just as well have applied it to Goethe, whose diplomatic nature he always defended, with the acuity of a lover secretly realising that he is not in agreement with the object of his admiration, ' it is such a mind that Kant means when he says that we can imagine an intellect that is not like our own, but intuitive. The knowledge that we arrive at by a slow process of analytical thought and pro-longed drawing of conclusions *that* mind beheld and in the same instant profoundly comprehended. Hence came his gift for understanding the age, the present, and for cajoling the spirit of it, never offending it, always making use of it. But since the spirit of the age was formed not only by revolutionary influences, but by the confluence of both the revolutionary and the counter-revolu-tionary views, Napoleon never acted in an entirely revolutionary and never in an entirely counter-revolutionary manner, but always in the spirit of both views, both principles, both tendencies, which had their conjunction in him ; hence he always acted in a manner that was natural, simple and great, never strained and brusque, always calm and temperate. Hence he never intrigued on a small scale, and his *coups* were always the result of his art of understanding and swaying the masses. Complicated slow intrigue is something to which petty analytical minds are inclined ; but the synthetically intuitive mind of the genius has its own miraculous way of linking up the possibilities that its time offers, in such a manner that it is soon in a position to use them for its own purpose.'

Heine may perhaps have meant this slightly differently from the way in which his admirer Arnheim understood it. But Arnheim did very much feel that this description applied also to himself.

97   *Clarisse's mysterious powers and missions.*

CLARISSE in the room . . . Walter was somehow mislaid. What she had was an apple and her dressing-gown. These, the apple and the dressing-gown, were the two springs from which an unregarded thin rivulet of reality flowed into her consciousness. Why did it seem to her Moosbrugger was musical ? She did not know. Perhaps all murderers were musical. She knew that she had written a letter to His Highness Count Leinsdorf about this matter ; she even remembered vaguely what she had written, but it seemed a long way off and she had no way of getting at it.

But the Man Without Qualities was unmusical, wasn't he ?

Since no proper answer occurred to her, she left this thought where it was and passed on.

After a while, however, something did occur to her : Ulrich is the Man Without Qualities. And a man without qualities can't be musical, of course. But he can't be unmusical either, can he ?

She passed on.

He had said of her : You're both girlish and heroic.

She repeated : ' Girlish and heroic ! ' Warmth flooded into her cheeks. From this dictum arose a duty that she could not define.

Her thoughts were thrusting in two directions, as in a skirmish. She felt attracted and repelled, without knowing to what and by what. Finally some faint sensation of tenderness that was, though how she did not know, somehow the remains of it, tempted her to go and look for Walter. She stood up and put the apple aside.

She was sorry that she always tormented Walter. She had been no more than fifteen when she had first noticed that she was able to torment him. She only needed to exclaim in a decided tone of voice that something was in fact not as he maintained it was, and he would tense up—no matter how right whatever he had been saying was ! She knew he was afraid of her. He was afraid she might go mad. He had once let it slip out, and then quickly tried to cover it up again. But since then she knew he was thinking about it. She thought it very beautiful. Nietzsche said : ' Is there such a thing as a pessimism of strength ? An intellectual inclination towards what is harsh, dreadful, malignant? A depth of the anti-moral tendency ? A desire for the terrible as the one worthy enemy ? ' Such words, whenever she thought them, set up a sensual stimulus in her mouth that was as bland and strong as milk, and she could hardly swallow.

She thought of the child that Walter wanted from her. That was something else he was afraid of. Understandably, too, if he believed she might go mad some day. It made her feel tenderness towards him, even when she refused herself violently.

But she had forgotten that she had been going to look for Walter. Now there was something going on in her body. Her breasts were filling up, a thicker bloodstream was pressing through the veins of her arms and legs, and she felt a vague urgency driving against bladder and bowels. Her slender body grew inwardly deep, sensitive, alive, strange to her, one thing after the other. . . . A child lay imponderably shining and smiling in her arms. . . . From her shoulders the golden mantle of the Mother of God streamed out in light, folds falling to the floor, and the congregation sang. Now it was outside her—the Lord was born unto the world !

But no sooner had that happened when her body sprang together again, closing the gap over the image, like timber after ejecting a wedge. Once more she was slender, all herself, was disgusted, felt a cruel gladness. She wasn't going to let Walter get away with it as easily as that ! ' It is my will that your triumph and your freedom shall yearn for a child ! ' she chanted to herself. ' Living memorials you shall build, over and above yourself. But I want you to be built in body and soul first ! ' Clarisse smiled. It was that smile of hers that was like the narrow licking flames from a fire covered by some great boulder.

Then it occurred to her that her father had been afraid of Walter. She cast back to some years earlier. This she was used to ; Walter and she liked to ask each other : " Do you remember ——— ? " and then a vanished light streamed magically out of the distance, back upon the present here and now. That was beautiful. They loved it. It can be the same as when one has been walking bad-temperedly for hours and hours, and turns back, and suddenly the whole empty road that has been journeyed over lies transformed in far perspective, a lovely satisfaction now. But they never looked at it like that ; they took their reminiscences very seriously indeed. And so it seemed to her tremendously exciting and complicated that her father, the ageing painter, at that time a figure of authority for her, had been afraid of Walter, who had brought the modern age into his house, while Walter had been afraid of her. It was rather like when she had put her arm round her friend Lucy Pachhofen, having to say ' Papa ', knowing all the time that Papa was Lucy's lover ; for that had been going on at the same time.

Clarisse felt the heat flushing into her cheeks again. She was acutely interested in trying to call to mind the peculiar whimpering sound, that quite alien whimpering, of which she had told Ulrich. She took up a looking-glass and tried to rediscover the face with the lips tightened in anguish that she must have had in that night when her father came to her bed. She could not manage to produce the sound that had escaped from her breast under the pressure of temptation. She reflected that the sound must still be inside her breast at this moment, just as it had been then. It was a sound without mercy or scruple of any kind ; but it had never again risen to the surface. She laid the looking-glass aside and looked round warily, her gaze testing the surroundings, confirming her consciousness of being alone. Then, feeling through her skirt, with her finger-tips she sought the velvety black birthmark that had something so very queer about it. In the hollow of the groin, half hidden by the thigh, at the rim of the hair, which there grew a little irregularly, leaving room for it—there it was. She let her hand rest on it, closed her mind to all thought, and lay in wait for the change that must now come about. And instantly she felt it. It was not the soft streaming of lust, but her arm grew stiff, taut as a man's arm ; it seemed to her that if she could once lift it properly she would be able to smash up everything with it.

She called this spot on her body the Devil's eye. At this spot her father had turned back. The Devil's eye had a gaze that penetrated through her clothes. This gaze ' held ' men, the ' glittering eye ' held them ' spellbound' and drew them on, but would not let them move for as long as Clarisse willed it so. Clarisse thought a good many words in quotation-marks, giving them special emphasis, just as in writing she underlined many words with thick strokes of the pen ; and words so framed in emphasis then had a tensed meaning, were tense rather as her arm was now. Who had ever thought that one could really ' hold ' something ' with one's eye ' ? And she was the first person to hold this expression in her hand like a stone that could be flung at a target. It was part of the smashing force of her arm. And over all this she forgot the whimpering she had wanted to think about, and was thinking of her younger sister Marion. At the age of four Marion had to have her hands tied up at night, because else, not knowing what they did, they went under the bed-clothes out of pure delight in what was pleasant, like two young bears to a hollow tree where there's a honeycomb. And later on she, Clarisse, had once had to tear Walter away from Marion. Sensuality was passed round in her family as wine was among the peasants of the vine-lands. It was a fate. She bore a heavy burden. But for all that her thoughts now went wandering back into the past ; the tension in her arm relaxed, giving way to a natural condition, and her hand lay forgotten on her lap.

At that time she had still been on terms of formality with Walter. Really she owed him a great deal. It was he who had brought the news that there were modern people who could not stand anything but cool, clear furniture and in their rooms hung pictures on which the truth was shown. He read aloud to her— Peter Altenberg, for instance, little stories of little girls bowling their hoops among love-maddened tulip-beds, their eyes as brightly, sweetly innocent as *marrons glacés*. And from that moment on Clarisse knew that her slim legs, which to her had seemed still childish, were just as significant as a scherzo by ' oh I don't know whom '.

At that time they were all on summer holidays together, a large circle of people, several families of acquaintances who had all rented villas on the shores of a lake ; and all bedrooms were crowded with friends, male and female, who had been invited to come and stay. Clarisse shared a room with Marion, and at eleven o'clock Herr Dr. Meingast sometimes came to their room on his secret rounds by moonlight, to have a chat with them. He, who was now a famous man in Switzerland, had then played the part of master of revels and every mother's idol. How old had she been then ? Either between fifteen and sixteen, or between fourteen and fifteen. That was when Meingast's pupil Georg Gröschl had come along too, who was only a little older than Marion and Clarisse. And that evening Herr Dr. Meingast had seemed absent-minded, delivering only a short talk on moon-beams, parents insensitively asleep, and modern-minded people, and suddenly disappeared, apparently having come merely in order to leave sturdy little Georg, his great admirer, alone with the girls. Georg was now silent, probably feeling shy, and the two girls, who had up to then been answering Meingast, were also silent. But then Georg must have clenched his teeth in the dark ; he went up to Marion's bed. The room received some faint light from outside, but in the corners where the beds were there was an impenetrable towering bulk of shadows, and Clarisse could not be sure what was happening ; all she could make out was that Georg seemed to be standing upright beside the bed, looking down at Marion. But he had his back turned to Clarisse and Marion did not utter a sound, just as though she were not in the room at all. This lasted for a long time. But in the end, while Marion remained as motionless and soundless as ever, Georg detached himself from the shadows, like a murderer ; for an instant in the bright patch of moonlight in the middle of the room his shoulder and side were visible, pallid ; and then he came over to Clarisse, who had quickly lain down again and pulled the bedclothes up to her chin. She knew that now the secret thing that had happened at Marion's bed would happen again, and she was rigid with suspense as Georg stood mutely at her bedside, with, as it seemed to her, his lips pressed queerly tight together. Finally his hand came like a snake and began to busy itself with Clarisse. What else he did she was not sure ; she had no clear notion of it and could not make head or tail even of the little that she perceived of his movements through her excitement. She herself felt no desire or pleasure at all—that came only later—and at the moment there was only an intense, nameless, frightened excitement. She kept quiet as a trembling stone in a bridge over which a heavy vehicle passes infinitely slowly, and was unable to say anything, letting it all happen. After Georg had let her go, he disappeared without a word, and neither of the two sisters knew for certain whether the other had experienced the same thing as herself. They had no more called to each other for help than asked each other for sympathy, and years passed before they exchanged the first words about the incident.

Clarisse had found her apple again and was nibbling at it, chewing it in little bites. Georg had never betrayed himself or referred to what had happened, except that perhaps in the period immediately afterwards he had now and again made stonily significant eyes at them. Today he was a smart, rising young lawyer in the civil service. Marion was married. Meingast's career, however, had been more eventful.

Meingast shed his cynicism when he went abroad and became what outside the universities is called a famous philosopher. He always had a throng of pupils, male and female, gathered around him. Only a short time ago now he had written a letter to Walter and Clarisse, announcing that he was intending to visit his homecountry shortly in order to be able for a while to work undisturbed by his followers ; he had also asked whether they would be able to have him to stay, as he had heard that they lived ' on the borderline between Nature and the metropolis '. And perhaps this was really the starting-point of all the roads that Clarisse's thoughts had gone this day. ' Oh lord, what a weird time that was ! ' she thought. And now she remembered too : it had been the summer before the summer with Lucy. Meingast used to kiss her then whenever he felt like it. ' You will permit me to kiss you now,' he would say politely before he did so. He also kissed all her girl friends, and Clarisse even knew of one whose skirt she had never again been able to look at without thinking of hypocritically modest, lowered eyelids. Meingast had told her about it himself, and Clarisse—and after all she was only fifteen then !—had said to the completely grown-up Herr Dr. Meingast, when he told her of his adventures with her girl friends : " You're a swine ! " Using this coarse word, reviling him, caused her a pleasure that was like being booted and spurred. All the same, she had been afraid that in the end she too would not be able to resist ; but when he asked her for a kiss she did not dare to refuse, because she was afraid of appearing silly.

But when Walter kissed her for the first time, she said very solemnly : " I promised Mamma never to do this sort of thing." That was just the difference. Walter talked as beautifully as the Scriptures, and he talked a great deal, art and philosophy surrounding him like great hosts of clouds surrounding the moon. He read aloud to her. But for the most part he merely kept on gazing at her, at her among all her girl friends ; and that was all there was to their relationship at first. And this was just as when the moon looks down : one simply folds one's hands. Actually their relationship progressed also by means of holding of hands—a tranquil holding of hands, wordless now, in which there lay a unique and binding power. Clarisse felt her whole body purified by the touch of his hand. If he ever gave her his hand absently and coolly, it made her quite unhappy. " You don't know what it means to me ! " she would say pleadingly. For by that time they were already on close terms, in secret. He developed in her an understanding for mountains and beetles ; for up to then all she had seen in Nature was a landscape that her father or one of his colleagues would paint and sell. All at once her critical sense was awakened where her family was concerned. She felt herself new and changed.

Now too Clarisse remembered exactly what it had been about the scherzo. " Your legs, Fräulein Clarisse," Walter had said, " have more to do with real art than all the pictures your father paints." There was a piano in the house they were staying in that summer, and they used to play duets together. Clarisse learned from him. She wanted to rise beyond her girl friends and her family. Nobody understood how anyone could play the piano on beautiful summer days instead of going out boating or bathing; but she had pinned her hopes to Walter, she had even then, from the very beginning, resolved to become 'his woman' and marry him. Whenever he spoke to her sharply for playing a wrong note, everything in her would seethe, yet pleasure was predominant. And indeed Walter did snap at her sometimes, for the spirit knows no compromise; but only at the piano. Outside the realm of music it sometimes still happened that she was kissed by Meingast, and on one moonlight boating expedition, when Walter was rowing, quite of her own accord she laid her head on Meingast's chest as he sat beside her in the stern. Meingast was uncannily good at such things, and she did not know where it would take her. On the other hand, once after their piano lesson, when it happened for the second time at the very last moment, as they were already at the open door, that Walter seized her from behind and kissed her hard, she had only had the quite unpleasant sensation of not being able to get any air, and tore herself away from him. For all that, she had made up her mind that whatever might happen between her and the other one, this was the one she must not let go!

There is something queer about such things. Herr Dr. Meingast's breath had something about it in which resistance melted, something that was like pure clear air in which one feels happy without noticing the air itself. Walter, on the other hand, who always, as Clarisse had long known, suffered from a slow digestion, corresponding to the hesitant slowness of his decisions, had something 'set' in his breath, which was partly too hot, partly musty and paralysing. Such psycho-physical elements had played a strange part right from the beginning; nor did it surprise Clarisse, for nothing seemed more natural to her of all people than Nietzsche's saying that a man's body was his soul. There was no more genius in her legs than in her head; they both had exactly the same amount of it, they themselves were the genius; her hand, touched by Walter, instantly set going a current of resolutions and assurances that flowed from the crown of her head to the soles of her feet, but which was without words. And her youth, once she had been aroused to self-certainty, rebelled against the convictions and other follies of her parents, simply with the freshness of a hardened body that despised all feelings even remotely reminiscent of voluptuous connubial beds and the magnificence of Turkish carpets, such as were so popular with the strict and moral elder generation. And that was why the physical element later went on playing a part that she regarded differently from the way other people may regard it.

But here Clarisse called a halt to her reminiscences. Or rather, it was not quite so ; it was more that her reminiscences all at once, and quite without the impact of landing on firm ground, set her down again in the present. For all this and what was still to follow she had wanted to tell her friend ' without qualities '. Perhaps Meingast was taking up too much space in it all at the moment ; for soon after that eventful summer he had vanished, making his escape abroad, and then there had begun that tremendous transformation in him that had turned the frivolous *bon vivant* into a famous philosopher. Since then Clarisse had seen him only in passing, without their having paid tribute to the past. But as she considered it now in her thoughts, the part she had had in his transformation was clear to her. Much else had happened between her and him in the weeks before his disappearance— without Walter and in Walter's jealous presence, displacing Walter, spurring Walter on and driving him high—spiritual thunderstorms, yet madder hours such as make a man and a woman go out of their minds before a thunderstorm, and hours of calm after the storm had worn itself out, when all passion was shed, hours that lay like the green of meadows after rain in the pure air of friendship. Clarisse had had to let all sorts of things have their way with her, and let them not unwillingly, but the inquisitive child had afterwards defended herself in her own fashion by giving her unbridled friend a piece of her mind. And because Meingast in that last period before he departed had already grown more serious in his friendship, almost magnanimous and melancholy in his rivalry with Walter, today she was firmly convinced that she had drawn upon herself everything that had clouded his spirit before he went to Switzerland and that she had thus made it possible for him to transform himself so unexpectedly. She was strengthened in this view by what took place between herself and Walter immediately after that. She could no longer quite distinguish those long past years and months from each other ; but after all, it did not matter much when this had happened and when that. The main thing was that, after the increase (filled with resistance on her side) in intimacy with Walter, there had been a dreamy rapturous time, with walks together and confessions and a spiritual taking possession of each other, all of which was at the same time packed with those innumerable little, infinitely tormenting, and yet joyful aberrations to which two lovers get carried away when they are still lacking exactly as much in resolute courage as they have already lost in chastity. That was just as if Meingast had bequeathed his sins to them to be lived through once again with a higher meaning, lived out, indeed, to the highest meaning, and so exhausted ; and it was in this way that they both saw it. And today, when Clarisse set so little store by Walter's love that she was often revolted by it, she saw even more clearly that the cravings of the thirst of love, which had driven her to such a degree of mania, could not have been anything but an incarnation—which, she knew, meant a manifestation in the flesh—of something unfleshly, of something that was a meaning, a mission, a destiny, such as is laid up among the stars for those who are elect.

She was not ashamed. It was rather that she could have wept when she compared the Then and the Now. But the fact was that Clarisse had never been able to weep ; she just tightened her lips, and it turned into something resembling her smile. Her arm, kissed all the way to the arm-pit, her leg, watched over by the Devil's eye, her pliant body, a thousand times twisted by the beloved's yearning and, like a rope, twisting back again, all were permeated with the wonderful feeling that goes with love : the sense of being, in every movement that one makes, of mysteriously great importance. Clarisse sat there feeling like an actress in the interval. Admittedly she did not know what was to come of things. But she was convinced that the infinite mission of all who loved was to keep themselves as they had been for each other in their sublimest moments. And there was her arm, there were her legs, and her head was poised on her body, uncannily ready to be the first to perceive the sign that could not fail to appear.

It is perhaps difficult to make out what Clarisse meant. But for her it was all quite plain. She had written a letter to Count Leinsdorf, calling for a Nietzsche Year and, at the same time, for the setting free of the woman-killer and perhaps his exhibition in public, as a memorial to the calvaries of those who had to collect and take upon themselves the scattered sins of all the others. And now too she remembered why she had done it. Someone must be the first to speak up. Very likely she had not expressed herself well, but that didn't matter. The main thing was to begin, to make an end of the long-suffering and the putting up with things. It was historically established that the world from time to time—and behind that the phrase ' æon to æon ' tolled like two bells, which one could not see although they were somewhere close at hand—had need of such beings, people who could not join in the doing and the lying of it all, and hence caused a disagreeable stir. So far the case was clear.

And it was also clear that people who caused a disagreeable stir must come to feel the pressure of the world. Clarisse knew that mankind's great geniuses almost always had to suffer, and she was not surprised that many days and weeks in her life had been subject to a leaden pressure, just as if a heavy slab had been laid upon them ; but it had always passed off again. And so it was with all human beings. The Church in its wisdom had even introduced times of mourning and mortification, in order to draw the mourning together all in one and to prevent it from happening that half-centuries at a time should be drenched in hopelessness and callousness—which had been known to happen.

It is more difficult to deal with certain other moments in Clarisse's life, moments all too liberated and lacking in counter-pressure, when sometimes a word was enough to make her, as it were, go off the rails. Then she was beside herself, outside herself, somewhere else—she could not tell where. But she was by no means absent ; on the contrary, it would be more correct to say she was intent, introverted somewhere in a profounder kind of space there was (in some way beyond the grasp of ordinary imagining) inside the space that her body took up in the world. But why seek words for something that did not lie on the road of words ? After a while she would in any case land among the others again, only with some faint bright tickling in her head, as after nose-bleeding. Clarisse realised that these were dangerous

moments that she sometimes experienced. They were obviously
preparations and tests. As it was, she had the habit of thinking
of several things at once, just as a fan may be flicked open and
shut, and one leaf is half inside, half under the other, and whenever that becomes too confused, it is understandable that there
should be an urge to give a jerk and slip right out. Many people
may feel the need ; the only thing is that they cannot quite do it.

And so Clarisse experienced intimations and forebodings in the
same spirit in which other people pride themselves on their
memory or their iron digestion, saying they could eat splintered
glass. Clarisse, however, had proved more than once that she
could really take something upon herself ; her strength had been
tested on her father, on Meingast, on Georg Gröschl. With
Walter some exertions had still to be made ; there things were,
though slowing up, still in flux. But for some time now Clarisse
had had the intention of proving her strength on the Man Without
Qualities. She could not have said exactly since when. But it all
hung together with this name that Walter had invented and Ulrich
had approved. Formerly—this she had to admit—in earlier years
she had never paid serious attention to him, even though they had
been quite good friends. But ' Man Without Qualities '—that
reminded her, for instance, of playing the piano, that is to say, of
all those states of melancholy, leaps of joy, outbreaks of anger,
through which one races, and yet without their being quite real
passions. To this she felt akin. From here the way led straight
to the assertion that one must refuse to do anything that one could
not do with all one's soul, and there she was right in the middle of
the churned-up, deep reality of her marriage. A Man Without
Qualities does not say No to life, he says Not Yet, saving himself
up ; this she had understood with the whole of her body. Perhaps
this was the meaning of all the moments in which she stepped out
of herself : that she was meant to become mother of the Divine
Child. She remembered the vision that had come to her hardly
a quarter of an hour ago. ' Perhaps every mother can become
mother of God,' she thought, ' if she makes no concessions, is not
false and does not strive, but brings forth what is in her very
depths, as a child. Always assuming that she achieves nothing for
herself ! ' she added mournfully. For the thought was by no
means purely agreeable to her ; it filled her with that sensation,

divided between torment and bliss, of being sacrificed for something. And though her vision had been as if, among the branches of a tree, all among the leaves suddenly flickering like candles, an image had appeared and an instant later the wood had closed up again, now her mood remained permanently changed. Some chance a moment later afforded her the discovery, meaningless to any other human being, that the word ' birth ' was contained in the word ' birthmark '; for her this signified as much as if her destiny had suddenly been written in the stars. The wonderful thought that for the sake of giving birth the woman must take the man into herself, both as mother and as lover, made her feel soft and excited. She did not know how this thought had come to her, but it melted away her resistances and yet gave her power.

But she was still far from trusting the Man Without Qualities. There were many things he did not mean the way he said them. When he asserted that one could not carry out one's ideas and that he did not take anything quite seriously—that was only a way of hiding, she understood that clearly. They had scented each other out and recognised each other by signs—and this while Walter was thinking that Clarisse was sometimes mad ! And yet there was in Ulrich something sinister and vicious, something that diabolically clung to the easy way the world ambled on. He must be set free. She must go and fetch him.

She had said to Walter : Kill him. It had not amounted to much. She had not been quite sure what she meant by it. But what it came to was that something must be done to tear him out of himself, and that one must not shrink from anything.

She had to wrestle with him.

She laughed, rubbing her nose. She walked up and down in the darkness. Something must be done about the Collateral Campaign. What, she did not know.

98

Concerning a State that perished for want of a name.

THE train of events is a train unrolling its rails ahead of itself. The river of time is a river sweeping its banks along with it. The traveller moves about on a solid floor between solid walls ; but the floor and the walls are being moved along too, imperceptibly, and yet in very lively fashion, by the movements that his fellow-travellers make. It was an incalculable piece of good fortune for Clarisse's peace of mind that this notion had not yet turned up among all those that had occurred to her so far.

Count Leinsdorf, for his part, was also proof against it. He was armoured against it by the conviction that what he was engaged in was practical politics.

The days rocked from side to side, running into weeks. The weeks did not stand still, but wreathed together into chains. There was continually something happening. And when there is continually something happening, one easily gets the impression that one is achieving something real and practical. For instance, the state rooms of the Palais Leinsdorf were to be thrown open to the public on the occasion of a grand entertainment in aid of children suffering from pulmonary tuberculosis, and this event was being led up to by exhaustive conferences between His Highness and His Highness's major-domo, in which certain days were named by which certain operations had to be concluded. The police at the same time organised a jubilee exhibition, at the opening of which Society appeared in full force, and the President of Police in person had called on His Highness in order to deliver his invitation. When Count Leinsdorf entered and was welcomed by his host, the President of Police recognised the ' voluntary helper and honorary secretary ' at the Count's side, and, when he was about to be introduced to him all over again, quite super-fluously, the President had the opportunity of showing off his legendary memory for faces and names : he had the reputation of either knowing every tenth citizen personally or at least being informed about him. Diotima came too, accompanied by her husband, and all who were present were looking forward to the appearance of a member of the Imperial family, to whom some of them were to be presented. It was unanimously agreed that the exhibition was quite fascinating and a tremendous success.

It consisted of a close combination of pictures hanging on the walls and souvenirs of great crimes arranged in glass-fronted cabinets and cases. Among them were burglars' jemmies, blow-lamps and so on, forgers' apparatus, lost buttons that had constituted clues, and the tragic tools of notorious murderers, with their stories attached to them. The pictures on the walls, in contrast with this arsenal of terrors, presented edifying scenes from the life of the police. Here were to be seen : the worthy policeman helping some little old woman across the street ; the solemn policeman standing over a corpse just washed up from the river ; the brave policeman flinging himself forward and catching the bridles of shying horses ; an allegory, ' The Police Force as the Guardian Angel of the City ', the lost child among the motherly policemen at the station ; the burning policeman, carrying in his arms a girl he had just rescued from a house on fire ; and yet a great many more such pictures, such as ' First Aid ', ' Alone on the Beat ', and photographs of doughty policemen with years of service dating back to 1869, together with descriptions of their careers and framed poems celebrating the works of the police as a whole or of individual functionaries. Its highest official, the head of the Ministry that in Kakania bore the psychological-sounding name ' for interior affairs ', in his speech declaring the exhibition open drew his listeners' attention to these pictures, saying that they showed the spirit of the police as something truly of the nation and the people, and referred to admiration for such a spirit of helpfulness and stern discipline as a rejuvenating well-spring of morality, in a time when art and life inclined only too sorely towards a cowardly cult of happy-go-lucky sensualism.

Diotima, standing beside Count Leinsdorf, full of her own aspirations and endeavours in the cause of modern art, felt ill at ease ; and she went to great pains to gaze into the air with an expression at once gentle and unyielding, in order that this very excellent body of men might feel that in Kakania there were other ways of thinking than the Minister's.

Her cousin, who was observing her, during this speech, with the respectable thoughtful air appropriate to the honorary secretary of the Collateral Campaign, suddenly in all this packed crowd felt a warily light hand laid on his arm and to his amazement recognised Bonadea at his side. She had come with her husband, that high judicial personage, and was exploiting the moment when all necks were craned towards the Minister and the Archduke standing next to him to approach her faithless lover. This audacious move was the result of long planning. Upset and wretched at her beloved's desertion of her in a moment when she had been filled with the mournful urge to—figuratively speaking— bind fast the loose end of the frivolously fluttering banner of her desires, she had occupied herself in these last weeks solely with thoughts of how to win him back. He was avoiding her, and scenes of ' having it out ', thrust on him by her, only put her at the disadvantage that is the lot of one who clamours for companionship when the chosen partner would rather be left alone. So she had made up her mind to force her way into the circle that her beloved daily frequented. Furthermore, included in this purpose was a second one, that of exploiting the professional connection her husband had with the abominable murderer, Moosbrugger, and her lover's intention of in some way alleviating this murderer's lot—of exploiting this for her own ends, in order to forge certain inner links with both sides. It was for this reason that she had recently been bothering her husband quite a good deal with talk about the interest that influential circles were taking in welfare work for criminal lunatics ; and when it became known that the police were organising this exhibition, and its formal opening was announced, she had got him to take her with him, her instinct telling her that this was the long-sought philanthropic air at which she would make Diotima's acquaintance.

When the Minister had concluded his speech and the crowd began to circulate, she did not budge from her much-disconcerted ex-lover's side. Together with him she moved along, looking at the blood-stained instruments, in spite of her almost unsurmountable horror of them.

" You said people could prevent all this sort of thing if they only wanted to," she murmured, reminding him, like a good child bent on showing how it attends to what it is told, of their last more detailed discussion on this subject. And a little while later she smiled, letting the crowd press her close to him, and made use of the opportunity to whisper : " You once said in the right circumstances every person is capable of any weakness."

Ulrich felt himself considerably embarrassed by her ostentatious way of walking along at his side ; and because his *inamorata*, in spite of all the diversionary tactics he tried, was making steadily towards the place where Diotima stood and he could not very well give her a serious lecture on the subject in front of all these people, he realised that the day had come when he had no alternative but to introduce to each other the two women whose acquaintance he had hitherto done all he could to prevent.

They were already very close to a group of which Diotima and His Highness formed the centre when Bonadea exclaimed loudly, in front of one of the glass cases :

" Oh, do look, there's Moosbrugger's knife ! "

There indeed it lay, and Bonadea gazed at it, entranced, as if she had opened a drawer and come upon grandmamma's first cotillon-favour.

Her friend made a swift decision and, inventing an appropriate pretext, asked his cousin if he might introduce to her a lady who wished to make her acquaintance and who was known to him as being passionately interested in all endeavours for the good, the true, and the beautiful.

And thus it could not quite be said that little happened in the rocking passage of the days and weeks ; and the police exhibition, together with all that was bound up with it, was actually the least of it all.

In England, for instance, they had something far more magnificent, about which there was much talk in society here : it was a doll's house that had been presented to the Queen, built by a famous architect, with a dining-room three feet long in which there hung miniature portraits by famous modern painters, bedrooms in which hot and cold water came out of real taps, and a library with a little book all made of gold, in which the Queen pasted photographs of the royal family, a railway time-table and a sailing-list in microscopic print, and about two hundred tiny volumes in which famous authors had with their own hands written poems and stories for the Queen. Diotima possessed the two volumes of the luxury edition of the English book about it, which had just appeared, with expensive illustrations of all that was most interesting, and it was to this book that she owed an increased attendance on the part of the highest Society at her at-home evenings.

But elsewhere too there were all sorts of things going on all the time, things for which it was not so easy to find words at once, so that it all went, like a tattoo of drums in the soul, ahead of a Something that had not yet come round the corner into sight. For instance, the Imperial-Royal telegraph employees went on strike for the first time and in an extraordinarily disturbing way, which was called ' working to rule ' and which consisted simply of their observing all official regulations in the most punctilious and conscientious manner ; it turned out that following out the regulations exactly brought all work to a standstill much faster than the wildest anarchy could have done. Like the story of the Captain of Köpenick in Prussia (who, as is remembered even to this day, by putting on a uniform bought at an old-clothes shop had turned himself into an officer, had stopped a patrol in the street and with its aid and that of the Prussian virtue of obedience to orders had taken possession of a municipal treasury), ' working to rule ' was something that tickled the sense of humour and at the same time, in some subterranean way, set staggering the ideas that were the basis of the disapproval one felt obliged to express. At the same time it was to be read in the news that His Majesty's government had entered into an agreement with the government of some other majesty with a view to securing peace, reviving trade, and effecting cordial collaboration and respect for the rights of the nations, but also envisaging measures to be taken in the event of these aims' being jeopardised or even threatened with being jeopardised. Permanent Secretary Tuzzi's Minister had a few days later made a speech in which he demonstrated the urgent necessity for close solidarity between the three Continental empires, which could not afford to ignore modern social developments and must form a common front, in the common interest of the dynasties, against social innovations. Italy was involved in a military campaign in Libya. Germany and England had a Baghdad problem. Kakania was making certain military preparations in the South, in order to show the world that it would not allow Serbia to expand to the sea, but would only permit a railway-connection. And on a par with all events of this kind came the confession made by the world-famous Swedish actress Vogelsang that she had never before in her life slept as well as on the first night after her arrival in Kakania and had been delighted with the policeman who, having rescued her from the enthusiasm of the crowd, had then asked for permission to press her hand in gratitude with his own two hands. And so one's thoughts came round again to the police exhibition. There was a great deal going on, and one was aware of it. One thought well of what was done by oneself, and thought the same thing dubious if it was done by others. Every schoolboy could understand the details of what was going on, but as regards the whole there was nobody who quite knew what was really happening, except a few persons, and even they were not sure whether they knew. Only a short time later it might all just as well have happened in a different order or the other way round, and everything would have looked pretty much as it always did, and as indeed it always does except for certain changes that inexplicably establish themselves in the course of time, forming the shiny track that is left by the snail of history.

It is understandable that in such circumstances a foreign embassy is faced with a difficult task if it is to communicate a clear statement of what is actually going on. The diplomatic envoys would have liked to draw on Count Leinsdorf for their enlightenment, but His Highness put obstacles in their way. Every day he found anew in his work the contentment that solid achievement can bestow, and his countenance showed the foreign observers the radiant calm that indicated operations proceeding in good order. Department One wrote, Department Two answered ; when Department Two had answered, Department One had to be informed, and it was usually best to suggest talking it over in person. When Department One and Two had agreed, it was decided that nothing could be done about the matter. And so there was always something to do. There were, besides, innumerable little minor considerations to be borne in mind. One was working, of course, hand in glove with all the various Ministries ; one did not want to cause any offence to the Church ; one had to take account of certain persons and social connections : in short, even on days when one did nothing in particular, there were so many things one must avoid doing that one had the feeling of being very active indeed.

His Highness had a proper appreciation of this. " The higher destiny places a man," he was in the habit of saying, " the more clearly he recognises that all that matters is a few simple principles, and above all a firm will and activity well planned." And once he held forth on this subject in more detail to his ' young friend '. Taking as his point of departure the German endeavours to achieve national unity, he admitted that between 1848 and 1866 quite a number of really clever people had had their say in politics. " But then," he continued, " this fellow Bismarck came along. At least there was one good thing about him, he showed people how to conduct politics. It can't be done with speeches and cleverness ! He had his seamy side, but he did see to it that since his time, wherever the German tongue is spoken, everyone knows that there's nothing to be hoped for in politics from cleverness and speech-making, but only from silent thought and action ! "

Count Leinsdorf uttered similar views at the ' Council ' too, and the representatives of foreign powers, which sometimes sent their observers along, found it difficult to form an exact picture of his intentions. Arnheim's interest was regarded as a matter of importance, and so was the attitude taken by Permanent Secretary Tuzzi ; and the general conclusion was that there was a clandestine understanding between these two men and Count Leinsdorf, an understanding the political aim of which remained concealed, for the present, behind vigorous moves to distract attention, these moves being conducted by Frau Tuzzi, the Permanent Secretary's wife, with her pan-cultural endeavours. If due consideration is given to how successfully Count Leinsdorf, without exerting himself in the very slightest, deceived the curiosity of even hardened observers, it will be seen that he cannot be denied that gift for practical politics which he believed himself to possess.

But gentlemen of the kind that on ceremonial occasions appear in tail-coats adorned with gold-embroidered foliage and ' scrambled egg ' also clung to the practical-political prejudices of their _métier_ ; and since they found no tangible phenomena on their quest into the remoter depths of the Collateral Campaign, they soon concentrated their attention on something that was the cause of most of the unresolved phenomena in Kakania and was called 'the unliberated nations'.

Nowadays people talk as if nationalism were exclusively the invention of armaments manufacturers. But it would be worth looking for a rather broader explanation, and to this Kakania made an important contribution.

The inhabitants of this Imperial and Royal Imperial-Royal Dual Monarchy found themselves confronted with a different problem. They were supposed to feel themselves to be Imperial and Royal Austro-Hungarian patriots, but simultaneously Royal Hungarian or Imperial-Royal Austrian patriots. Their not incomprehensible slogan, in the face of such difficulties, was 'United we stand!' In other words, *viribus unitis*. But for this the Austrians needed to make a far stronger stand than the Hungarians. For the Hungarians were first and last only Hungarians, and counted only incidentally, among people who did not understand their language, as also Austro-Hungarians. The Austrians, on the other hand, were primarily nothing at all, and in the view of those in power were supposed to feel themselves equally Austro-Hungarians and Austrian-Hungarians—for there was not even a proper word for it. And there was no such thing as Austria, either. The two parts, Hungary and Austria, matched each other like a red-white-and-green jacket and black-and-yellow trousers. The jacket was an article in its own right; but the trousers were the remains of a no longer existent black-and-yellow suit, the jacket of which had been unpicked in the year 1867. The Austrian trousers since then were officially known as 'the kingdoms and lands represented in the Council of the Imperial Realm', which naturally meant nothing at all, being a name made up of names; for these kingdoms, for instance the entirely Shakespearean kingdoms of Lodomeria and Illyria, no longer existed either and had not yet existed even at the time when there was still a whole black-and-yellow suit in existence. And so if one asked an Austrian what he was, he naturally could not answer : 'I am from the non-existent kingdoms and lands represented in the Council of the Imperial Realm.' If only for this reason he preferred to say : 'I'm a Pole, a Czech, an Italian, a Friulian, a Ladin, a Slovene, a Croat, a Serb, a Slovak, a Ruthenian, or a

Wallachian.' And that was nationalism, so called. Imagine a
badger that does not know whether it is a badger or a brock, a
creature that has no conception of itself; it is not surprising if in
some circumstances it is thrown into fits of terror by its own tail.
This was, however, the relationship the Kakanians had to each
other, regarding themselves and one another with the panic and
dismay of limbs hampering each other, united as they stood, from
being anything at all. Since the earth has existed no being has
ever died for want of a name. All the same, this is what happened
to the Austrian and Hungarian Austro-Hungarian Dual Monarchy:
it perished of its own unutterability.

For those not well acquainted with Kakania's history it may
be not without interest to learn in what manner a well-versed
and high-ranking Kakanian like Count Leinsdorf came to terms
with this difficulty. First of all, in his watchful mind he carefully
sliced off Hungary, of which he, as a wise diplomat, never spoke,
just as people do not speak of a son who has struck out for independence against his parents' will, even though they hope he will
yet come to a bad end. What remained, however, Count Leinsdorf referred to as ' the nationalities ' or even as ' the Austrian
tribes '. This was a very subtle invention. His Highness had
studied constitutional law, and there had found a definition, of
more or less world-wide acceptance, according to which a people
had a claim to count as a nation only if it possessed its own
characteristic constitution; from this he drew the conclusion that
the Kakanian nations were at best nationalities. On the other
hand, Count Leinsdorf knew that man can find his full, true
destiny only within the higher framework that is the community
life of a nation, and because he did not like to think of this being
withheld from anyone, he deduced from all this the necessity that
the nationalities and tribes should be incorporated within the
larger framework of a State. He believed, furthermore, in a
divine order, even if this order was not always transparently clear
to the human eye; and in his revolutionary ' modern ' hours,
which he was sometimes subject to, he was even capable of thinking that the idea of the State, so strongly confirmed in modern
times, might conceivably be nothing but the divinely established
idea of sovereignty only just beginning to manifest itself in a
rejuvenated form. However that might be—as a practical poli-

tician he was against carrying one's thinking too far and would even have accepted Diotima's view that the idea of the Kakanian State was the same as that of universal peace : the main thing was that there *was* a Kakanian State, even if without a proper name, and that a Kakanian nation had to be invented to go with it. He was in the habit of illustrating this with the example that nobody was a schoolboy who did not go to school, but that the school remained a school even when it was empty. The more the nationalities rebelled against the Kakanian school, which was trying to make one nation of them, the more—accordingly—did it seem to him that the school was necessary. They strongly emphasised that they were nations, demanding back long-lost historical rights, ogling brother-tribes and other kin beyond their borders and quite openly calling the Empire a prison from which they wanted to be liberated. Count Leinsdorf, however, all the more soothingly called them tribes. He emphasised the incompleteness of their condition every bit as much as they themselves did ; only he wanted to perfect this condition by turning the tribes into the Austrian nation, and whatever did not fit in with his plan, or was all too like rebellion, he in his well-known manner declared to be results of their continuing lack of maturity, and it was his opinion that the best means of dealing with this sort of thing was a wise blend of shrewd tolerance and punitive benevolence.

When Count Leinsdorf created the Collateral Campaign, it was therefore immediately regarded among the nationalities as a mysterious pan-German conspiracy. The interest that His Highness showed in the police exhibition was held to be linked up with the secret police and was interpreted as confirming his sympathy with the latter. All this was known to the foreign observers, who had heard as many frightful things about the Collateral Campaign as they could wish for. It was in their minds while they listened to accounts of the reception given to the actress Vogelsang, of the Queen's Doll's House, and the telegraph-office strike, or when they were asked for their views on the recently published international agreements. And although the words about the spirit of austerity that the Minister had used in his speech could be interpreted as the announcement of a policy, if one wished to interpret it so, they nevertheless had the impression that to an unprejudiced scrutiny the opening of the much-talked-of police exhibition did not reveal the slightest element of anything deserving of comment. But still, like everyone else, they had the impression that something general and vague was going on, which for the moment still evaded scrutiny.

99

Of demi-intelligence and its fruitful complement. Also of the likeness between two epochs, of Aunt Jane's lovable nature, and the pernicious nonsense known as the New Age.

IT was indeed impossible to get any systematic picture of what went on in the 'Council's' sessions. The general tendency among progressive people at that time was to be in favour of an 'active spirit'; it had been recognised that it was the duty of men of brain to take over, if necessarily by force, the leadership of the men of brawn. Besides that, there was something known as Expressionism. Nobody could say exactly what it was, but as its name implied, it was a sort of *pressing out*; perhaps of constructive visions, although these, when contrasted with artistic tradition, seemed to be destructive too, so that one might as well simply call them 'structive', which commits one to nothing, and 'a structive conception of the world' sounds pretty good. But that was by no means everything. The general attitude was turned towards the day and the world, from within outwards, but there was also already a tendency from without inwards. Individualism and the intellectual attitude were also considered out of date and egocentric; love was once again entirely discredited; and people were on the verge of rediscovering the healthy mass effect of cheap and trashy art on the purified souls of men of action. What one 'is' changes, it seems, just as quickly as 'what is being worn' and has in common with it the fact that nobody, probably not even the people who make fashion their business, knows the secret of who it really is that ' is ' and ' wears '. Anyone who rebelled against this, however, would infallibly make a slightly ridiculous impression reminiscent of a man who has got caught between the poles of a faradic machine and who twitches and jerks about violently without anyone's being able to see whom or what he is struggling with. For the counter-agent does not consist of the people who are sharp-witted enough quickly to exploit the given commercial situation ; it is made up of the fluid, gaseous insubstantiality of the general state of affairs itself, and of the way this state of affairs, originating in innumerable different quarters, concentrates, and of its unlimited capacity to form combinations and permutations. Added to all this there is, on the recipient's side, also the lack or the breakdown of valid, up-holding, and classifying principles.

To try to find any solid point in this flux of phenomena is about as difficult as trying to knock a nail into a fountain-jet of water. Yet there is something in it that seems to remain constant. For what happens, for instance, when that fickle species, Man, takes it upon itself to call a tennis-player a genius ? It is leaving some-thing out. And when it calls a race-horse a genius ? It is leaving even more out. It always leaves something out, whether it calls a football-player scientific or a swordsman witty, or speaks of a boxer's tragic defeat. In fact it always leaves something out. It exaggerates ; but what causes the exaggeration is the inexacti-tude, just as in a small town the inexactitude of people's idea of things is the cause of the main storekeeper's son being taken for a man of the world. There will be *something* in it, of course. And why should the element of surprise that goes with a champion's activity not be reminiscent of that in a genius, and his thought-processes not remind us of those of an experienced research-scientist ? Naturally there is something else, and of course much more, that is not in accord ; but this additional element is for ordinary purposes either not perceived at all or at least perceived only reluctantly. It is regarded as uncertain ; and so it is passed over and omitted. Indeed, what this age demonstrates when it talks of the genius of a race-horse or a tennis-player is probably less its conception of genius than its mistrust of the whole higher sphere of things.

This is now the place to speak of Aunt Jane, who was recalled to Ulrich's memory as a result of his leafing through old family albums that Diotima had lent him and comparing the faces in them with the faces that he saw at her house. It so happened that as a boy Ulrich had often spent long periods staying with a great-aunt whose dear friend for immemorable ages had been Aunt Jane. Originally she had not been an aunt at all. She had come into the house as the children's piano-teacher, and though in this capacity she had not gained any great glory she had won much affection, for her principle was that there was little sense in prac-tising the piano if one was not, as she said, ' a born musician '. It gave her more pleasure to see the children climbing trees. And in this way she became not only an aunt to two generations but also, through the retroactive effect of the years, the old friend of her disappointed employer's youth.

' Ah yes—little Mucki,' Aunt Jane would say, for instance, full of feeling that was impervious to the passage of time, so full of indulgence and admiration for little Nepomuk (who by that time was in reality Uncle Nepomuk and forty years of age) that to this day her voice was still vividly alive for anyone who had ever heard it. This voice of Aunt Jane's was as though dusted with flour, positively as if one had dipped one's bare arm into very fine flour. It was a husky voice, mild and as it were done in batter ; and this was because she drank a great deal of black coffee and with it smoked long, thin, strong Virginia cigars, which, together with the effects of age, had made her teeth black and worn. And, what was more, if one looked into her face one might easily have believed that the quality of her voice must be connected with the innumerable little fine lines that covered her skin like the lines of an etching. Her face was long and gentle-looking, and to the later generations it seemed never to have changed, as little as anything else about Aunt Jane. She wore one and the same dress all her life long, even if, as certainly seems probable, it existed in a multiplicity of reproductions. It was a tight-fitting encasement of black ribbed silk reaching to the ground, allowing for no physical excesses of any sort, and was finished off by a row of many little black buttons, like a priest's soutane. At the top a narrow stiff stand-up collar just peered forth, its corners bent over to reveal the Adam's apple and the skin of the fleshless throat, in which little tremulous gullies appeared at every pull at the cigar. The tight sleeves were finished off with stiff white cuffs. And the whole turn-out was topped with a fair, gingery, slightly curly wig, which had a parting in the middle and had obviously been meant for a man. With the passing of the years a little of the canvas began to be visible along this parting; but what was even more touching was the two places where the grizzled hair at the temples could be seen next to the bright hair of the wig, the only sign that Aunt Jane had not remained the same age all her life long.

It might be thought that she was by many decades an anticipation of the mannish type of woman that was later to come into fashion. But this was not so, for in her masculine breast there beat a very womanly heart. One could also quite believe that she had once been a very famous pianist, who had later lost touch with her time; for that was what she looked like. But this was also not so, for she had never been more than a music-mistress. The mannish coiffure and the soutane both originated in the fact that as a girl Aunt Jane had had a passionate admiration for the Abbé Liszt, whom during one short period she several times met socially; and somehow then too her name had assumed its English form. And she kept faith with that encounter, like a love-sick knight wearing his lady's colours into his grey old age, without ever having craved for more; and in Aunt Jane's case this was more touching than if she had had days of glory of her own and in her retirement had gone on wearing the uniform of those times.

There was something similar about the secret of her life, a secret that in the family was communicated to the children when they reached years of comparative discretion, and only after solemn admonitions to respect it—rather like a ritual initiation in adolescence. Jane had been no longer a young girl (for a fastidious soul is long in making its choice) when she found the man she loved and, against her family's wishes, married. This man was of course an artist, even though through the great wrongs he had suffered and the ill-luck of his small-town provincial circumstances only a photographer. However, a short time after they were married he was already running up debts like a genius and drinking furiously. Jane deprived herself for his sake. She went to the tavern after him and fetched him back to the gods. She wept in secret and in front of him, at his feet. He looked like a genius, with a mighty mouth and proud hair, and if Jane had been capable of injecting the passion of her desperation into him he would, with the misfortune of his vices, have been as great as Lord Byron himself. But the photographer put obstacles in the way of such a transference of feelings. After a year he left Jane with her peasant servant-girl, who was with child by him, and not long afterwards died in considerable misery. Jane cut a lock of hair from his superb head, and kept it. She took to herself the illegitimate child that he had left, and brought it up with great self-sacrifice. She seldom spoke of that past. If life is stupendous one cannot also demand that it should be easy.

In Aunt Jane's life, then, there was no lack of romantic hardship. But later, when the photographer in his earthly imperfection had long ceased to cast any spell on her, it was rather as though the imperfect substance of her love for him had also mouldered away, leaving as its residue the eternal form of love and enthusiasm ; at a far remove that experience had an effect scarcely different from that of a really tremendous experience. But that was altogether what Aunt Jane was like. Her intellectual content was presumably not very great, but its spiritual form was quite beautiful. Her attitude was heroic, and such attitudes are unpleasant only as long as they have the wrong content ; when they become quite empty they are once again like faith and the flickering of flames. Aunt Jane lived on nothing but tea, black coffee and two cups of beef-tea daily. In the little town where she lived nobody stopped and turned round to stare when she passed along the street, for they all knew she was a good person ; more than that, indeed, people felt a certain veneration for her because she was such a good person and yet had never lost the capacity to look as it was clearly her heartfelt wish to look, though no one knew what really went on in her heart.

And so that was pretty much the story of Aunt Jane, who died long ago, at a great age. 'And Great-aunt is dead, and Uncle Nepomuk is dead—and why did they all ever live, come to think of it ?' Ulrich wondered. But at this time he would have given much to be able to have a talk again with Aunt Jane. He turned over the leaves of the thick old albums with photographs of his family in it, which had somehow or other come to Diotima, and the further he turned back towards the beginnings of that new art of picture-making the more proudly, it seemed to him, did the people face the camera. There they were, one foot placed on a pile of cardboard boulders wreathed in paper ivy, or, if they were officers, with their legs straddled and the sword between ; or if they were girls, they laid their hands in their laps and opened their eyes very wide ; if they were free and independent men their trousers rose upward from the ground in a bold romantic sweep, without a crease, rather like curling smoke, and their coats had a rounded swing to them, a suggestion of a fine free gale that had blown away the rigid dignity of the bourgeois frock coat. That must have been somewhere or other between 1860 and 1870, when the technique of photography had got past its first beginnings. The revolution of the 'forties by then lay far back in the past, a wild and chaotic time, and the style of life had become subtly different, in a way nobody quite remembers any more. And the tears, embraces, and confessions in which the bourgeoisie had sought its soul at the beginning of its epoch no longer existed either. But just as a wave ripples out over the sand, this nobleness of mind had now arrived at the style of dress and at a certain individual *élan* ; these may not be quite the best words for it, but at the moment all we have is the photographs. That was the time when photographers wore velvet jackets and imperials, looking like painters, and painters designed large cartoons on which they drilled whole companies of significant figures ; and to ordinary people this time seemed to be exactly the right time for a process of immortalisation to have been invented for them as well. It only remains to be added that people of any other time can hardly have felt so full of genius and magnificence as precisely the people of that time, among whom there were fewer unusual people—or they succeeded more rarely in rising to eminence among the others —than ever before.

And in turning over the pages Ulrich often wondered whether there was a connection between that time—when a photographer could think himself a genius because he drank, wore an open-necked shirt, and by the aid of the most modern process proved the nobility of soul that he himself possessed to be present also in all those of his contemporaries who poised before his lens—

and his own time, when only race-horses were honestly thought to possess genius, on account of their superlative ability to stretch themselves out and contract again. The two epochs looked different. The present looked proudly down upon the past, but if the past had happened to have come along later it would have looked proudly down upon the present. Yet in the main both amounted to pretty much the same, for in both cases it was inexactitude and the ignoring of the decisive differences that played the greatest part. A part of what was great was taken for the whole, a remote analogy for the fulfilment of the truth; and the emptied-out skin of a great word was stuffed according to the fashion of the day. Such things worked magnificently, even though they did not last long. The people who talked in Diotima's drawing-room were not even entirely wrong about anything, because their concepts were as vague in outline as figures are in the steam of a wash-house. 'Oh, these concepts on which life hangs as the eagle hangs on his own wings!' Ulrich thought. 'These innumerable moral and artistic concepts of life that are by their very nature as delicate as hard mountain-ranges blurred in the distance!' On such people's tongues all these concepts multiplied simply by being turned round and round, and it was impossible to speak of any of their ideas for a while without suddenly finding oneself entangled in the next.

This sort of people had in all ages regarded themselves as constituting the New Age. That is an expression like a bag in which one tries to catch the winds of Æolus. It is the perpetual excuse for not getting things straight, for not reducing them to order, which means their own order, their own objective order, but merely fitting them into the illusory complex of an out-and-out absurdity. And yet there is in this a confession of faith. In these people there lived, in the queerest way, the conviction that it was their mission to bring order into the world. If one were to name what they did to this end *demi-intelligence*, it would become apparent that the other half of the whole, the unnamed, or—to name it now—the stupid, the never exact and never correct half that is complementary to this demi-intelligence, is precisely the one possessing an inexhaustible fertility and capacity for self-renewal. There was life in it, mutability, restlessness, and constant change of standpoint. But doubtless they themselves felt how it was. It shook them, it blew like a gust through their heads. They belonged to a nerve-racked age, and there was something wrong, each individual thinking himself intelligent and yet all together feeling themselves barren. If they had talent in addition —and their inexactitude was far from excluding the possibility of it—then the way it was in their heads was as if one were to see the weather and the clouds, the railways, telegraph-wires, trees and animals and the whole moving picture of our good old world through a narrow window dim with dust and cobwebs ; and no one was very quick to notice it about his own window, but every-one noticed it about the windows of the others.

Ulrich had once, for the fun of it, asked them for exact state-ments of what they meant. They had looked at him disapprovingly and called his demand a mechanistic view of life, and scepticism, asserting that the most complicated things of all could only be solved in the simplest way, so that the new age, once it has sloughed off the present, would look quite simple. Ulrich, in contrast with Arnheim, did not impress them at all. Aunt Jane would have patted his cheek and said : " I know just how they feel. You put them off by being so serious."

100

General Stumm invades the State Library and gathers some experience with regard to librarians, library attendants, and intellectual order.

GENERAL STUMM had observed his ' brother-in-arms's ' lack of success and showed signs of wishing to comfort him.

" What a futile lot of talky-talky ! " he said in indignant criti-cism of the members of the ' Council '. And after a while, although he had received no encouragement, he began, still rather excitedly and yet with a certain complacency, to confide in Ulrich.

" You remember," he said, " I was set on finding the great

redeeming idea that Diotima is in search of, and on laying it at her feet. It turns out that there are a very great many important ideas, but one of them, after all, must be the most important of them. That's only logical, isn't it ? So then it's only a matter of getting them into order. You yourself said this was a resolve worthy of a Napoleon. You remember ? And then you gave me a quantity of excellent advice, such as is only to be expected of you. But I never got to the point of turning it to account. And so, to cut a long story short, I've taken the matter in hand in my own way."

He had recently gone in for horn-rimmed glasses instead of the *pince-nez* he had been in the habit of wearing whenever he wanted to look closely at a person or an object, and he now took them out of his pocket and put them on.

One of the most important principles in the art of generalship, he said, was to get a clear idea of the enemy's strength.

" So," he went on, " I told them to get me a reader's ticket for our world-famous Imperial Library, and under the guidance of a librarian, who very obligingly put himself at my disposal when I told him who I was, I penetrated into the enemy lines. We walked along the ranks, in that colossal store-house of books. And I don't mind telling you I wasn't particularly overwhelmed —rows of books like that are no worse than a garrison parade. Only, after a while I couldn't help starting to do sums in my head, and with an unexpected result. You see, what I *had* been thinking was that if I were to read a book a day, of course it would be very exhausting, but sooner or later I would get to the end of it and by then I ought to have some claim to a certain position in the intellectual world, even supposing I skipped a few. But what d'you think the librarian told me ? There we were, going on and on without getting to the end of it, and so after a while I asked him how many books there actually were in that crazy library of his. Three and a half million volumes, he told me ! When he told me that, we had just got to approximately the seven-hundred-thousandth. And from that moment on I couldn't stop doing sums. I'll spare you the details, but when I was back at the Ministry I worked it out on paper—it would have taken me ten thousand years to carry out my plan !

" At that moment I felt as though I were rooted to the spot, and the whole world seemed nothing but an enormous hoax. I assure you, even now that I've calmed down again I'm convinced there's *something radically wrong* !

"You may say one doesn't really need to read every single book. My retort to that is—in warfare, too, one doesn't need to kill every single soldier, and yet every single one is necessary. Now you will say every single book is necessary too. But there you are, you see, even *there* there's something wrong. For it isn't true. I asked the librarian !

"My dear chap, what I was thinking was simply this—after all, this fellow lives among these millions of books, knows every one of them, knows where each one is, and so he ought to be able to help me. Of course I wasn't going to ask him point-blank : 'How do I find the most beautiful idea in the world ? ' It would have sounded just like the beginning of a fairy-tale, and even I'm smart enough to realise that. Anyway, even when I was a youngster I couldn't stand fairy-tales. But what is one to do in such a case ? In the end I had to ask him *something* of the sort ! On the other hand, my sense of discretion stopped me from telling him the truth and leading up to the question by telling him about the Campaign Committee and asking the fellow to set me on the track of the noblest aim for it. I didn't feel I was authorised to do that. So in the end I resorted to a little stratagem. 'Oh, by the way,' I began all innocently, 'by the way, I mustn't forget to ask how it is you always manage to find the right book in all this endless collection.' I said it just the way I thought Diotima would say it, you know, and I threw in a touch of awed admiration just to butter him up a bit.

"And sure enough, he began to purr and wriggle about and asked, very eagerly and helpfully, what it was in particular I was looking for. Well, that was a bit awkward for me. 'Oh well, all sorts of things,' I said, dragging it out.

"'I mean, what question or what author are you interested in, General ? ' he asked. 'Military history ? '

"'Oh no, not a bit of it. Something more like the history of peace.'

"'History proper ? Or current pacifist literature ? '

"No, I said, it wasn't as easy as all that. For instance, a compendium of all great humanitarian ideas—was there, I asked him

cunningly, anything like that ?   I dare say you remember the
amount of work I've had them do on the subject already.

" He didn't say anything.

" ' Or a book on the realisation of the quintessential ? ' I asked.

" ' Ah, something on theological ethics ? ' he suggested.

" ' By all means theological ethics, if you like, but,' I insisted,
' there must be something in it about good old Austrian culture
and a bit about Grillparzer.'   You know, I think there must have
been such a thirst for knowledge blazing in my eyes that the
fellow suddenly took fright and thought I might be going to
empty him to the dregs.   And when I added something about,
well, about some sort of railway time-table that would make it
possible to get cross-connections between ideas going in every
direction, it was uncanny how polite he became, offering to take
me into the catalogue room and leave me there, though actually
it's against the rules, it's only meant to be used by the librarians.
And so then there I really was, in the holy of holies.   I assure you,
I felt as though I'd stepped inside a huge head.   All around—
nothing but those shelves with the pigeon-holes for the books,
and everywhere ladders for climbing up, and on the desks and
tables nothing but catalogues and bibliographies, you know, the
concentrated extract of knowledge, and not a sensible book to
read anywhere.   Nothing but books about books !   It positively
reeked of brain-phosphorus, and I'm not flattering myself when
I say I felt as if I'd really got somewhere.   But of course when the
chap was going to leave me on my own, a queer feeling came over
me, almost uncanny, I'd call it—awe-inspiring and uncanny.
He goes rushing up a ladder like a monkey, darting at a book,
aiming straight at it from down below, the very one he wants,
fetches it down for me, and says : ' Here I have a bibliography of
the bibliographies for you, General—you know what that is, I
suppose—an alphabetical index of the alphabetical indexes of the
titles of the books and papers that have been written in the last
five years on progress in ethical problems only in the field of moral
theology and *belles lettres*.'   Or that's more or less what he told
me, and was on the point of slipping away.   But I grabbed him
by the lapel just in time and held on to him tight.   ' My dear
sir,' I exclaimed, ' you mustn't go and leave me without revealing
the secret of how you yourself find your way about in this—' well,

I couldn't stop myself from saying 'looney-bin', for that was what I suddenly felt about it, so I said, 'how you find your way about in this looney-bin of books.' He must have misunderstood me. Afterwards I remembered that lunatics are supposed to have a habit of calling other people loonies. Anyway he kept staring at my sword, and I could hardly keep a hold of him. And then he gave me a thorough shock. When I didn't let go of him at once, he suddenly pulled himself up, visibly rearing up in his wobbly pants, and said in a peculiar slow and significant way, as if he were being forced to betray the secret of those precincts, ' General,' he said, ' so you want to know how it is I know every book ? I can certainly tell you that : because I never read any of them ! '

"You know, that really was almost too much for me ! But when he saw how taken aback I was, he explained what he meant. The secret of all good librarians is that they never read any of the literature they have charge of, except the titles and the tables of contents. ' Anyone who lets himself go any further into a book than that is lost as a librarian,' he instructed me. ' He will never get a view of the thing as a whole.'

" ' So,' I asked him, all agog, ' you never read any of the books ? '

" ' Never. Only the catalogues.'

" ' But you're a man of academic qualifications ? '

" ' Oh yes. In fact I lecture in my subject at the university. Librarianship is a science in its own right,' he explained. ' How many systems do you think there are, General,' he asked me, ' according to which books are arranged, preserved, their titles catalogued, misprints and defective title-pages corrected, and so on ? '

" I must confess, when he left me there on my own, there were only two things I really wanted to do : either to burst into tears or to light a cigarette. And there I was in a place where I couldn't do either !

" And what do you think happened ? " the General went on delightedly. " As I'm standing there, completely baffled, an old attendant, who must have been watching us, comes up, pads respectfully round me a few times, then stops, looks at me, and begins to speak in a voice that's all soft either from the dust of the books or from the foretaste of a tip. ' Are you looking for something in particular, sir ?' he asks me. I shake my head, but the old chap goes on : ' Lots of gentlemen from the Staff College come in here. You've only got to tell me, sir, what subject you're specially interested in at the moment, sir. Julius Cæsar ? Prince Eugene ? Count Daun ? Or would it be something modern ? Military statutes ? Budget debates ? ' I assure you, the old codger talked so sensibly and knew such a lot about what's in the books that I gave him a tip and asked him how he did it. And what d'you think he said ? He started off again telling me that when the chaps from Staff College have to write an essay, they often come to him and ask for books. ' And sometimes they curse a bit too, when I bring them the books,' he went on, ' and talk about the nonsense they have to learn. And that's the way the likes of us pick up all sorts of things. Or in comes the parliamentary Deputy who has to draw up the report on the education budget and asks me what material was used by the parliamentary Deputy who drew up the report the year before. Or maybe it's the bishop who's been writing about a certain sort of beetle for the last fifteen years. Or one of the professors from the university comes and complains he's been asking for a particular book for three weeks without getting it, and then we have to go through all the shelves to see whether it's got put back in the wrong place, until it comes out in the end that he's had it at home for the last two years, and never brought it back at all. And that's the way it's been, sir, for nigh on forty years now. By that time you get an instinct for what people are after and what they read when they're after it.'

" ' All the same, my dear man,' I said to him, ' it isn't as easy as all that to explain what I want to read.'

And what do you think he answers ? He gives me a quiet look and nods and says : ' If I may respectfully say so, sir, it's only natural for such things to happen. Only just a little while ago a lady was talking to me, and she said exactly the same thing. Perhaps you know her, sir—the lady is the wife of Permanent Secretary Tuzzi from the Foreign Office.'

" Well, what do you say to that ? You could have knocked me down with a feather. And when the old chap saw how it was, upon my word, he brought me along all the books Diotima had

had reserved. And whenever I go to the Library now, it's positively like a secret spiritual marriage, and now and then I make a careful pencil-mark in the margin, or write a word in, knowing she'll find it next day and won't be able to guess who has got inside her head, making her think about what it all means."

The General paused for a blissful moment. But then he pulled himself together, a look of grim seriousness came over his face, and he went on :

"Now brace yourself up for a minute for all you're worth, because I'm going to ask you something. We're all convinced—aren't we ?—that our era is just about the best ordered one there has ever been. I know I did once say in Diotima's presence that it's mere prejudice to think so, but of course it's a prejudice I have myself. And now I'm confronted with the fact that the only people with a really reliable intellectual order are the library attendants, and I ask you—no, I don't ask you—after all, we've talked about it before, and naturally I've thought it all out again in the light of my recent experiences. And I'd like to put it this way. Imagine you drink brandy. Right ? Well and good, in certain circumstances. But suppose you go on and on and on drinking brandy. You follow me ? Well, at first you get drunk, and later you get d.t.'s, and in the end you're buried with military honours and the chaplain mumbles something over your grave about unflinching devotion to duty. Have you imagined it ? Well, if you have—and it doesn't take much doing—now imagine water. And imagine you have to go on drinking it till you're drowned in it. And now imagine eating till your intestines are tied into knots. Now imagine drugs—quinine or arsenic or opium. What for ?—you're going to ask me. But now, dear old boy, I'm coming to the most magnificent of my propositions. Imagine *order*. Or rather, imagine first of all a great idea, and then one still greater, then another still greater than that, and so on, always greater and greater. And then on the same pattern imagine always more and more order in your own head. At first everything's as neat and tidy as an old maid's sitting-room and as clean as a Horse-Guards stable. And after that it's as splendid as a brigade in battle formation. And after that again it's as crazy as when you come out of the mess in the middle of the night and shout orders

at the stars : ' Cosmos, 'shun ! Eyes right ! ' Or let's say in the
beginning order is like when a recruit is still falling over his own
feet and you teach him how to pick 'em up. Then it's like when
you dream you've suddenly been made War Minister over everyone else's head. But now, just imagine a complete universal
order embracing all humanity, in a word, a state of perfect
civilian order. Take my word for it, it's sheer entropy, rigor mortis,
a landscape on the moon, a geometrical plague !

" I had a chat about it with my library attendant. He suggested
I should read Kant or something of the sort, something about
the limitations of intellectual concepts and of the faculty of perception. But frankly, I don't want to do any more reading. I
can't help having a slightly queer feeling that now I understand
why in the army, where we have the highest degree of order, we
also have to be prepared to lay down our lives at any moment. I
can't quite explain why. At a certain stage order somehow creates
a demand for bloodshed. And now I'm seriously worried by the
thought that your cousin may in the end, with all her endeavours,
go and do something that will do her a great deal of harm—and
I shall be less able to help her than ever ! Do you follow me ?
As for the arts and sciences and all they achieve on the side in the
way of great and admirable ideas—all honour to them of course.
Far be it from me to say anything against that ! "

101   *The hostile relatives.*

IT was at this time that Diotima also had a talk with her cousin.
Behind the eddies swirling insistently, unremittingly, through her
rooms, one evening there arose a lagoon of stillness by the wall
where he was sitting on a little settee, and she came like a tired
dancer and sat down beside him. Nothing like this had happened
for a long time. Since those drives of theirs about the countryside, and as though it were the consequence of them, she had
avoided being with him at all ' off duty '.

Diotima's face was faintly blotchy and flushed from heat or fatigue.

She rested her hands on the settee, saying : " How are you ? " and then nothing more, though there was every reason why she should have said something more, but merely gazing straight in front of her, with slightly bowed head. There was a suggestion about her as of ' grogginess ', if it may be put in terms of the boxing-ring. She did not even bother to see that her dress hung well, as she sat there, rather hunched up.

Her cousin thought of tousled hair, a peasant girl's skirts and bare, bright legs. What remained, if one thought away the artificial adornment with which she was tricked out, was a fine, sturdy wench, and he had to restrain himself from simply taking her hand in his fist, as peasants do.

" And so Arnheim is not making you happy," he observed calmly.

She might have rebuked this surmise, but, evidently fighting with somewhat strange emotions, she remained silent. Only after a while she retorted : " His friendship makes me very happy."

" I got the impression that his friendship was a worry to you."

" Oh, indeed, I assure you ! " Diotima drew herself up and regained her lady-like self-possession. " Do you know who is a worry to me ? " she asked, doing her best to strike the lightly conversational note. " Your friend the General ! What does the man want ? Why does he come here ? Why does he keep on staring at me ? "

" He's in love with you ! " her cousin exclaimed.

Diotima laughed nervously. Then she went on : " Do you know, I shudder from head to foot when I set eyes on him. He makes me think of death."

" A figure of Death unusually well-disposed to life, if one looks at him with an impartial eye."

" Evidently I am not impartial. I can't explain it to myself. But I am seized with panic when he comes up to me and explains that I make ' outstanding ' ideas ' stand out ' on an ' outstanding ' occasion. I'm overcome with an indescribable, incomprehensible, dream-like sense of dread ! "

" Of him ? "

" Of what else ? He's a hyena ! "

Her cousin could not help laughing.

She went on chafing and scolding, uncontrolled as a child.
" He goes creeping round, waiting for our splendid endeavours
to collapse in ruins ! "

" And that is probably what you're afraid of. O grand cousin,
do you remember that I have been prophesying that collapse
all along ? It is inevitable. You must brace yourself to meet
it."

Diotima looked at Ulrich haughtily. She remembered very
well indeed. More than that, at this moment she recalled the
words she had spoken to him when he paid his first call, and they
were words of the very kind to cause her pain now. She had
expounded to him that it was a great privilege to be allowed to
summon a whole nation, nay more indeed, the whole world, to
come to itself in the midst of all this materialism and remember
the spirit, the mind. She had wanted nothing outworn, nothing
in the way of ' recapturing the past '. And for all that, the gaze
she bestowed upon her cousin at this moment was that of someone above these things rather than of someone who had got
above herself. She had mused upon a Universal Year, she had
gone in quest of a revival, some value, some content in culture
that would crown all. She had been now close to it, now farther
away. She had wavered much and suffered much. The last
several months seemed to her like a long sea-voyage, with the
sensation of being lifted high by the waves and dropped down
again, over and over again and always in the same way, so that
now she could scarcely distinguish what had been earlier and what
later. And she sat now, like a traveller sitting on a bench after
tremendous exertions—on a bench that, thank heaven, does not
move about—and for the moment wanting to do nothing but, say,
follow with his gaze the smoke curling upward from his pipe.
Indeed, so intense was this feeling in Diotima that she actually
formulated in her mind this simile of an old man sitting in the
late afternoon sunshine. She seemed to herself like someone
who has great, impassioned battles all behind him.

In a weary voice she said to her cousin : " I have been through
a great deal. I have changed very much."

" Shall I be any the better off for it ? " he asked.

Diotima shook her head, smiling, though without looking at him.

" Then I will tell you a secret," Ulrich said suddenly. " It is Arnheim who's behind the General, not myself. You know you've always put all the blame for his being here on me. But do you remember what I told you when you took me to task about it ? "

Diotima did remember. ' Keep him off,' her cousin had said. But *Arnheim* had said she should go ahead and make the General a welcome guest. What she felt at this moment can hardly be described ; it was rather as if she were sitting in a cloud that rose swiftly over her own eyes. But an instant later the settee was again hard and solid under her, and she said : " I don't know how this General ever came to be here. *I* didn't invite him. And Herr Doktor Arnheim, whom I asked about it, of course, doesn't know anything either. There must have been some kind of mistake."

Her cousin yielded only a little ground. " I know the General from the old days," he declared, " but we met again for the first time here. It's naturally very probable that he does do a little spying about here on behalf of the War Ministry, but he is also anxious to help you. And I have it from his own lips that Arnheim goes to a strikingly great amount of trouble about him."

" Because Arnheim takes an interest in everything ! " Diotima retorted. " He advised me not to rebuff the General, since he believes in his good faith and sees his influential position as something that can be of use to our endeavours."

Ulrich shook his head vigorously. " Just listen to the squawking going on all round him ! " he burst out so sharply that people standing nearby overheard and the lady of the house felt acute embarrassment. " He puts up with it because he's rich. He has money, he agrees with everyone, and he knows they will all go out of their way to do propaganda for him."

" Why should he do that ? " Diotima asked disapprovingly.

" Because he's vain ! " Ulrich continued. " Immoderately vain ! I don't know how to make the full meaning of this statement comprehensible to you. There is such a thing as vanity in the Biblical sense, which means the turning of emptiness into cymbals and sounding brass. The man is vain who thinks himself enviable when on his left hand the moon is rising over Asia and on his right Europe's light is fading as the sun goes down. That is how he once described to me a trip he had made across the Sea of Marmora ! Very likely the moon rises more beautifully behind the flower-pot on some love-sick little girl's window-sill than it does over Asia."

Diotima was wondering where they could go in order not to be overheard by the people strolling about. " You are irritated by his success," she said in a low voice, leading him through the rooms. Then with a deft manœuvre she contrived it so that they walked through the door and out into the hall. All the other rooms were packed with guests.

" Why," she now began again, " why are you so hostile towards him ? It is a way of making difficulties for me."

" I—make difficulties for you ? " Ulrich asked in amazement.

" But I might be seized with the wish to have a thorough talk with you, might I not ? Only so long as you adopt this attitude, I can't confide in you at all ! " She stopped, standing in the middle of the hall.

" Please do go ahead and confide in me whatever you want to," Ulrich begged her. " You and he have fallen in love with each other, that I know. Is he going to marry you ? "

" He has offered it," Diotima replied, without regard for the lack of certain privacy here where they were talking. She was overwhelmed by her own feelings and took no offence at her cousin's unseemly bluntness.

" And you ? " he asked.

She blushed like a schoolgirl being subjected to questioning. " Oh," she answered hesitantly, " that's a problem involving great responsibility. One mustn't let oneself be swept into doing or thinking anything unjust. And where really great experiences are concerned, it doesn't matter so much what one does anyway."

These words made no sense to Ulrich, since he knew nothing of the nights in which Diotima overcame the voice of passion and attained to that unmoving justice of the soul whose love floats as evenly as the scales of a balance. And so he got the feeling that it would for the present be better to abandon the road of straight-forward talk. And he said :

" I should very much like to have a talk with you about my

relations with Arnheim, because in these circumstances I'm sorry you have the impression of there being hostility. I believe I understand Arnheim very well. You must realise this—what is going on in your house, something that in compliance with your wishes I shall call a synthesis, is something he has experienced innumerable times before. Intellectual stirrings, where they occur in the form of convictions, immediately occur likewise in the form of the opposite convictions. And where they are embodied in what is called a great intellectual personality, the moment admiration is not freely accorded to this personality from every side they feel as insecure as in a cardboard box that has been thrown into the water. We are—or at least, in Germany one is—moved by love for recognised personalities, and behave like the drunks who fall on a stranger's neck and after a while fling him off again, and both for equally obscure reasons. And so I can very clearly imagine what Arnheim feels. It must be like a kind of sea-sickness. And when he remembers, in such surroundings, what can be achieved with wealth, by making skilful use of it, after a long voyage by water he suddenly has solid ground under his feet again. He will notice how each proposal, suggestion, wish, indication of readiness, or achievement strives to come closer into the orbit of wealth, and this is, in fact, an image of the mind itself. For even ideas that want to gain power cling to ideas that already have power. I don't know how to put it. The difference between an idea with genuinely lofty aspirations and an idea trying to elbow its way to the top is so slight that it can hardly be defined. But once the false association with what is great takes the place of worldly poverty and purity of spirit, what also pushes its way in—and of course rightly—is the pseudo-great, whatever passes for great, and finally whatever is simply inflated to greatness by means of advertisement and commercial adroitness. Then you get Arnheim, in all his innocence and all his guilt ! "

" Your thoughts take a very holy turn today," Diotima replied acidly.

" I admit he's little concern of mine. But I must say the way he accepts the mixed effects of outer and inner greatness, trying to make a model humanitarianism out of it, is almost enough to exasperate me into frantic holiness."

" Oh, how wrong you are ! " Diotima burst out eagerly. " You picture a *blasé* rich man. But to Arnheim wealth is an incredibly urgent and all-pervading responsibility. He devotes himself to his business as someone else might devote himself to a human being entrusted to his care. And to be effective in the world is a matter of profound necessity to him. He makes himself pleasant to people because one must bestir oneself in order, as he says, to be stirred. Or was it Goethe who said that ? He once explained it to me at length. He takes the view that one can begin to effect the good only when one has begun to be effective in *some* way. I confess, though, I have sometimes rather felt, myself, that he consorts a little too much with all and sundry."

While they were talking they had been walking to and fro in the empty hall, where there were only looking-glasses and coats hanging from hooks. Now Diotima stopped, laying her hand on her cousin's arm.

" This man, whom fate has in every way distinguished above others," she said, " has the modest principle that the individual alone is no stronger than a sick person abandoned by all. Surely you can agree with him there ? When someone is lonely he rushes into a thousand exaggerations ! "

She looked down at the floor as though she were searching for something there, and at the same time could feel her cousin's gaze fixed on her eyelids.

" Oh, I might talk about myself," she went on. " I have been very lonely just recently. But I can see it in you too. You are embittered and not happy. You are out of joint with your environment, as one sees from all your opinions. You have a jealous nature, you are in opposition to everything. I will confess to you frankly that Arnheim has complained to me about your rejecting his friendship."

" Do you mean he has told you that he wishes for my friendship ? It's a lie ! "

Diotima glanced up and laughed. " There you go exaggerating again ! We both wish for your friendship. Perhaps for the very reason that you are like that. But now I must go back to the beginning and explain. Arnheim made use of the following examples—" She hesitated for a moment and then thought better of it. " No, it would lead too far. To cut a long story short, Arnheim says one must use the means that one's time puts into one's hands. In fact, he says, one should always act in the spirit of two attitudes, never entirely in a revolutionary way and never entirely in an anti-revolutionary way, never fully loving, and also never fully hating, never following an inclination, but developing everything one has in oneself. But that is not the calculated cleverness that you attribute to him. On the contrary, it is the sign of an all-embracing, synthetically simple nature that breaks through all superficial differences—a lordly nature ! "

" And what has this to do with me ? " Ulrich asked.

The effect of this objection was to tear to shreds the recollection of a conversation about scholasticism, the Church, Goethe, and Napoleon, and with it the mists of culture that had condensed about Diotima's head. She suddenly and very distinctly saw herself sitting beside her cousin on the long low shoe-cupboard where in the intensity of her emotion she had drawn him down beside her and saw his back stubbornly trying to avoid the other people's coats hanging behind him. Her hair had become ruffled by them and had to be tidied. While she was doing this she replied :

" But you are the very opposite of that ! You would like to re-create the world in your own image ! You are always going in for some form of ' working to rule '—as the frightful expression is." She was very glad that she was able to give him such a thorough piece of her mind. But at the same time she was aware that they must not go on sitting where they were, for at any moment some guests might leave or come into the hall for other reasons. " You are always full of criticism," she went on. " I don't remember your ever having a good word to say of anything. Out of sheer opposition you praise everything that is intolerable nowadays. If in the midst of the dry desert of our godless age one tries to rescue for oneself a little feeling and intuition, one can be sure that you will enthusiastically defend specialisation, disorder, the negative side of existence."

While she was speaking, she smiled and got up, and then gave him to understand that they must find some other place.

They could only go back into the rooms or, if they wanted to continue their conversation, hide from the others. The Tuzzis' bedroom could have been reached even from here through a door concealed in the wallpaper, but it seemed to Diotima too intimate, after all, to take her cousin in there, especially as every time the apartment was rearranged for a reception an incalculable disarray mounted up in that room. So all that remained in the way of refuge was the two servants' rooms. The thought that it would be a gay mixture of gipsy behaviour and the housewife's duty to keep an eye on things to make, for once, an unheralded inspection of Rachel's room, in which she otherwise never set foot, was decisive. As they went along, after she had made a slight apology for the suggestion, and then when they were in the little room, she continued to speak urgently to Ulrich.

" One gets the impression," she said, " that you try to countermine Arnheim at every opportunity. Your contradictoriness distresses him. He is a great example of the man of today. Therefore he has and needs contact with reality. You, on the other hand, are always about to leap into the impossible. He is all affirmation and quite balanced. You are really asocial. He strives for unity and is to his very finger-tips eager for decision. You confront this with an amorphous attitude. He has a feeling for what is already in existence and stands firm. But you ? What do you do ? You act as though the world were only about to begin tomorrow. That's the way you talk, isn't it ! From the very first day, as soon as I told you that we were given an opportunity to do great things, you adopted this attitude. And while one regards this opportunity as an act of destiny and feels one has been brought together with others in the decisive moment and is, so to speak, waiting, with a silent question in one's eyes, for an answer, you simply behave like a naughty boy making a nuisance of himself ! "

She felt the urge to gloss over their delicate situation there in the maid's bedroom by talking very sensibly ; and by scolding her cousin in rather exaggerated terms she gathered courage to face this situation.

"And if I am like that, what use can I be to you ? " Ulrich asked.

He was sitting on little Rachel's little iron bed, and Diotima was sitting on the little cane-bottomed chair, an arm's length from him.

And now he received an admirable answer from Diotima.

" If," she said without any obvious connection to what they had been talking about, " I were ever to behave thoroughly badly and immorally in front of you, I am sure you would be as wonderful as an archangel ! "

She herself was taken aback by what she had said. She had only meant to give an illustration of his contradictoriness and make a small joke about his probably being kind and thoughtful when one did not deserve it. But in her unconscious mind a spring had gushed forth, pouring out words that instantly, the moment they were uttered, struck her as fairly nonsensical, although they surprisingly seemed to be bound up with herself and her relationship to this cousin of hers.

Ulrich felt this. He looked at her without speaking. Then, after a pause, he asked :

" Are you very . . . are you immoderately in love with him ? "

Diotima looked at the floor. " What unsuitable expressions you use ! After all, I'm not a schoolgirl with a ' crush ' ! "

But her cousin was insistent. " I ask for a reason that I can roughly define—I ask because I wonder whether you have come to know the desire that all human beings have—and I think also of the most dreadful creatures over there in your drawing-room—to strip to the skin, put their arms round each others' shoulders and, instead of talking, burst out singing. But then you would have to go from one to the other and press a sisterly kiss upon his lips. If you find the whole thing too indecent, I might go as far as to allow nightshirts."

Diotima answered at random : " What nice ideas you have ! "

" But you see, I—*I* have known that desire, though I admit it was long ago. There have in fact been very respectable people who asserted that this was really the way things should be on earth."

" Then it's your own fault if you don't do it ! " Diotima exclaimed shortly. " And anyway, one needn't paint such a ridiculous picture of it." She had remembered that her adventure with Arnheim was something for which there was no name, something arousing the desire for a life in which social differences would banish and action, soul, mind and dream would all be one.

Ulrich did not answer. He offered his cousin a cigarette.

Diotima took it.   And as the aromatic clouds filled the ' modest chamber ' Diotima wondered what Rachel would think when she sniffed in the air the traces of this visit.   Should they open the window ?   Or should she explain to the girl the next morning ? Oddly enough it was precisely the thought of Rachel that made her decide to stay ; she had been on the brink of putting an end to this colloquy, which was becoming all too strange, but the privileges of intellectual superiority and the smell of cigarette-smoke, inexplicable to her maid, the token of a mysterious visit, somehow became one and the same, and she enjoyed it.

Her cousin scrutinised her.   He was rather surprised at himself for having spoken to her in this way, but he continued.   He felt a longing for companionship.

" I will tell you," he said now, " under what conditions I might be so seraphic.   For I suppose seraphic is not too grand an expression for one's not merely enduring one's fellow-man physically, but even so to speak touching him under his psychological loin-cloth without shuddering."

" Except if he is a woman ! " Diotima interpolated, thinking of the ba.l reputation that her cousin enjoyed in the family.

" Not even excepting that ! "

" You are right !   What I call loving the human being in the woman is something that occurs fantastically seldom."   In Diotima's view Ulrich had for some time been developing in a way that made his opinions very closely resemble her own : but still, what he said always missed the point and was not quite adequate.

" I shall now describe it to you seriously," he said stubbornly.

He sat leaning forward, his forearms resting on his muscular thighs, and gazing gloomily at the floor.   " Nowadays we still say : I love this woman and I hate that man, instead of saying they attract me or repel me.   And to come one step nearer to precision one ought to add that it is I who awaken in them the capacity to attract or repel me.   And to take yet another step nearer to precision one ought then to add that they bring out in me the qualities that make for that.   And so on.   One can't say where the first step is made, for the whole thing is a functional interdependence like that between two bouncing balls or two electric circuits.   And of course we've known for a long time that we ought to feel like that too, but we still prefer by far to be the cause, the first cause, in the magnetic fields of feeling that surround us. Even if one of us admits he's imitating someone else, he expresses it in such a way as to make it seem an active achievement. That's why I asked you, and why I ask you, have you ever been immoderately in love or angry or desperate. For then, if one has any power of observation worth mentioning, one realises very precisely that in the highest excitement of one's whole being one is no better off than a bee on a window-pane or an infusorium in poisoned water : one undergoes an emotional storm, one dashes blindly in all directions, one runs a hundred times up against the impenetrable, and once, if one is lucky, one escapes through an opening into freedom, and afterwards, of course, in a rigid state of consciousness, one explains as the result of planned action."

" I must object," Diotima remarked. " That's a hopeless and undignified way of looking at feelings that may decide a person's whole life."

" Perhaps what you have in mind," Ulrich replied, swiftly glancing up, " is that boring old argument about whether man is his own master or not. If everything has a cause, then one can't help anything, and all that sort of thing ? I must confess it hasn't interested me for a single quarter of an hour in the whole of my life. It is the sort of question put by an age that—without anyone's having become aware of it—has become obsolete. It comes from theology, and apart from jurists, who still have a great deal of theology and the smell of burning heretics in their nostrils, the only people who care about causes nowadays are the members of the family, who say : You are the cause of my sleepless nights, or : The fall in the price of wheat was the cause of his misfortune. But ask a criminal, after you have given his conscience a good shaking-up, how he came to do it ! He doesn't know—not even if the balance of his mind was not disturbed even for a single instant while he did it."

Diotima drew herself up straighter. " Why do you so often talk about criminals ? You seem particularly fond of crime. That must mean something, surely ? "

" No," her cousin retorted. " It means nothing. At the most a certain stimulus. Ordinary life is an intermediate state made up

of all our possible crimes. But now that we have used the word
' theology ', there's something I'd like to ask you."

"I suppose now you're going to ask whether I've ever been
immoderately in love or jealous before ? "

"No. Just consider—if God has preordained all things and
has foreknowledge of all things, how can human beings sin ? It's
a question asked of old. And you see, it's still quite a modern
sort of question to raise. An uncommonly fascinating conception
of God that was, by the way—the conception of Him as an intri-
gant. You offend against Him with His own consent. He forces
human beings into error at which He will then be affronted. Not
only does He know it all in advance—one could of course think
of plenty of examples of such resigned love—He actually causes
it to be so ! The situation we all find ourselves in nowadays in
relation to each other is a similar one. The personality is losing
the significance that it has had up to now as a sovereign issuing
edicts from on high. We are coming to understand its evolution
according to the pattern imposed on it, we are coming to understand the influence its environment has on it, the types according
to which it is constructed, its disappearance in moments of very
intense activity—in short, the laws regulating its formation and
its behaviour. Just think—the laws of the personality, cousin !
That is much like speaking of a trade union of solitary poisonous
snakes or a chamber of commerce for highwaymen. For since
laws are, I should say, the most impersonal thing there is in the
world, the personality will soon be no more than an imaginary
meeting-point for all that is impersonal, and it will be difficult to
find for it the honourable standpoint that you don't want to do
without . . ."

So her cousin spoke.

At one point when she got a chance, Diotima objected : " But
my dear man, surely one ought always to do everything as personally as one possibly can ! " And when he had finished she
said : " You are really very theological today. This is the first
time I see you from this side."

Once again she had that look of being a tired dancer sitting out.
A fine sturdy wench. . . . In some obscure way she herself felt
this in every fibre of her being.

She had been avoiding her cousin for weeks, or it might even have been months. But she rather liked him, this man of her own age. He looked dashing in evening dress, in the faintly lighted room, black and white as a knight templar ; this black-and-whiteness had something of the fervour of a cross. She glanced round the modest little bedroom. The Collateral Campaign was far away, and beyond that again lay the great passionate struggles that she had been through. This room was simple as duty itself, the only touch of alleviation being the pussy-willows and the unused coloured picture-postcards stuck into the corners of the looking-glass.—So it was between these, garlanded by the glories of the capital, that Rachel's face appeared when the girl looked at herself in the glass. And where was it she washed ?—Diotima thought vaguely. Oh yes, in that narrow cupboard with the lid that lifted up, there was a tin basin, of course. And then Diotima thought to herself : ' This man wants to and yet won't."

She gazed at him calmly, all the kindly listener.

' Does Arnheim really want to marry me ? ' she wondered. He had said so. But then he had not pressed the matter further. He had so much else to talk about. But even her cousin ought really, instead of talking about things of remote interest, to have asked : ' So then how does it all stand ? ' Why didn't he ask ? It seemed to her that he would certainly understand if she were to tell him in detail about her inner struggles. ' Shall I be any the better off for it ? ' he had asked, in his characteristic way, when she had told him that she had changed. What impudence ! Diotima smiled.

Come to think of it, what these two men had in common was that they were rather odd. Why had her cousin no good word to say of Arnheim ? She knew that Arnheim wished for his friendship. But, to judge by his own violent remarks, Ulrich was also preoccupied with Arnheim. ' And how he misunderstands him ! ' she thought once more. ' One simply can't cope with it.' And besides, it was now not only that her soul rebelled against the body that was married to Permanent Secretary Tuzzi ; at times too her body rebelled against the soul that Arnheim's hesitant and extravagant love was causing to pine at the edge of a desert, over which perhaps only yearning set up the delusive mirage that quivered in the air. She would have liked to share her grief and her weakness with her cousin. She had a liking for the determined one-sidedness that he generally displayed. Arnheim's poised and balanced many-sidedness was, of course, something that must be rated higher, but in the moment of decision Ulrich would not waver like that, in spite of his theories, which all aimed at dissolving everything into utter vagueness. She could feel this, though she did not know what made her feel it. It was probably bound up with what she had felt about him from the very beginning of their acquaintance. If at this moment Arnheim seemed to her a tremendous effort, a kingly burden weighing upon her soul, a burden that towered up over her soul in all directions, everything that Ulrich said seemed to have only one effect, which was that one became so involved in hundreds of kinds of awareness that one lost the awareness of responsibility and suddenly found oneself in a suspicious state of freedom. She suddenly felt the need to make herself heavier than she was. And though she did not quite know why, somehow this reminded her of how once as a young girl she had carried a little boy out of some danger, and while she carried him in her arms he had stubbornly kept on prodding her in the stomach with his knees, fighting to get away. The vividness of this memory—which came into her mind as unexpectedly as though it had come down the chimney into this lonely little room—quite threw her off her balance. ' Immoderately ? ' she wondered. Why did he keep on asking her that ? As if he thought she couldn't be immoderate !

She had forgotten to listen to what he was saying. Without waiting to make sure whether it was at all relevant, she simply interrupted him, she swept aside all he was talking about, and in reply to everything and once and for all and laughing (only her belief that she was laughing was perhaps not quite reliable in the sudden heedless excitement of it) she said : " But I *am* immoderately in love ! "

Ulrich smiled, looking into her eyes. " You're quite incapable of it," he said.

She had stood up, and now, her hands on her hair, turned to him with a look of amazement.

" In order to be immoderate," he expounded calmly, " one must first be quite precise, objective, and matter-of-fact. Two selves that know how questionable the self is nowadays hold on to each other—that's the way I picture it, if at all costs it has to be love and not merely some ordinary activity—and become so inter-linked with each other that one seems to be the cause of the other when they feel themselves changing into greatness, and they float like a veil. In such a state of things it is tremendously diffi-cult to make no false moves, even if one has been making the right ones for some time. The simple fact is, it's difficult to feel the right thing in the world. Quite contrary to a general pre-judice, it calls for something that practically amounts to pedantry. Incidentally, here's what I particularly wanted to say to you. You greatly flattered me, Diotima, when you ascribed to me the potentialities of an archangel, and I refer to it in all modesty, as you will see in a moment. For only if human beings were com-pletely objective and matter-of-fact—and that's almost the same, after all, as being impersonal—only then would they also be all love. Because only then would they be all feeling and emotion and thought. And all the elements that make up a human being are affectionate, for they all yearn towards each other. Only man himself is not so. And so being immoderately in love is some-thing that you might not even at all like. . . ."

He had tried to say this as unsolemnly as possible. In order to manage his facial expression the better he even lit another cigarette.

Diotima too, not knowing what else to do, accepted one he offered her.

She adopted a jokingly defiant expression and blew the smoke high into the air in token of her independence ; for she had not quite understood what he was talking about. But the occurrence as a whole was having its strong effect on her—the fact that quite suddenly, here in this little room where they were alone together, her cousin chose to say all this to her, and yet did not make the slightest effort, so natural in such circumstances, to take her hand or touch her hair, although both of them certainly felt the attrac-tion that the two bodies exerted on each other in this confined space, and felt it like a magnetic current. . . .

'And supposing now one were to . . . ?' she wondered. But what could one do in this room, anyway ? She looked around. Behave like a hussy ? But how did one set about it ? Supposing she were to dissolve ? ' Dissolving ' was a schoolgirl expression that suddenly occurred to her—meaning ' into tears '. Supposing she suddenly did what he had demanded ? And undressed, put her arm round his neck and sang (what should she sing ?) ? Play the harp ? She looked at him, smiling. He seemed to her like a naughty brother in whose company one could get up to any mischief one liked. Ulrich smiled too. (But his smiling was like a blank window ; for after having yielded to the seduction of this talk with Diotima, he merely felt ashamed of it.) And yet here and now she had a foreboding of the possibility of being in love with this man. It seemed to her very much like what, in her view, modern music was like—quite unsatisfying, but full of excitement because it was so utterly different.

And while she assumed that she naturally had a clearer premonition of this than he had, the thought of it, as she stood there before him, made her legs begin to glow with secret heat. For this reason, with the air of one who decides the conversation has been going on a good deal too long, she somewhat abruptly said to her cousin :

" My dear man, we are behaving in the most impossible fashion. Stay here for a moment by yourself, while I go ahead and put in an appearance again among our guests."

102 *Love and strife in the Fischel family.*

GERDA waited in vain for Ulrich's visit. The truth was he had forgotten his promise, or at any rate thought of it only at times when he had other things to do.

" Don't bother about him," Frau Klementine said, when Director Fischel grumbled. " We were good enough for him in the old days. I dare say he aims higher now. If you go and look him up you'll only make it worse. You're much too clumsy for that sort of thing."

Gerda felt a longing for this friend who was older than herself. She wished he were there, at the same time knowing she would

wish him away if he were to come. For all her three-and-twenty
years she had not yet had any ' experiences ', except for a certain
Herr Glanz, who, with her father's encouragement, was cautiously
wooing her, and her Christiano-Germanic friends, who sometimes
seemed to her less like men than schoolboys. ' Why does he
never come ? ' she wondered whenever she thought of Ulrich.
In the circle of her friends it was regarded as beyond dispute that
the Collateral Campaign indicated the beginning of the intellectual and spiritual destruction of the German nation, and she was
ashamed of his being involved in it. She would gladly have heard
what he himself thought about it, and hoped he had reasons that
would exculpate him.

" You missed your chance to be in this whole affair," her
mother said to her father. " It would have been a good thing for
Gerda. It would have given her something else to think about.
All sorts of people go to the Tuzzis'."

It had come out that he had neglected to answer His Highness's invitation. Now he was suffering for it.

The young people whom Gerda called her ' comrades in the
spirit ' had settled down in his house like Penelope's wooers,
there arguing about what a young man of German blood should
do about the Collateral Campaign.

" There are circumstances under which a financier must show
the spirit of a Mæcenas ! " Frau Klementine insisted, when her
husband asserted violently that he had not taken on Hans Sepp,
Gerda's ' spiritual guide ', as a tutor for her, spending his good
money on him, only to have *this* come of it.

For so it was. Hans Sepp, the student, who did not show the
slightest sign of being able to keep a wife now or in the future,
had come into the house as a tutor and, through nothing but the
conflicts prevailing there, had developed into a tyrant. Now, at
Fischel's, he took counsel with his friends, who had become
Gerda's friends, as to how to save the Germanic nobility, which at
Diotima's (and it was said of Diotima that she made no distinction between persons of her own race and of alien races) had
' been ensnared in the meshes of the Jewish intellect '. And even
if, when this was discussed in Leo Fischel's presence, it was
generally tempered with a certain tone of impartiality and objectivity, he still heard enough of a vocabulary and of principles that

got on his nerves. Alarm was expressed about the fact that in a century to which it was not given to produce great symbols such an experiment should be made at all, since it must lead to out-and-out catastrophe. And the expressions ' highly significant ', ' the way to the heights of humanity ', and ' the free human values ' were in themselves enough to make the *pince-nez* quiver on Fischel's nose every time he heard them. In his house such concepts now flourished as ' formative life-thought, ' ' the graph of spiritual growth ', and ' soaring action '. He discovered that every fortnight an ' hour of purification ' was held under his roof. He demanded an explanation. It turned out that it meant reading Stefan George together. Leo Fischel looked up the name in his old encyclopædia in a vain attempt to find out who this was. But what most annoyed him, old-style liberal that he was, was the fact that these young puppies, when talking about the Collateral Campaign, referred to all the high civil servants, bank presidents, and learned and scientific personages who were taking part in it as ' inflated mannikins ' ; and that they asserted in a *blasé* manner that nowadays there were no more great ideas, or at any rate that there was no longer anyone capable of understanding them ; and that they even declared ' humanity ' was an empty word and only the nation or, as they called it, ' nationhood and tradition ' could be allowed to be something real.

" ' Humanity ' doesn't mean anything to me, Papa," Gerda answered when he tackled her on the subject. " The meaning's gone out of it now. My nation, though, is something solid ! "

" Your nation ! " Leo Fischel then exclaimed, and prepared to launch forth into a speech about the great prophets and his own father, who had been a lawyer in Trieste.

" I know," Gerda interrupted him. " But my nation is that of the spirit. *That's* what I'm talking about."

" I'll lock you up in your room till you come to your senses ! " her father declared. " And I'll forbid your friends the house. People who spend all their time worrying about their conscience instead of getting on with their work are simply undisciplined."

" I know your way of thinking, Papa," Gerda retorted. " You older people think you are entitled to humiliate us because you support us. You're all patriarchal capitalists.

Such discussions came about not infrequently, Leo Fischel's paternal anxiety being what it was.

" And what do you think you'd live on if I weren't a capitalist ? " the master of the house demanded.

" I can't be expected to know everything," Gerda declared, and that was her usual way of cutting short any such elaboration of the argument. " But I do know that scientists, educationists, spiritual pastors, political thinkers and other men of action are already at work creating new values for belief ! "

And then it would sometimes happen that Director Fischel made one more effort and asked ironically : " I suppose you yourselves are these spiritual pastors and political thinkers ? " But if he did, it was only in order to have the last word. In the end he was always glad that Gerda did not notice to what an extent something irrational was, by sheer force of repetition, beginning to make him afraid that he would have to surrender. It reached such a pitch that on several occasions he concluded such an argument by actually beginning, in a gingerly way, to praise the orderliness of the Collateral Campaign, by way of contrast to the wild counter-effects going on in his own house ; but this he did only when Klementine was not within earshot.

What lent Gerda's resistance to her father's admonitions the quiet obstinacy of martyrdom was—as Leo and Klementine also obscurely felt—something like a breath of innocent lustfulness being wafted about this house. Among the young people many things were discussed about which Gerda's parents maintained a resentful silence. Even what they called national feeling, this fusion of their everlastingly contending separate egos into dreamed-of unity, which they referred to as ' the Germano-Christian commonweal ', had, when contrasted with the gnawing love-relations of their elders, something of the winged Eros about it. Old heads on young shoulders, they despised ' desire ', the ' inflated lie of crude wallowing in sensual existence ', as they called it, but talked so much about supra-sensuality and a fervour not of the flesh so that involuntarily, and by sheer contrast, the amazed listener began to feel in his soul something like affection for the thought of sensuality and downright physical passion. Even Leo Fischel had to admit that the ruthless eagerness with which they talked at times made the listener feel the roots of their ideas going down into his very legs, which he himself disapproved of, for he insisted that great ideas were something lofty to which one must look up.

Klementine, on the other hand, said: " You shouldn't just sweep everything aside like that, Leo."

" How can they assert that ' property is the death of the mind ' ? " he then began the quarrel with her. " Is my mind dead ? I shouldn't wonder if yours is at least half dead, taking their silly talk so seriously ! "

" You don't understand it, Leo. They mean it in a Christian spirit. They want to leave the old way of life behind and reach a higher life even on earth."

" That's not Christian, it's simply crack-brained ! " Leo retorted.

" Perhaps after all it isn't the realists that see true reality, but those who turn their gaze inward," Klementine suggested.

" I could laugh ! " Fischel declared. But he was wrong there : he was nearer to weeping. Inwardly he wept at being powerless, unable to keep the upper hand over the intellectual and spiritual changes going on around him.

Nowadays Director Fischel felt a need of fresh air more often than hitherto. After his day's work he was not in a hurry to get home, and if it was still daylight when he left the office he liked to stroll about for a while in one of the city's gardens, even though it was winter. He had a liking for these gardens that dated back to his days as a ' junior '. For some reason, which he himself could not make out, the city council had in the late autumn had the iron folding chairs newly painted, and here now they stood, all fresh green, piled up against each other by the sides of the snow-white paths, and stimulating the imagination with their bright look of spring. On and off Leo Fischel would sit down on one of these chairs, all alone and muffled up to the ears, at the edge of a playground or a walk, and watch the nursemaids, with their charges, assuming an air of winter-time health in the sunshine. The children played diavolo or threw little snowballs, and the little girls made big eyes like grown-up women—' ah dear yes,' Fischel thought, ' just the same eyes that in the face of a beautiful grown-up woman make one think with delight that she has the eyes of a child . . .'

He found it a pleasant relief to watch the little girls at play, in their eyes love still floating in the fairy pool from which the stork would later fetch it. And at times, too, he watched the nurse-maids and governesses. In his youth he had often enjoyed this sight, at that time when he still stood gazing into life's shop-window, lacking the money to walk inside, and at the most could ponder on what his destiny might later bring him. It had turned out shabbily enough, he thought. And for a moment that brimmed with the tension of youth it seemed to him that he sat again surrounded by white crocuses and green grass.

Afterwards, then, when his sense of reality brought him back to awareness of snow and green paint, he thought every time, oddly enough, of his income. Money meant independence. But the whole of his salary went on the needs of the family and the ' something put aside ' that prudence demanded. And so—he reflected—one ought to do something else as well, apart from one's job, in order to make oneself independent—perhaps turn to account the knowledge one had of the Stock Exchange, just as the higher-up directors did.

But such thoughts came to Leo only when he was watching the little girls at their play, and he rejected them, because he was far from feeling he had the temperament needed for speculation. He was manager of a department, bearing the merely honorary title of director ; he had no prospect of rising above this ; and he at once conscientiously intimidated himself with the thought that a poor toil-worn back like his had long been far too bent to be able to straighten up in freedom now. He did not know that he thought this solely in order to erect an insurmountable barrier between himself and the pretty children and their nannies that here, in these moments in the gardens, for him took the place of all life's allurements. For even in the disgruntled mood that kept him from going home he remained an incorrigible family man ana would have given everything only to be able to transform the circle of Hell at home into a circle of angels floating round a paternal divinity, Titular Director Fischel.

Ulrich also had a liking for these gardens and walked across them whenever his errand took him that way. So it came about these days he ran into Fischel again. And Fischel instantly remembered all he had had to suffer at home because of the

Collateral Campaign. He expressed his dissatisfaction at the fact that his young friend thought so lightly of invitations from his (the young friend's) old friends—and he could throw himself into this way of looking at it with all the more sincerity since even casual friendships in the course of time become every bit as old as do the most intense.

Fischel's old young friend declared that it gave him really the greatest of pleasure to see Fischel again, and lamented the ridiculous activities that had hitherto prevented him from calling.

Fischel complained of the way everything was going to the dogs and how bad business was. And morality was crumbling on all sides. Everything nowadays was so materialistic and rushed.

" And I was just thinking I could safely envy you ! " Ulrich countered. " Surely the business man's occupation must be a downright sanatorium for the soul ! At least it's the only occupation with an ideally clean basis."

" It's that all right ! " Fischel confirmed. " The business man served the cause of human progress, contenting himself with a fair profit. And, for all that," he added with sombre melancholy, " he's every bit as badly off as anyone else ! "

Ulrich declared his readiness to walk home with him.

When they arrived, they found an atmosphere that was already strained to breaking-point.

All the friends had assembled, and a tremendous battle of words was in full swing. These young people were either still at school or in their first or second term at the university, excepting some who were at work learning some business. They themselves no longer knew what had forged their circle. It had been a matter of personal contacts. Some had got to know each other in nationalist students' fraternities, others in the Socialist or the Catholic youth movement, and others again when rambling or camping in a group of *Wandervögel*.

One would not be entirely at error in assuming that the only thing they all really had in common was Leo Fischel. A spiritual movement, if it is to have permanence and solidity, needs a body : and this body was Fischel's apartment, together with the refreshments provided and a certain controlling of social intercourse by Frau Klementine. Gerda went with the apartment, and Hans Sepp went with Gerda, and Hans Sepp, the student with the impure complexion and the soul that was all the purer, was, though not their leader (because these young people acknowledged no leader), certainly the one among them most inspired by passion. At times, of course, they met elsewhere, and then a girl other than Gerda dispensed hospitality. This, however, did not alter the fact that the nucleus of the movement was as described.

For all this it was as remarkable an enigma whence these young people's spirits came from as is that of how a new disease comes into existence or a long series of winning numbers turns up in a game of chance. When the sun of old-style European idealism began to fade out and the white spirit began to grow dark, many torches were passed on from hand to hand—ideas, those torches of the mind—and heaven alone knows where they had been stolen from or invented !—and, flaring here and there, they became that dancing pool of flame, a small community in the spirit. And so it was that in those last years before the Great War carried this to its foregone conclusion there had also been much talk, among the younger generation, of love and a sense of fellowship. Above all the young anti-Semites in the house of Bank-Director Fischel all felt themselves to be under the ægis of such an all-embracing love and sense of fellowship. True solidarity and community of feeling were the workings of an inner code of law, and the deepest, simplest, most perfect, and also the first, of these was the law of love. As has already been pointed out, this did not mean love in any lower, sensual sense ; for physical possession was an invention of Mammon and operated only in such a way as to disunite and divest life of its meaning. And of course one could not love *everyone* without discrimination. But one could respect each individual's character in so far as he strove, in genuine human endeavour, with the strictest sense of being responsible to and for himself. So in the name of love they wrangled together about everything.

But on this day a united front had been formed against Frau Klementine, who so much liked to feel young again and who admitted in her heart of hearts that connubial love really did have a close connection with the money-grubbing servitude imposed by capitalism, but could not bring herself to permit harsh criticism of the Collateral Campaign on the grounds that Aryans were capable of creating symbols only when they were exclusively among themselves. Frau Klementine was only just managing to hold on to her temper, and on Gerda's cheeks there were round red spots of rage because her mother could not be got to leave the room.

When Leo Fischel came home with Ulrich, she made secret signs to Hans Sepp, urging him to break off.

Hans said conciliatingly : " People of our epoch are altogether incapable of creating anything great ! " and believed that with this remark he had reduced the subject to an impersonal formula that everyone was by now quite familiar with.

At this moment, however, Ulrich unfortunately joined in, asking Hans, with a touch of malice aimed at Fischel, whether this meant he did not believe at all in progress.

" Progress ! " Hans Sepp exclaimed patronisingly. " You only need to make the comparison with the men who lived a hundred years ago, before there was any such thing as progress—Beethoven ! Goethe ! Napoleon ! Hebbel ! "

" H'm," Ulrich remarked. " The last of them happens to have been an infant in arms at that time."

" Exact figures are something these young people despise," Director Fischel declared delightedly.

Ulrich did not take that up. He knew that Hans Sepp had a jealous contempt for him, but he himself in many ways rather liked Gerda's weird friends. And so he sat down among them and continued :

" Undeniably, in individual branches of human skill we have been making so much progress that we have thoroughly got the feeling we can't catch up with it. Isn't it possible that this is what produces the feeling there is no progress ? After all, progress, surely, is the product of all joint efforts, and one can actually say in advance that the progress that is really made will always be precisely what nobody wanted."

Hans Sepp turned his dark shock of hair at Ulrich like a quivering horn.

" There you are—you say it yourself ! ' What nobody wanted ! ' A lot of cackling, first this way and then that ! Hundreds of ways, but no way ahead ! In other words, ideas—but no soul ! And no character ! The sentence leaps out of the page, the word leaps out of the sentence, the whole thing is no longer

a whole—as Nietzsche said. Quite apart from the fact that
Nietzsche's egomania is also one of life's anti-values ! Just tell
me of a single solid ultimate value from which you, for instance,
take your bearings in life ! "

"At the drop of a hat ! I like that ! " Director Fischel protested.

But Ulrich asked Hans : " Do you really find it utterly impossible to live without an ultimate value ? "

"Yes," Hans said. " But I admit it means I shall always be
unhappy."

"The devil take you ! " Ulrich said, laughing. " Everything
we can do depends on our not being too strict, waiting for the
highest knowledge and understanding. The Middle Ages did
that, and remained ignorant."

"That is a very moot point," Hans Sepp answered. " I
maintain that *we* are ignorant."

"But you must admit that our ignorance is manifestly of an
extremely fortunate and varied kind."

From the background a drawling voice grumbled : " Varied !
Knowledge ! Relative progress ! Those are concepts belonging
to the mechanistic mode of thought prevailing in an era corrupted
by capitalism ! I need scarcely say more. . . ."

Leo Fischel was also grumbling to himself. So far as could be
gathered, he was of the opinion that Ulrich was paying far too
much attention to these disrespectful boys. He pulled a newspaper out of his pocket and disappeared behind the outspread
pages.

But Ulrich happened to find it amusing. " Is the modern
middle-class house," he asked, " with its six rooms, servant's
bathroom, vacuum cleaner and so on, compared with the old
houses that have high ceilings, thick walls and beautiful arch-
ways, progress or not ? "

"No ! " Hans Sepp shouted.

"Is the aeroplane progress compared with the mail-coach ? "

"Yes ! " Director Fischel shouted.

"The machine compared with handicrafts ? "

"Handicrafts ! " Hans shouted.

"The machine ! " shouted Fischel.

"It seems to me," Ulrich said, " that every progressive step is also a retrogressive step. Progress exists always only in one particular sense. And since our life as a whole has no sense, there is as a whole no progress either."

Leo Fischel lowered his newspaper. " Do you think it better to be able to cross the Atlantic in six days or to have to spend six weeks on it ? "

" I should probably say it's definitely progress to be able to do both. However, our young Christian friends deny that as well."

The circle was taut as a drawn bow. Ulrich had paralysed the discussion, but not the aggressive spirit.

He went on quietly : " But one can also sa ythe contrary : if our life contains progress in particular instances, then there is also sense in it in particular instances. But once there has been any sense in, for example, sacrificing human beings to the gods or burning witches or powdering one's hair, then that does remain one of life's meaningful feelings, even if more hygienic habits and humane customs are steps in progress. The mistake is that progress always wants to make a clean sweep of the old meaning."

" So you mean to say we ought to go back to human sacrifice after having successfully got over those ages of abominable darkness ? " Fischel asked.

" I wouldn't be so sure about darkness ! " Hans Sepp answered in place of Ulrich. " When you devour an innocent hare, that is dark. But when a cannibal makes a meal of a stranger, reverently and to the accompaniment of religious ceremonies, we simply don't know what goes on in him ! "

" There must really have been something to be said for the ages we have left behind," Ulrich agreed with him. " Or else so many perfectly nice people couldn't once have approved of them. I wonder whether that could be turned to account for us, without great sacrifices ? And perhaps the very reason why we still go on sacrificing so many human beings today is that we have never clearly put to ourselves the question as to the correct way of overcoming humanity's earlier notions ? The relations between all these things are obscure and difficult to express."

" But to your way of thinking the desideratum always remains nothing but a total or a balancing of accounts, all the same ! " Hans Sepp burst out, now turning against Ulrich. " You believe in bourgeois progress in just the same way as Director Fischel, only you express it in as involved and perverted a way as possible, so that nobody can catch you out ! "

Hans had expressed the opinion of his friends.

Ulrich turned to look in Gerda's face. He wanted to take up the thread of his thoughts again in a leisurely way, ignoring the fact that Fischel and the young people were just as ready to hurl themselves upon him as upon each other.

" But, Hans," he said, beginning again, " you do strive towards a goal, don't you ? "

" Something strives—in me—through me," Hans Sepp answered curtly.

" And is it going to get there ? " Leo Fischel let himself be carried away into asking this sarcastic question, and with that, as all but he himself realised, went over to Ulrich's side.

" I don't know about that," Hans answered gloomily.

You ought to get on and pass your exams—that would be progress ! " Leo Fischel could not stop himself making this remark too, so irritated was he. But he was irritated not less by his friend than by the callow youths.

At this point something like a general explosion occurred.

Frau Klementine cast an imploring glance at her husband. Gerda tried to forestall Hans, and Hans struggled for words, which finally poured forth in yet another attack on Ulrich.

" You may be sure," he shouted at him, " in the last resort even you don't think a single thought that Director Fischel couldn't think ! "

With this, he rushed out of the room, and his friends bowed angrily and then stormed after him. Director Fischel, bludgeoned by the looks his wife was giving him, pretended he had just remembered his obligations as master of the house and disappeared, muttering, into the hall in order to say a last soothing word to the young men. Only Gerda, Ulrich, and Frau Klementine were left in the room. Frau Klementine heaved several sighs of relief because the air was now cleared ; then she rose. And to his surprise, Ulrich found himself alone with Gerda.

103   *The temptation.*

GERDA was visibly excited when they were left alone. Ulrich took her hand. Her arm began to tremble, and she freed herself.

" You don't know," she said, " what it means to Hans to have a goal. You make fun of it. And that's cheap, of course. It seems to me your thoughts have become even more obscene than they used to be ! " She had been groping for the strongest possible word, and now was shocked by it herself.

Ulrich tried to catch hold of her hand again.

She drew her arm close to her side. " We don't want just that ! " she exclaimed. She thrust the words at him with violent contempt ; but her body swayed.

" I know," Ulrich mocked. " Everything that goes on among you people is supposed to meet the highest demands. That is precisely what makes me unable to resist taking up the attitude you have so amiably described. And you can't imagine how much I used to like talking differently to you in the old days."

" You have never been different," Gerda retorted swiftly.

" I have always been inconsistent," Ulrich said simply, searching her face. " Would it amuse you if I were to tell you something of what goes on at my cousin's ? "

In Gerda's eyes now something flickered that was clearly distinct from the uneasiness that Ulrich's proximity caused her ; for she was burning with expectation of this information, in order to pass it on to Hans, and she was trying to conceal this.

Ulrich noted this with some satisfaction, and just as an animal, scenting danger, instinctively changes its course, he began with something else.

" Do you remember the story I told you about the moon ? " he asked her. " I should like first of all to tell you about something else of the same kind."

" You'll only tell me another pack of lies ! " Gerda snapped.

" As far as possible, I won't. I dare say you remember from your lectures how it is in the world when people want to know whether something is a law or not? Either one starts out with reasons for believing it is a law, as for instance in physics or chemistry, and even though the observations never produce the value one is in search of, still they do lie in a definite pattern all around it, and from that one reckons it out. Or, as so often happens in life, one has no such reasons, and is faced with a phenomenon of which one doesn't quite know whether it is a law or an accident. Then the matter becomes humanly exciting. For one first of all turns one's pile of observations into a pile of figures. One divides them into categories, to see which numbers lie between this value and that, between the next and the one after that, and so on. And from that one arranges them in distributive series. The result is that the frequency of the events has or has not a systematic increase or decrease. One gets a stationary series or a distributive function. One calculates the degree of aberration, the mean deviation, the degree of the deviation from an arbitrary value, the central value, the normal value, the average value, the dispersion, and so forth, and with all these concepts one examines the given event."

Ulrich expounded this in a calm explanatory tone, and it would have been hard to be sure whether he was trying to gain time for reflection or whether it amused him to hypnotise Gerda with scientific talk. Gerda had moved some distance away from him. She was sitting in an armchair, leaning forward, with a furrow of concentration between her eyebrows, looking down at the floor. When anyone talked in such a matter-of-fact way, appealing to her pretensions to intellect, her ill-humour was daunted; she felt the simple security that it had lent her vanishing away. She had been to the *Realgymnasium* and had done some terms at the university, skimming a mass of new knowledge that could not be fitted into the old framework of the classical and humanist outlook. Such an education leaves many young people nowadays with the feeling that it is entirely inadequate, while ahead of them the new age lies spread out like a new world whose ground cannot be worked with the old tools. She did not know where the things that Ulrich was talking about led to: she believed him because she was in love with him, and disbelieved him because she was ten years younger than he and belonged to another generation, one that felt itself to be fresh and energetic, and both these attitudes began to merge in the vaguest possible way while he went on talking.

" And then," he continued, " there are observations that look exactly as though they constituted a natural law, yet without having any basis that we could regard as such. The regularity of numerical series is at times just as great as that of laws. I am sure you have heard the usual examples at some sociology lecture or other. For instance, the statistics of divorce in America. Or the proportion between the male and female birth-rates, which is, of course, one of the most constant ratios. And then you know that every year there is a fairly constant number of conscripts that try to escape military service by means of self-mutilation. Or that every year approximately the same percentage of the population of Europe commits suicide. Furthermore, the annual rates of theft, rape, and, if I am not mistaken, bankruptcy remain approximately the same. . . ."

At this point Gerda's resistance tried to break through.

" You're not trying to explain progress to me, are you ? " she exclaimed, doing her utmost to put a great deal of scorn into this surmise.

" But of course I am ! " Ulrich retorted, without letting himself be put off. " This is somewhat vaguely known as the law of large numbers. Meaning more or less that one person commits suicide for this reason and another for that reason, but that when you have a very large number the accidental and personal element ceases to be of interest, and what is left is—well, what *is* left ? This is what I want to ask you. For, as you see, what remains is what every one of us, as a lay person, without more ado refers to as the average, the thing, that is, as to which nobody has the slightest idea what it really is. Allow me to add that attempts have been made to explain this law of large numbers by logical and formal means, so to speak, as a self-evident fact. On the other hand, it has also been asserted that such regularity of phenomena that are not causally related to each other cannot be explained at all by the usual intellectual operations, and, besides many other analyses of this phenomenon, the assertion has been made that this is not only a matter of single events but also of unknown laws of totality. I don't want to bother you with the details, which I no longer have at my fingertips anyway, but without doubt it would be very important to me personally to know whether what is behind this is laws of collectivity or whether it is simply that by some irony of nature particularity arises out of the fact that nothing in particular happens and the highest meaning turns out to be something that can be got at by taking the average of what is most profoundly senseless. It would surely make a decisive difference to our approach to life if we could know definitely one way or the other ! For however it may be, every possibility of leading an ordered life rests on this law of large numbers. And if it were not for this law of averages, nothing might happen in one year, and there would be no certainty about anything for the next year, famines would alternate with plenty, there would be either no children or too many, and mankind would flutter to and fro between its heavenly and hellish possibilities, as little birds flutter when someone goes up to their cage."

" Is that all true ? " Gerda asked hesitantly.

" You ought to know that yourself."

" Of course. I do know something about it where the details are concerned. But I don't know whether this is what you meant a little while ago when everyone was arguing. What you said about progress only sounded as if you were trying to annoy everyone."

" That's what you always think. But what do we know about what our progress is ? Nothing at all ! There are many possibilities of what it might be, and I have just mentioned yet another one."

" What it might be ! That's the way you always think. You'll never try to answer the question as to how it ought to be ! "

" You people are in such a hurry. There always has to be a goal, an ideal, a programme there for you—something absolute. And what comes of it in the end is only a compromise after all, an average ! Won't you admit that in the long run it's wearisome and ridiculous always to do and demand the utmost, merely in order to produce some mediocre result ? "

This was at bottom the same conversation as that with Diotima. The external form of it was different, certainly, but behind that one might have gone on from one into the other. And that too made it obvious how little it mattered which woman was sitting there : a body that, once introduced into a given intellectual magnetic field, set certain definite processes going. Ulrich contemplated Gerda, who gave no answer to his last question.

A thin girl, she sat there with a little furrow of discontent between her eyes. And there was another deep, perpendicular furrow visible at the low-cut neck of her blouse. Her arms and legs were long and delicate. A limp springtide, shot with the harsh glow of a too early summer—that was the impression he received, together with the whole impact of the wilfulness that is locked up in such a young body. He was overcome by a queer mixture of aversion and composure, for he suddenly had the feeling that he was closer to a decision than he thought and that this young girl was called to play her part in bringing it about. And involuntarily he now in fact began to talk of the impressions he had received of what in the Collateral Campaign was referred to as ' the younger generation ', and concluded with words that surprised Gerda.

" They are very radical there too, and they don't like me there either. But I pay them back in the same coin, for in my own way *I* am radical, and there is no kind of disorder I can stand less than the intellectual kind. I should like to see ideas not only elaborated, but also correlated. I want not only the oscillation but also the density of the idea. That is what you, my indispensable friend, disapprove of. You say that I only talk about what might be instead of about what ought to be. I don't confuse these two things. And this is probably the most anachronistic quality that one can have, for nothing nowadays is so alien to anything as strictness and the emotional life are to each other, and our exactitude in mechanical things has unfortunately developed to such a point that it regards its proper complement as being the inexactitude of life. Why don't you understand me? You're probably quite incapable of it, and it's perverted of me to take the trouble of confusing a mind like yours, which is so happily in harmony with the spirit of the age. And candidly, Gerda, I sometimes ask myself whether I am not wrong. Perhaps it is the very people I can't stand who are doing what I once wanted. Perhaps they do it wrong, do it brainlessly, one running in one direction and one in another, each with one notion in his beak, which he considers the only one in the world, each of them thinking himself fright-

fully clever, and all of them together believing that the age is
condemned to sterility. But perhaps it's the other way round,
and each one of them is stupid but all of them together are fertile ?
It appears that nowadays every truth comes into the world split
into two mutually antagonistic falsehoods, and this too may be a
way of arriving at a suprapersonal result ! The average, the sum
of the experiments, then no longer comes about in the individual
case, which becomes unbearably one-sided, but the totality is
like an experimental community. To cut a long story short—do
be indulgent towards an old man, whose solitariness sometimes
drives him to excesses ! "

" How you do always hold forth to me about all sorts of
things ! " Gerda replied gloomily. " Why don't you write a
book about your ideas ? In that way you might help yourself
and us."

" But why should I write a book ? " Ulrich exclaimed. " After
all, I was born of a woman and not of an ink-well ! "

Gerda considered whether a book by Ulrich could in fact help
anyone. Like all the young people she was friends with she over-
rated the power of the written word. Everything in the apartment
was very quiet now that the two of them had fallen silent ; it
seemed that the Fischels, husband and wife, had left the house
soon after their indignant guests. And Gerda could feel the
pressure caused by the proximity of the more powerful male
body, as she always felt it, contrary to all her convictions, whenever they were alone together ; she revolted against it and began
to tremble.

Ulrich noticed this, got up, put his hand on her frail shoulder
and said to her : " I'll make a suggestion to you, Gerda. Let us
assume that in matters of morality it is exactly the same as in the
kinetic theory of gases : everything swirls about chaotically, each
thing doing what it likes, but if one calculates what in a manner
of speaking has no cause to arise out of it, one finds that is the
very thing that does really arise ! Let us therefore assume too
that a certain quantity of ideas is swirling about in the present
time. It produces some most probable average value. This
shifts very slowly and automatically, and that is what we call
progress or the historical situation. But what is most important
is that our personal, individual motion doesn't matter in the least

in all this. We may think and act to the right or to the left, high or low, in a new way or an old way, wildly or with circumspection : it is of no consequence at all to the average value. And to God and the universe *that*'s all that matters—*we* don't count ! "

While he was saying this he made some approach to clasping her in his arms, although it was only with an effort that he could bring himself to do so.

Gerda grew angry. " You always begin by being meditative," she exclaimed, " and what comes out then is nothing but the common gobbling of a turkeycock ! " Her face was aflame, with round flecks of colour, her lips seemed to be sweating, but there was something beautiful about her indignation. " The very thing you make of it is the thing *we* don't want ! "

At that Ulrich could not resist the temptation to ask in a low voice : " Possession kills desire ? "

" I don't want to talk to you about it ! " Gerda retorted in an equally low voice.

" It's one and the same whether it's possession of a human being or of a thing," Ulrich went on. " I know that too. Gerda, I understand you and Hans better than you think. What is it you and Hans want ? Tell me."

" There you are—nothing ! " Gerda exclaimed triumphantly. " It can't be said in words. Papa too keeps on saying : ' Get clear about what you want. You'll see it's nonsense.' Everything's nonsense when you get clear about it ! If we are rational, we shall never get beyond platitudes ! Now you'll have some objection to make again, you with your rationalism ! "

Ulrich shook his head. " And how about the demonstration against Count Leinsdorf ? " he asked gently, as though that had something to do with it.

" Oh, so you spy on us ! " Gerda exclaimed.

" Assume that I spy, if you like, but tell me, Gerda. So far as I am concerned you are welcome to assume that too."

Gerda looked embarrassed. " Nothing in particular. Well, just one of those demonstrations of German youth. Perhaps a march past his house, with shouts of abuse. The Collateral Campaign is an infamy ! "

" Why ? "

Gerda shrugged her shoulders.

" Do sit down again," Ulrich begged her. " You over-estimate all that. Let's talk quietly for once."

Gerda obeyed.

" Now listen and tell me whether I understand your situation," Ulrich continued. " So you say that possession kills desire. In saying that you are thinking primarily of money and of your parents. They of course are souls that have been killed. . . ."

Gerda made a haughty gesture.

" Well then, instead of talking about money, let's talk straight-away about every kind of possession. The man who possesses himself. The man who possesses his convictions. The man who lets himself be possessed, by another or by his own passions or merely by his habits or by his successes. The man who wants to conquer something. The man who wants anything at all. Do you reject all that ? You want to be rovers. Roaming rovers, Hans once called it, if I am not mistaken. Roving towards some other meaning and form of existence ? Am I right ? "

" In all you say you are horribly right. The intellect can imitate the soul ! "

" And the intellect belongs to the possession group ? It measures, weighs, divides, collects—just like an old banker ? But haven't I told you a whole lot of stories today which have remark-ably much of our soul clinging to them ? "

" That's a cold soul ! "

" You're absolutely right, Gerda. And so now I only need to tell you why I'm on the side of the cold souls or even of the bankers."

" Because you're a coward ! "

Ulrich noticed that in speaking she bared her teeth like a little animal in mortal terror.

" As God is my judge, I am," he replied. " But if there is nothing else you believe me capable of, at least you will believe I would be man enough to break out along a lightning-conductor, or even down the narrowest ledge of the wall, if I were not convinced that all attempts to escape would only lead straight back to Papa ! "

Gerda had been refusing to have this talk with Ulrich since the time when a similar one had taken place between them. The feelings that were its subjects belonged only to her and Hans ; and even more than Ulrich's scorn she feared his approval, which would have delivered her over to him, quite helpless, before she even knew whether he was in good faith or blaspheming. From the moment a little while ago when she had been surprised by his mournful words, the consequences of which she had to bear now, it was clearly perceptible how violently she wavered in her own mind.

But it was also somewhat similar with Ulrich. He was far from taking a vicious pleasure in his power over this girl. He did not take Gerda seriously, and since this included an intellectual repugnance, he generally said disagreeable things to her. But for some time now the more energetically he played the part of counsel for the world in her presence, the more weirdly he felt himself drawn by the wish to confide in her and as it were show her his inner being without either deceit or glossing over of anything, or to contemplate hers in a nakedness like that of a slug. Therefore he gazed thoughtfully into her face and said :

" I could let my eyes rest between your cheeks as the clouds rest in the sky. I don't know whether the clouds like resting in the sky, but ultimately I know every bit as much as all the Hanses in the world about the moments when God takes hold of us as of a glove and slowly, slowly turns us inside out over His fingers ! You people make it too easy for yourselves. You sense a negative aspect to the positive world in which we live and announce curtly that the positive world belongs to parents and the older generation, and the world of the shadowy negative to the new younger generation. Now, I don't exactly want to be a spy for your parents, dear Gerda, but I put it to you that when it comes to choosing between a banker and an angel the more solidly real and honest-to-goodness nature of the banker's occupation does count for something ! "

" Would you like some tea ? " Gerda asked sharply. " Let me offer you some hospitality ! You shall be entertained by the daughter of the house at her very best." She had pulled herself together again.

" Let us assume you'll marry Hans."

" But I don't *want* to marry him ! "

" One must have some aim. You can't go on for ever living on being in opposition to your parents."

" Some day I shall leave the house, I shall be independent, and we shall remain friends ! "

" Please, Gerda darling, just for once let us assume that you'll be married to Hans or something of the sort. It certainly can't be avoided if everything goes on the way it's going. And now work out for yourself how you will brush your teeth in the morning, or how Hans will cope with an income-tax demand, in a world-renouncing state of mind."

" Do I have to know that ? "

" Your Papa would say ' yes ', if he had any notion of world-renouncing states of mind. Unfortunately, ordinary people are very good at stowing the far-from-ordinary experiences in their ship of life so deep down in the hold that they never notice them. But let's take a simpler question—will you expect Hans to be faithful to you ? Faithfulness is part of the possession complex ! It ought to be acceptable to you if Hans lifted up his soul by rejoicing in another woman. Indeed, according to the laws you try to live up to you ought to consider that an enrichment of your own condition ! "

" Don't you go and believe," Gerda replied, " that we ourselves never talk about such questions ! One can't become a new being in a single stride. But it's very bourgeois to make that an argument against it ! "

" What your father is demanding of you is actually something quite different from what you think it is. He doesn't even assert that he is any wiser in these questions than you and Hans are. He simply says he can't understand what you are up to. But he knows that power is a very rational thing. He believes it has more sense than you and he and Hans all rolled together. How would it be if he were to offer Hans money so that at long last he could finish his studies without any further obstacle ? If he were to promise that after a period of trial he would, if not give him his blessing, at least withdraw his fundamental objection ? And if he only attached the condition that until the period of trial was over you should not communicate with each other in any way whatsoever, not even seeing each other in the way you do now ? "

" So this is what you are lending yourself to, is it ? "

" I just wanted to explain your Papa to you. He is a sinister deity of quite extraordinary superiority. He believes that money would bring Hans to the point where he'd like to have him—to the common sense of realism. In his view a Hans with a limited monthly income could not possibly go on being silly beyond all limits. But perhaps your Papa is a dreamer. I admire him, just as I admire compromises, averages, dry facts, dead figures. I don't believe in the Devil, but if I did, I should picture him as the trainer who drives Heaven on to record achievements. And I promised him to press you hard till nothing remained of your fancies, nothing except—well, plain reality."

Ulrich was far from having a clear conscience when he said this. Gerda stood before him all in flame, the anger in her eyes overlaid with tears.

All at once there was an open road ahead for Hans and her. But had Ulrich betrayed her or was he trying to help them? She did not know, and either possibility was of such a kind as to make her both unhappy and happy. In her confusion she mistrusted him, and yet she passionately felt that he was akin to her in all that she held sacred, only that he would not show it.

" Your father," Ulrich added, " naturally has the secret wish that I should in the mean time pay my court to you and give your thoughts a new direction."

" That is out of the question ! " Gerda exclaimed in a strained voice.

" I dare say it is out of the question between us," Ulrich agreed gently. " But it can't go on like this either. I've already gone too far." He tried to smile, and in doing so was utterly loathsome to himself. He really did not want all this to happen. He could feel the irresoluteness of this soul and despised himself because it aroused an impulse of cruelty in him.

And at that very instant Gerda looked at him with horror in her eyes. Suddenly she seemed as beautiful as a fire that one has come too near to—almost without form, only a warmth paralysing the will.

" You ought to come and see me some day," he suggested. " Here one can't talk as one likes." And the nihilism of masculine ruthlessness was as a stream of light pouring from his eyes.

" No," Gerda said, all resistance.

But she averted her gaze, and sadly Ulrich saw—as though with this turning away of her eyes she had again become really visible to him—the figure of the young girl standing before him, breathing heavily, a girl neither beautiful nor ugly. He sighed deeply and out-and-out sincerely.

104 *Rachel and Soliman on the war-path.*

IN the Tuzzi household, between the exalted tasks allotted to it and the multitude of ideas that assembled in it, there was a flitting, lissom, enraptured, exotic creature at work. This little maid, Rachel, was like a Mozart aria for a lady's waiting-maid. Opening the door, she would stand with arms half outstretched to receive the coat discarded by the visitor. On such occasions Ulrich sometimes wondered whether she had at all acknowledged him as someone related to her master and mistress, and would try to look into her eyes. But Rachel's eyes either avoided his gaze or met it blankly, like two lustreless patches of velvet. He thought he remembered that, when her glance had met his for the first time, it had been different, and a few times on such occasions he observed another pair of eyes, out of a dark corner of the hall, moving towards Rachel like two big white snails. These were Soliman's eyes. But the question whether this boy was the cause of Rachel's reserve remained open, because Rachel responded to his gaze as little as to Ulrich's and withdrew quietly as soon as she had announced the visitor.

The truth was more romantic than curiosity could suppose. Since Soliman, with his wilful defamations, had succeeded in involving Arnheim's radiant figure in obscure machinations, and even Rachel's childlike admiration for Diotima had suffered under this change, all that there was in her of an impassioned desire for good behaviour and ministering love, had focused on Ulrich. Since, having been persuaded by Soliman that one must keep a watch on what went on in this house, she had become an eager listener at key-holes and an eavesdropper while waiting on the guests, and had also listened in to more than one conversation between Permanent Secretary Tuzzi and his wife, it had not escaped her that the position Ulrich occupied between Diotima and Arnheim was half that of an enemy and half that of a person loved ; and this corresponded entirely to her own feeling, oscillating between revolt and remorse, for her unsuspecting mistress. Now too she recollected very clearly that she had long ago noticed that Ulrich wanted something from her. It did not occur to her that he might have taken a liking to her. Though—since she had been turned out of her home and wanted to show her family in Galicia that she could nevertheless get on in the world—she doubtless cherished the hope that she would strike lucky, inherit an unexpected fortune, discover she was the disinherited child of high-ranking parents, or have the chance of saving a prince's life, still, the simple possibility that she might attract some gentleman among her lady's visitors, who would make her his mistress or even marry her, did not occur to her at all. This was why she merely held herself in readiness to do Ulrich some great service.

It was she and Soliman who had sent the General an invitation, after it had come to their knowledge that he was a friend of Ulrich's : though admittedly it was also done because things had to be set moving and the entire lie of the land made a general seem a very suitable personage to this end. But because Rachel was acting in hidden, hobgoblinish alliance with Ulrich, it was inevitable that between her and him whose movements she watched over so eagerly there should arise that overwhelming affinity that turned all the secretly observed motions of his lips, eyes, and fingers into actors to whom she clung with the passion of a person who finds his own insignificant existence set upon a vast stage. And the more intensely she noticed that this mutual relationship contracted her bosom no less violently than a tight dress does when one crouches at a key-hole, the more depraved she felt herself to be because she did not more resolutely resist Soliman's sombre wooings, with which she was beset at the same time. This was the reason, unknown to Ulrich, why she met his curiosity with the awed passion of one intent on showing herself to be a well-trained, model serving-maid.

Ulrich asked himself in vain why this little creature, by Nature formed for amorous sportings, should be so chaste that it almost

seemed here was a case of the mutinous frigidity that is not un-
common in slightly-built women. However, he changed his
mind about that, and was perhaps, indeed, a little disappointed
when one day he was a witness of a surprising scene.

Arnheim had just arrived, Soliman had squatted down in the
hall, and Rachel had withdrawn as swiftly as ever. Ulrich took
advantage of the momentary little stir caused by Arnheim's
arrival to go back into the hall and get a handkerchief from his
overcoat pocket. The light had been switched off again, but
Soliman was still there and he did not realise that Ulrich, blotted
out by the shadow in the doorway, only went through the motion
of opening and shutting the door, as though he had once more left
the hall. Soliman rose cautiously and with great care produced a
large flower from under his jacket. It was a beautiful white arum
lily. He contemplated it for a while and then set out, on tip-toe,
past the kitchen. Ulrich, who remembered where Rachel's
room was, followed quietly and saw what happened. Soliman
stopped outside the door, pressed the flower to his lips, and then
fixed it to the handle, hastily twisting the stem round it twice
and squeezing the end of it into the key-hole.

It had been difficult to extract this lily from the bunch without
being noticed on the way and to hide it for Rachel. And Rachel
appreciated such attentions for what they were worth. To be
caught and dismissed amounted, for her, to the same as death and
the Day of Judgment, and for this reason it was of course bur-
densome to her that wherever she was, wherever she went or
stood, she had to be on her guard against Soliman. It was anything but a pleasure to her to be suddenly pinched in the leg by
him, reaching out from some hiding-place of his, and not to be
at liberty to scream. Yet it could not fail to make an impression
on her that another being should offer her attentions involving
dangers to himself, in the most devoted way spying out each of her
steps, and testing her character in difficult situations. This little
monkey was speeding up matters in a way that seemed to her
senseless and dangerous : that was what Rachel felt, yet at times,
quite against her principles and in the midst of all the tangled
expectations that filled her head, she felt a sinful yearning, whatever great and important things might be waiting for her at a
further distance, first of all to make abundant use of those thick

lips everywhere lurking in wait for her, the lips of a Negro king's son, that seemed to be created for her, the serving-maid's, service.

One day Soliman asked her whether she was brave. Arnheim was spending two days in the mountains in the company of Diotima and several of her friends and had left him behind. The cook had twenty-four hours off, and Permanent Secretary Tuzzi was having his meals at a restaurant. Rachel had told Soliman about the cigarette stubs and ash that she had found in her room, and Diotima's unuttered question as to what the girl would think about it was answered by the girl's and Soliman's agreement in the surmise that something was going on in the Council that called for some increase of activity on their part too. When Soliman had asked if she was brave he went on to tell her he meant to steal from his master the documents proving his high birth. Rachel did not believe in the existence of this evidence, but all the entrancing complications round about had conjured up in her the irresistible desire to have something happen. They agreed that she should keep on her little white cap and frilled apron when Soliman called for her and took her to the hotel, so that it would look as if she had been sent on an errand by her employers.

And then, when they went out into the street, under the frilly lace-trimmed bodice of her apron such a smouldering heat rose in her breast that there was something like smoke before her eyes and she could not see. But Soliman boldly summoned a cab ; he had recently got into the way of having a great deal of money, since Arnheim was often very absent-minded. So now Rachel too plucked up courage and there, in broad daylight, stepped into the cab as though it were her function, her daily work, to go driving about town with a little Negro. The bright morning streets flashed past, full of those smartly-dressed idlers to whom the streets rightly belonged, while Rachel again felt her heart thumping as though she were committing a theft. She tried to lean back in the cab as correctly as she had observed Diotima doing ; but above and below, wherever she came into contact with the upholstery, a confused rocking movement broke upon her. The cab was a closed one, and Soliman took advantage of her attitude, as she leaned back, to press the broad ink-pads of his lips upon her mouth : it might be seen through the windows, but the cab was dashing along, and a sensation suggestive of the simmering of some aromatic fluid poured out of the billowing cushions into Rachel's back.

The black boy would not be deprived of the pleasure of driving up to the very door of the hotel. The men-servants with their black taffeta sleeves and green baize aprons grinned when Rachel got out of the cab, the porter peered through the glass door while Soliman paid, and Rachel felt as though the pavement were giving way under her feet. But then it seemed to her that Soliman must after all have great influence in the hotel, for nobody stopped them as they walked through the enormous pillared entrance-hall. There were some solitary gentlemen sitting about in armchairs, who followed Rachel with their eyes, and this once again overwhelmed her with shame. But then she was going up the stairs, and she soon became aware of the many chambermaids, dressed in black like herself, with white caps, only slightly less prettily ; and this made her feel somewhat as an explorer must feel when, wandering across an unknown and perhaps dangerous island, he encounters human beings for the first time.

After this Rachel for the first time in her life beheld apartments in a smart hotel. Before doing anything else Soliman locked all the doors ; then he felt himself in duty bound to kiss his little friend once again. These kisses, which had recently become customary between Rachel and Soliman, held something of the glow of children's kisses ; they were more like reassurances than like anything dangerous and weakening, and even now, when they were for the first time alone in a locked room, nothing seemed more urgent to Soliman than to shut this room up even more romantically. He pulled down the blinds and stopped up the keyholes to the corridor. And Rachel, for her part, was too excited by these preparations to think of anything but her own daring and the shame of possible discovery.

Then Soliman led her to Arnheim's cupboards and trunks, and all were open except one. It was therefore clear that only in this one could the secret be hidden. The black boy took the keys out of the trunks that were open and tried them. None of them turned the lock. All this time Soliman kept up a ceaseless chatter, pouring out his whole store of camels, princes, and mysterious messengers, and his defamations of Arnheim. He borrowed a hair-pin from Rachel and tried to pick the lock with it. When this turned out to be unavailing he tore all the keys out of the cupboards and chests, spread them out before him where he kneeled, crouched there thoughtfully gazing at them, and paused in order to reach some new decision.

" There, you see how he hides from me ! " he said to Rachel, rubbing his forehead. " But I may as well show you everything else first."

And so he simply spread out the bewildering riches out of Arnheim's trunks and cupboards before Rachel, who crouched on the floor, with her hands clamped between her knees, staring at all these things in eager curiosity. The intimate belongings of a man used to the greatest luxuries wealth could provide were something she had never seen before. Her own master was certainly not badly dressed, but he neither had the money to buy the most refined inventions of tailors and shirt-makers and manufacturers of all the luxurious objects used in the house and on travels, nor did he feel the need for them. Even her mistress had nothing to compare with the exquisite things, feminine in their delicacy and complicated in their use, that this immeasurably rich man possessed. Something of Rachel's former awed reverence for the Nabob awoke in her again, and Soliman was puffed up with pride in the overwhelming impression he created with his master's property, hauling everything out, showing how all the gadgets worked, and eagerly explaining all the mysteries. Rachel was beginning to grow tired when she was all at once struck by a strange realisation : she recollected distinctly that for some time now similar things had been making their appearance among Diotima's underclothing and personal possessions. They were not so numerous or so costly as these, but compared with the former monastic simplicity they were decidedly more akin to what she saw here than to what she had seen in the more severe past. At this moment Rachel was invaded by the outrageous conjecture that the relationship between her mistress and Arnheim might be less spiritual than she had supposed.

She turned red to the roots of her hair.

Her thoughts had never touched upon this territory since she had entered into service with Diotima. Her eyes had gulped down the splendour of her mistress's body like a powder in its paper, without her attaching to that any thoughts as to how this splendour might be turned to account. Her satisfaction at living in association with exalted beings had been so great that in all this time the so easily seducible Rachel had never thought of any man as something really of another sex, but only as being different in the romantic fashion of something in a novel. In this high-mindedness she had grown even more childlike, being transported back, as it were, into the period before puberty, the period when one is so all unselfishly aglow with admiration for the greatness and grandeur of others ; and this was the only explanation of the fact that Soliman's tall stories, at which a cook might laugh scornfully, in her case met with indulgence and enraptured weakness. But while Rachel now sat crouching on the floor, seeing the thought of an adulterous relationship between Arnheim and Diotima as it were exposed before her, the long impending change came about—an awakening out of an unnatural psychic state into the mistrustful carnal state of the world.

In a single flash she became wholly unromantic, somewhat cross, a stout-hearted body believing that even a servant-girl might come into her own some day. Beside her, Soliman squatted before his outspread bazaar, having collected together all that she had especially admired, and was trying to stuff into the pocket of her apron, by way of a present, everything that was not too big. Now he leapt up and swiftly set to work at the locked trunk again with a pocket-knife. Wildly he declared that before Arnheim returned he was going to draw a large sum of money out of the bank with his master's cheque-book—for in matters of money the crazy little devil had rather unchildlike ideas—and flee with Rachel ; but first of all he must get hold of his documents.

Rachel, who had been kneeling, stood up, resolutely emptied her pocket of all the presents he had stuffed into it, and said : " Stop chattering ! I must go. What's the time ? " Her voice had become deeper. She smoothed her apron and adjusted her cap.

Soliman at once felt that she was not going to play the game any more and that she was suddenly older than himself. But before he could object, Rachel was kissing him goodbye. Her lips did not tremble as they had before, but pressed themselves into the juicy fruit of his face, while she, the taller of the two, bent his head back, holding it tight so long that he was almost suffocated. Soliman struggled, and when she let him go he felt rather as if a stronger boy had been holding him under water, so that for the first instant all he wanted was vengeance for the violence done to him.

But Rachel had already slipped through the door, and though the glance that was all he sent in pursuit of her was, to begin with, angry as a fiery-tipped arrow, as it burned further it fell softly into ash. And Soliman gathered up his master's possessions from the floor in order to put them away again. He had become a young man who wished to gain something that was by no means unattainable.

105 *Being sublime lovers is no joke.*

DIRECTLY after the trip into the mountains Arnheim had gone abroad for longer than usual. This use of the expression ' gone abroad ', which he himself had involuntarily got into the habit of using, was odd, since properly speaking it ought to have been said that he had ' gone home '. For this reason, as for many others of the same kind, Arnheim felt that it was becoming urgently necessary to arrive at a decision. He was haunted by unpleasant daydreams such as his austere mind had never previously experienced. One was particularly persistent : he saw himself and Diotima standing on a high church-steeple, with the land spreading out green at their feet for a moment, and then they jumped off. To intrude by night, and devoid of all chivalry, into the Tuzzis' bedroom and shoot the Permanent Secretary obviously came to the same thing. He might also have vanquished him in a duel, but this seemed less natural : this fantasy was already loaded with too many of the attributes of reality, and the closer Arnheim came to reality, the more unpleasantly the inhibitions increased. Finally, one might, in a manner of speaking, also have approached Tuzzi with a frank request for his wife's hand. But what would Tuzzi say to that ? It would mean entering into a situation full of possibilities for making oneself ridiculous. And even assuming for the sake of argument that Tuzzi would behave decently and the scandal would be hushed up as far as possible—indeed even assuming there were no scandal at all, since at that time divorce was already beginning to be tolerated even in the best circles—the fact would remain that an old bachelor always made himself slightly ridiculous by a late marriage, rather like a married couple to whom yet another child is born at the time of their silver wedding.

And if Arnheim was really bent on doing something of this kind, then his responsibility towards the firm would at least have demanded that he should marry a rich American widow or a woman of old and noble family with connections at Court, and not the divorced wife of a middle-class civil servant. For him every act, including the sensual, was permeated with responsibility. In an age when there was as little responsibility for what one did or thought as in the present it was by no means merely personal ambition that raised such objections, but positively a suprapersonal urge to bring the power that had grown under the hands of the Arnheims (this organism that had grown up primarily out of a craving for money, but which now had long grown beyond that, having developed its own mind and its own will, and which had to enlarge itself and establish itself more firmly, which could fall ill, which would rust if it rested !) into harmony with the powers and hierarchies of life, a matter of which, so far as he knew, he had never made a secret even to Diotima. Of course, an Arnheim might permit himself to marry even a goose-girl if he wished ; but this he could permit himself only in a personal way, and above and beyond that it would still remain betrayal of a cause to a personal weakness.

It was nevertheless a fact that he had proposed marriage to Diotima. He had done so, if for no other reason, because he wanted to forestall the situations involved in adultery, which were not in harmony with a grand moral attitude to life. Diotima had pressed his hand gratefully and, with a smile reminiscent of the best models provided by art through the ages, replied to his offer in the following words : ' It is never those whom we embrace that we love most deeply. . . .'

After this answer, which was as equivocal as the seductive

yellow at the heart of the chaste lily, Arnheim had lacked the determination to renew his proposal. But in place of it there arose conversations of a general nature, in which the words ' divorce ', ' marriage ', ' adultery ' and others of the same kind showed a remarkable tendency to recur. So it was, for instance, that Arnheim and Diotima repeatedly had a profound discussion on the treatment of adultery in contemporary literature. It appeared to Diotima that this problem was always treated entirely without any sense of those great values, propriety, renunciation, and heroic self-denial, but merely from a sensual point of view, which was unfortunately the very same opinion that Arnheim held, so that all that was left to him was to add that appreciation of the deep moral mystery of the individual had today been almost universally lost. This mystery consisted in not indulging oneself in everything. Every age in which everything was permissible had made those living in it unhappy. Propriety, abstinence, chivalry, music, morality, poetry, the forms, the social veto, all this had no deeper purpose than that of giving life a restricted and definite shape. There was no such thing as boundless happiness. There was no great happiness without great prohibitions. Even in commerce one must not chase after every advantage, or else one would not get anywhere. Limitation was the secret of the phenomenal world, the secret of strength, of happiness, of faith and of the task of asserting oneself, a tiny being such as one was, in the cosmos. This was how Arnheim expounded it, and Diotima could not but agree with him.

It was in a certain sense a deplorable consequence of such understanding that it lent the concept of legitimacy an abundance of meaning that it no longer generally possesses for ordinary mortals. However, great souls have a yearning for legitimacy. In hours of exaltation one senses the perpendicular severity of the universe. And the merchant, though he rules the world, respects kingship, aristocracy and clergy as pillars of the irrational. For the legitimate thing is simple as everything great is simple, having no need of mere intellect. Homer was simple. Christ was simple. Time and again the great minds come back to simple principles, nay, one must have the courage to say, to moral commonplaces, and all in all, therefore, there is no one for whom it is so difficult to act against tradition as it is for truly free souls.

Such understanding, however much it may go to the heart of the matter, is not favourable to the intention of trespassing upon somebody else's marriage. So these two found themselves in the position of people who are linked by a splendid bridge in the middle of which there is a hole, merely a few yards wide, preventing their coming together. Arnheim regretted most fervently that he had no spark of that desire which is one and the same in all things and can sweep a man just as easily into an ill-considered business deal as into an ill-considered love-affair, and, regretting this as he did, he began to expatiate on the subject of desire. Desire was, according to him, precisely the feeling that went with the merely intellectual culture of our age. No other feeling was so unequivocally focused on its purpose as this. It struck fast like an arrow that had penetrated ; it did not swarm away into ever new distances like a flock of birds. It impoverished the soul, just as arithmetic and mechanics and brutality impoverished it. Thus did Arnheim speak disapprovingly of desire, while he felt it buffeting and racketing about in the dungeons below, like a blinded slave.

Diotima tried a different approach. She stretched out her hand to her friend and implored : " Let us be silent ! The word can accomplish great things, but there are things still greater ! The true truth between two people cannot be uttered. As soon as we speak, doors close. The word does better service to the unreal communications. One speaks in those hours when one does not live. . . ."

Arnheim concurred. " You are right. The self-confident word gives an arbitrary and poverty-stricken form to the invisible motions of our inner being."

" Do not speak ! " Diotima urged him once more, laying her hand on his arm. " I cannot help feeling that we bestow a moment of life upon each other by remaining silent."

After a while she withdrew her hand and said with a sigh :

" There are minutes when all the hidden jewels of the soul lie revealed ! "

" A time will perhaps come," Arnheim said, elaborating this, " and there are already many signs that it is near, when souls will behold each other without the mediation of the senses. The souls unite when the lips separate ! "

Diotima pursed her lips, so that they became suggestive of a little crooked tube such as a butterfly dips into the flowers. She was in a state of extreme spiritual intoxication. Slight delusions of reference are probably a property of love as of all states of exaltation. Everywhere that words fell a portentous significance lit up, stepped forward like a veiled deity and dissolved again into silence. Diotima knew this phenomenon from lofty hours of solitude, but never before had it been heightened to such a degree, to the limits of barely endurable happiness ; there was within her an anarchy of overflowing richness, an enhanced mobility of the divine that was as though on skates, and more than once it seemed to her as though she must the next moment fall down in a swoon.

Arnheim buoyed her up with great pronouncements. He created delays and breathing-spaces. Then once again the outspread net of great and significant thoughts dangled there below them.

The agonising thing about this outspread happiness was that it did not allow for any concentration. It was constantly radiating tremulous waves, which rippled out into circles but never pressed together to form a current of action. Nevertheless, Diotima had now got so far that at least in her own mind she had at times regarded it as sensitive and superior to prefer the dangers of adultery to the crude catastrophe of broken lives and smashed careers, and Arnheim had long come to the moral decision not to accept this sacrifice and to marry her. Hence in one way or the other they could take possession of each other at any moment, and they both knew it. What they did not know, however, was how they were to bring it about by an act of will, for happiness swept their souls—which were created for it—upward to such solemn heights that there they suffered from a fear of making any unlovely movement, a fear quite natural to people who have a cloud under their feet.

Their minds had never left unquaffed anything of all the grandeur and beauty that life poured out before them ; yet in their highest exaltation this state suffered some strange damage. The wishes and vanities that at other times filled their lives then lay far below them like little toy houses and farmyards in the valley, with all the cackling, barking and other excitements swallowed up in the stillness. What remained was silence, vacancy, and depth.

' Is it possible that we are elect beings ? ' Diotima wondered, gazing around her on this emotional pinnacle, with a foreboding of something agonising and unimaginable. It was not only that she herself had experienced lesser degrees of such states ; even an unreliable man like her cousin had something to say about them, and recently a great deal had been written on the subject. If the accounts could be trusted there were times, every thousand years or so, when the soul was nearer to an awakening than at other times, as it were being born into reality through the medium of certain individuals upon whom it imposed tests quite different from anything one could read or talk about. In this connection she suddenly recalled the mysterious arrival on the scene of the General who had not been invited. And in a low voice she said to her friend, who was groping for new words, while agitation flung a tremulous arc through the air between them :

" Intellect is not the only means of understanding between two people ! "

And Arnheim replied : " No." His gaze met hers as horizontally as a beam from the setting sun. " As you have said yourself, the true truth between two people cannot be uttered in words. Every effort is only an obstacle in its way."

106

Does modern man believe in God or in the head of the world concern? Arnheim's lack of resolution.

ARNHEIM was alone. He was standing thoughtfully at a window of his hotel apartment, looking down at the leafless tops of the trees whose branches interwove in a grille under which the people, bright or dark, formed the two moving, snaky lines, brushing against each other, of the *corso* that began at this time of day. The great man's lips were parted in an irritable smile.

Up to now he had never had any difficulty in defining what he considered soulless. What, nowadays, was not soulless ? It was easy enough to recognise the individual exceptions for what they were. Far back in his memory Arnheim heard the music of an evening's chamber-concert. Friends were staying with him at his castle in the Mark Brandenburg. The Prussian lime-trees cast their fragrance on the air. These friends were young musicians who were very hard up, and yet they sent their enthusiasm resounding out into the evening. There was soul in that. Or to take another case : a short time ago he had refused to continue paying an allowance that he had for a while made to a certain artist. He had expected that this artist would be angry with him and feel himself to have been left in the lurch before he had succeeded in making a reputation ; he would have to be told that there were other artists as well in need of support, or something similar, all of which would be unpleasant. But it turned out quite differently. This man, when Arnheim had seen him on his last visit home, had merely looked at him hard, shaken his hand, and declared : ' You have put me in a difficult situation, but I'm convinced that a man like you never does anything without pro- found reasons.' That showed a manly soul, and Arnheim was not disinclined to do something for this man again some time in the future.

So it can be seen that even today there is soul to be found in many individual cases. This had always seemed important to Arnheim. But soul, if one has to enter into direct and uncon- ditional association with it, constitutes a serious menace to sin- cerity. Was there really a time approaching when souls would commune with each other without the mediation of the senses ? Was there any aim—of the same value and importance as the realistic aims of life—in communing with each other in the way that some inner urge had recently been compelling him and this wonderful woman, his friend, to do ? He did not for an instant believe that it was so, when he thought about it soberly ; neverthe- less it was clear to him that he was encouraging Diotima to believe it.

Arnheim was in a peculiar state of dichotomy. Moral riches are closely related to material riches : that he was well aware of. And it is easy enough to see why it is so. For the soul replaces morality by logic ; if a soul has morality, there are actually no longer any moral problems for it, but only logical ones. The soul asks itself whether what it wants to do falls under this commandment or that, whether its intention is to be interpreted this way or that, and much more of the same kind, all of which is the same as when a crowd of people that has been wildly dashing along has gymnastic discipline imposed on it and, when the signal is given, swings to the right, extends arms, bends its knees. But logic presupposes the existence of experiences that can be repeated. It is clear that wherever events followed upon each other as in a vortex where nothing ever returns we could never formulate the profound discovery that A equals A or that the greater is not the lesser, but we should simply dream—a state that every thinker abhors. And so too the same applies to morality, and if there were nothing that could be repeated, then nothing could be demanded of us either, and without the privilege of making demands on human beings, morality would be no pleasure to anyone. This quality of repeatability, which is inherent in morality and intellect, is also inherent, and to the highest degree, in money. Money positively consists of this quality and, so long as it is constant in value, breaks down all the pleasures of the world into those little blocks of purchasing power by means of which one can build up whatever one likes. Money is therefore moral and reasonable ; and since, as is well known, the converse is not the case, i.e. not every moral and reasonable being has money, it may be concluded that these qualities originally lie with money, or at least that money is the crown of a moral and reasonable existence.

Now of course Arnheim did not think in precisely this way, thinking for instance that education and religion were the natural consequence of property, but he assumed that property created the obligation to have them. But he liked to stress the fact that the spiritual powers did not always understand enough about the active powers of life and could only rarely be acquitted of the charge of still having some traces of unworldliness, and he, the man with the large view, came to quite other conclusions above and beyond this. For every weighing up of things, every drawing up of an account of things, every sort of measuring, also presupposes that the object to be weighed or measured does not change during those mental operations ; and wherever this nevertheless happens, all one's acuteness of perception must be applied to the task of finding something immutable even in the mutation itself. Thus money is akin to all the powers of the mind, and it is on its pattern that the scientists and scholars split the world up into atoms, laws, hypotheses, and weird and wonderful mathematical symbols ; and out of these fictions the technicians build up a world of new objects. This was as familiar to this owner of a gigantic industry, well informed as he was concerning the nature of the forces in his service, as the moral concepts of the Bible are to an average German novel-reader.

Now, this need for the unequivocal, for the repeatable and the solid, which is the precondition of success in thinking and planning—so Arnheim reflected, gazing down at the street—in the spiritual field is always satisfied by means of a form of violence. Anyone who wants to build on rock in dealing with human beings must confine himself to making use of the lower qualities and passions, for only what is most intimately bound up with egoism has permanence and can be counted upon in all circumstances ; the higher intentions are unreliable, contradictory, and as changeable as the wind.

The man who knew that sooner or later empires would have to be governed in the same way that factories are run looked down on the swarming of uniforms, on haughty faces no bigger than nits, with a smile that was a blend of superiority and melancholy. There could be no doubt of it : if God were to return today in order to establish the Millennium among us, not a single practical and experienced man would have confidence in the enterprise unless the Last Judgment were supplemented by machinery for carrying out the sentences, with solid prisons, as well as police, gendarmerie, armed forces, a sedition act, government departments, and the rest of it, in order to restrict the incalculable capacities of the soul to the two basic facts that the future inhabitant of heaven can only be made to do what he is told either by intimidation and a tightening of the screws or by offering bribes to his desires, but in any case only by ' strong measures '.

But then Paul Arnheim would step forward and say to the Lord : ' Lord, to what end ? Egoism is the most reliable quality in human life. The politician, the soldier, and the king with its help have ordered Thy world by cunning force. That is the tune to which human life is lived. Thou and I must admit it. Abolishing compulsion would mean a weakening of order. Our first task is to make man capable of great things, although he is a mongrel cur.' And while speaking thus Arnheim would modestly smile up at the Lord, calm and composed, lest it be forgotten how important it still was for every man to acknowledge the great mysteries in all humility. And then he would continue his speech : ' But is not money a method of managing human relationships that is every bit as sure as physical force, and one that allows us to do without the crude application of the latter ? It is spiritualised force, a pliant, highly developed and creative form, a unique form, of force. Does not commerce rest on cunning and compulsion, on outwitting and exploiting the other ? But the difference is that here they are civilised, wholly transferred into man's psyche, and even, indeed, garbed in the guise of his liberty. Capitalism, as the organisation of egoism based on a hierarchy that develops from the capacity to get hold of money, is positively the greatest and at the same time also the most humane form of order that we have been able to develop to Thy Glory. Human action cannot provide any measurement more exact ! '

And Arnheim would advise the Lord to organise the Millennium on business principles and entrust the administration of it to a big business man, one, it went without saying, who must also have encyclopædic knowledge and a philosophic outlook. For, after all, religion pure and simple was something that had hitherto always got the worst of it, and compared to the insecurity of its existence in heroic ages, it too would receive great advantages from commercial management.

Thus Arnheim would have spoken, for a voice somewhere deep within him distinctly told him that one could no more do without money than without reason and morality.

But another voice, equally deep within him, told him equally distinctly that one ought audaciously to renounce reason, morality, and the whole of rationalised existence. And precisely in those dizzy moments when he felt no other urge than to plunge, a wandering satellite, into the blazing solar mass that was Diotima, this voice almost became the more powerful one. Then the way that thoughts went on growing seemed to him as strange and extraneous as the growing of nails and hair. A moral existence then appeared to him as something dead, and a hidden distaste for morality and order made him blush. Arnheim fared not otherwise than the whole age in which he lived. This age worshipped money, order, knowledge, calculating, measuring, and weighing —all in all, that is, the spirit of money and its kin—and at the same time deplored this. While in its working hours it hammered and reckoned, and outside them behaved like a horde of children who are driven from one extravagance to another by the pressure of ' Well, what shall we do now ? ', which at bottom has a bitter and disgusting taste, it could not help hearing an inner admonition to undergo a change of heart. This is dealt with by the principle of division of labour : for such premonitions and inner sorrow humanity has its special sort of intellectuals, those who make and those who hear the confessions of the age, jobbers in absolution, literary Lenten preachers and literary evangelists whom it is particularly important to have in the world if personally one cannot manage to carry out their principles ; and what constitutes pretty much the same sort of moral ransom-money is the phrase-making and funds that the State annually sinks in cultural schemes that have no solid basis.

This division of labour was also exemplified in Arnheim himself. Sitting in one of his directorial offices and checking sales figures, he would have been ashamed to think otherwise than commercially and technically ; but as soon as it was no longer the firm's money that was at stake, he would have been ashamed not to think the other way round and insist that mankind must be made capable of evolving upwards on some other way than the erroneous path of regularity, rules and regulations, norms, and the like, the results of which are so utterly lacking in inner meaning and are in the last resort inessential. There is no doubt of it that this other way is what is called religion. Arnheim had written books about it. In these books he had also called it myth, the return to simplicity, the realm of the soul, the spiritualisation of economics, the essence of action, and the like, for there were many sides to it ; or to be precise, there were exactly as many sides to it as he observed in himself when he was selflessly thinking about himself, as befits a man who sees great tasks confronting him. But clearly it was his destiny that this division of labour should collapse in the decisive hour. In the very moment when

he wanted to cast himself into the flame of his emotion or felt the
urge to be as great and integral as the heroic figures of mythical
times, as untrammelled as only the truly aristocratic man can be,
as unreservedly religious as love demands when its nature is
essentially comprehended—in the very moment, that is to say,
when he wanted to fling himself down at Diotima's feet reckless of
his beautifully creased trousers and, indeed, of his future—some
inner warning voice held him back. It was the voice of reason
awakening at the least propitious moment—or, as he said irritably
to himself, the voice of the hoarding and calculating instinct that
nowadays everywhere raised its ugly head against the grand conception of life, the mystery of feeling. He hated this voice, at the
same time knowing that it was not so very wrong. For assuming
it ever came to that honeymoon—what form would life with
Diotima take then after that honeymoon ? He would return to
his business and would deal with the rest of life's problems in
partnership with her. The year would be divided between
financial operations and recreation in the midst of Nature, in the
animal and vegetative part of one's own existence. A great,
truly humane marriage of action and repose, of the human needs
and the beauty of life, would perhaps be possible. That was very
good, that was doubtless what he vaguely had in mind as a goal.
According to Arnheim's views nobody had the energy for great
financial operations who did not know complete relaxation and
self-abandon, that undesirable state of seclusion, far from the
madding crowd, lying on the beaches of solitude, as it were clad
only in a loin-cloth ; but some wild mute state of contentment
raved in Arnheim, for all this was in contradiction to the sense of
the emotional alpha and omega that Diotima aroused in him.
Every day when he set eyes again on this classical beauty with the
slight rounding out of curves that was more pleasing to a modern
taste, he was plunged into bewilderment and felt his strength
melting away, felt his incapacity to absorb this poised and balanced
being, harmoniously moving in its own orbit, into his inner being.
That was anything but a loftily humane feeling ; it was hardly a
humane feeling at all. In this condition there lay the whole void
of eternity. He stared into the beauty of his beloved with a gaze
that seemed to have been seeking her for a thousand years, and
now, when it was as though it had discovered her, suddenly found

its occupation gone, and the result was an incapacity closely resembling stupor, an amazement that was almost imbecile. Emotion had by now ceased to respond to such excessive demand, which could in fact no longer be compared to anything but the wish to have the beloved and oneself together shot out of a cannon into interstellar space.

The ever-tactful Diotima had found the right words for this also. In one such moment she recollected that even in his day the great Dostoievsky had established the connection between love, imbecility and inner holiness ; but, for all that, people of today, who did not have his devout Russia at their backs, doubtless had need of a preliminary and special redemption if they were to put the idea into practice.

These words expressed what Arnheim felt at the bottom of his heart.

The moment when they were uttered was one of those moments full of supra-subjectivity and at the same time of supra-objectivity that are like a stopped-up trumpet on which one cannot blow a single sound, in that they send the blood into one's head. Nothing in that moment was unimportant, from the smallest cup on a shelf, Van-Goghishly asserting itself in the room, to the human bodies, which, at once swelled and pointed as they were by the Unutterable, seemed to be only squeezing themselves into this space.

Appalled, Diotima said : " Now I should like to be gay and jocular. Humour is such a wonderful thing. It floats free of all desires, high above the manifested world."

Arnheim smiled in response to this. He had stood up and begun to walk up and down the room. ' Suppose I were to tear her to pieces,' he wondered. ' Supposing I began to roar and dance. . . . Supposing I put my hand down my throat to tear out my heart for her. . . . Would then perhaps a miracle happen ? ' But as he cooled down he ceased to ask himself these things.

This scene had now vividly returned to his memory. His glance once more rested icily on the street below. ' It would truly need the miracle of some redemption first,' he thought. ' Another species of mankind would have to inhabit the earth before one could begin thinking of how such things could be put into practice.' He ceased to make the effort to puzzle out how redemption could be achieved, and from what ; all he knew was that everything needed to be different. He went back to his desk, which he had left half an hour earlier, back to his letters and telegrams, and rang for Soliman to tell his secretary to come.

And while he was waiting for his secretary's arrival and in his thoughts was already rounding out the first sentence of an economic statement he was about to dictate, this experience of his crystallised within him, taking on a beautiful and significant moral form.

'After all, a man conscious of his responsibilities,' Arnheim told himself with conviction, 'even when he gives of his soul, must expend only the interest, and never the capital!'

107 *Count Leinsdorf achieves an unexpected political success.*

WHEN His Highness spoke of a European family of nations that was to throng jubilantly round the aged Emperor and patriarch, he always tacitly excluded Prussia. Perhaps he now did this even more fervently than before, for Count Leinsdorf felt undeniably troubled by the impression that Herr Dr. Paul Arnheim was making; every time he went to see his dear friend Diotima, he came upon either the man himself or traces of him, and he did not know any more than Permanent Secretary Tuzzi what to make of it.

Now, as had never happened in earlier days, every time she gazed soulfully at him Diotima noticed the swollen veins on His Highness's hands and neck and the light tobacco-coloured skin from which there emanated the characteristic odour that old men have; and even though she took care to pay all due reverence to this great nobleman, something in the radiance of her favour had nevertheless undergone a change—a change as from summer sunlight to winter sunlight.

Count Leinsdorf was not given to fancifulness and had not much taste for music, but since he had had to put up with Herr Dr. Arnheim it happened curiously often that he had a faint ringing in his ears as of the kettle-drums and cymbals of an Austrian military march, or that when he closed his eyes he was disturbed by a billowing in the darkness, which came from black-and-yellow flags moving there in throngs. And such patriotic visions seemed also to come as visitations to yet other friends of the Tuzzi family. At least, though wherever he turned the talk he heard was full of deep respect for Germany, still, when he suggested that the great patriotic Campaign might perhaps in the course of events take on a little barbed tip directed against the brother-Empire, that deep respect was lit up by a cordial smile.

His Highness had here, within his own field, stumbled upon an important phenomenon. There are certain family feelings that are particularly intense, and one of them was the dislike of Germany that prevailed generally in the European family of nations before 1914. Perhaps Germany was the intellectually and spiritually least unified country, and hence a country that offered everyone something to suit his own dislikes ; it was the country whose old-time culture had been the first to fall under the wheels of the new era and be sliced up into high-flown phrases for the catch-penny purposes of commercialism : it was, further-more, aggressive, grasping, boastful and dangerously lacking, like every excited crowd, in responsibility for its actions. But all this was, after all, only European, and it should not have been anything but, at most, a little bit too European for all the other Europeans. What it comes to is simply that there must be entities, which one might call displeasure images, to which disgust and disharmony cling, as it were the residue of a smouldering fire such as life nowadays leaves behind. Out of the potentiality, the It-May-Be, suddenly, to the boundless amazement of all concerned, the actual thing, the It-Is, arises, and whatever chips off during this highly disorderly process, whatever does not fit, whatever is superfluous and does not satisfy the mind, seems to form that hatred, suspended in the atmosphere and setting up tremors among all living creatures, which is so characteristic of present-day civilisation, and which replaces a lost contentment with one's own doings by an easily attainable discontent with the doings of others. The attempt to concentrate this displeasure on specific entities is merely something that is part of the oldest psychotechnical apparatus mankind possesses. So it was that the magician drew forth the carefully prepared fetish from the sick man's body, and so it is that the good Christian projects his defects into the good Jew, asserting that it is *he* who has lured him into publicity stunts, usury, journalism, and the like more. In the course of the ages people have blamed thunder, witches, the socialists, the intellectuals, and the generals, and in the last years before the war, for special reasons that are of no account whatever in comparison with the importance of the principle itself, one of the most magnificent and popular means of satisfying this queer need was Prussian Germany. For the world has lost not only God but the Devil as well. Just as it projects the Evil into displeasure-images, it projects the Good into pleasure-images, wishful fantasies, day-dreams, which it reveres for doing what one finds it impossible to do in one's own person. One lets other people exert themselves while one sits there comfortably looking on : that is sport. One lets other people talk the most wildly one-sided extravagances : that is idealism. One shakes off the Evil, and what gets splashed with it is the images of one's displeasure. So everything gets its place in the world and fits into some hierarchy. But this technique of hagiolatry and fattening up of scapegoats by means of projections into the outer world is not without its dangers, for it fills the world with the tensions of all the inner conflicts that have not been fought out. Men slaughter each other or fraternise with each other, never rightly knowing whether they are doing it quite seriously, because, after all, one part of oneself is outside oneself and all that happens seems to go on half in front of reality, or half behind it, as a sort of sword-play in a mirror, a sham fight of hate and love. The ancient belief in dæmons, which held heavenly or hellish spirits responsible for all the good and evil that came one's way in life, worked much better, more accurately and neatly, and one can only hope that as developments in psychotechnics progress we shall get back to it again.

Kakania was a particularly, indeed an exceedingly, suitable country for intercourse with images of pleasure and displeasure ; life there had, in any case, a touch of unreality, and it was above all to the intellectually most refined Kakanians, who felt themselves to be the heirs and representatives of that renowned Kakanian culture leading from Beethoven to Viennese operetta, that it seemed entirely natural to be in fraternal alliance with the Germans of the Reich and at the same time not to be able to endure them. One was glad to see these Germans get a little rebuff here and there, and whenever one thought of their successes one always became a shade concerned about the state of affairs at home. This state of affairs at home, however, consisted in the main of the fact that Kakania, a State that had originally been as good as any and better than many others, had in the course of the centuries somewhat lost interest in itself. Since the Collateral Campaign had begun it had several times become noticeable that world history was a story made up in the same way as other stories : that is to say, the authors seldom had anything new to say and where complications of plot and ideas are concerned are much given to plagiarism. But this calls for something else as well, which has not yet been mentioned, and it is nothing other than the pleasure of story-telling ; it calls for that conviction, which comes so easily to an author, that his story is a good story, and for the passion of authorship, which, as it were, enlarges an author's ears and lends them a glow in which all criticism simply melts away.

Count Leinsdorf had this conviction and this passion, and it was also to be found even in his friendships ; but further away in Kakania it had been lost and people had for a long time been looking around for a substitute. There the story of Kakania had been replaced by that of the nation, a story on which the authors were still at work, and it was being treated quite in that European taste that finds its edification in historical novels and costume dramas. The result was the remarkable fact, which perhaps has not yet been properly appreciated, that people who had to settle some quite ordinary matter together, such as building a school or appointing a station-master, in doing so found themselves talking about the year 1600, or A.D. 400, and quarrelling about which candidate was the more suitable in the light of the colonisation of the Lower Alps in the period of the great migrations, as well as in the light of the battles fought during the Counter-Reformation, and tricked out these arguments with those notions of high-mindedness and rascality, of the homeland, loyalty and masculinity, that more or less correspond to the generally prevailing nature of people's reading. Count Leinsdorf, who attached no importance to literature, was ceaselessly amazed at this, all the more when he reflected how well off, at bottom, were all the peasants, artisans and townsfolk whom he happened to see on his journeys through the countryside of his Bohemian estates, which were populated by Germans and Czechs; and he therefore decided there was a special virus, some loathsome agitation, that caused them from time to time to break out into tempestuous discontent with each other and with the wisdom of the government, behaviour which seemed all the more incomprehensible in that in the long intervals between such feverish attacks, and whenever they did not happen to be reminded of their ideals, they got on peaceably and contentedly with everyone.

State policy in this matter, which is to say, that well-known Kakanian policy for dealing with national minorities, in the long run, however, amounted to this: that in approximately half-yearly alternations the government now took a punitive line against some rebellious minority, and now wisely gave ground before it, and just as in a U-tube the fluid rises on one side when it sinks on the other, so policy towards the German minority varied inversely. This minority played a very special part in Kakania, for the great mass of its representatives had always wanted only one thing, namely that the State should be strong. It had held on longest to the belief that there must after all be some sense in Kakanian history; and only gradually, as it came to understand that in Kakania one could begin as a traitor and end as a cabinet minister, but also, conversely, continue one's career as a minister by going in for high treason, did it too begin to feel itself an oppressed nationality. Perhaps similar things have happened in other countries too; but what was peculiar to Kakania was that *there* there was no need of anything in the way of revolutions and upheavals to produce all this, because as time went on everything began to happen according to the pattern of a natural, quietly pendulating development, simply by virtue of the vagueness of terms, and finally there was nothing left in Kakania but oppressed minorities and a supreme circle of persons who were the actual oppressors and who regarded themselves as being outrageously hoaxed and pestered by the oppressed. In this circle there was deep concern over the fact that nothing ever happened, so to speak, over a lack of history, and a firm conviction that some day at long last something must happen, something must be done. And if this were to turn against Germany, as seemed to be in the nature of the Collateral Campaign, that was not regarded as entirely unwelcome; first of all because one always felt somewhat put in the shade by one's brothers in the Reich and secondly because, feeling German as one did in ruling-class circles, one could find no better way of demonstrating Kakania's impartial role than in such an unselfish manner.

It was therefore completely understandable that in these circumstances nothing should be more remote from His Highness than the notion that his enterprise might be pan-Germanic. But that it passed for such was evident from the fact that the Slavonic groups were gradually beginning to disappear from among the 'officially classified minorities', whose wishes were to be dealt with by the various committees of the Collateral Campaign; and the foreign envoys after a while began to hear such dreadful stories about Arnheim, Permanent Secretary Tuzzi and a German plot against the whole Slavonic element, that something of it even came to His Highness's ears in the muted form of rumour, confirming his anxious awareness that even on days when nothing in particular was happening one was engaged in activity of a difficult nature because there was so much that one must not do. But since he was a practical politician he was not slow to make a counter-move, and in doing so, unfortunately, he made his calculations on such a magnificent scale that at first they took on the aspect of an error in the art of statesmanship. The thing was that the leadership of the propaganda committee—the committee, that is, whose function it was to make the Collateral Campaign *popular* in character—was still vacant, and Count Leinsdorf made up his mind that he would choose Baron Wisnieczky for this position; he especially based his considerations on the fact that Wisnieczky, who had been a cabinet minister some years previously, had been a member of a government that was brought down by the German nationalist parties and that he therefore enjoyed the reputation of having carried on an insidious anti-German policy.

For His Highness had a plan of his own. Right from the beginning of the Collateral Campaign it had been one of his ideas to win over precisely that section of Kakanians of German descent who felt less allegiance to their country than to the German nation. However much the other 'racial groups' might refer to Kakania as a prison, which indeed they did, and however they might give public expression to their love for France, Italy, or Russia, as the case might be, these were, so to speak, more remote enthusiasms, and no serious politician could make the mistake of putting them on one level with the enthusiasm certain Germans had for the German Empire, which held Kakania in a geographic stranglehold and until only one generation ago had formed a unity with it. It was to these German apostates, whose machinations evoked the most painful of all emotions in Count Leinsdorf because he was himself a German, that he had been referring when he uttered his celebrated dictum : 'They'll come of their own accord!' This dictum had meanwhile attained the status of a political prophecy, one in which much confidence was placed by the members of the patriotic Campaign, and its meaning was approximately that the 'other national groups in Austria' must be won over to patriotism, for only when one had been successful in this would all the German circles see themselves compelled to join in, since it is, of course, much more difficult to hold aloof from something that everyone else is doing than to refuse to be the first to begin. So the road to the Germans led first of all against the Germans and to favouritism towards the other nationalities. This was something that Count Leinsdorf had long recognised, and, what was more, when the decisive hour came, he acted on this recognition ; and it was precisely this that made him put His Excellency Baron Wisnieczky at the head of the propaganda committee, he being, in Leinsdorf's view, a Pole by birth but a Kakanian by conviction.

It would be difficult to decide whether His Highness was conscious that this choice was an affront to the German idea, something for which he was later reproached ; in any case it is probable that he must have assumed that in this way he was serving the true German idea. Only the consequence was that German circles too now instantly began intense activity against the Collateral Campaign, so that on the one side the Campaign in the end came to be regarded as an anti-German conspiracy and was publicly combated as such, whereas on the other side it had been considered pan-German from the very beginning, which was the reason why it had been avoided to the accompaniment of cautious excuses. This unexpected result did not escape His Highness, and in all quarters it aroused grave concern. However, Count Leinsdorf also found such tribulations extraordinarily bracing. When he was repeatedly asked about it in an anxious way both by Diotima and by other leaders of the Campaign, he turned to these faint-hearted ones a face that was impenetrable but full of devotion to duty, and made the following reply :

"This attempt of ours has not quite succeeded at the very beginning, but anyone who sets out to achieve great things must not let himself be dependent on the success of the moment. In any case, interest in the Collateral Campaign has risen, and if we only stand firm the rest will look after itself."

108 *The 'unredeemed' nationalities and General Stumm's thoughts about the semantic complex 'redemption'.*

HOWEVER many words are uttered at every moment in a big city in order to express its inhabitants' personal wishes, there is one that is never among them, the word ' redeem '. It seems fair to assume that all the others, the most passionate words and those used to express the most complicated relationships, even including those relationships clearly defined as exceptions, are being shouted or whispered by multitudes of voices all the time—for instance : ' You're the biggest crook I've ever come across ' or ' There is no other woman as heart-stirringly lovely as you '. These highly personal experiences could in fact be graphically represented by means of beautiful statistical curves showing their mass distribution throughout the whole city. But never does one living man say to another : ' You can redeem me ! ' or ' Be my redeemer ! ' One can tie him to a tree and leave him to starve ; one can maroon him on a desert island together with the woman he has been wooing in vain for months past ; one can make him forge cheques and then find someone who will save him : in any of these situations all the words in the world will pour forth from his mouth, but quite definitely so long as he is truly moved, he will not utter the words ' redeem ', ' redeemer ', or ' redemption ', although from the linguistic point of view there could be no objection to them at all.

And yet the peoples united under the Kakanian crown called themselves ' unredeemed nationalities '.

General Stumm von Bordwehr mused. By virtue of his position in the War Ministry he had ample knowledge of the difficulties, caused by its national minorities, that Kakania had to contend with ; for where the budget was concerned it was the army that first felt the effects of the wavering policy, influenced by hundreds of different kinds of considerations, that resulted from these difficulties. Only a short time ago the War Minister had been white with rage over the necessity of withdrawing an urgent financial bill, because an unredeemed nationality had demanded concessions in return for its vote in favour of granting the necessary funds, and these concessions the government could not possibly make without unduly stimulating other minorities' craving for redemption. So Kakania remained defenceless against the enemy without. For it had been a matter of heavy expenditure on the artillery, in order to replace the army's completely obsolete guns, whose range compared with that of other countries' guns as a knife compares with a spear, by new guns that were to compare with those of others as a spear compares with a knife, and now this had once again been prevented for an unconscionable time to come. It could not be asserted that General Stumm had on this account been in a suicidal frame of mind, but annoyances on a large scale may, after all, first manifest themselves in many apparently unconnected trivialities, and it was doubtless connected with this defencelessness, to which Kakania was condemned as a result of its insufferable inner strife, that Stumm began to think about redeeming and all that was unredeemed, all the more since in his semi-civilian capacity at Diotima's he had for some time been hearing the word ' redemption ' until he was sick and tired of it.

His first view was that it simply belonged to that group of words, on which linguistics have not yet cast adequate light, which we call ' high-falutin '. His natural soldierly common sense told him that it was so. But apart from the fact that this sense of his had been confused by Diotima (Stumm had, after all, heard the word 'redeeming' for the first time from her lips and had then been quite delighted, and even today, in spite of the artillery bill, when it came from her it was still wafted along with such a sweet enchanting fragrance that what has been called the General's first view was actually the second view he had had of it) the 'high-falutin' theory did not seem to meet the case for yet another reason: the individual members of the 'redemption' group of words only needed to be furnished with a pleasant little lack of gravity and they instantly came tripping off the tongue. 'You are positively my salvation, my redemption!' or something of the sort—which of us has not said that at some time, so long as it was led up to by nothing more than, say, ten minutes of impatient waiting or some other inconvenience of an equally trifling kind? And so it became clear to the General that it was not so much the words to which healthy instinct objected as the implausibility of the claim that what they referred to was serious. And indeed, when Stumm asked himself where, except at Diotima's and in politics, he had ever heard any talk of redemption or salvation, he realised that it had been in churches and cafés, in art journals, and in Herr Dr. Arnheim's books, which he had read with admiration. In this way it became obvious to him that what was expressed in such words was not a natural, simple, human happening, but something abstract, some general complication or other. To redeem or to yearn for redemption seemed from any point of view to be something that could only be done by one spirit in relation to another.

The General shook his head in amazement over the fascinating discoveries that he had made in the course of this special duty. He switched on the round red light over his office door to indicate that he was holding an important conference; and while outside the door his officers, with their despatch-cases under their arms, turned away, sighing, he went on with his speculations.

The people of intellect, whom he now encountered wherever he went, were not contented. They had some objection to make about everything; everywhere too little or too much was being done for their liking; things never seemed to be right in their eyes. Little by little he had become fed up with them. They resembled those unfortunate sensitive people who always manage to be sitting in a draught. They complained indignantly about excessive bookishness and about illiteracy, about coarseness on the one hand, and over-refinement on the other, about aggressiveness and about indifference; wherever their eyes turned, there was sure to be something too much or too little, some cleft gaping open! Their thoughts were never at peace, beholding that eternally wandering element, the final, undefined factor in all things, which never finds its proper place anywhere. And so they finally became convinced that the age in which they were living was fated to be one of spiritual barrenness and could only be redeemed from that condition by some remarkable happening or some quite remarkable person. This was how, among what were called intellectual people, there at that time arose the popularity of the semantic complex ' redemption '. There was a conviction that everything would come to a standstill if some Messiah did not come soon. This was, as the case might be, a medical Messiah, who would redeem the healing art from the academic researches that went on while people fell ill and died without getting help or, say, a poetic Messiah capable of writing a drama that would sweep millions of people into the theatres and yet at the same time be utterly original and unique in its spiritual sublimity. And apart from this conviction that every single human activity could in fact only be restored to its proper condition through the agency of a special Messiah, there was of course also the simple and in every respect wholesome desire for a strong-armed Messiah to deal with the situation as a whole. So that age just before the Great War was a rather Messianic age, and if even whole nations wanted to be redeemed, that did not really amount to anything special and unusual.

Admittedly it did seem to the General that this could not be taken any more literally than anything else that people went about saying. ' If the Redeemer were to return today,' he said to himself, ' they would bring His Government down just like any other.' Going by his own personal experience, he conjectured that it was all like this because people wrote too many books and articles for the newspapers. ' How wise it is,' he thought, ' to have an army regulation prohibiting officers from writing books without special permission.' He was slightly startled, not having felt such a violent wave of loyalty for a fairly long time. There was no doubt about it, he himself was doing too much thinking ! That came from being in contact with the civilian mind : the civilian mind had obviously lost the advantage of having a solidly established view of the world. This was something the General recognised quite clearly, as a result of which he now saw all this talk about redemption from yet another aspect.

General Stumm's mind strayed back to memories of divinity and history lessons long ago, in order to clear up this new problem. It would be hard to say what he was thinking, but if one could have lifted it bodily out of him and carefully ironed it out, it would probably have looked more or less as follows.

To begin briefly with the religious aspect : so long as one believed in religion one could throw a good Christian or a pious Jew down from any storey one liked in the edifice of hope or prosperity, and he always landed, so to speak, on his spiritual feet. That was because, in the interpretation of life that they gave mankind, all religions had included an irrational, incalculable final factor that they called the inscrutability of God ; if mortal man could not get things to work out right, he only needed to think of this final factor, and his spirit could rub its hands contentedly. This falling on one's feet and rubbing of one's hands is called ' knowing what one believes in ', and it is something that modern man has lost. He must either entirely give up the habit of thinking about his life, something in which many people indulge, or he gets into that strange state of conflict in which he has to think and yet apparently never can reach the point of satisfaction. This conflict has in the course of the ages just as often taken on the form of a complete scepticism as that of a renewed complete subjection to the faith ; and the form it most frequently takes on today is doubtless that of the conviction that without the spirit there can be no human life worthy of the name, but that with too much of the spirit there cannot be any, either. It is on this conviction that our civilisation is wholly based. It takes the greatest care to provide money for educational and research institutions, but never too much money, only such as is in appropriate subordinate proportion to the sums it expends on entertainment, motor-cars, and armaments. It everywhere opens the road to the able man, but it takes good care that he should also be an able man of business. It gives its recognition, after some resistance, to every idea, but this automatically works in such a way that the counter-idea also profits from it. All this looks like some tremendous weakness and carelessness ; but it is undoubtedly also a perfectly conscious effort to let the spirit know that the spirit is not everything ; for if it should ever happen, even once, that any one of the ideas that motivate our life were taken seriously— uncompromisingly seriously, so that nothing were left of the counter-idea—our civilisation could scarcely continue to be the sort of civilisation it is !

The General had podgy little babyish hands. He clenched one of them and brought it down on the top of his desk with a thump as with a padded glove, the sensation this gave him confirming his view that a strong hand was absolutely necessary. As an officer, he knew what he believed in all right. The irrational factor in it bore the names honour, discipline, Supreme Commander of the Forces, Service Regulations Part III, and, summarising all this, it consisted in the conviction that war was nothing but the continuation of peace by stronger measures, a forceful kind of order, and one without which the world could not survive. The gesture with which the General had thumped his desk would have been faintly ludicrous if a fist were something merely athletic and not also something mutinous, a sort of indispensable supplement to the mind. Stumm von Bordwehr had had almost all he could stomach of civilian life. He had discovered that the library attendants were the only people who had a sound general view of the civilian mind. He had hit upon the paradoxical element in excessive order, which was that its perfection inevitably brought inactivity in its train. He had a funny feeling almost amounting to an explanation of why it was in the army that the highest degree of order prevailed and together with it the readiness to lay down one's life. He had worked out that for some indefinable reason or other order created a need for bloodshed. Worried, he told himself that he must not go on working at this pressure !

'And what then *is* the spirit, anyway ? ' the General asked himself rebelliously. ' I mean, it doesn't walk at midnight, dressed up in a white shirt. So what else can it be but a certain order that we impose on our impressions and experiences ? But then,' he concluded resolutely, on a happy inspiration, ' if the spirit is nothing but ordered experience, in a properly ordered world there isn't any need of it !'

With a sigh of relief Stumm von Bordwehr switched off the ' in conference ' light outside his door, and went up to the looking-glass and smoothed his hair, in order to efface all signs of emotional stress before any of his subordinates came into the room.

109   *Bonadea, Kakania, systems of happi-ness and equipoise.*

IF there was anyone in Kakania who did not understand any-thing about politics and did not want to know anything about them either, it was Bonadea. And yet there was a connection between her and the unredeemed nations : Bonadea (not to be confused with Diotima—Bonadea, the Good Goddess, goddess of chastity, whose temple by a freak of fate became the scene of debauches, Bonadea, the wife of an eminent legal personage, a president of the *Landesgericht* or something of the sort, and the unhappy mistress of a man who was neither worthy of her nor sufficiently in need of her) had a system, and Kakanian politics had none.

Bonadea's system had hitherto consisted in leading a double life. Her ambition was satisfied by the fact that she belonged to a family circle that could be referred to as of high standing, and in her social intercourse too she had the satisfaction of passing for a highly cultivated and well-bred woman. But there were certain lures to which her spirit was exposed that she gave way to on the pretext that she was the victim of an over-stimulated constitution or, alternatively, that she had a heart that led her into committing follies ; for follies of the heart are honourable in much the same way as romantically political crimes, even if their accompanying circumstances are not always completely beyond reproach. In this the heart played the same role as honour, discipline, and Service Regulations Part III in the life of General Stumm, or as the irrational factor in every ordered attitude to life—this final factor that ultimately creates order in everything that the intellect cannot settle.

But there had been one fault in the working of this system : it divided Bonadea's life into two conditions, and the transition from one to the other was not made without heavy losses. For however eloquent the heart might be before one of her lapses, it was equally discouraged afterwards, and she whose heart it was was constantly being flung to and fro between a psychic state that was maniacally effervescent and one that drained away in inky blackness, two states between which there was rarely a middle state. Nevertheless, it was a system. That is to say, it was not a mere play of uncontrolled instincts, to be compared, for instance, with the way that people once used to see life as an automatic squaring of accounts between pleasure and pain, with a certain balance on the side of pleasure, but included a considerable number of intellectual arrangements for faking these accounts.

Every person has such a method of interpreting the accounts of his impressions in his own favour, so that the result is more or less the minimum daily allowance of pleasure necessary to support life in all ordinary circumstances. A person's pleasure, his enjoyment of life, may also, however, consist of pain and unpleasure ; such differences in kind are of no importance, for, as is well known, there are happy melancholics, just as there are funeral marches that float in their element as imponderably as a dance floats in its own. Probably the contrary can also be asserted, namely that many cheerful people are not an iota happier than sad ones, for happiness is every bit as much of a strain as unhappiness ; all this is more or less like flying on the principle of lighter or heavier than air. But there is another obvious objection. For would this not mean the rich were right with their age-old adage that no poor man need envy them, since it is only an illusion after all that their money would make him happier ? It would merely confront him with the task of elaborating another system of life instead of his own, and one the pleasure-economics of which could at best only leave him with the same small balance of happiness that he has anyway. Theoretically this means that the family without a roof over its head, if it has not frozen to death in an icy winter's night, will be just as happy, when it sees the first rays of the morning sun, as the rich man who has to get out of his warm bed ; and in practice what it comes to is that every person bears the burden with which he has been loaded as patiently as a donkey, for a donkey that is only just a little bit stronger than the weight of its burden demands of it is happy. And indeed this is the most reliable definition of personal happiness that one can arrive at, so long as one considers only a solitary donkey. But the fact is that personal happiness (or equipoise, contentment, or whatever one may call the automatic inner aim of the personality) is self-contained only in so far as a stone is in a wall or a drop of water is in a river, through which there flow the forces of tensions of the totality. What a person himself does and feels is of minor importance in comparison with everything that he must assume others do and feel, in relation to him, in an orderly and proper manner. No human being lives only in his own equipoise ; everyone supports himself on the equipoise of the strata surrounding him. And so the individual's little pleasure-factory is affected by a highly complicated sort of moral credit-system, something of which there will be more to say later, because it is no less essential to the psychic balance-sheet of the community as a whole than to that of the individual.

Since Bonadea's efforts to win her lover back had not been successful, and this made her believe that it was Diotima's intellect and energy that had robbed her of Ulrich, she was boundlessly jealous of this woman. But, as easily happens to weak personalities, in admiration for her rival she had found a certain explanation and compensation that partly reconciled her to her loss. She had been in this condition for some length of time now, and she had managed to be received by Diotima now and then on the pretext of some modest assistance to the work of the Collateral Campaign, without however being drawn into the circle that frequented the house ; and she imagined that there must be a certain understanding between Diotima and Ulrich on this point. So she suffered under the cruelty of the two of them, and since she was also in love, what came into existence in her was the illusion of some incomparable purity and selflessness of feeling. In the mornings, when her husband had left the house—a moment she looked forward to impatiently—she would very often sit down in front of the looking-glass, behaving like a bird preening its plumage. Then she would curl her hair with curling-tongs, and twist it and twine it until it took on a form somewhat resembling Diotima's Grecian knot. She combed and brushed and produced little curls, and even if the effect as a whole was a trifle absurd, she did not notice it, for what smiled back at her out of the glass was a face that in its general outline was now a remote reminder of the divinity.

The sureness and beauty of a being whom she admired, and that being's happiness, then rippled up in her, in the little, shallow, warm waves of a mysterious though not yet profoundly completed union ; and this was like sitting at the edge of a vast ocean, dabbling one's feet in the water.

This behaviour, comparable to an act of religious worship— for from the time when primitive man crept bodily into the masks of the gods down to the rites and ceremonies of civilisation this happiness of devout imitation, which can overpower the flesh, has never quite exhausted its significance—gained an additional hold on Bonadea because she loved clothes and externals with an intensity that was a sort of compulsion. This Bonadea, gazing at herself in the looking-glass, wearing a new dress, was quite incapable of imagining that a time might come when instead of leg-of-mutton sleeves, long, bell-shaped dresses, and a curl in the middle of the forehead, one would wear knee-length skirts and have one's hair cropped like a boy's. Nor would she have denied the possibility of it ; her brain was simply incapable of absorbing such a notion. She had always dressed the way a lady must dress, and every six months, when she contemplated the new fashions, felt a reverence as though face to face with eternity. Even if an appeal to her power of reasoning had forced her to admit the transience of these things, it would not in the least have diminished her reverence for them. She absorbed the tyranny of the world into her own being, undiluted, and the times when one turned down the corner of visiting-cards, or sent one's friends New-Year greetings, or took off one's gloves at a ball, lay as far behind, in the times when one did *not* do these things, as for other people the time a hundred years ago : that is to say, wholly in the realm of the unimaginable, impossible, and out-of-date. And this was why it was so comical to see Bonadea without clothes on ; she was then denuded of all ideal coverings too and was the naked victim of an inexorable compulsion that overwhelmed her with the non-human violence of an earthquake.

However, this periodic decline and fall of her civilised condition amid the upheavals of an insensate and oppressive world of matter had now ceased to occur, and since Bonadea had been devoting such mysterious care to her appearance she had been living—and this had not happened since her twentieth year—the illicit part of her life in the role of a widow. Experience shows that in general women who devote excessive care to their appearance are relatively virtuous, for the means then displace the aim ; it is just as with great sporting champions, who often make bad lovers, with all too martial-looking officers, who are bad soldiers, and with those particularly intellectual-looking masculine heads, which often turn out to be blockheads. But with Bonadea it was not merely a question of distribution of energy ; she had really begun to apply herself to her new life with a quite astonishing excess of self-abandonment. She pencilled her eyebrows with the loving care of a painter and slightly enamelled her forehead and cheeks, so that they were heightened out of their naturalism into that faint exaggeration, that remoteness from reality, which is peculiarly in the style of sacred art. The body was settled, quiveringly, into the pliant corset, and for the large breasts, which she had always felt to be somewhat in the way and humiliating because they had seemed to her all too feminine, she all at once felt a sisterly affection. Her husband was not a little surprised when, tickling her neck with his finger, he was told : ' Mind my hair ! ' or when, having asked : ' Aren't you going to give me your hand ? ', he got the answer : ' I can't possibly, I'm wearing my new dress.' But the power of sin had, as it were, slipped out of the bonds in which the body generally held it and was like a new-born star moving across the sky in the transfigured new world of a Bonadea who, in this unaccustomed and mildly diminished radiance, felt herself freed of her ' overstimulation ', as though the loathsome scales of leprosy had fallen from her. For the first time since they had been married her husband asked himself suspiciously whether there might be some third person troubling his domestic peace.

What had happened was however nothing but a phenomenon belonging to the sphere of systems of life. Clothes, if they are lifted out of the fluidity of the present and regarded, in their monstrous existence on a human figure, as forms *per se*, are strange tubes and excrescences, worthy of the company of such facial decorations as a ring through the nose or a disc extending the lip. But how enchanting they become when they are seen in combination with the qualities they bestow on their wearer! What happens then is nothing less than when some tangle of lines drawn on a piece of paper is suddenly infused with the meaning of some great word. Let us imagine that the invisible goodness and elect nature of a human being were suddenly to loom up behind his head as a halo floating golden as the yolk of an egg and big as the full moon (as one sees in pious old paintings), while he was taking his walk in the park or was just putting a sandwich on his plate at a tea-party : without a doubt it would be one of the most tremendous and shattering experiences possible. And such a power of making the invisible, and even, indeed, the non-existent, visible is what a well-made dress or coat demonstrates every day !

Such objects are like debtors who pay back the sums we lend them with fantastic interest ; and in fact there *are* only debtor-objects. This quality that clothes have is also possessed by convictions, prejudices, theories, hopes, belief in anything, thoughts ; indeed, even thoughtlessness possesses it, in so far as it is only by virtue of itself that it is penetrated with a sense of its own rightness. All of them, by endowing us with the properties that we lend them, serve the purpose of placing the world in a light that emanates from us, and fundamentally this, precisely this, is the task for which everyone has his own special system. By exercising great and manifold skill we manage to produce a dazzling deception by the aid of which we are capable of living alongside the most uncanny things and remaining perfectly calm about it, because we recognise these frozen grimaces of the universe as a table or a chair, a shout or an outstretched arm, a speed or a roast chicken. We are capable of living between one open chasm of the sky above our heads and one slightly camouflaged chasm of the sky beneath our feet, feeling ourselves as untroubled on the earth as in a room with the door locked. We know that life ebbs away both out into the inhuman distances of interstellar space and down into the inhuman construction of the atom-world ; but in between there is a stratum of forms that we treat as the things that make up the world, without letting ourselves be in the least disturbed by the fact that this signifies nothing but a preference given to the sense-data received from a certain middle distance. Such an attitude lies considerably below the potentiality of our intellect, but precisely this proves that our feelings play a large part in all this. And in fact the most important intellectual devices produced by mankind serve the preservation of a constant state of mind, and all the emotions, all the passions in the world are a mere nothing compared to the vast but utterly unconscious effort that mankind makes in order to maintain its exalted peace of mind. It seems to be hardly worth while to speak of it, so perfectly does it function. But if one looks into it more closely one sees that it is nevertheless an extremely artificial state of mind that enables man to walk upright between the circling constellations and permits him, in the midst of the almost infinite *terra incognita* of the world around him, to place his hand with dignity between the second and third buttons of his coat.

And in order to achieve this, not only does every man need his own artifices, the idiot every bit as much as the sage, but these personal systems of artifice are, furthermore, artfully built into the institutions for the maintenance of society's and the community's moral and intellectual equilibrium, which fulfil the same function on a larger scale. (This interlocking is like that of Nature itself, where the influence of all the universe's magnetic fields extends into the earth's magnetic field, though no one becomes aware of it, for the simple reason that this is why what happens on earth happens the way it does. And the intellectual relief that this brings about is so great that under undisturbed conditions the wisest of men, and for that matter ignorant little girls too, to themselves appear very clever and good.)

But from time to time, after there have been such states of contentment, which might in a certain sense also be called compulsive states of feeling and volition, the contrary seems to befall us, or, to resort once more to the terminology of the mental hospital, what then suddenly sets in on the earth is a tremendous flight of ideas, at the end of which the whole of human life is arranged round new centres and axes. The ultimate cause of all great revolutions, which lies deeper than the effective cause, is not in the accumulation of unwholesome conditions, but in the exhaustion of the cohesive factor that has enabled the souls to enjoy an artificial contentment. One cannot do better here than apply to this the saying of a celebrated early schoolman, which in Latin goes ' Credo ut intelligam ' and which may be somewhat freely translated into contemporary terms as : ' Lord, O my God, grant my spirit a production credit ! ' For every human creed is probably only a special case of the general principle of the credit-system. In love as in commerce, in science as in the long jump, one has to have faith before one can win, before one can reach one's aim, and it would be an odd thing if this were not true of life as a whole. However well-founded its order may be, it always includes a piece of voluntary belief in this order, indeed, this indicates, as though the thing were a plant, the place where growth began ; and once this belief, which cannot be accounted for and for which there can be no compensation, is exhausted, collapse soon follows : epochs and empires crumble just as commercial concerns do when they lose their credit.

And so this consideration of the principles of psychic equilibrium leads from the beautiful example of Bonadea to the melancholy one of Kakania.

For Kakania was the first country in this present stage of evolution from which God withdrew His credit, enjoyment of life, belief in itself, and the ability that all civilised nations have to spread around them the useful illusion that they have a mission. It was an intelligent country, and it sheltered within its frontiers a fair number of cultivated persons. Like all cultivated persons in all parts of the world these people dashed about in an unsettled state of mind amidst a tremendous upheaval of noise, speed, innovation, legal disputes and everything else that belongs to the optical and acoustic landscape of our lives ; like all other people they daily read and heard several dozen news-items that made their hair stand on end, and were prepared to become excited about them, indeed even to do something about them, but nothing ever came of it because some moments later the stimulus had already been displaced from the consciousness by other and more recent stimuli ; like all other people they felt themselves to be surrounded by murder, manslaughter, passion, self-sacrifice, and greatness, which came about somehow in the tangle that had formed around them, but they could not reach these adventures because they were held captive in an office or in some other professional institution, and when towards evening they were let out, the accumulated tension for which they had no more use exploded in the form of entertainment that did not entertain them. And there was one additional factor in the case of the cultivated persons, if they did not dedicate themselves to love as exclusively as Bonadea did : they no longer had the boon of credit and had not acquired the gift of deceit. They no longer knew what became of their smiling, their sighing, their thoughts. To what purpose had they been thinking ? Why had they smiled ? Their opinions were accidental, their likings had been there of old, somehow everything was there, floating in the air, ready-made, and one ran full tilt into it ; and they could not do anything, or leave anything undone, wholeheartedly, because they had no unifying law. So it was that the cultivated person was the man who felt that there was some debt steadily rising higher and higher and that he would never be able to pay it off; he was the man who saw the inevitable bankruptcy drawing nearer, and either inveighed against the age in which he was condemned to live, although he liked living in it just as much as anyone else, or flung himself, with the courage of one who has nothing to lose, upon every idea that held out a promise of change for him.

This of course was the same throughout the world. But when God withdrew His credit from Kakania, He did something special in that He made all its nationalities realise the difficulties of civilisation. There they had been sitting prettily like bacteria in their culture-medium, without worrying about whether the sky was as round overhead as it ought to be, or the like ; but all at once they began to feel they were in a tight place. Though man does not usually know it, he must believe he is something more in order to be capable of being what he is ; he must somehow have the sense of that something more above him and around him. But at times he may be suddenly deprived of it. Then he lacks something imaginary. Nothing whatsoever had happened in Kakania, and in earlier days one would have thought that this was simply the old, unobtrusive Kakanian way of life ; but now this lack was as distressing as not being able to sleep or not being able to understand. And so it was easy for the intellectuals, after they had persuaded themselves that it would all be different if each nation within the Empire had its own way of life, to convince the Kakanian national minorities of the same thing. This was, in fact, a sort of substitute for religion, or a substitute for the dear good Emperor in Vienna, or simply an explanation of the incomprehensible fact that there were seven days in the week. For there are many inexplicable things, but people cease to feel them when they sing their national anthem. Of course that would have been the moment when a good Kakanian could have replied to the question as to what he was with the enthusiastic answer : ' Nothing ! ' For this Nothing would, again, have meant something that could turn a Kakanian into anything of all that had never yet existed. But the Kakanians were not so defiant by temperament and contented themselves with half, each nationality merely doing its utmost to do what seemed to it good with the other. Naturally it was difficult, in a situation like this, to imagine pains one was not suffering oneself. And after two thousand years of education in altruism one has become so unselfish that even when things have to go badly with either you or me, one always gives the other preference. However, it would be wrong to form a picture of this notorious Kakanian nationalism as something particularly savage. It was more an historical than a real process. The people there rather liked each other. Admittedly they hit each other over the head and spat at each other, but this they did only because of higher cultural considerations, just as it also happens that, for instance, a man who would not hurt a fly, if he were alone and eye to eye with it, when he is seated under the image of the Crucified One in a court of law will condemn another man to death. And one is justified in saying that every time when their higher selves gave them a little respite the Kakanians sighed with relief and—good little tools as they were for eating and drinking, having been created to that end like all other human beings—were greatly amazed at their experiences as the tools of history.

110   *Moosbrugger's dissolution and preservation.*

MOOSBRUGGER was still in prison, waiting for the psychiatrists to come and examine him once more. It was a compact
quantity of days. The individual day did, of course, stand out
once it was there, but by evening it was already sinking back into
the crowd again. True, Moosbrugger encountered convicts,
warders, corridors, courtyards, a little patch of blue sky, a few
clouds that moved across that patch, as well as food and water,
and now and again someone in authority who was concerned
with his case ; but these impressions were too faint to assert
themselves permanently. He had neither a watch nor the sun to
go by, neither work nor time. He was always hungry. He was
always tired, from wandering around on his seven square yards,
something that makes a man more tired than wandering around
for miles. He was bored with everything he did, as though he
had had to stir a pot of glue. But when he thought back over
the whole thing, then it seemed to him as if day and night, a
meal-time and yet another meal-time, inspections and checkings,
one after the other, ceaselessly went whizzing past ; and he got
some amusement from that. The clock of his life had gone
wrong : it could be moved on or back. He liked that. It was
his sort of thing. Things that lay far back in the past and
things quite fresh and new were no longer kept artificially
apart ; but when it was all there at once, then what they called
' at different times ' was no longer entwined with it like a scarlet
thread that one has to tie round a twin baby's neck because
one can't tell one from the other. Everything non-essential
vanished out of his life. When he thought about this life of his,
he had long slow talks with himself in his own head, and as he
talked put the same weight on the short as on the long syllables ;
then life sang quite a different song from what a man heard every
day. Often he would linger over one word for a long while, and
when at last he moved on, leaving it, without quite knowing how,

after some time the word would all at once turn up somewhere else. He laughed with pleasure because no one knew what things came his way.

It is hard to find an expression for this unity of his being that he at times achieved. It is probably easy enough to imagine human life flowing along like a stream ; but the movement that Moosbrugger was aware of in his life was like a stream flowing through a large quiet lake. Flowing insistently onwards, it was also one with what was behind it, and the actual course of life almost disappeared in it all. He himself had once in a half-waking dream got the feeling from this that he had been wearing the Moosbrugger of his life like a threadbare coat on his back, and out of it now, when he sometimes opened it a little, the most weird and wonderful lining came gushing forth in silken waves as big as the dark woods.

He no longer cared what was going on there outside. Somewhere there was a war. Somewhere there was a big wedding. The King of Baluchistan's coming, he thought to himself. Everywhere there were the soldiers drilling, the tarts walking up and down their beat, the carpenters standing high up in the rafters. In the taverns in Stuttgart the beer came pouring out of the same sort of crooked yellow taps as in Belgrade. When you were on the road, there was everywhere the gendarme asking for your papers. Wherever you went, they stamped them. Everywhere either there were bugs or there were none. Everywhere either work or no work. The women were all the same. The doctors in the hospitals were all the same. When you were leaving your work in the evening, people were there in the streets, with nothing to do. It was always the same, everywhere. People never thought of anything new. When the first aeroplane had flown through the blue sky over Moosbrugger's head, that had been very nice. But then there was one aeroplane after another, and one looked just like the other. That was a different sort of sameness from the way the wonders of his thoughts were all the same. He could not make out how it came about, and wherever he had gone, it had always been there in his way. He shook his head.

' What a world ! ' he thought. ' To hell with it ! '

To hell with it, or to the hangman with him. . . . He didn't stand to lose much either way. . . .

And yet sometimes, as though absent-mindedly, he would go to the door and quietly fiddle about at the place where the lock was, on the other side. Then an eye would look in through the peep-hole from the corridor, and there would be an angry voice scolding him. From such affronts Moosbrugger quickly withdrew, back into the cell, and then it was that he felt himself imprisoned and deprived. Four walls and an iron door are nothing much if a man goes in and out. And there is nothing special about bars in front of an unfamiliar window, and if a bench or a wooden table is firmly fixed to the floor, that is only right and proper. But in the moment when a man can no longer deal with these things as he wants to, well, something happens that doesn't make sense at all. These things, made by human beings, servants, slaves, of which he doesn't even know what they look like, begin to get uppish. They pull him up short. When Moosbrugger noticed how the things were ordering him about he felt pretty much like smashing them up, and it was a struggle to convince himself that fighting with these servants of the law would be beneath his dignity. But the twitching in his hands was so violent that he began to be afraid that one of his ' turns ' was coming on.

Seven square yards of the whole wide world had been picked out, and on them Moosbrugger went to and fro. Incidentally, the way that sane people, not in prison, thought was very much like the way he thought. Although a short time earlier they had been greatly interested in him, they had quickly forgotten him. He had been fixed into his place like a nail that has been driven into the wall ; once it is in nobody notices it any more. Other Moosbruggers had their turn now. They were not himself, they were not even the same sort of people, but they fulfilled the same function. It had been a sexual crime, a sombre affair, a shocking murder, the act of a madman, the act of one who was only half responsible for his actions, an encounter such as really every person ought to be on his guard against, a satisfactory intervention on the part of the criminal investigation department and the law. . . . Such more or less meaningless generalisations, such flying-squads of *clichés*, rounded up the incident, which was now drained of life and interest, spinning it in, enwrapping it, at some place in their wide net. Moosbrugger's name was forgotten ; the details were forgotten. He was left to be ' a squirrel, a hare, or a fox '—the more precise distinction having lost its value; the public mind preserved no definite concept of him, only the dim, wide planes of overlapping general concepts, which were like the grey glimmer in a telescope that is wrongly focused.

This failure to correlate, the cruelty of a sort of thinking that juggles with the concepts that suit its purpose without bothering about the load of suffering and life that lends weight to every decision—this was something that the collective psyche had in common with Moosbrugger's. But what in his crazed brain was a dream, a fairy-tale—the damaged or queer spots in the mirror of the mind, which did not reflect the image of the world but let the light through—in the case of society as a whole was lacking; or at the most there was something of it present here and there in an individual and his obscure excitement.

And what had an exact bearing on Moosbrugger, on this particular Moosbrugger and none other, this one who was for the time being housed upon these particular seven square yards of the world, his food, surveillance, treatment according to official instructions, removal to a penitentiary life or to death—all this was deputed to a comparatively small group of people who had a completely different attitude. Here eyes peered suspiciously in the execution of their duty, and voices reprimanded for the slightest offence. Never did less than two warders come into his cell. Irons were put on him when he was taken through the corridors. This was all done under the influence of the fear and caution that were associated with the particular Moosbrugger in this small area, but which were somehow in queer contrast with the treatment he met with in general. He often complained about this display of caution. But then the warder, the governor, the doctor, the priest, whoever happened to be listening to his protests, looked at him blankly and told him that he was being treated according to regulations.

So regulations had now become a substitute for the interest the world had once taken in him, and Moosbrugger thought : ' You've got a long rope round your neck and can't see who's pulling on it.' He was roped, as it were round a corner, to the world that was outside. People, most of whom did not think about him at all, indeed did not even know anything about him, or to whom he meant no more than an ordinary hen in an ordinary village street means to a professor of zoology at the university, were at work together preparing the doom that, in a disembodied way, he could feel tugging at him. A young lady in an office was typing an addendum to his case. A registrar was classifying this according to an ingeniously thought-out filing-system. A *Ministerialrat* was drawing up the latest directive regarding the execution of the sentence. Some psychiatrists were engaged in controversy about the dividing-line between the purely psychopathic constitution found in certain forms of epilepsy and this condition as it occurred in other syndromes. Jurists wrote about the relation between the factors that would mitigate the guilt and the factors that would modify the sentence. A bishop made a public statement about the general decline of morality, and someone who owned a shoot complained to Bonadea's justice-dispensing husband about the excessive increase in the number of foxes, thus strengthening this eminent legal man's attitude in favour of the inflexibility of the principles of the law.

It is such impersonal items and events that go to make up personal events, in a way that for the present eludes description. And when Moosbrugger's case was shorn of all the individual romantic elements that concerned none but himself and the few human beings whom he had murdered, all that was left of it amounted to little more than approximately what could be gathered from the list of references to works cited that Ulrich's father had enclosed in a recent letter to his son. Such a list looked more or less like this : AH. — AMP. — AAC. — AKA. — AP. — ASZ. — BKL. — BGK. — BUD. — CN. — DTJ. — DJZ. — FBgM. — GA. — GS. — JKV. — KBSA. — MMW. — NG. — PNW. — R. — VSgm. — WMW. — ZGS. — ZMB. — ZP. — ZSS. Addickes *ibid*. — Aschaffenburg *ibid*. — Beling *ibid*. and so on. Or, translated into words : Annales d'Hygiène Publique et de Médecine légale, ed. Brouardel, Paris ; Annales Médico-Psychologiques, ed. Ritti . . . etc., etc. making a list a page long even when reduced to the briefest of abbreviations. What it comes to is that truth is not a crystal one can put in one's pocket, but an infinite fluid into which one falls headlong. One need only think of each of those abbreviations linked up with hundreds, or at least dozens, of printed pages, each page linked up with a man with ten fingers, a man who writes it, and for each of his fingers ten disciples and ten opponents, each disciple and each opponent also with ten fingers, and to each finger the tenth part of a personal idea, and one gets a faint picture of what truth is like. Without it not even the celebrated sparrow can fall from the house-top. Sun, wind, and food brought it there, and illness, hunger, cold, or a cat killed it; but none of this could have happened without biological, psychological, meteorological, physical, chemical, social and all the other laws, and it is really quite soothing to be merely in search of such laws instead of being, as is the case in morals and jurisprudence, oneself engaged in manufacturing them.

For the rest, so far as Moosbrugger himself was concerned, he had, as is already known, a great respect for knowledge, something of which he unfortunately possessed only such a small portion, but he would never have understood his situation completely even if he had known what it was. He had an obscure awareness of it. His condition seemed to him unstable. His huge and powerful body did not quite hold together. The open sky sometimes peered right into his skull . . . just as had often happened in the old days, when he was on the road. And never, even if now it was at times positively disagreeable to him, was he rid of a certain grave exaltation, which poured into him through the prison walls out of all the surrounding world.

So there he was, the wild, captive possibility of a dreaded deed, like an uninhabited coral island in the midst of an infinite ocean of scientific papers extending invisibly all around him.

111 *So far as jurists are concerned, there are no semi-insane people.*

STILL, a criminal often has a very easy time of it in comparison with the strenuous intellectual work in which he obliges academic lawyers and other learned persons to engage. The offender

simply takes advantage of the fact that in Nature the transitions
from mental health to mental disease are smooth and imper-
ceptible. The jurist, however, in such a case has to assert that
'the arguments *pro* and *contra* the existence of the individual's
capacity to exert his will, or of an awareness of the criminal
nature of the act, cut across each other and cancel each other out
to such an extent that the verdict arrived at on any system of
reasoning must inevitably be problematic'. For there are logical
reasons why a jurist must bear in mind that 'in discussing one
and the same act no possibility can be admitted of there being
any mingling of two states', and he will not permit 'the principle
of moral freedom in relation to physically conditioned states of
mind to be lost in a vague mist of empirical thought'. He does
not go to Nature for his concepts; what he does is to penetrate
into Nature with the flame of intellect and the sword of the moral
law. And in this connection a controversy had broken out in the
committee set up by the Ministry of Justice for the purpose of
bringing the criminal code up to date, a committee of which
Ulrich's father was a member.

However, it had taken some time, and some admonitions
urging him to fulfil his filial duty, to get Ulrich to the point where
he made a proper study of his father's representation of the problem and all the supplementary material.

His 'affectionate father'—for that was how he signed even the
bitterest of his letters—had made the assertion, which was likewise a demand, that a partially insane person should be acquitted
only if it could be established in evidence that among that person's delusions there were some of such a nature that, if they had
not been delusions, they would have justified the act or cancelled
the liability to punishment.

Professor Schwung, on the other hand—perhaps because he
had been the old man's friend and colleague for forty years, which
must, after all, lead to a violent difference of opinion sooner or
later—had made the assertion, which was likewise a demand, that
such an individual, in whom the state of being responsible for his
actions and the state of not being responsible for his actions, since
from a juristic point of view they could not exist side by side,
could only alternate with great rapidity, was to be acquitted only
if and when it could be proved in evidence with relation to the

particular act of volition under discussion that in precisely the moment when that act of volition took place it had been impossible for the offender to control it.

That was the point of departure. For a layman it is not difficult to see that it may be no less difficult for the criminal not to over-look any moment of sane volition in the instant when he performs the act than not to overlook any notion that might constitute his liability to a penalty. But it is after all not the function of aca-demic jurisprudence to make people's thinking and moral behaviour a bed of roses ! And because both these learned jurists were equally convinced of the dignity of the law and neither could win the majority of the committee over to his side, they charged each other first of all with error, and then in swift succession with a lack of logic, deliberate misunderstanding, and a lack of high ideals. They did this at first within the bosom of the irresolute committee. Later, however, when committee meetings began to be very sticky, then had to be adjourned, and finally had to be suspended for long periods, Ulrich's father wrote two pamphlets, ' Penal Code Paragraph 318 and the True Spirit of the Law ' and ' Penal Code Paragraph 318 and the Polluted Well-Springs of Jurisprudence ', and Professor Schwung re-viewed them in the journal, ' The Academic Legal World ', which Ulrich found included among the papers his father had sent him.

In these pamphlets there occurred a great deal of And and Or, for it was necessary to ' clear up ' the question whether the two views could be combined by an And or must be separated by an Or. And by the time the committee reassembled after a long interval, it too had split into an And and an Or party. Apart from this, however, there was also a party that supported the plain proposal to make the degree of soundness of mind and respon-sibility for actions rise and fall proportionately with the rising and falling of intensity of effort in terms of psychic energy that would suffice, in the given pathological circumstances, to maintain self-control. This party was opposed by a fourth, which insisted that before all else there must be a clear and definite decision as to whether a criminal could be said to be responsible for his actions at all ; for diminution of responsibility for one's actions logically presupposed the existence of responsibility for one's actions, and if the criminal was in part responsible for his actions, then he must suffer the penalty with his entire person because this part was not otherwise accessible in terms of criminal law. This party met with opposition from yet another, which, while granting the principle, pointed out, however, that Nature, which produced semi-insane persons, did not keep to it ; for which reason those persons could enjoy the benefits of the law only in the form that although there could be no mitigation of their guilt, in view of the circumstances there should be some modification of their punishment. So there were also formed a ' soundness of mind ' party, and a ' responsibility ' party, and only when these too had split up into enough fractional parties were the issues revealed on which there had not yet been any difference of opinion.

No professional man today, of course, bases his arguments on the arguments of philosophy and theology ; but as perspectives—that is to say, something as empty as space and yet, like space, telescoping the objects in it—these two rivals on the quest for ultimate wisdom do everywhere keep on invading the optics of each special subject. And so in this matter too the carefully avoided question whether it was justifiable to regard every human being as morally free—in other words, the good old question about the freedom of the will—constituted a perspectival centre of all the various differences of opinion, although it was outside the sphere of what they were concerned with. For if man is morally free, he must in practice be subjected, by means of penalties, to a compulsion in which, theoretically, no one believes ; if, on the contrary, he is regarded as not being free, but as the meeting-place for irrevocably linked natural processes, then, though one may cause him effective discomfort by means of penalties, one cannot consider him morally accountable for what he does. On this question there arose, therefore, yet another party, which proposed to divide the criminal into two parts : one zoological and psychological part, which did not concern the judge, and one juridical part, which, although it was only a fiction, was in a legal sense free. Fortunately this proposal remained confined to theory.

It is difficult to do justice to justice in brief. The commission consisted of about twenty academic lawyers, who were capable of adopting several thousand points of view towards each other, as can easily be worked out by simple arithmetic. The laws that were to be revived had been in operation since 1852, which meant that there was an additional complication in the fact that the matter to be dealt with was of long standing and therefore was not lightly to be replaced by another. And of course, in any case, the static institution of the law cannot follow all the intellectual jumps of whatever happens to be the prevailing fashion in thought —as one member of the commission rightly pointed out. The need for approaching the problem in this conscientious way is best seen from the fact that according to statistics about seventy per cent. of all persons who injure us by committing crimes are quite certain to slip through the meshes of the law; so it is obvious that all the closer attention must be paid to the percentage that *is* caught. Of course all this may have become a little better since that time. In any case, it would be wrong to think the real purpose of our description of the affair is to mock the icicles and ice-ferns that intellect caused to proliferate in the heads of these learned men of the law, something that has always been a source of great amusement to many people whose intellectual climate tends more to produce slush. On the contrary, let it be pointed out that it was masculine severity, arrogance, moral soundness, unassailability, and complacency, that is to say, all qualities of mind and heart and to a great extent virtues that it is to be hoped (as the expression goes) we shall never lose, which prevented the learned members of the commission from making unprejudiced use of their intelligence. They treated the boy, Man, as though they were elderly schoolmasters and he were a pupil entrusted to their care, one who only needed to be attentive and willing in order to ' make good progress ' ; and what this aroused was nothing other than the pre-1848 political emotions of the generation before their own. Admittedly the psychological knowledge these jurists had was about fifty years out of date ; but that sort of thing tends to happen when one has to work a part of one's own field of knowledge with one's neighbour's tools, and as soon as circumstances are favourable the deficiency is quickly made good. All the same, there is something that remains permanently behind the times, because it does somewhat plume itself on its permanence ; this is the heart of man, and, what is more, especially of the man who is thorough. Never is the

ntellect so dry, hard, and intricately twisted as when it has a
ittle weakness, an old weakness, of the heart !

This weakness ultimately led to a furious outburst. When
he battles had sufficiently weakened all those concerned and prevented any progress being made with the work, more and more
voices were raised suggesting a compromise, which was to look
pretty much as all formulas look that are devised to glue up an
unbridgeable gap with fair words. There was a certain inclination
to agree on that well-known definition according to which those
criminals are termed ' of sound mind ' whose intellectual and
moral qualities do in fact make them capable of committing a
crime, and not, in any circumstances, those *without* those qualities.
And this is an extraordinary definition, having the advantage that
it makes it very difficult to qualify as a criminal and would positively entitle such persons to combine the right to wear a convict's uniform with the sporting of an academic degree.

But at this point Ulrich's father, envisaging the imminent
balminess of the Jubilee Year and also envisaging a definition that
was as round as an egg, so that he took it for a hand-grenade that
had been flung at him, underwent what he called his sensational
conversion to the social school of thought. The social view tells
us that the criminally ' degenerate ' person cannot at all be considered from a moral aspect, but only according to the degree in
which he is dangerous to society as a whole. What follows from
this is that the more dangerous he is the more he is responsible for
his actions. And what follows again from this, with compelling
logic, is that the criminals who are apparently least guilty, that is
to say, those who are insane or of defective mentality, who by
virtue of their nature are least susceptible to the corrective
influence of punishment, must be threatened with the harshest
penalties and in any case with harsher penalties than sane persons, in order that the deterrent force of the punishment may be
equal for all.

It could reasonably be expected that Professor Schwung would
now in vain search far and wide for an objection to this social
view. And so indeed it seemed to be. But for this very reason
he resorted to methods that were the immediate occasion of
Ulrich's father's also, for his own part, leaving the path of jurisprudence, which looked like petering out in further deserts of

controversy within the committee, and appealing to his son now to turn to account, to the behoof of the good cause, those connections with highly placed—and indeed also with the most highly placed—circles which he had procured for him. For what his colleague Schwung had done was this : instead of making any attempt at a sober and scholarly refutation he had at once maliciously seized on the word ' social ' and, in a newly published attack, insinuated that it was ' materialistic ' and infected with ' the Prussian idea of the State '.

' My dear son,' Ulrich's father wrote, ' I did of course immediately point out the Roman antecedents of the ideas held by the social school of juristic thought, thus making it clear that they are anything but Prussian in origin, but this may well turn out to be futile as a means of dealing with this denunciation and defamation, which is aimed, in a diabolically venomous way, at creating the repellent impression which it is bound to create in *high quarters*, an impression only too easily created by the thought of materialism, as indeed by that of Prussia. These are reproaches against which it ceases to be possible to defend oneself. Here is, on the contrary, the dissemination of a rumour so indefinable that in *high quarters* it will receive practically no examination, and the necessity of having to pay any attention whatsoever to it is likely to bring the innocent victim into no less disrepute than the unscrupulous author of the denunciation. I, who have all my life long scorned to make use of backstairs methods, therefore see myself compelled to request you . . . ' And so on, and so on, the letter continued to its end.

112

Arnheim sets his father Samuel among the gods and forms the resolution to secure Ulrich for himself. Soliman wants to learn more about his royal father.

ARNHEIM had rung and sent for Soliman. It was a long time since he had felt the urge to talk to him, and now the young imp had gone off and was wandering about somewhere in the hotel.

Ulrich, in his antagonism, had at last succeeded in touching Arnheim to the quick.

Of course it had never escaped Arnheim that Ulrich was working against him. Ulrich did not do it deliberately. It was simply that he exerted an influence such as water does on fire, as salt does on water ; he was endeavouring, almost without his own will, to cancel out any influence Arnheim might have. Arnheim was sure that Ulrich abused even Diotima's confidence, in order to make unfavourable or scornful remarks about him in private.

Arnheim admitted to himself that nothing of this sort had happened to him for a long time. The usual methods by which he achieved success were of no avail here. For the effect a great and integral man has is like the effect of beauty : it can no more stand up to a denial of its existence than a balloon can stand up to having holes drilled into it or a statue to having a hat put on its head. A beautiful woman becomes plain as soon as she fails to please, and although a great man, if no notice is taken of him, may become something greater still, he nevertheless ceases to be a great man. Not that Arnheim confessed as much to himself in these words, but he did think : ' I cannot endure contradiction, because it is only the intellect that thrives on contradiction, and I despise anyone who possesses only intellect ! '

Arnheim assumed that it would not be difficult for him, by some means or other, to render his opponent harmless. But he wanted to win Ulrich over ; he wanted to influence him, educate him, and compel his admiration. In order to make this easier for himself, he had persuaded himself that he liked Ulrich, that he had a profound and paradoxical affection for him ; yet he would not have been able to give any reasons for it. He had nothing to fear from Ulrich and nothing to expect from him. Arnheim knew perfectly well that he had no friend in either Count Leinsdorf or Permanent Secretary Tuzzi, and for the rest things were going, even though rather slowly, the way he wished them to go. Ulrich's counter-influence paled before the influence Arnheim exerted, remaining an, as it were, unearthly protest ; the only thing it seemed to be able to do lay perhaps in postponing Diotima's decision, by having a faintly paralysing effect on that wonderful woman's resolution. Arnheim had cautiously analysed this and now could not help smiling at the thought of it. Mournfully, was it, or maliciously ? Such distinctions, in cases of this kind, amount to very little. He considered it only fair that his opponent's rational, critical mind and antagonistic attitude should, without knowing it, have to work in his service ; this was a victory of the profounder cause, one of the wonderfully clear, self-disentangling complications in life. Arnheim felt this was the noose of destiny that bound him together with the younger man and lured him into making concessions that the other did not understand. For Ulrich was not open to any wooing ; he was as insensitive as an imbecile to social advantage and seemed either not to notice or not to appreciate the offer of friendship.

There was something that Arnheim called Ulrich's wit. What he meant by this was, among other things, this inability, on the part of a man who had ' a first-class mind ', to recognise the advantages life offered and to adjust that mind to the great objects and opportunities that would be able to bestow dignity and stability on him. Ulrich showed that he held the ridiculous contrary view that life must adapt itself to the mind. Arnheim saw him in his mind's eye : as tall as himself, younger, without the traces of flabbiness that he could not fail to notice in his own body, and with something uncompromisingly independent in the face. This last he attributed, not quite without envy, to Ulrich's being the descendant of generations of ascetic-living scholars (for that was how he pictured Ulrich's origins). Here was a face that looked more careless of all considerations of money and appearances than a flourishing dynasty of specialists in refuse-refinement had enabled their descendant to be ! Yet there was something missing in this face. It was life that was missing : the marks of life itself were terrifyingly missing !

In the moment when Arnheim saw this, in a flash of extreme clarity, it was so disturbing that it made him realise once more how greatly he was taken with Ulrich. It was a face of which one might almost have predicted some great misfortune. He mused on the conflicting sensation of envy and anxiety this caused him ; here was a mournful satisfaction, such as may be felt by someone who escaped into safety, but through cowardice. And suddenly a violent upsurge of envy and disapproval flung up the thought that he had unconsciously been at once seeking and avoiding : it flashed upon him that Ulrich was doubtless a man who would expend not only the interest but the entire capital of his soul if circumstances required it of him.

Yes, this was, oddly enough, also part of what Arnheim meant by Ulrich's wit. At this moment, recalling the expression he had himself coined, it became completely clear to him : the notion that a man might let himself be swept away by passion, as it were beyond the limits of the atmosphere in which a human being could breathe, struck him as a sort of joke.

When Soliman sidled into the room and came to stand before his master, Arnheim had almost quite forgotten why he had sent for him ; yet he felt the soothing effect of having a living and devoted creature there with him. With an air of grave reserve Arnheim paced up and down the room, and the black disc of the boy's face turned this way and that, following him.

" Sit down," Arnheim commanded, and, turning on his heel in the corner he had just reached, he remained standing there, and began : " There is a passage in *Wilhelm Meister* where the great Goethe with a certain passionate intensity utters a maxim for right living, which is : ' Think in order to act, act in order to think ! ' Do you understand that ? No," he said, " I suppose you can't really understand it . . . " And having answered his own question he relapsed into silence.

' It is a prescription that contains all the wisdom life can give,' he thought. ' And the man who would like to be my enemy is acquainted with only half of it, with *thinking*.' It occurred to him that this too might be part of what he meant by being ' merely witty '. He recognised Ulrich's weakness. Wit came from witting, knowing, and here was a piece of wisdom on the part of language, for it revealed the intellectual origins of this quality, and how spectral it was, how poor in feeling. The witty man is always inclined to live, as it were, by his wits, overriding the ordained frontiers where the man of true feeling calls a halt. And with this realisation the matter of Diotima and the entirety of the soul's capital was all at once seen under a more pleasing aspect.

Thinking thus, Arnheim said aloud to Soliman : " It is a maxim that contains all the wisdom life can give, and it was following this maxim that I decided to make you go without books and set you to work."

Soliman did not answer. He adopted a profoundly solemn expression.

" You have seen my father several times," Arnheim said suddenly, and asked : " Do you remember him ? "

Soliman thought it suitable to roll his eyes, showing the whites.

And Arnheim went on, musingly : " You see, my father practically never reads books. How old do you think my father is ? " But once again he did not wait for an answer, and himself added : " He is over seventy now, and still has his fingers on the strings wherever there is anything going on that is of interest to our firm."

Once more Arnheim paced up and down in silence. He suddenly felt an irresistible desire to talk about his father, but he could not say all he meant. Nobody knew better than he that deals sometimes went wrong even when his father was conducting them ; but nobody would have believed that if he had told them, for as soon as someone has the reputation of being a Napoleon, he wins even his lost battles. So for Arnheim there had never been any other chance of asserting himself alongside his father, than the one he had chosen, that of putting culture, politics, and society into the service of business. It seemed to please old Arnheim, too, that the younger Arnheim knew so much and was so accomplished. But when there was an important question to be decided, and it had been discussed and analysed for days on end from the point of view of the technique of production and of finance, of economics and of its bearing on civilisation, the old man would express his gratitude, would not infrequently give orders for the opposite of what had been proposed, and would answer all the objections and protests anyone made only with a helpless, stubborn smile. Often, indeed, even the directors shook their heads over this way of his, but sooner or later it would always turn out that the old man had been right, in one way or another. It was rather as though an old huntsman or alpine guide had had to sit listening to a meteorologists' conference, and in the end, of course, had decided according to the prophetic twinges his rheumatism caused him ; and at bottom this was not at all surprising, either, for there are many problems in which rheumatism is a much surer guide than science, and anyway it is not exclusively the exactness of the forecast that matters, because after all things always turn out differently from the way one expects anyway, and the main thing is to be cunning and tough in adjusting oneself to their waywardness. So it should not really have been difficult for Arnheim to understand that an old hand at the game knows and can do a great deal that cannot be forecast by theoretical means ; and yet it was a fateful day for him when he discovered that old Samuel Arnheim had intuition.

" Do you know what intuition is ? " Arnheim asked, still lost in his thoughts, as though he were groping after some shadow of an excuse for his desire to speak of it.

Soliman blinked hard, as he always did when he was cross-examined about something he had been told to do and had forgotten.

And once again Arnheim swiftly corrected himself. " My nerves are on edge today," he said. " Of course you can't possibly know. But pay attention to what I am now going to tell you. Making money, as you can imagine, often gets us into situations that are not quite in good style. This perpetual effort to keep on working out sums, and to extract some profit out of everything, is in contradiction to the shape of greatness in which life can be moulded, and has been moulded in more fortunate epochs. Mankind has contrived to extract from murder the aristocratic virtue of courage, but to me it seems questionable whether anything similar can be successfully done with mere figures. There is no real goodness of heart in figures—no dignity, no depth of character. Money turns everything into a mere concept. It is unpleasantly rational. Whenever I see money, I never can help thinking—whether you understand this or not—of fingers testing it mistrustfully, a great deal of clamour, and a great deal of mere brain-work, and they are all images that are equally abhorrent to me."

He broke off and sank back again into his solitude. He remembered how when he was a child his relations had patted him on the head, saying that he had a good little head on his shoulders. A good little head for figures. How he hated that attitude! What was reflected in the bright gold pieces was the rational outlook of a family that had worked its way up in the world! He would have scorned to feel ashamed of his family; on the contrary, it was above all in the highest circles that he insisted on speaking, modestly and with dignity, of his origins. But the rational outlook his family had was something he dreaded as though, like all-too-lively talking and fluttering gestures of the hands, it were a family weakness that made him 'impossible' on the loftiest heights mankind could attain.

Here probably was the origin of his veneration for the irrational. Aristocracy was irrational : that came very near to sounding like a joke about the nobility not being very bright, but Arnheim knew what he meant by it. He only needed to remember how, since as a Jew he had not been able to become an officer of the reserve and since, being an Arnheim, he could not, on the other hand, occupy the lowly position of a non-commissioned officer, he had simply been declared unfit for military service. To this day he refused to see only a lack of sense in this, appreciating as he did the code of honour that lay behind it. This recollection caused him to add some further remarks to what he had been saying to Soliman.

" It is possible," he continued, picking up the thread where he had dropped it, for in spite of all his distaste for method he was methodical even in his digressions, " it is possible, indeed it is probable that nobility has not always signified what we today mean by an aristocratic outlook. In order to gain possession of all the lands and estates upon which its titles of nobility were later based the aristocracy must have been no less calculating and assiduous than a business man is today, indeed it is even possible that the business conducted by a business man is the more honourable of the two. But in the land itself there is a hidden strength—understand me rightly, I mean this strength has always lain in the very soil of the fields, in hunting, in warfare, in belief in heaven, and in the essential quality of those who till the earth— in short, it was implicit in the physical life of those people who bestirred their brains less than their arms and legs. In their proximity to Nature lay the strength that ultimately made them dignified, well-bred, and averse to everything low and mean."

He wondered whether he had not let his mood lure him into saying too much. If Soliman did not understand the meaning of what had been said, then the boy was capable of having his veneration for the aristocracy diminished by his master's words.

But now something unexpected happened. Soliman had for some time been shifting about restlessly, and now he broke out with a question to his master.

" Excuse me, please," Soliman asked, " my father is a king ? "

Arnheim looked at him, taken aback. " I don't know anything about that," he said half sternly, half in amusement. But as he gazed at Soliman's solemn, almost angry face, something like a touch of sentiment came over him. He liked to see how seriously the boy took everything. ' He's utterly witless,' he thought to himself, ' and really quite tragic.' In some way it seemed to him that witlessness amounted to the same as gravity and roundedness of life. In a gently didactic tone he continued, in reply to the boy's question : " There is little reason to believe that your father is a king. I am more inclined to think he must have followed some lowly occupation, for I found you with a troupe of acrobats in a seaside town."

" What did I cost ? " Soliman interrupted searchingly.

" My dear boy, how can I possibly remember that today ? Not much, anyway, I dare say. Oh, certainly not much ! But why should you worry about that ? We are born in order to create our own kingdom ! Next year, perhaps, I shall send you to take a course of commercial training, and after that you could make a start as a learner in one or other of our offices. Naturally it will depend on you what you achieve, but I shall keep an eye on you. You might, for instance, later represent our interests in some place where coloured people now have some say in affairs. One would of course have to go very carefully in doing that, but still, the fact that you are a Negro might produce a number of advantages for you. And only in doing such work would you come to understand completely how much benefit you have had from the years under my immediate supervision. And one thing I can tell you now : you belong to a race that still has something of the nobility of Nature herself. In the mediæval tales of chivalry black kings always played an honourable part. If you cultivate what there is in you of spiritual nobility, your dignity, your goodness of heart, frankness, courageous love of truth, and the still greater courage of being able to keep yourself from the intolerance, jealousy, resentment and petty nervous spitefulness that stigmatises most people nowadays—if you can do that, you will also be sure to make your way as a business man, for it is our function to offer the world not only goods, but also a better way of life."

As Arnheim had not talked to Soliman so intimately for a long time, he felt that talking so would make him ridiculous to a witness of the scene ; but there was no witness and, besides, what he said was only the top layer overlying deeper associations of ideas, which he kept to himself. So what he was saying about the aristocratic outlook and the historical rise of the aristocracy moved, somewhere deeper within him, in precisely the opposite direction to the words he was uttering. There the thought thrust itself upon him that never since the beginning of the world had anything developed solely out of spiritual purity and good intentions ; everything had developed only out of beastliness, which in time had sown all its wild oats and exhausted itself, and what arose out of it all in the end was the great, pure, noble outlook ! Quite obviously—he reflected—the rise of the nobility is not based, any more than is the rise of a rag-and-bone business to a world-wide commercial undertaking, solely on relations that can be definitely said to partake of a lofty humanism ; and yet out of one there arose the silver age of the *dix-huitième siècle*, and out of the other there arose Arnheim. In other words, life was unequivocally confronting him with a task that he believed he could most properly define in the profoundly dichotomous question : what measure of beastliness is necessary and permissible in order to create greatness of outlook ?

Another layer of Arnheim's thoughts had meanwhile, however, at intervals pursued what he had said to Soliman about intuition and rationality, and suddenly he remembered with great vividness the first time he had told his father that he—the old man—did business by intuition. Having intuition was at that time fashionable with all the people who could not quite justify their actions by reason ; it played more or less the same part as is nowadays played by being ' a fast worker '. Everything that one did wrong, or that did not utterly satisfy one in one's innermost heart, was justified on the grounds that it was done for the sake of or by means of intuition ; indeed, intuition was used for everything, in cookery as much as in writing books. But old Arnheim knew nothing of this, and, being taken unawares, he actually glanced up at his son in surprise. And his son felt this as a great triumph.

" The making of money," the younger Arnheim had said to the elder, " forces us into a mode of thinking that is not always truly in good style. At the same time, it is probable that we big business men are called upon to take over the leadership of the masses at the next turning-point in history, and we don't know whether we shall be spiritually capable of it or not ! Yet if there is anything in the world which can give me the courage to face that, it is you, for you have a gift of vision and will-power such as in the grand ancient times was possessed by the kings and prophets who were still guided by God. The way you set about a deal is a mystery, and I should like to say that all the mysteries that elude calculation are of the same quality, whether it is the mystery of courage, or that of invention, or that of the stars ! "

With distressing clarity Arnheim now again saw how old Arnheim's eyes, which had been raised to look at him, after his first sentences had dropped again to the newspaper, from which they were not to be raised on any later occasion when the younger man talked of business and intuition.

This was the relationship that had always existed between father and son, and in a third stratum of his thoughts, as it were in the very canvas of these memory-pictures, Arnheim had it all well in hand, even now. In his father's superior talent for business, which always oppressed him, he saw something like a primal power that must remain unattainable for him, the complicated son ; and in so thinking he shifted the model out of the realm of things for which he would for ever strive in vain, and into a realm he could not enter, thus incidentally providing himself with letters patent where his own descent was concerned. This dual service worked very nicely. Money turned into a supra-personal, mythical power, for which only the most original and genuine people were wholly a match, and he set his ancestor among the gods, just as the old warriors had done, who doubtless had also thought their mythical forefather, in spite of all the awe he inspired, just a shade primitive in comparison to themselves.

But in a fourth stratum of his thoughts he knew nothing of the smile that hovered over that third stratum, and thought exactly the same thoughts over again, but seriously, meditating on the role that he still hoped to play on this earth. These strata of thought are of course something that is not to be taken literally, as though they were superimposed on each other like different strata in the structure of the earth ; it is merely a convenient expression for something porous, flowing from various directions, which is the stuff of thought under the influence of strong emo-tional conflicts. All his life long, after all, Arnheim had had an almost morbidly sensitive dislike of wit and irony, a dislike that probably originated in a quite considerable hereditary tendency to both. He had suppressed this tendency, because it had always seemed to him the quintessence of the ignoble and of all that went with the intellectual *canaille*, but precisely now, at this period, when his emotions were at their most aristocratic and positively hostile to intellect, the tendency became active in relation to Diotima : when his feelings were already, as it were, on tip-toe, he was often tempted by the diabolical possibility of escaping from his sublime emotion by means of one of those pointed and pertinent jokes about love that he had not infrequently heard from the lips of low-placed or coarse persons. And coming up through all these strata, emerging on the surface again, he all at once found himself gazing in astonishment into Soliman's glumly attentive face, which looked like a black punch-ball on which unintelligible words of wisdom had come raining down like blows. ' What a ridiculous situation I have got myself into ! ' Arnheim thought.

Soliman looked as though he were asleep with open eyes, no more than a body seated on a chair, by the time his master came to the end of this one-sided conversation. And now the eyes began to move, but the body did not stir yet, as though it were still waiting for the word that would awaken it.

Arnheim noticed this, and what he saw in the black boy's gaze was an avid desire to learn more about whatever intrigues had brought a king's son to be a valet. This gaze, this looking out as it were with claws extended to clutch and hold, made Arnheim think suddenly of the under-gardener who had stolen things from his collection, and he said to himself, with a sigh, that he would probably always lack the ordinary common acquisitive instinct. It struck him now that this might also sum up his relation to Diotima. With a painful stirring of emotion he felt how on the heights of his life there was a cold shadow dividing him from everything he ever touched.

This was no easy thought for a man who had just stated the principle that one must think in order to act and who had always striven to make all greatness his own and to stamp all the pettier aspects of life with the imprint of his own distinction. But the shadow had laid itself between him and the objects of his desire, in spite of the will-power in which he had never been lacking, and to his surprise Arnheim thought he could recognise with certainty that this shadow was somehow related to those gossamer-glimmering states of awe that had cast their veils over his youth, and in just such a way as if some wrong handling of them had transformed them into an almost imperceptibly thin sheet of ice. Only he could not find an answer to the question why it did not melt even when confronted with Diotima's world-renouncing heart. But, like a very unpleasant jab of pain in a part of his body that had only been waiting for a touch, now once again the thought of Ulrich occurred to him. All at once Arnheim realised that the same shadow lay over the other man's life—but *there*, what a different effect it had !

Of all the passions that human beings have, there is one that is seldom allotted the place that is due to it on the grounds of its intensity ; and this is the passion of a man who is irritated to the point of jealousy by another man's personality. The realisation that his impotent annoyance about Ulrich at some profounder depth resembled the hostile encounter of two brothers who had not recognised each other gave him a very intense and at the same time comforting sensation. With eager interest Arnheim considered both their personalities from this point of view. The crude acquisitive instinct, the urge to get what advantage one could out of life, was something Ulrich had even less of than he had himself; and the sublime acquisitive urge, the wish to make the dignities and distinctions of this life one's own, was something he lacked in a positively infuriating way. This man was without any craving for the weight and substance of life. His matter-of-fact objective zeal, which was undeniable, was not zealous to acquire possession of the thing, whatever the thing might be. Arnheim would positively have felt reminded of his employees if the selflessness that in their case amounted to being ' keen on their work ' had not, as exemplified in Ulrich, taken on a character that was uncommonly supercilious. It might be truer to say that here was a man possessed who did not wish to have possessions. Or what was evoked, perhaps, was the thought of one fighting for a cause in voluntary poverty. It seemed possible to express it, too, by saying he was an out-and-out theoretical being; only that again did not quite fit the case, because one really could not call him a ' theoretical man ' at all. At this point Arnheim recollected having once expressly told him that his intellectual capabilities were not equal to his practical ones. Yet if one regarded him from a practical point of view, the man was utterly impossible.

So Arnheim's thoughts went this way and that, and indeed not for the first time; but in spite of the doubts about himself that had taken hold of him today he found it impossible to grant Ulrich superiority over himself on any single count, and so he came to the conclusion that the decisive difference probably lay in the fact that Ulrich was deficient in something or other. And yet for all this there was something about the man as a whole that was fresh, untried, and free, and Arnheim admitted to himself, somewhat reluctantly, that this positively reminded him of the ' Mystery of the Whole ' that he himself possessed and which he felt to be made questionable by the existence of this other man. For how would it be possible, if it were a matter only of what was accessible to the weighing and measuring side of the intelligence, to get from a man who was so utterly not a realist the same uneasy sensation of ' wit ' that Arnheim had learned to fear when it manifested itself in such an all-too-exact expert in reality as his own father was?

' What it comes to is that the man as a whole lacks something ! ' Arnheim thought. But as though it were only the other side of this certainty, almost at the same instant he was quite involuntarily struck by the thought : ' There's soul in him ! '

The man had reserves of as yet unexhausted soul. Since this was an intuitive discovery, Arnheim could not have explained exactly what he meant by it ; but somehow or other what it came to was that every human being, as he knew, in the course of time dissolved his soul in intelligence, morality, and lofty ideas, which was an irreversible process, and in this his best-beloved enemy the process had not been completed, so that something was left over, something with an ambiguous charm that could not quite be defined, though it could be recognised by the unusual combinations it formed with elements drawn from the sphere of all that was soulless, rational, and mechanical, elements that could no longer be properly reckoned as belonging to the ' values ' of ' culture '.

While he was turning all this over in his mind and instantaneously adjusting it to the mode of expression he used in his philosophical works, Arnheim had, of course, not had an instant in which to credit any of it to Ulrich as a merit, even, at the worst, as his one and only merit, so strong was the sense of having made a discovery ; it was he himself who was building up these ideas, and he felt like a music master discovering the potential splendour of a voice that had not yet been raised in song.

His thoughts cooled off only at the sight of Soliman's face. Soliman had obviously been staring at him for a long time and now thought the moment had come to ask more questions. The consciousness that it was not given to everyone to arrive at his discoveries with the aid of such a dumb little semi-savage enhanced Arnheim's sense of happiness at being the only person who knew his opponent's secret, even though there was still much that was not defined or clear in its implications for the future. The affection he felt now was merely the affection that a usurer feels for the victim in whom he has invested his capital. And perhaps it was the sight of Soliman that suddenly inspired him with the resolution to draw into his orbit, at any price, this man who seemed to him to be the differently embodied adventure of his very self, and to do it even if he had to adopt him as a son ! He smiled at this over-hasty enthusiasm for an intention that must have time to mature, and at the same time cut short anything that Soliman, whose face was twitching with tragic curiosity, might try to say, by announcing :

" That's quite enough now. It's time for you to go round to Frau Tuzzi with the flowers I ordered. If there's anything else you want to ask me, perhaps we can see about it some other time."

113

Ulrich converses with Hans Sepp and Gerda in the pidgin-language of the frontier district between the super-rational and the sub-rational.

ULRICH honestly did not know what he could do to fulfil his father's wish that he should, out of enthusiasm for the social school of thought, pave the way for a personal discussion with His Highness and other highly placed patriots. And so he went to see Gerda, in order to get the matter right out of his mind.

He found Hans with her, and Hans went straight in to the attack.

" So you are standing up for Director Fischel ? "

Ulrich replied evasively with the counter-question whether Gerda had told him about it.

Yes, Gerda had told him.

" And what then ? Do you want to hear why ? "

" Yes, please, I do ! " Hans said imperiously.

" That isn't so simple, my dear Hans."

" Don't call me your dear Hans ! "

" Well then, my dear Gerda," Ulrich said, turning to her, " it's far from simple. I've talked about it such a frightful lot already— I thought you understood me ? "

" Oh, I understand you all right, but I don't believe you," Gerda answered, trying, by the way she said it and looked at him, to give some conciliating air to her answer in spite of her hostile alliance with Hans.

" We don't believe you," Hans burst in, at once stopping this
more amiable turn the talk seemed to be taking. " We don't
believe you can be serious about it. You have picked all that up
somewhere ! "

" What ? You mean, I suppose—you mean what one can't—
can't quite express ? " Ulrich asked, instantly realising that Hans's
impudence referred to his own private conversation with Gerda.

" Oh, one can express it all right if one means it seriously ! "

" I don't seem able to. But I can tell you a story."

" *Another* story ! You seem to go in for story-telling quite in
the style of old Daddy Homer ! " Hans exclaimed even more
impudently and brazenly.

Gerda gazed at him imploringly.

But Ulrich would not be put off. " I was once very much in
love," he continued. " I must have been about the same age
as you are now. Actually I was in love with being in love—with
the altered condition I was in—and less with the woman who went
with it. At that time I came to know all about the things that
you, your friends, and Gerda, make such a great mystery of. That
is the story I was going to tell you."

The two young people were taken aback to find the story
turned out to be so short.

" So you were once very much in love—— ? " Gerda asked
hesitantly, in the same instant feeling annoyed at having asked
such a question in front of Hans and with the grisly curiosity of
a schoolgirl.

But Hans broke in : " Why on earth should we talk about
such things at all ? It'd be more to the point if you would tell
us what your cousin is up to—your cousin who's got into the
hands of all these intellectual bankrupts."

" She's in search of an idea," Ulrich replied, " that will
gloriously show the whole world the spirit of the land we live in.
Wouldn't you like to help her with some suggestion ? I shall be
glad to act as a go-between."

Hans uttered a scornful guffaw. " Why do you try and pretend
you don't know we're going to wreck this campaign ? "

" And why actually are you so indignant about it ? "

" Because it's a tremendous organised piece of infamy against
German-kind in this country ! " Hans said. " Do you really

not know there's a very promising counter-movement developing ? The German National League has had its attention drawn
to the machinations of this Count Leinsdorf of yours. The
German League For Physical Culture has already entered a protest against this affront to the German spirit. The Federation of
Arms-Bearing Fraternities in the Austrian Universities is going
to make a statement in the next few days regarding this menace of
slavonification, and the Union of German Youth, to which I
belong, will not let the matter rest, even if we have to march
through the streets ! " Hans had drawn himself up and recounted
this with a certain degree of pride. Yet he added : " But of course
none of that is what really matters ! These people overrate
external circumstances. The decisive thing is that in this country
nothing whatsoever can possibly succeed ! "

Ulrich asked what the reason for this was.

The great races had all created their own myth at the very
beginning of their history. Was there any such thing—Hans
asked—as an Austrian myth ? A primitive Austrian religion ?
Or epic ? Neither the Catholic nor the Protestant religion had
originated here. The art of printing and the traditions of painting
had come from Germany. The ruling house had been provided
by Switzerland, Spain, and Luxembourg. Engineering and so
forth had come from England and Germany. The most beautiful
cities, Vienna, Prague, and Salzburg, had been built by Italians
and Germans, and the army had been organised on the model of
Napoleon's. Such a State had no business to try anything of its
own. There was only one possibility of salvation for it, and that
was union with Germany. " And so now," Hans concluded, " I
suppose you know everything you wanted to get out of us ! "

Gerda was not sure whether she ought to be proud or ashamed
of him. Her attraction towards Ulrich had recently flared up
again, even if the very human wish to play a role herself was
much more adequately satisfied by her younger friend. The
remarkable thing was that this girl was confused by two contradictory inclinations, one to become an old maid and the other to
abandon herself to Ulrich. This second inclination was the natural
consequence of the love she had been feeling for years, a love, it
must be added, that did not burst into flame, but smouldered
listlessly within her ; and her feelings resembled those of someone

who loves an unworthy person and whose soul is affronted and tormented by the body's contemptible tendency towards submission. In strange contrast with this, but perhaps linked with it, after all, simply and naturally as a yearning for peace, there was the foreboding that she would never marry and, having come to the end of all her dreams, would lead a solitary, quietly active life. This was by no means a wish born of convictions, for Gerda did not see clearly where she herself was concerned; it was rather more one of those forebodings that our body sometimes has much sooner than our mind. The influence that Hans exerted on her was also connected with this. Hans was an ordinary-looking lad, bony without being tall or strongly built, who wiped his hands in his hair or on his clothes and was always looking at himself in a small round tin-framed pocket-mirror, because he was incessantly worried about some pimple on the muddy skin of his face. But it was exactly like this that Gerda pictured the first Roman Christians, who, defying the persecutions, had their gatherings in the catacombs below ground—exactly like this, except probably for the pocket-mirror. After all, ' exactly so ' did not mean agreement in all the details; it meant chiefly the common presence of a general and fundamental sense of terror, which she associated with her mental images of Christianity : the washed and anointed saints had always been more to her taste, but confessing oneself a Christian for her meant making a sacrifice that one owed to one's character. In this way the higher obligations had for Gerda taken on a slight, stuffy smell of the detestable, and this formed an ideal combination with the mystical outlook of which Hans had opened the realms to her.

Ulrich knew this outlook very well. We must perhaps be grateful to spiritualism for the fact that with its quaint messages from the Beyond, which suggest the spirits of deceased cooks, it satisfies the crude metaphysical craving to shovel down spoonfuls of, if not God, then at least the spirits, like some pabulum that, partaken of in darkness, slips icily down the gullet. In older times this craving to get into personal touch with God or any of the heavenly hierarchy—which allegedly happened when one was in the condition of ecstasy—in spite of the frail and to some extent weird forms that it took on did nevertheless give rise to an intermingling of a crude earthly attitude with the experiences that occurred in an extremely unusual and quite indefinable condition of intuitive apprehension. The metaphysical was merely the physical as it was projected into that condition, a mirror-image of earthly desires ; for people believed they saw then whatever contemporary notions made them have a lively expectation of being able to see. Now it is, however, precisely the notions emanating from the intellect that change with the times and become incredible. If anyone were today to declare that God had spoken to him, had seized him painfully by the hair and drawn him up to Himself, or had slipped into his breast in some not entirely comprehensible but intensely sweet way, nobody would believe in these particular images in which he clothed his experience, least of all, naturally, the professional men of God, because they, as children of a rational age, have a thoroughly human fear of being compromised by hysterical adherents in a state of exaltation. The consequence of this is that one has either to regard experiences that were numerous and well-defined in the Middle Ages, as also in pagan Antiquity, as delusions and pathological phenomena, or to conjecture that they contained something that remains independent of the mythical terms in which it has hitherto always been expressed : that is to say, a pure core of experience that ought to stand up even to being investigated according to strict empirical principles and which then, it goes without saying, would constitute a matter of extreme importance long before one got to the second question as to what conclusions were to be drawn from this with reference to our relations to the supramundane realm. And while faith, having been organised into the system of theological reason, everywhere has to fight a hard battle against doubt and opposition from the rational attitude prevailing nowadays, it seems in fact that the naked fundamental experience—peeled out of all the traditional terminological husks of faith, detached from the old religious concepts—this fundamental experience that perhaps cannot even any longer be called an exclusively religious one, this experience of mystic rapture, has extended vastly and now constitutes the soul of that multiform, irrational movement which haunts the age in which we live like a nocturnal bird that has strayed into the daylight.

A grotesque particle of this manifold movement was represented by the circle and vortex in which Hans Sepp played his part. If one had counted up the ideas that ebbed and flowed inside that group—which, however, would not be permissible according to the fundamental principles prevailing there, which were opposed to number and measure—one would have encountered first of all a timid, entirely platonic demand for trial marriage and companionate marriage, indeed for polygamy and polyandry; then, further, where problems of art were concerned, the abstract outlook, focused on universal and eternal values, that then existed under the name of Expressionism and which contemptuously turned its back on mere appearances, the shell, the 'banal visual externals' of things, precisely those externals whose faithful representation had, incomprehensibly enough, a generation earlier been accounted revolutionary; and in harmonious alliance with this tendency towards the abstract, this tendency to portray an 'essential vision' of the spirit and the world by direct means, without bothering much about externals, one would also have found a taste for all that was most down-to-earth and limited, namely for German 'traditional' and 'folk' art, to which these young people felt themselves bound in dutiful allegiance and service by virtue of their German souls. And so one would have found there too, all higgledy-piggledy, the most splendid of the leaves and grasses that could be picked up on the roads of time to build a nest for the spirit. Among them there were, above all else, luxuriantly lush conceptions of the rights, duties, and creative energy of youth; and these played so great a part that they must be considered in more detail.

The present age, according to these conceptions, did not acknowledge that youth had any rights: until a human being reached his majority he was practically without rights. His father, mother, or guardian could dress him, house him, feed him, just as they liked, reprimand and punish him and even, according to Hans Sepp, wreck his life, so long as they did not overstep the far-flung limits of the law, which granted children, at most, the same sort of protection from cruelty that was granted to animals. The child belonged to his parent as the slave belonged to his master, and through his economic dependence became a chattel, a mere object in the capitalist system. This 'capitalist ownership of the child', which Hans had originally found expounded somewhere or other and then elaborated for himself, was the first thing about which he taught his astonished disciple, Gerda, who had up to then felt perfectly well looked after at home. Christianity, he declared, had lightened only the wife's yoke, and not the daughter's ; the daughter vegetated, for she was forcibly kept a stranger from life. After this preparation he instructed her in the child's right to build up its education on the laws of its own personality. The child was creative because it was growth : it was self-creative. It was kingly, because it imposed its ideas, feelings, and fantasies on the world. It did not want to have anything to do with the accidental, ready-made world with which it was confronted ; it set out to build its own world of ideals. It had its own sexuality. Adults committed a barbaric sin, destroying the child's creativeness by robbing it of its world, suffocating it with the dead matter of traditional knowledge and training it for certain purposes that were alien to it. The child was non-purposive ; its creativeness was play, a delicate process of growth. If it was not forcibly disturbed, it acquired nothing but what it genuinely absorbed into its being. Every object that it touched was alive. The child was a universe, a cosmos. It beheld the ultimate, the Absolute, even if it could not express it. But the child was killed by being taught to understand purposeful aims, by being fettered to that ordinary common repetitiveness that was so falsely called reality !

That was what Hans Sepp said.

When he began to implant this doctrine in the Fischel household he was already twenty-one, and Gerda was no younger. Incidentally, Hans had for a long time had no father, and continually relieved his feelings by being rude to his mother, who kept a small shop by means of which she supported him and his brothers and sisters ; there was therefore really no immediate reason for him to have such a philosophy of the oppressed on behalf of all poor children.

And Gerda, absorbing this doctrine, wavered between a mild pedagogic interest in the education of future mankind and the immediate belligerent exploitation of these ideas in her relationship to her father and mother. Hans Sepp, on the other hand, had a much more thorough-going attitude and formulated the slogan : ' We all ought to be children ! ' His obstinacy in insisting on the child's embattled condition may have had its origin in an early craving for independence. In the main, however, it was all owing to the fact that the jargon of the youth movement, which was then coming into full swing, was the first language that helped his soul to find utterance, and, like any proper language, it inevitably led him from one word to another, with each word saying more than the speaker had really known he was going to say. So, for example, the proposition that we all ought to be children led to the most important discoveries. What it came to was that the child should not reverse and renounce its own nature in order to become a father or a mother ; for that was done only in order to be a ' citizen ', a slave of the world, bound and ' utilitarianised '. Thus it is really citizenship that makes a human being old, and the child puts up a fight against being turned into a citizen. In this way the difficulty that at the age of twenty-one one is not supposed to behave like a child is swept away, for this fight continues from birth until old age and is only ended when the world of bourgeois values has been destroyed by the world of love. This was so to speak the higher aspect of Hans Sepp's doctrine, and all this Ulrich had in the course of time learnt from Gerda.

Ulrich had also discovered a connection between what these young people called their love, or, alternatively, ' community ', and the consequence of a queer, savagely religious, unmythologically mythical, or perhaps, after all, merely infatuated condition with which he was deeply concerned—without their knowing it, however, because he confined himself to casting ridicule on the traces it left in them. It was in the same manner that he now took up the subject with Hans, asking him point-blank why he would not try making use of the Collateral Campaign for the advancement of the ' community of those perfected in renunciation of the ego '.

" Because it won't do ! " Hans retorted.

The discussion that now sprang up between the two of them would inevitably have made a strange impression on an impartial observer, somewhat reminding him of conversation carried on in the jargon of the underworld, although this particular jargon was in fact simply the pidgin-language of secular and spiritual infatuation. It is therefore preferable to give more the gist than the actual words of this talk.

' The community of those perfected in renunciation of the ego ' was an expression hit upon by Hans. It was nevertheless not without meaning ; the more selfless a human being feels himself to be, the brighter and intenser do the things of this world become, and the lighter he makes himself, the more does he feel himself exalted. It may be assumed that everyone has experiences of this kind. But they must not be confused with mere jollity, cheerfulness, light-heartedness, or the like, for those are only the substitutes for it that serve a lower, if not, indeed, a corrupt, purpose. Perhaps the genuine state should not be called exaltation at all, but a discarding of the coat of mail : of the coat of mail, Hans explained, in which the ego was encased. A distinction must be made, he said, between two different ramparts surrounding the human being. One was transcended every time he merely did something good and unselfish ; but that was only the lower rampart. The higher rampart consisted in the selfness that was to be found even in the most selfless human being. That was simply Original Sin. Every sensual perception, every sensation, even that of abandonment, was, as we experienced it, more of a taking than a giving, and there was scarcely any way of escaping from this armour, this state of being permeated with egoism. Hans gave a list of examples. Knowledge was nothing but appropriation of an alien object ; one killed it, tore it up and devoured it, like an animal. A concept was a slain thing, now lying motionless for ever. Conviction was the now stone-cold relationship that could never change again. Research meant establishing. Character was only inertia with regard to development. Knowing a person thoroughly amounted to no more than no longer being moved by that person. Insight was merely one kind of sight. Truth was the successful attempt to think functionally and inhumanly. In all these relationships there was extermination, iciness, a demand for property and petrification and a mixture of egoism with a matter-of-fact, cowardly, treacherous, false selflessness.

And when and where was love itself (Hans asked, although he only knew the innocent Gerda) anything but the desire for possession or self-abandon in return for the same ?

Ulrich agreed, cautiously and with modifications, with these not entirely coherent assertions. It was true, he said, that even

passive suffering and self-renunciation left a mite over for ourselves. A pale and, as it were, merely grammatical shadow of
egoism overcast all our doings so long as there was no such thing
as a predicate without a subject.

But Hans disagreed violently. He and his friends argued about
how one should live. Sometimes they assumed that each one
must primarily live for himself and only secondarily for all the
others. Another time they were convinced that each one could
have only one really true friend, but that this one friend in his
turn needed another friend, in which way the community appeared
to them as a union of souls forming a circle, resembling the spectrum or other progressive series. But what they most liked to
believe was that there existed a spiritual law of communal awareness, which was merely overshadowed by egoism, a vast inner
source of life, still unexhausted, to which they ascribed fantastic
potentialities. Not even a tree, fighting for its existence in the
forest and sheltered by the forest, can seem more vague to itself
than is the vagueness with which sensitive people nowadays feel
the dark warmth of the mass, its dynamic force, and the invisible
molecular processes of its unconscious cohesion, which remind
them with every breath they draw that the greatest and the
smallest alike are not alone.

Ulrich felt the same. He did, indeed, see clearly that the tamed
egoism of which life was made up resulted in an orderly structure,
whereas the breath of community remained merely a quintessence
of unclarified interconnections, and where he himself was concerned he had a tendency towards isolation. But he was peculiarly
affected when Gerda's young friends made their wild assertion
about the great wall that had to be surmounted.

Hans recited the articles of his faith, now in a monotonous
chant, now with gasps and ejaculations, his eyes staring straight
ahead, seeing nothing. There was an unnatural division, he said,
running through all Creation, splitting it in two like an apple, the
two halves of which were doomed to dry up and shrivel. Therefore one had nowadays to appropriate by artificial and unnatural
means that with which one had previously been united. This
division, however, could be done away with by some sort of
opening up of one's own being, a change of attitude ; for the
more a person could forget himself, blot himself out, get away from

himself, the more forces would be liberated in him and become available for the community, just as if they had been set free from a wrong amalgamation of elements ; and at the same time, the closer he drew to the community, the more he was bound to become himself. For, if one followed Hans, one learnt among other things that the degree of true originality did not lie in vain idiosyncrasy, but arose out of the opening up of one's own being, leading, by increasing degrees of participation and devotion, to the possibility of in this way achieving the highest degree of a community of those who would be entirely absorbed by the world, perfected in their selflessness.

These propositions, which were, it seemed, entirely devoid of substance, set Ulrich dreaming about how one might give them a real content. But he merely asked Hans, in a cool tone, how he meant to go about this opening up of his being, and all the rest of it, in practice.

Hans replied with a flood of high-flown words : the transcendent ego in the place of the sensual ego, the Gothic ego in place of the naturalistic one, the realm of the numinous in place of the phenomenal world, pure and unconditional experience . . . All these, and similar formidable expressions, came gushing forth, and were fathered on the quintessence of his indescribable experiences—as is, incidentally, a widespread custom that, though it is damaging to the cause itself, nevertheless tends to enhance its dignity. And because the experiences and states of which he caught glimpses at times, perhaps indeed frequently, never granted him more than some brief moments of contemplation, he went further and asserted that the things of the Beyond nowadays did not reveal themselves more clearly than in the jerking flashes accompanying an extracorporeal vision that was, naturally, difficult to hold on to and the sediment of which was to be found, if at all, in great works of art. He was soon talking of ' the symbol ', which was his favourite expression for these and other supernaturally grand manifestations of life and finally of the Germanic experience proper to those who had even a few drops of Germanic blood in their veins, the experience of creating and beholding these things. In this way, in a sublime variation on the nostalgic ' the good old days ' pattern, he managed to explain quite comfortably that a lasting apprehension of the essence of things belonged to the past and was denied to the present. And the argument had, after all, started from precisely this assertion.

Ulrich was irritated by this superstitious claptrap. He had been wondering for a long time what there really was in Hans to attract Gerda. She sat there, pale, taking no active part in the conversation. Hans Sepp had a grand theory of love, and probably she found in it the deeper meaning of her own existence.

Ulrich now gave the conversation a new turn by asserting—though not without all sorts of reservations on the subject of entering into such discussions at all—that the highest degree of feeling to which a person could rise did not originate in either the ordinary egoistic attitude in which one appropriated everything that came one's way, nor, as Hans and his friends maintained, in what might be called enhancement of the self by opening up and abandonment, but was actually a static condition in which nothing ever changed, like still waters.

Gerda brightened up and asked what exactly he meant by that.

Ulrich replied by saying that Hans had all the time been speaking—even though to some extent in very arbitrary disguises—about love and nothing else : about the saint's love, the anchorite's love, the love that overflowed the banks of desire, the love that had always been described as a loosening up, a dissolution, indeed as a reversal of all worldly relations, and which in any case signified not merely an emotion but a change in a person's whole way of thinking and perceiving.

Gerda looked at him probingly, as though she were trying to find out whether he, with all his knowledge, which so far outstripped her own, had somehow discovered this too, or whether what was happening was that it was from this secretly beloved man himself, as he sat here beside her, not showing much sign of any emotion, that there came forth the strange radiation which unites two beings though the bodies do not touch.

Ulrich felt the probe. It was all as though he were speaking in some strange language in which he could go on talking fluently, but only externally, without the words having any roots in him.

"In this state," he said, "in which one oversteps the limits that are generally imposed on one's actions, one understands everything, because the soul only accepts what is of its own nature. In a certain sense it already knows everything that it is about to discover. Lovers can't tell each other anything new. And there isn't such a thing as recognition between them, either. For all that the lover recognises of the being he loves is that this other causes him, in some indescribable way, to be in a state of inner activity. And recognising a person whom he does not love for him means drawing that other into the sphere of his love, where the other is then like a blank wall on which the sunlight lies. And recognising an inanimate object does not mean spying out its qualities one after the other. It means that a veil falls away, or a frontier is erased somewhere beyond the world of sense-perception. The inanimate thing also enters, unknown as it is, but full of trust, into the companionship of those who love. Nature and the spirit that is peculiar to lovers look into each other's eyes. Here there are two directions of one and the same act. It is a flowing in two directions, and a burning at both ends. And recognising a person or a thing without there being a relation between it and oneself is then simply impossible. For taking notice means taking something *from* the things—they keep their shape, but seem, even while they keep it, to crumble inwardly into ashes. Something of what they are evaporates. All that is left is their mummies. That too is why there is no truth for lovers. Truth would be a blind alley, an end, the death of the thought that, so long as it lives, resembles the breathing edge of a flame, where light and darkness lie breast to breast. How can any one thing light up, in a flash of recognition, in a being who is all light within ? What need is there for alms, for the small change of security and the unequivocal, where everything is superabundance ? And how can one still desire anything for oneself alone, even though it should be the loved object itself, when one has experienced how those who love no longer belong to themselves, but have to squander themselves on everything that comes their way, four-eyed intertwined beings that they are ? "

Anyone who has mastered this language can go on using it indefinitely without any effort. That is then like walking with a lighted candle in one's hand, its delicate ray falling on one after the other of life's complexities, and all of them looking as though in their usual manifestation, as they looked in the solid light of everyday, they had merely been crude misunderstandings. How

impossible then, for instance, the function of the word ' possess '
appears when one applies it to lovers ! But does it reveal wishes
of a finer sort to want to possess principles ? and the respect of
one's children ? ideas ? oneself ? This unwieldy movement of
attack, as though on the part of some ponderous animal that
crushes its prey with its entire weight, is nevertheless, quite
justifiably, the fundamental and favourite expression of capitalism ; and in it there can be seen the connection between those
who have property and possessions in bourgeois life and those
who are the owners of knowledge and skills—for that is what
bourgeois life has made of its thinkers and artists—while love
and asceticism stand on one side, brother and sister, a solitary
pair. And are this brother and sister not, when they stand
together, without any aim or target, in contrast with life, which is
all aims and targets ? But the words ' aim ' and ' target ' come
from the language of gunmen. So do not ' aimless ' and ' target-
less ' in their original context signify as much as not being one
who kills ? So through the mere act of following up the track
that language leaves behind—a blurred but revealing trail !—
one stumbles upon the way that everywhere the crudely altered
meaning has pushed into the place of more circumspect relationships, which are now quite lost. This is like a complex that is
everywhere perceptible but nowhere tangible.

Ulrich saw no sense in continuing to discuss such ideas with
Hans. Still, Hans could not be blamed, either, for believing that
by pulling at a certain place one could turn the whole fabric of
things inside-out, the only difficulty being that people had lost the
instinct for where that place was.

He had repeatedly interrupted Ulrich and finished his sentences
for him.

" If you want to look at these experiences with a scientist's eyes,
you won't see anything in them but what a bank-clerk would see
too ! All empirical explanations are only apparent explanations !
They don't take us out of the circle of low, sensually perceptible
knowledge ! Your urge for knowledge would like to reduce the
universe to no more than mechanical thumb-twiddling on the part
of what you call natural forces ! "

Of such a kind were his objections and interpolations. He was
now rude, now enthusiastic. He could feel that he had put his

case badly, and he blamed this on the presence of this stranger, this man who prevented his being alone with Gerda ; for if he had been alone with her, he knew, the words he had used, though the same words, would have been quite different, rising up into the air like glittering fountains, or falcons circling. He could feel that this was really one of his grand days. At the same time he was very much amazed and annoyed at hearing Ulrich talking so easily and at length in his place.

The fact was, however, that Ulrich had not been talking at all like a scientist. He had, on the contrary, said much more than he was prepared to stand up for, and yet he did not feel he had been saying anything he did not believe. He was borne along by suppressed fury about it all. It is necessary to be in a strangely exalted, slightly inflamed mood if one is to talk like this, and Ulrich's mood was half-way between that state and a state caused by the sight of Hans, with his greasy towsled hair, his dirty complexion, the disagreeably intrusive gestures he made, and the torrent of his foaming talk, in which there was yet a veil of something belonging to his innermost being, like skin from a flayed heart. But to be quite exact, Ulrich had all his life long been half-way between two such impressions of this matter. He had always been capable of holding forth about it as fluently as he did today, and of half believing in it at the same time ; and yet he had never got beyond this dilettante facility, because he did not believe in the meaning of his words. And in the same way he now took equal pleasure and displeasure in this conversation.

But Gerda took no notice of the mocking objections that he for this reason sometimes interpolated, as though in parody. Her only feeling was that he had been revealing himself. She gazed at him almost anxiously. ' He's much softer than he'll admit,' she thought while he was talking, and she was made defenceless by a feeling as though a baby were groping at her breast.

Ulrich caught her eye. He knew about almost everything that went on between her and Hans, because, since she was frightened by it, she felt the need to relieve her heart by at least throwing out hints, and he was easily able to supplement them. They regarded possession of each other, which is generally the young lovers' goal, as the beginning of spiritual capitalism, something that they hated, and they believed they scorned the passion of the body, while they also scorned the sobriety of common sense, which was suspect from being a bourgeois ideal. So they clung to each other in a non-corporeal or semi-corporeal embrace ; they sought to ' affirm ' each other, as they called it, and felt that tremulously tender union of personalities which comes about when two people gaze at each other, let themselves slip into the invisible rippling waves within each other's breast and head, and, in the moment when they are sure they understand each other, feel that each is borne within the other and is one with the other. In hours that were not quite so sublime, however, they contented themselves with ordinary admiration for each other. At such times they somehow felt that they resembled great and famous paintings or were re-enacting stirring dramatic scenes, and they were amazed, when they kissed each other, to think that—to make use of a proud saying—millennia were gazing down upon them. For they did kiss each other. In spite of the fact that they declared the crude sensation there was in love of the ego's cringing inside the body to be just as ' low ' as a doubling up with stomach-ache, their limbs did not entirely conform with their souls' point of view, but of their own accord pressed hard against each other. Afterwards they were both always quite upset and bewildered. Their frail philosophy was no match for their awareness that there was nobody about, for the twilight in the room around them, and for the furiously increasing power of attraction exerted by two bodies nestling close together ; and Gerda especially— who as the girl was the more mature of the two—then felt the craving for a consummation of these embraces—felt it with the innocent intensity a tree might feel if something were preventing it from coming into bud in the springtime. These half-embraces, as savourless as children's kisses and as undefined as the caresses of the old, always left them shattered and, as it were, high and dry. Hans adjusted himself to it the better of the two, for as soon as it was past he could look back on it as a test of his convictions.

" It is not given to us to be possessors," he instructed her. " We are rovers, progressing from one level to the next."

And when he noticed how Gerda's whole body was quivering with frustrated desire, he made no bones about accusing her of weakness, if not indeed of a residue of non-Germanic heredity.

At such times he felt like Adam who walked with God and whose manly heart was yet destined to be turned away from faith again by what had once been his rib.

Gerda despised him then. And this was probably the reason why, formerly, at any rate, she had told Ulrich as much as possible about it all. She was vaguely aware that a grown man would do both more and less than Hans, who, after he had insulted her, would come like a child and bury his tear-stained face between her legs. And, being just as proud of her experiences as she was bored with them, she held out the knowledge of them to Ulrich, in the frightened hope that he would say something to destroy the agonising beauty of it.

Ulrich, however, seldom talked to her in the way she expected. He usually chilled her with mockery, for although this was the reason why Gerda refused to trust him, he knew quite well that she was in a perpetual state of longing to subject her personality to his, and that neither Hans nor anyone else had as much power over her mind as he himself might have had. He absolved himself of responsibility by saying that any other real man would inevitably have had the same effect on her, the effect something like salvation after that guttersnipe obscurantist Hans. But while he was now reflecting on all this and suddenly feeling himself again recollected and alert, Hans had turned things over in his mind and begun another attempt to go over to the attack.

" All in all," he said, " you have committed the worst mistake that anyone can, by trying to express in conceptual terms what occasionally elevates an idea just an iota over the level of the conceptual. But I dare say that is, after all, simply the difference between you learned gentlemen and the like of us. First," he added proudly, " one must learn to live it, and then perhaps one learns to think it ! " And as Ulrich smiled, he flashed out as though with a stroke of wrathful lightning : " Jesus was a seer when he was only twelve, and didn't need to become a doctor of the law first ! "

This provoked Ulrich into breaking the silence to which Gerda's confidence committed him and giving Hans a piece of advice that betrayed knowledge of facts that he could only have been made acquainted with by her. For he retorted : " I don't know why, if you want to live it, you don't go the whole hog. I would take Gerda in my arms, discard all the qualms my reason caused me, and keep my arms round her until our two bodies had either crumbled to ashes or, following the transformation of the meaning, turned back upon themselves in the very way we can't imagine ! "

Hans, feeling a stab of jealousy, looked not at him but at Gerda.

Gerda turned pale and was obviously embarrassed. The words ' I would take Gerda in my arms and keep my arms round her ' had had on her the effect of a secret promise. At this moment it was a matter of complete indifference to her how one should most logically imagine the ' other life ', and she was sure that if Ulrich really wanted to he would do everything just as it ought to be.

Hans, angry at Gerda's treachery, which he could feel, denied that what Ulrich was talking about would necessarily work. The epoch was not propitious, he said. The first souls to take flight would have to take off from a mountain, just like the first aeroplanes, and not from the lowlands of an epoch like the present. Perhaps there must first come a man who would deliver the rest of mankind from its fetters before the sublime thing could be achieved ! He did not seem to be entirely convinced that in no circumstances could *he* be that saviour ; but that was his own affair, and apart from this he denied that the present time, which was one of spiritual low pressures, was capable of producing such a saviour.

Now Ulrich said something about how many saviours there were going about nowadays. Any respectable chairman of any local club passed for one ! He was convinced that if Christ Himself were to come again, He would fare even worse than the last time. The newspapers and book-clubs that went in for moral uplift would find His tone not ' pleasant ' enough, and the great international press would not be likely to throw its columns open to Him !

This now got them once more to where they had been at the beginning. The discussion was at the same stage as when it had started, and Gerda drooped.

But one thing was different. Without showing any sign of it, Ulrich had begun to feel slightly involved in all this. His thoughts were not with what he was saying. He looked at Gerda. Her body was angular, her skin looked tired and dull. The faint breath of old-maidishness that hung about her all at once became obvious to him, though probably it had always been of major importance in inhibiting him from ever really getting on with this girl who was in love with him. It was something to which, of course, Hans also contributed, with the semi-physical implications of his cloudy notions about ' fellowship ' and ' community ', which likewise doubtless had something about them that was not entirely out of the key of old-maidishness.

Ulrich found Gerda unattractive, and yet he felt an urge to continue the conversation with her. This reminded him that he had invited her to come and see him. She had not given any sign whether she had forgotten the suggestion or was still thinking of it, and he did not get an opportunity to ask her about it privately. It left him with an uneasy sense of regret and also of relief, as when one feels a danger passing over that one has noticed too late.

114

The state of affairs gradually becomes critical. Arnheim is very gracious to General Stumm. Diotima prepares to sally forth into the Illimitable. Ulrich indulges in fanciful talk about the possibility of living in the same way as one reads.

HIS HIGHNESS had expressed the urgent wish that Diotima should inform herself about the famous Makart pageant in the 'seventies, which had united the whole of Austria in enthusiasm. He himself could still remember the tapestry-hung wagons, the heavily caparisoned horses, and the trumpeters, and the pride that people took in their mediæval costumes, which transported them out of the everyday monotony of their lives. So it came about that Diotima, Arnheim, and Ulrich had been in the Imperial Library, looking through contemporary material. As Diotima, with disdainfully curling lips, had foretold when talking to His Highness, the result was quite impossible : people could no longer be transported out of the everyday monotony of their lives with such pseudo-spiritual gewgaws. And as they came out of the Library, this beautiful woman announced to her companions that she felt impelled to rejoice in the bright sunshine and the fact that it was 1914—this year only a few weeks old, which was such an advance on that mouldering past. On the stairs, Diotima had declared that she wished to walk home. But they had scarcely come out into the daylight when they ran into the General, who was about to go through the great doorway on his way into the Library and who, because he was no little proud at being found engaged in such an erudite activity, immediately said he would be delighted to turn back and enlarge Diotima's escort by joining them. Hence it came about, after they had gone only a few yards, that Diotima discovered she was tired and required a cab. However, there was no sign of a free cab at the moment, and so they all stood there in front of the Library, in the square, as it were at the bottom of a rectangular box, open at the top, of which three sides consisted of glorious old façades and the fourth was formed by a long, low-built mansion and the asphalt street in front of it, which glittered like an ice-rink, with the motor-cars and carriages dashing along. But not one of these vehicles responded to the beckoning and signalling of these four people, who stood waving like shipwrecked sailors until they grew tired of it, or forgot, and only now and then repeated the gesture half-heartedly.

Arnheim himself carried a big book under his arm. This was something he took pleasure in doing, the attitude being at once condescending and respectful towards the life of the mind. He was talking eagerly to the General.

" I am glad to find you too are an *habitué* of libraries. It is a good thing," he expounded, " to seek out the mind in its own house, but nowadays it has become rare with men in public life."

General Stumm replied that he knew this library very well indeed.

Arnheim found this very laudable. " What we have nowadays is almost nothing but writers, and nobody who reads the books," he continued. " Have you ever asked yourself, General, how many books are printed annually ? If I remember right, there are over a hundred books a day published in Germany alone. And more than a thousand periodicals are founded every year ! Everyone writes. Everyone uses every idea as though it were his own, whenever it suits him. Nobody feels any responsibility towards the situation as a whole. Since the Church has lost its influence, there is no longer any authority, and it is chaos in the midst of which we live. There is no educational model and no educational principle. In these circumstances it is only natural that feeling and morality should drift without an anchor, and the most stable of people begin to waver ! "

The General felt his mouth becoming dry. It could not be said that Herr Dr. Arnheim was actually speaking to him : he was a man standing in an open square and thinking aloud. It occurred to the General that a great many people talk to themselves in the street while hurrying along somewhere ; or, more correctly, many civilians, for a soldier in the ranks would be locked up for doing so and an officer would be sent to the psychiatric clinic. It made Stumm feel thoroughly uncomfortable to stand there, philosophising in public, as it were, in the middle of the capital of the Empire. Apart from the two of them there was only one other, a silent man, present in the sunshine on the square, and he was of bronze and high upon a large slab of stone. The General did not recall whom he represented and, in fact, had really noticed him now for the first time. Arnheim, who followed the General's gaze, asked who it was. The General apologised for his ignorance.

" And to think that he was put up there in order that we should venerate him ! " the great man commented. " But that's the way it is, I suppose. In every minute of our lives we are moving among institutions, problems, and requirements of which we know only the last bit, so that the present is continuously reaching back into the past. If I may put it so, the floor of time is always giving way beneath us and our feet go through into the cellars below, while we imagine ourselves to be in the top storey of the present ! "

Arnheim smiled. He was making conversation. His moving lips flickered ceaselessly in the sunshine, and the lights in his eyes kept changing as though they were signals from a steamer far out at sea.

Stumm felt more and more uneasy. He found it difficult to keep on showing that he was paying attention, when there were changes of subject so many and so unusual, while here he was standing served up to the public view, in uniform, on this salver of a square. In the cracks between the cobbles there was grass growing ; it was last year's grass and looked improbably fresh, like a corpse that has been lying in the snow ; indeed it was altogether remarkable and disturbing that there should be grass growing between the cobbles here, when one reflected that a few paces further on the asphalt was polished smooth, as was in keeping with the times, by the motor-cars driving over it. The General began to suffer from a nervous fantasy that if he had to go on listening much longer he might suddenly find himself going down on his knees and eating grass in front of everybody. It was not clear to him why he should do that. But, as though in search of protection, he looked round, to see what had become of Ulrich and Diotima.

These two had taken shelter under a wall where there was a thin veil of shadow, and all that could be gathered from their low-voiced talk was that they were involved in an argument. . . .

" That's a hopeless way of looking at things ! " Diotima said.

" What is ? " Ulrich asked, more mechanically than curiously.

" There *are* individualities in life, after all ! "

Ulrich tried to catch her eye from where he stood at her side. " Good heavens," he said, " we've been over all this before ! "

" You have no heart ! Or else you wouldn't always talk like that ! " she said gently. From the cobbles on which the sun had been shining there was warmer air rising up her legs, which were enclosed in the long skirts like the legs of a robed statue, inaccessible and, for the world, non-existent. She gave no sign that she was aware of it. It was a caress that had nothing to do with any being, any man.

Now there seemed to be a pallor, a blankness in her eyes. But that might have been merely an impression caused by her reserve in a situation where she was exposed to the glances of passers-by.

Turning to Ulrich, she said with an effort :

" When a woman has to choose between duty and passion, what then should she rely on if not on her character ? "

" You needn't choose ! " Ulrich retorted.

" You go too far ! " his cousin whispered. " I wasn't speaking of myself ! "

Since he made no reply to that, the two of them remained silent for a while, both gazing out over the square with the same hostile stare.

Then Diotima asked : " Do you think it possible that what we call our soul might issue forth from the shadow in which it is usually wrapped ? "

Ulrich looked at her, disconcerted.

" In special and privileged human beings," she supplemented.

" Have you come to trying to get into rapport with spirits ? " he asked incredulously. " Has Arnheim introduced you to a medium ? "

Diotima was disappointed. " I shouldn't have expected you to misunderstand me like that ! " she said reproachfully. " When I said 'issue forth from the shadow' I meant out of the insub-stantiality, out of that glimmering concealment in which we some-times sense the presence of the unusual. It is spread out like a net, tormenting us because it neither holds us fast nor lets us go. Don't you think there must have been times when it was different ? When the inner life was more intensely noticeable, when individual human beings went along an illumined path—in a word, went along what used to be called the holy path, and miracles became reality because they are nothing but an ever-present, different kind of reality ! "

Diotima was amazed at the sureness with which she found her-self saying all this, without any special heightening of her mood, as it were with solid ground under her feet.

Ulrich was secretly furious, but, what was more to the point, he was shocked to the core. ' So it's come to this, has it,' he said to himself, ' that this giant hen has begun talking exactly like me ? ' Before his mental eye he again saw Diotima in the shape of a colossal hen that was about to peck at a little worm, which was his soul. The childish terror of old, the dread of the Tall Lady, reached out for him, mingled with another curious sensation : he found it pleasant to be as it were spiritually consumed by this stupid affinity with a person who was related to him. The affinity was of course only an accident, and all nonsense. He did not believe either in the magic of kinship or in the possibility that he could ever, even in the most dismal state of drunkenness, take his cousin seriously. But recently something in him had been undergoing a transformation ; he was growing soft ; his inner attitude, which had always been that of an attacker, was gradually loosening up and showing a tendency to turn into a desire for tenderness, dreams, kinship, or heaven knows what, which also manifested itself in the fact that the counter-mood that was at war with this, a mood of ill will, sometimes would break out of him quite unexpectedly.

That was why now too he made fun of his cousin. " If you believe that," he said to her, " I consider it your duty either publicly or secretly, but as quickly as possible, to become Arnheim's ' out-and-out ' mistress ! "

" Please do not say such things ! I have not given you any right to speak of that ! " Diotima rebuked him.

" I must speak of it ! Until a short time ago it was not clear to me precisely what the relationship was between you and Arnheim. But now I see it clearly, and you seem to me like a person who is in all seriousness trying to fly to the moon. I would never have thought you capable of such madness."

" I have already told you I am capable of being immoderate," Diotima said, gazing into the air with what was meant to be a daring expression ; but the sunlight made her screw up her eyes so that she looked almost merry.

" These are the delirious ravings of starved love," Ulrich said, " and they pass off when satisfaction is achieved." He wondered what Arnheim might have up his sleeve where his cousin was concerned. Was he regretting his proposal and trying to cover his retreat by turning it all into a farce ? But then it would have been simpler to go away and not come back again. After all, a man who had been occupied with business all his life long must surely be capable of the callousness necessary for such a step. He remembered having observed in Arnheim certain signs that, in a man who was getting on in years, indicated passion : the face was sometimes greyish-sallow, slack, and tired, and looking into it was like looking into a room where at noon the bed was still unmade. He guessed that the most likely explanation was the havoc caused by two almost equally strong passions fighting each other to a standstill. But since he was incapable of imagining the passion for power intensified to the degree in which it ruled Arnheim, Ulrich could not appreciate the violence of the measures that love took to combat this.

" What a strange person you are ! " Diotima said.   " Always different from what one would expect ! Wasn't it you yourself who talked to me about seraphic love ? "

" And you think one can really do that ? " Ulrich asked absent-mindedly.

" Of course one can't do it in the way you described ! "

" So Arnheim loves you seraphically ? " Ulrich began to laugh softly.

" Do stop laughing ! " Diotima said in vexation, and there was a faint hiss in her voice.

" Of course you don't know what I'm laughing about," he said apologetically.   " I am laughing, in a manner of speaking, out of excitement.   You and Arnheim are sensitive beings.   You go in for poetry.   I am utterly convinced that you are sometimes touched by a breath—well, by a breath of something or other— the question is only *what* it is.   And so now you want to get to the bottom of it all, with all the thoroughness that your idealism makes you capable of ? "

" Don't you yourself always say one must be precise and thorough ? " Diotima retorted.

Ulrich was slightly taken aback.   " You are mad ! " he said. " Forgive my saying so—you are mad ! And *you* must not be so ! "

Meanwhile Arnheim had been telling the General that the world had for the last two generations been undergoing the great-est of revolutions : the end of the soul was in sight.

It gave the General a start.   Heavens above, here was some-thing new again ! To tell the truth, up to this moment he had thought, in spite of Diotima, that there was really no such thing as ' the soul ' ; at the Military College and in the regiment one had snapped one's fingers at such churchy sort of talk.   But now that here was a manufacturer of guns and armour-plating talking about it as calmly as if he could see it standing somewhere nearby, the General's eyes began to shift uneasily and gloomily, goggling into the translucent air round about.

But Arnheim did not wait to be asked for explanations ; the words flowed from his lips, out of the pale pink slit between the clipped moustache and the little pointed beard. He pointed out that since the decline of the Church, that is to say, more or less since the beginnings of the bourgeois age, the soul had been undergoing a process of shrinking and withering. Since then it had lost God, and all stability of values and ideals, and today mankind had reached a stage where it lived without morality, without principles, indeed even without experiences.

The General did not quite understand why one could not have experiences if one had no morals. So Arnheim opened the big volume, bound in pigskin, that he held in his hand and which contained an expensive facsimile of a manuscript so valuable that it could not be taken out of the building even by such an unusual mortal as he was. The General beheld an angel whose wings extended, horizontally, across two pages on which there was also represented dark earth, golden sky, and strange streaks of colour that might have been clouds. He was gazing at a reproduction of one of the most moving and glorious of early mediæval paintings, but since he did not know this and since he was an old hand at fowling, and well acquainted with portrayals of it, all that he could make of it was that a winged creature with a long neck, which was neither a human being nor a snipe, must indicate some aberration to which his companion wished to draw his attention.

And here was Arnheim with finger extended, pointing to it, and saying thoughtfully : " Here you have before your eyes what the creatrix of the Austrian Campaign would like to restore to the world . . . ! "

" Quite, quite," Stumm answered. Evidently he had failed to appreciate the thing properly, and so now he must be careful what he said.

" This grandeur of expression, utterly simple though it is," Arnheim went on, " makes it utterly clear to us what our age has lost. What does all our science signify compared to this ? Patchwork ! Or our art ? Extremities without a body to unite them ! Our minds lack the secret of integrity, and that, you see, is why I am so moved by this Austrian plan to bestow an all-uniting example and a great communal idea upon the world, even if I do not think it entirely feasible. I am a German. Everything in the world today, everywhere, is so noisy and crude, and in Germany it is even more so than anywhere else. In every country people strain and toil from morn to night, whether they are at work or amusing themselves, but in Germany they get up even earlier and go to bed even later than anywhere else. Everywhere in the world there is the spirit of cold figures and brute force, which has lost contact with the soul, but in Germany we have more business men than anywhere else, and our army is the strongest." He gazed about him in the square with a look of delight. " In Austria all that has not yet gone so far. Here there is still something of the past, and people still have something of man's primal intuition. If such a thing is still possible at all, then it is only from here that salvation could come, delivering the German spirit from rationalism. But I fear," he added, sighing, " it is hardly likely to happen. Nowadays a great idea encounters too much resistance. The only use great ideas have nowadays is to prevent each other from being overmuch misused. We are living, so to speak, in a state of moral peace armed to the teeth with ideas."

He smiled over his jest. And then something else occurred to him :

" You know, the difference between Germany and Austria, this difference of which we have just been talking, always makes me think of billiards. It is just the same with playing billiards—everything goes wrong if one tries to do it according to calculation instead of by feeling."

The General had guessed that he was intended to feel flattered by the phrase about armed moral peace, and he wished to give a token of his attentiveness. He did understand something about billiards, and so he said : " Of course I may be wrong, but I play snooker myself, and skittles too, and I never heard there was any difference between the German and the Austrian style of play."

Arnheim closed his eyes and reflected. " I myself never play billiards," he said after a moment, " but I know that one can play the ball high or low, from the right or from the left. One can strike the second ball head on or merely graze it. One can hit hard or lightly. One may choose to make the cannon stronger or weaker. And I am sure there are many more such possibilities. Now, I can imagine each of these elements being graduated in all directions, so that there are therefore an almost infinite number of possible combinations. If I wished to state them theoretically, I should have to make use not only of the laws of mathematics and of the mechanics of rigid bodies, but also of the law of elasticity. I should have to know the coefficients of the material and what influence the temperature had. I should need the most delicate methods of measuring the co-ordination and graduation of my motor impulses. My estimation of distances would have to be as exact as a nonius. My faculty of combination would have to be more rapid and more dependable than a slide-rule. To say nothing of allowing for a margin of error, a field of dispersal, and the circumstance that the aim, which is the correct coincidence of the two balls, is itself not clearly definable, but merely a collection of only just adequately surveyable facts grouped round an average value."

Arnheim spoke slowly and in a manner that compelled attention, as though pouring something drop by drop out of a phial into a glass. He did not spare his companion a single detail.

" And so you will see," he continued, " I should need to have all the qualities and to do all the things that I cannot possibly have or do. You are, I am sure, enough of a mathematician yourself to appreciate that it would take one a lifetime even to work out the course of an ordinary cannon-stroke in such a way. This is where our brain simply leaves us in the lurch ! And yet I can go up to the billiard-table with a cigarette between my lips and a tune in my head, so to speak with my hat on, and, hardly bothering to survey the situation at all, take my cue to the ball and have the problem solved in a twinkling ! General, it is the same thing that is always happening in life ! You are not only an Austrian, you are an officer too, and so you will understand what I mean when I say that politics, honour, war, art, all the decisive processes in life, are completed outside the scope of the conscious intelligence. All man's greatness has its roots in the irrational. Even we business men do not work things out by brainwork, as you may believe. No, we learn—I speak, naturally, of the leading men— the little men may very well count their pennies—we learn to regard our really successful inspirations as a mystery that defies all attempts at analysis. Anyone who does not care deeply about feeling, morality, religion, music, poetry, form, discipline, chivalry, generosity of mind, candour, and tolerance—believe me, anyone who does not care deeply about these things will never make a business man on the grand scale. That is why I have always admired the soldier's profession—particularly in Austria, based as it is here on age-old traditions—and I am delighted that you are giving Frau Tuzzi your support. It relieves me of some anxiety. Your influence, taken with that of our younger friend, is extremely important. All great things are based upon the same qualities. Great obligations are a blessing, General ! "

Carried away by his feelings, he shook Stumm by the hand. Then he added :

" Very, very few people know that real greatness has no foundations in reason. I mean, everything strong is simple."

Stumm von Bordwehr fought for breath. He could hardly make sense of a word of all this, and felt an urgent desire to rush headlong into the Library, where he had been going, and spend hours reading up all these points, the exposition of which the great man at his side obviously intended by way of flattery to him. Finally, however, out of this springtide storm whirling in his head there came a ray of surprising lucidity. ' Damn it all,' he said to himself, ' the fellow wants to get something out of a chap ! ' He looked up.

Arnheim was still holding the book in both hands, but was making a serious effort to stop a cab. His face was slightly flushed and excited-looking, as is that of a man who has just been exchanging ideas with another.

The General was silent, as one is silent out of respect after some weighty utterance has been made. If Arnheim wanted something from him, then he, General Stumm, could also want something from Arnheim that would be to the advantage of the ' Service '. This thought opened up such possibilities that Stumm for the time being put off thinking about whether it was all really true. But if the angel in the book had suddenly lifted his painted wings in order to let clever little General Stumm have a glance underneath, the General could not have felt happier and more bewildered than he did.

In the corner where Diotima and Ulrich were standing the following question had meanwhile been raised : should a woman in Diotima's difficult position make an act of renunciation, or should she let herself be carried away into committing adultery, or should she take a third course and do something that was a mixture of the first two, belonging to the first man physically, perhaps, and spiritually to the second man, or perhaps physically to no one ? This third condition was like a song without words for her to go by ; there was only the sublime sound of the music of it. And Diotima still stuck austerely to the principle that she was certainly not speaking of herself, but only of ' a woman '. Her glance, armed for anger, checked Ulrich every time his words began to fuse the two into one.

And so he found himself talking in a roundabout way too. " Have you ever seen a dog ? " he asked. " Oh, you only think you have ! You always just see something that appears to you, more or less correctly, to be a dog. It hasn't all the doggy quali- ties, and it has got something or other that's personal, which no other dog has. Well then, how are we ever to do ' the right thing ' in life ? We can only do something that is never ' the ' right thing, but always somehow more and somehow less than right.

" And has a tile ever fallen from a roof exactly according to the law of falling bodies ? Never ! Even in the laboratory things don't behave the way they're supposed to. They diverge irregu- larly and chaotically in all directions, and there is something of a fiction in our regarding that as being due to experimental errors on our part and supposing that somewhere midway there is indeed a true value.

" Or consider—one finds certain stones and calls them diamonds because of some properties common to them all. But one of these stones comes from Africa and another comes from Asia. One is dug out of the earth by a Negro, the other by an Asiatic. Perhaps this difference is so important that it may cancel out what the two stones have in common—who knows ? In the equation ' diamond plus circumstances always equals diamond ' the utility-value of the diamond is so great that in comparison the value of the cir- cumstances simply vanishes. Yet it is possible to imagine spiritual circumstances in which the whole situation is reversed.

" Everything partakes of the universal, and in addition to this it is individual, something special to itself. Everything is true, and in addition to this it is wild and free and not comparable to anything. To me this makes it seem as though the personal quality of any given creature were precisely that which does not coincide with anything else. I once told you that the more truth we discover the less there is of the personal left in the world. There has for a long time been a war going on against individuality, which is steadily losing ground. I don't know how much of us will be left over in the end, by the time everything has been rationalised. Nothing, perhaps. But perhaps then, when the false significance that we attach to the personality has disappeared, we shall enter into some new realm of significance as into the most glorious adventure.

" And so how are you going to decide ? Ought ' a woman ' to act according to the law ? Then she may as well act according to the law society has set up, and be done with it. Morality is an entirely justifiable average and collective value, which is meant to be followed literally and without any divagations, wherever it is acknowledged. Individual cases, however, cannot be decided morally. There is less and less morality about them, the more they partake of the inexhaustibility of the universe ! "

" You have delivered a speech ! " Diotima said. She felt a certain satisfaction in the loftiness of these demands made upon her, but at the same time wished to demonstrate her superiority by not talking equally at random. " And so," she asked, " what is a woman, in the situation of which we have been speaking, to do in real life ? "

" Take it as it comes."

" But which ? Whom ? "

" Whichever turns up ! Her husband, her lover, her renunciation, her mixture of alternatives."

" Have you really any notion what that means ? " Diotima asked, feeling painfully reminded of how the exalted resolution to perhaps renounce Arnheim had its wings clipped every night by the simple fact that she slept in one room with Tuzzi.

Something of this thought must have conveyed itself to her cousin, for he asked bluntly :

" Will you try your luck with me ? "

" With you ? " Diotima answered, drawling. She tried to keep herself in countenance by means of some inoffensive mockery : " Perhaps, if this is an offer, you will expound just how you picture such a thing."

" Oh, certainly ! " Ulrich replied quite gravely. " You do read a great deal, don't you ? "

" Yes, of course."

" And how do you do it ? I can give you the answer at once : your preconceptions leave out whatever doesn't suit you. The same thing has already been done by the author. In the same way you leave things out in dreams and in your imaginings. So I offer you my conclusion that beauty or excitement comes into the world as a result of things having been left out. Obviously our behaviour in the midst of reality is a compromise, a medial condition in which the emotions prevent each other from developing to their full passionate intensity, blurring slightly into grey. Children, who have not yet acquired this attitude, are for that reason happier and also unhappier than adults. And I will at once add this : stupid people also leave things out. Stupidity is, after all, something that makes for happiness. I therefore suggest that we begin as follows—that we should try to love each other as though you and I were figures created by a poet and meeting in the pages of a book. In any case, however, let us leave out all the up-holstery of fatty tissue that is what makes reality look round and plump."

Diotima felt driven to make objections to this. She wished to turn the conversation out of this all too personal channel, and she wished, furthermore, to show that she understood something of the problems that had been touched upon.

" That is all very well," she answered. " But it is asserted that art is a holiday from reality, its function being that we should return to reality refreshed and invigorated ! "

" And I am unreasonable enough," her cousin retorted, " to assert that there must not be any such things as ' holidays '. What sort of life is it that one has to keep on riddling with holes called ' holidays ' ? Would we punch holes in a painting because it demands too much from us in appreciation of the beautiful ? Is it intended that there shall be holidays and rest-cures as an occasional relief from eternal bliss ? I confess to you that some-times I even find the thought of sleep downright disagreeable."

" Ah, there you are, you see ! " Diotima broke in, seizing upon this example. " You see how unnatural what you are saying is ! Just think of a human being without any need of ever leaving off and resting ! I cannot think of anything that so illuminates the difference between you and Arnheim as this does ! On the one side there is a mind that does not know the shadow-side of things, and on the other a mind that has developed out of the fullness of human life, with shadow and sunshine mingled ! "

" I don't mind admitting that I exaggerate," Ulrich confessed, quite unmoved. " You will recognise it even more clearly if we go into the question in detail. Let us think of, for instance, great writers. One may model one's life *on* them, but one cannot squeeze life itself out of them, like wine from grapes. What once moved them they have transfixed in such solid form that it confronts us like embossed metal, even from the spaces between the lines. And what have they really said, when it comes to the point ? Nobody knows. They themselves have never known it all of a piece. They are like a field over which the bees fly, and at the same time they are themselves a sort of flying this way and that. Their thoughts and feelings exhibit all the degrees of a transition between truths (or, of course, errors) which can, if it comes to the point, be defined and, at the other extreme, indefinable entities in a state of constant transformation that approach us of their own accord and elude us when we try to observe them.

" It is impossible to detach an idea in a book from the page in which it is enclosed. The thought signals to us like the look on the face of someone who is being swept past us in a crowd of other people, a face, a look, that looms up significantly for one brief instant. I dare say I'm again exaggerating slightly. But now I should like to ask you—what, after all, does happen in our life that is not like what I have been describing ? I shall say nothing of the precise, measurable, definable impressions that we have. But all the other concepts on which we base our lives are nothing but metaphors that have been left to congeal. Between how many different pictures of things does not such a simple concept as that, for instance, of manliness flicker and oscillate ! It's something like a little mist that changes shape at every puff of breath. And there's nothing in it that is solid—no impression, no order, nothing ! And so if, as I have said, in poetry we simply leave out all that doesn't suit us, all we are doing is to restore the primal condition of life."

" My dear cousin," Diotima said, " these reflections strike me as rather beside the point."

Ulrich had paused for a moment, and into the pause these words of hers fell.

" Yes," he said, " it does seem to be so. I hope I haven't been talking too loudly."

" You have been talking rapidly, quietly, and at length," she reassured him, a faint gibe in her voice. " All the same, you have not said a single word of what you meant to say. Do you know what you have been explaining to me all over again ? That reality should be abolished ! I must confess that after I had heard that remark of yours for the first time—I think it was on one of our expeditions—I couldn't get it out of my mind for a long while. I don't know why. But unfortunately you have again omitted to say how you mean to set about it ! "

" It is obvious that if I were to explain that I should have to talk for just as long again. But do you really expect it to be simple ? If I am not mistaken, you have spoken of wanting to fly away together with Arnheim into some sort of sanctity. So you imagine that as a kind of second reality. But what I have been saying means that we must regain possession of unreality. There is no more sense in reality now ! "

" Oh, Arnheim would scarcely be in agreement with *that* ! " Diotima commented.

" Of course he wouldn't. That's just the difference between us. He would like to bestow significance on the fact that he eats, drinks, sleeps, is the great Arnheim, and doesn't know whether to marry you or not, and to this end he has all his life long been collecting all the treasures of the mind."

Ulrich suddenly paused, and the silence lengthened.

At last, in a different tone, he asked : " Can you tell me why I should be having this conversation with you, of all people ? At this moment I find myself recalling my childhood. I was, though you will find it hard to credit, a good child, as mild as the air on a warm moonshiny night. I was capable of being bound-lessly in love with a dog, or a knife . . ." But then he left what he was saying unfinished.

Diotima looked at him doubtfully. Once again she remembered how intensely he had at one time been in favour of ' precision of feeling ', whereas today he spoke on the opposite side. He had once even gone so far as to reproach Arnheim with having insufficient purity of intention, and today he spoke in favour of 'taking things as they came'. And she was troubled by the fact that Ulrich was in favour of an intense life of feeling without any 'time off', whereas Arnheim had said, ambiguously, that one should never wholly hate or *wholly love*. She felt very ill at ease with these thoughts.

" Do you really believe then that there is any such thing as limitless feeling ? " Ulrich asked.

" Oh, there is such a thing as limitless emotion ! " Diotima replied, once again with firm ground underfoot.

" You know, I don't quite believe in it," Ulrich said absently. " Oddly enough we often talk about it, but it's the very thing we spend all our lives dodging as if we were afraid of drowning in it."

He noticed that Diotima was not listening. She was gazing uneasily at Arnheim, who was looking around for a cab.

" I'm afraid," she said, " we must release him from the General."

" I'll go and get a cab and take over the General myself," Ulrich offered.

And in the instant when he began to walk off, Diotima laid her hand on his arm and said in a tone of gentle agreement that was meant as a kindly reward for his endeavours :

" Any emotion that is not limitless is of no value."

115 *The tip of your breast is like a poppy-leaf.*

IN accordance with the law that times of great stability are followed by times of tempestuous upheaval, Bonadea suffered a relapse. Her attempts to get on closer terms with Diotima had been in vain, and nothing came of her splendid resolve to punish Ulrich by letting him see the two rivals for his love united in friendship and leaving him on one side—a fantasy over which she had spent much time dreaming. She had to swallow her pride and knock once more at her beloved's door ; but he seemed to have arranged things so that they were continually being disturbed, and the stories she told in explanation of why she was there again, even though he did not deserve it, were all wasted on his dispassionate friendliness. She was very much beset by the desire to make a frightful scene about this, but on the other hand her resolve to maintain a decorous demeanour made this impossible, so that in the course of time she came to feel an intense dislike of the virtues she had imposed on herself. By night the headache set up by unsatisfied desire was like a second head upon her shoulders, like some coconut whose shell had by a freak of Nature grown its monkeyish hair on the inside ; and after a while she was as full of impotent frenzy as a drinker who has been deprived of his tipple. In her thoughts she talked badly of Diotima, calling her a cheat and an insufferable hussy ; and her imagination provided coolly expert annotation to the noble, womanly sublimity that was the secret of Diotima's charm. The imitation of the other woman's appearance that had for a time given her such delight now became a prison, from which she broke out into wild and furious liberty. The curling-tongs and the looking-glass lost their power to turn her into the idealised image of herself, and with that the artificial state of consciousness in which she had been floating also collapsed. Even sleep, which Bonadea had always revelled in for all her conflicts in life, now kept her waiting sometimes for a while after she had gone to bed ; and this was so new that it affected her as being a morbid insomnia. In this state she now felt what everyone feels when he or she is seriously ill : that the spirit is taking flight, leaving the body in the lurch like a wounded soldier on the battlefield. When Bonadea lay suffering her trials of spirit as though she lay in redhot sand, all the clever turns of phrase she had admired Diotima for seemed to be miles away and she honestly despised them.

And when she could no longer bring herself to go and seek out Ulrich yet again, she once more thought out a plan to win him back to having natural emotions. It was of course the end of the plan that was finished first : Bonadea would invade Diotima's drawing-room when Ulrich was there with the siren. All those discussions at Diotima's had obviously been a mere blind while they flirted with each other instead of getting something done for the public weal. But now *Bonadea* would do something for the public weal; and with this the beginning of her plan was also completed. For nobody was bothering any more at all about Moosbrugger, and he was going to his doom while the rest of them were spinning phrases!

Bonadea was not for an instant surprised that it was once again Moosbrugger who came to her rescue in the hour of need. She would have thought him abominable if she had spent any time thinking about him; but all she thought was: ' If Ulrich takes such an interest in him, then I'll see to it he doesn't forget him!' Then, as she continued to brood over her plan, two little things occurred to her. She remembered that Ulrich had said, in the course of a discussion about this murderer, that every person had a second soul, which was always innocent, and that a person who was responsible for his actions could always do the other thing, but that a person who was not responsible for his actions never could. From this she drew something rather like the conclusion that she was going to be not responsible for her actions and that she would then be innocent, a condition that was, furthermore, not yet present in Ulrich and which should now be brought about in him, to his salvation.

With this aim before her she spent several evenings—smartly dressed up as though going to a party—strolling past Diotima's windows, and she never had to wait long before these windows were lit up, in token of activity within, all along the front of the house. What she had told her husband was that she was invited to go but that she never stayed long; and in the course of a few days, while she was still trying to screw up her courage, the lies she had told, and these evening strolls in front of a house where she had no business, set up a gradually intensified impulse that was soon to take her up the steps. She might be seen by acquaintances, or her husband might happen to pass that way and catch sight of her. The house-porter might notice her, or a policeman might wonder what she was doing and question her. The more often she repeated her stroll the larger did the dangers loom before her and the more probable did it become that something would happen if she were to hesitate much longer. Now, Bonadea had no small experience of slipping quickly into doorways or following paths on which she did not want to be seen, but on all previous occasions of this kind she had had with her, like a guardian angel, the consciousness that this was something inevitably associated with what she was after, whereas this time she was about to penetrate into a house where she was not expected and where it was quite uncertain what awaited her. She began to feel like an assassin who finds the whole thing turning out rather different from what he originally imagined and whom circumstances then sweep upwards into the state where the actual pistol-report, or the glitter of the drops of vitriol flying through the air, scarcely brings with it any heightening of his sensations.

Bonadea had nothing of *that* sort in mind, but she was in a similar state of spiritual isolation when at last she really pressed the door-bell and walked in.

Little Rachel unobtrusively approached Ulrich and told him that someone wished to speak to him outside, without revealing that this ' someone ' was an unknown lady, heavily veiled. When Rachel closed the drawing-room door again, as Ulrich came out into the hall, Bonadea flung the veil back from her face. At this moment she was firmly convinced that Moosbrugger's fate could not be left undecided for another instant, and she hailed Ulrich not in the manner of a mistress tormented by jealousy, but breathlessly, like a Marathon runner. Effortlessly lying, she told him in explanation of her presence that her husband had the previous day informed her that Moosbrugger would soon be past saving.

" There's nothing I hate so much," she concluded, " as murderers of that obscene kind. But in spite of that I have exposed myself to the risk of probably being regarded as an intruder here— anyway you must now go straight back to the lady of the house and to the most influential of her guests and raise this matter, if you still mean to get anything done ! "

She did not know what she expected. Was it that Ulrich, full of emotion, should thank her and summon Diotima forth, and that Diotima would then retire with her and him into some distant room ? Was it that Diotima might perhaps be lured out by catching the sound of voices in the hall, whereupon she, Bonadea, would make it clear to her that she, Bonadea, was far from being the person least fitted to take an interest in Ulrich's noble feelings ? Her eyes flashed and were moist. Her hands trembled. She raised her voice.

Ulrich was extremely embarrassed and kept on smiling in a desperate attempt to quiet her down and gain time to think out how he was to convince her that she must go away again as quickly as possible. The situation was difficult, and it might have come to an end with a fit of screaming or weeping on Bonadea's part, if Rachel had not come to his aid.

Little Rachel had all the time been standing there, not far from the two of them, her eyes wide open and shining. She had at once guessed at some romantic affair when the unknown beautiful lady, who was trembling all over, had asked to speak to Ulrich. She managed to hear most of the discussion, and the syllables of the name ' Moosbrugger ' resounded in her ears like reports from a gun. The sorrow, desire, and jealousy that throbbed and rang in this lady's voice carried her away too, although she did not know what it was all about. She guessed that the lady was Ulrich's mistress, and she herself instantly fell twice as much in love with him as before. She felt herself being swept along to perform some deed, just as though these two had been in full-throated song and she had felt impelled to lift up her voice and join in. And so it came that, with a glance imploring silence and secrecy, she opened a door and invited these two people to enter the only room not being used this evening. This was the first overt act of disloyalty to her mistress that she had ever committed and she was in no doubt as to what discovery would mean ; but the world was so beautiful, and glorious excitement is such an untidy state of mind, that she had no chance to think twice about it.

When the light flashed up and Bonadea gradually realised where she was, her legs almost gave way under her and the crimson flush of jealousy flooded into her cheeks : for what she saw, looking about her, was Diotima's bedroom. There were stockings, hair-brushes, and all sorts of other things strewn about, the flotsam and jetsam that was left behind when a woman had hastily changed from head to foot, dressing for a party, and her maid had had no time to tidy up or had left it, as was here the case, until the next morning, because then the room was due to be turned out anyway ; for on evenings when there was a big party the bedroom

came into use as a storage-place for furniture removed from the
other rooms in order to clear enough space. So the air was heavy
with the smell of all this furniture, tightly wedged together, and
of powder, soap, and scent.

" Silly thing for the girl to do," Ulrich said with a laugh.
" We can't stay here. But of course you shouldn't have come here
at all. There isn't anything to be done for Moosbrugger anyway."

" I oughtn't to have gone to all the trouble of coming here,
you say ? " Bonadea repeated in a very small voice. Her eyes
strayed. How, she wondered in anguish, could the girl have had
the notion of taking Ulrich into the inmost sanctum of the household if she had not been accustomed to doing so ? But she could
not bring herself to confront him with this piece of evidence.
Suppressing that, she said reproachfully but rather blankly :
" How can you manage to sleep soundly when such an injustice
is happening ? I sometimes don't sleep for nights on end, and
that is why I made up my mind to come in search of you."

She had turned her back on the room and was standing at the
window, staring into the opaque glimmering darkness that loomed
up towards her from outside. It might be trees ; or it might be
some deep courtyard into which she was looking down. In spite
of her excitement she was sure enough in her orientation to know
that this room did not look out upon the street. Possibly people
could see in, from other windows opposite ; and when she pictured to herself how she was standing here, together with her
faithless lover, in a flood of light, with the curtains not drawn,
before some unknown dark auditorium, and the scene her rival's
bedroom, she felt intense agitation. She had taken off her hat
and thrown her coat back, and her forehead and the warm tips
of her breasts touched the cold window-pane. Her eyes were
moist with tenderness and tears. Slowly she freed herself from
the fascination of the darkness and turned again to her lover, but
there was still something left in her eyes of the soft yielding
blackness into which she had been gazing, and it lent them a depth
of which she knew nothing.

" Ulrich ! " she said thrillingly. " You are not really bad !
You only pretend to be ! You put all the difficulties you can in
your own way, in order not to be good."

The situation once again became dangerous as a result of these unusually sensible words of Bonadea's. This, for once, was not just a woman dominated by her body and exhibiting a ridiculous yearning to find comfort in a high intellectual tone ; here it was the beauty of that body itself uttering its right to the gentle dignity of love.

Ulrich went up to her and put his arm round her shoulders. They turned back towards the darkness and looked out into it together. Dissolving in the seemingly illimitable obscurity was a faint glimmer of light that came from the house, so that it looked as if some dense mist filled the air with its soft pervasive presence. For some reason or other Ulrich had a very intense sensation of staring out into the crisp coolness of an October night, although in fact it was now nearly the end of winter, and it seemed to him the whole city was wrapped in it as in some huge woolly blanket. Then it occurred to him that one might just as well say a woolly blanket was like an October night. He felt a soft unsureness creeping on his skin, and drew Bonadea closer to him.

" Will you go in now ? " Bonadea asked.

" And prevent the injustice that is about to be done to Moosbrugger ? No. After all, I don't even know whether any injustice is really being done to him. What do I know about him ? I once had a fleeting glimpse of him in court, and I've read various things that have been written about him. It's as though I had dreamt that the tip of your breast was like a poppy-leaf. Am I therefore entitled to believe that it is really one ? "

He mused. And Bonadea also mused.

Ulrich thought : ' And isn't what it comes to really that even in broad daylight what one human being amounts to for another human being isn't much more than a string of symbols ? '

And Bonadea's reflections resulted in her saying : " Come, let us go away ! "

" That's impossible," Ulrich told her. " Somebody would ask what had become of me, and if anything were to leak out about your visit, it would cause a very undesirable sensation."

And after that they were united again in silence, and in staring out into the darkness, the two of them together in something that might have been an October night, or a night in January, or a woolly blanket, or sorrow, or happiness, without their being able to define it.

" Why do you never do the obvious thing ? " Bonadea asked.

All of a sudden he remembered a dream that he must have had quite recently. He was one of those people who dream seldom, or at least never have any recollection of their dreams, and it gave him a queer feeling to become aware of this memory, as it unexpectedly opened up and let him in. In the dream he had several times tried in vain to make his way across a steep mountainside, each time being driven back by a violent sensation of dizziness. Without going into the problem any more deeply he now knew that this experience referred to Moosbrugger, who, however, did not come into the dream at all. Besides that, since a dream image often has several layers of meaning, it was also symbolic in physical terms of the vain endeavours his mind was making and which had recently been manifesting themselves everywhere in his conversation and in his affairs, resembling nothing more than a striving onwards where there was no way, a perpetual inability to get beyond some given point. He could not help smiling at the ingenuous concreteness with which his dream had represented this : smooth rock and sliding screes, here and there a single tree as something to hold on to or a goal to make for, and besides that the violent increase in the steepness of the incline as he went on. He had tried higher up and lower down, each with the same lack of success, and he was becoming sick and dizzy. And then he said to someone who was with him that they had better drop the whole thing, for away down there at the bottom of the valley there was, after all, the easy road that everybody took. That was clear enough ! Furthermore, it seemed to Ulrich that the person with him might well have been Bonadea. Perhaps, too, he had really dreamt that the tip of her breast was like a poppy-leaf. Something vague and incoherent, something that for the groping emotion might very well be broad and jagged and of the dark bluish purple of a mallow, detached itself, like a mist, from some not yet illuminated cranny in the dream image.

At this moment his consciousness suddenly lit up with that special lucidity in which one sees behind the scenes of oneself and a glimpse of all that goes on there, though one may afterwards be quite unable to describe what one has seen. The relationship there is between a dream and what it expresses was something he knew about ; it was none other than that of analogy, of metaphor, a relationship that had often occupied his mind. A metaphor contains a truth and a falsehood, which are inextricably interlocked in one's emotions. If one takes it as it is and forms it with one's senses, giving it the shape of reality, what arises is dreams and art ; but between these two and real, full life there is a glass wall. If one takes it up with one's intellect, separating whatever does not accord from the elements that are in perfect concord, what arises is truth and knowledge, but emotion is destroyed. In the same way that certain species of bacteria split an organic substance into two parts, the human species by its way of living splits the original vital state of the metaphor into the solid matter of reality and truth, on the one hand, and, on the other, the glassy atmosphere of premonition, faith, and artefacts. It seems that between these two there is no third possibility. And yet how often something uncertain does come to a desired end if one only sets about it without taking too much thought !

Ulrich had the feeling that amid the tangle of streets through which his thoughts and moods had so often taken him he was now standing in the main square, where all the streets had their beginning. And he had hinted at all this in answering Bonadea's question why he never did the obvious thing.

Probably she did not understand what he meant. But without doubt this was one of her good days. She reflected for a while, pressed Ulrich's arm closer to hers, and summed it all up by saying : " Well, you don't *think* in dreams either. What happens is you experience some story or other."

That was almost true. He squeezed her hand. Suddenly she had tears in her eyes again. Slowly the tears coursed down her face, and from her skin, now drenched in their saltiness, there arose the indefinable ozone of desire. Inhaling it, Ulrich felt a great longing for that filmy, slippery state, for abandonment and oblivion. But he pulled himself together and gently led her to the door. At this instant he was sure that there was still something lying ahead of him and that he must not fritter it away in half-hearted attachments.

" You must go now," he said in a low voice, " and don't be cross with me—I don't know when we shall be able to see one another again—I have a great deal on my hands now, working out my own problems."

And the miracle happened : Bonadea put up no resistance and made no angrily haughty remarks. She was no longer jealous. She felt that she herself was ' experiencing a story '. She would have liked to enfold him in her arms ; she had an obscure feeling that he ought to be pulled down to earth again ; she would have liked best to make the sign of the cross over his forehead, protectively, as she did with her children. And this seemed to her so beautiful that it did not occur to her to see that it might signify the end. She put her hat on and kissed him, and then she kissed him once again through the veil, so that the threads of it glowed like red-hot window-bars.

With the aid of Rachel, who had been guarding the door and listening at the keyhole, it was possible for Bonadea to slip away unobserved, even though the party was already breaking up. As a reward, Ulrich pressed a big tip into Rachel's hand and said some words of praise to her for her presence of mind. Rachel was so ecstatic about both that, without her being aware of it, her fingers for some time continued to clutch not only the money but his hand too. At last, unable to help laughing, he patted her shoulder in a friendly way as she suddenly blushed scarlet.

116 *The two trees of life and the demand for a General Secretariat for Precision and the Spirit.*

ON that evening there had not been so many guests at the Tuzzis' as formerly. Attendance at gatherings of the Collateral Campaign had been falling off, and those who had come this evening left earlier than usual. Even the appearance of His Highness at the last minute—with the air, incidentally, of being worried and abstracted, and in fact being in a bad humour because he had received alarming news about the nationalist agitations that were being stirred up against his work—could not prevent the breaking up of the party. People lingered for a little on the assumption that the Count's arrival meant there was some special news, but then, when he gave no sign of having anything of the kind to report and paid scant attention to the remaining guests, even the last of them departed. So Ulrich, when he reappeared, found to his dismay that the rooms were almost empty. And a short time later the ' most intimate circle ' was alone in the deserted drawing-room, enlarged only by the presence of Permanent Secretary Tuzzi, who had come home in the meantime.

" Of course one can call an eighty-eight-year-old monarch of peace a ' symbol '," His Highness was declaring. " There we have a great idea. But this idea must also be given a political meaning ! Otherwise it is only too natural that interest should decline. That is to say—so far as I am concerned, don't you know, I have done what I could. The German Nationalists are in a rage about Wisnieczky, because they say he's a Slavophile, and the Slavs are in a rage too because they say that when he was in the government he was a wolf in sheep's clothing. But all this only goes to show that he is a genuinely patriotic figure standing above party quarrels, and I don't mean to drop him !

" On the other hand, it is now high time for us to enlarge on the cultural side, too, so that people have something positive to go on. Our enquiry in order to ascertain the wishes of participant sections of the population is progressing far too slowly. An Austrian Year or a Universal Year is quite admirable, of course. But I should like to put it like this : everything that's a symbol must in due course turn into something true. That is to say, so long as it is a symbol it stirs my heart, naturally, even though I don't know what it is all about, but after a while I turn away from the mirror of the heart and do something quite different, which has met with my approval in the meantime. I wonder do I make myself clear ? Our friend and hostess is doing her utmost, I know, and for months now there has been discussion going on here about the things that really matter most. And yet attendance is falling off, and I can't help feeling that we shall soon have to decide on something. On what, I don't know. Perhaps for a second steeple to St. Stephen's Cathedral, or for an Imperial and Royal colony in Africa—it doesn't matter much what. For I am convinced that then at the last moment perhaps something entirely different will come of it. The main thing is that the inventive talent of those taking part should, as it were, be harnessed in good time, so that it isn't wasted and lost."

Count Leinsdorf felt that he had spoken to some point.

It was Arnheim who spoke up in reply on behalf of the others. "What you say about the necessity of fertilising reflection by means of action at certain moments, and this even though the action should be merely provisional, is extraordinarily true—indeed it is true with regard to life in general. And in this connection it is in fact significant that for some time there has been a different mood prevailing in the circle that forgathers here. We are no longer contending with that chaotic multiplicity of problems which was the difficulty at the beginning. Almost no new proposals are being put forward now, and the older proposals are scarcely mentioned anywhere, or at any rate are not doggedly defended. The impression one receives is that on all sides there is now a lively awareness of the fact that acceptance of the invitation to participate creates the obligation to come to an agreement, so that the time has now come when any tolerably acceptable proposal would have a prospect of meeting with general approval."

"And how is it with us?" His Highness asked, turning to Ulrich, whom he had just noticed. "Is there some clarification to be seen there too?"

Ulrich had to admit that it was not so. An exchange of views that is conducted on paper can be much more luxuriously protracted than one that is conducted personally. Furthermore, the influx of reformist proposals was not decreasing, so that Ulrich was still founding Associations and referring them, in His Highness's name, to the various ministries, whose readiness to deal with them had, incidentally, shown a marked decline in recent weeks. It was thus that he now reported.

"No wonder!" His Highness commented, turning to the others. "Our people have a tremendous amount of fine patriotic feeling, but one would really need to be as well informed as an encyclopædia in order to satisfy them on all the points they bring up. It is simply becoming too much for the ministries, which only goes to show that, as I say, the time has come when we must intervene from above."

"In this connection, Count," Arnheim said, once more speaking up, "you may think it worth considering the fact that recently

General von Stumm has been arousing an ever-increasing degree of interest among the members of the Council."

Count Leinsdorf looked at the General for the first time. " What with ? " he asked, without in the least bothering to conceal the rudeness of the question.

" Oh, this is too embarrassing ! " Stumm von Bordwehr bashfully demurred. " That wasn't what I was after at all ! The role allotted to the soldier in the council chamber is only a modest one—that's a principle I stick to. But you'll remember, Count, that at the very first meeting and so to speak only carrying out my duty as a soldier, I suggested that if the committee set up to formulate a special idea should happen not to think of anything else, it might bear in mind that our Artillery has no modern guns and our Navy, for that matter, no ships—what I mean, not enough ships for the purposes of carrying out the defence of the country if that should ever become necessary."

" Well ? " His Highness interrupted him, and turned an amazed glance of enquiry upon Diotima, in unconcealed token of his displeasure.

Diotima raised her beautiful shoulders and let them sink again as in renunciation. She had become almost hardened to the fact that wherever she turned this podgy little General was sure to turn up, too, a pursuing nightmare, guided, as it seemed, by incomprehensible helpful powers.

" And the fact is," Stumm von Bordwehr went on at full speed before his bashfulness could get the better of him in the face of this success, " just recently opinions have been expressed that would justify someone coming forward with such a proposal for a start. What has been said, in fact, is that the Army and the Navy would be an idea in which all could share—and a great idea too, what's more—and very likely it would be a real pleasure to His Majesty as well. And how the Prussians would stare— oh, no offence, I hope, Herr von Arnheim ! "

" Oh no, the Prussians wouldn't be at all disconcerted ! " Arnheim waved that aside with a smile. " Besides, it goes without saying that whenever such Austrian matters are under discussion I am simply not present and only with all due extreme modesty make use of the permission granted me to stand by and listen in spite of that. . . ."

" Well, anyway," the General concluded, " opinions have in fact been expressed that the simplest thing would be not to go on talking it over much longer, but to settle on a military enterprise. Personally I'm inclined to think that it might be combined with some other proposal, perhaps with some great civilian idea. What I said, it isn't for a mere soldier-man to butt in, but the opinions that have come forward to the effect that anyway nothing better is likely to come of all this civilian thinking are actually opinions coming from a very high intellectual quarter."

Towards the end of the General's speech His Highness was listening with his eyes wide open in a fixed stare ; and only involuntary twitches of thumb-twiddling, which he could not quite suppress, betrayed the strain and the laborious effort of what was going on within him.

Permanent Secretary Tuzzi, whose voice was not usually heard on these occasions, now interjected, slowly and softly : " I hardly think the Minister for Foreign Affairs would have any objection to that ! "

" Ah, so the departments have been in touch on the subject already ? " Count Leinsdorf asked ironically and irritably.

" Your Highness has his little joke about the departments," Tuzzi replied in a tone that was all charm and equability. " But of course the War Ministry would be more likely to welcome world disarmament than to get into touch with the Ministry for Foreign Affairs ! " And then he went on to tell a little story : " I'm sure you know the story about the fortifications in the Southern Tyrol, which have been built during the last ten years on the urgent demand of the Chief of the General Staff. They are said to be magnificent, quite the latest thing. Of course they have also been equipped with electrically charged barbed wire and large searchlight installations, and underground diesel engines have been put in, to provide the current. So it can't be said we are at all behind the times. The only unfortunate thing is that the engines were ordered by the Artillery department, and the fuel is provided by the War Ministry's department of works, for that is the way it is prescribed by regulations, and as a result the installations can't be got working because the two departments can't come to an agreement about whether the match that has to be used to start the engine up is to be regarded as fuel and hence supplied by the department of works or as a machine-part and hence something that comes within the jurisdiction of the Artillery."

" Delightful ! " Arnheim said, knowing perfectly well that Tuzzi was confusing a diesel engine and a gas engine and that even with the latter it was a long time since matches had been used. This was simply one of those anecdotes that circulate in government departments, full of pleasant self-mockery, and the Permanent Secretary had told it in a tone of appreciative amusement over the whole lamentable affair.

Everyone smiled or laughed, and none more gaily than General Stumm.

" Of course, the people who are really to blame," he said, taking the joke a little further, " are the civilian people in the other departments. For the minute we order something that isn't properly provided for in the budget, the Finance Ministry comes dashing along to tell us we don't know the first thing about the way constitutional government works. So supposing war were to break out—which God forbid !—before the end of the financial year, at dawn on the first day of mobilisation we should have to telegraph to the commanding officers of these fortifications, instructing them to go out and buy matches, and if there were none to be had in those mountain villages, there'd be nothing for it but to conduct the war with the matches the officers' batmen carry in their pockets ! "

The General had perhaps really gone a little too far in his elaboration of the joke, and through the thin web of the comical the menacing seriousness of the state in which the Collateral Campaign found itself suddenly became apparent once again.

His Highness said meditatively : " In the course of time . . ." but then thought better of it, on the grounds that in a difficult situation it is wiser to leave the talking to other people. He said no more.

The six people were silent for a moment, as though they were all standing round a dark well and gazing down into it.

" No," Diotima said, " that is impossible ! "

' What ? ' all their instantly raised glances seemed to ask.

" Then we should be doing what Germany is reproached with doing—arming ! " she concluded. Her soul had paid no attention to the anecdote, or had forgotten it already, and was still lingering over the matter of the General's success.

" But what is to happen ? " Count Leinsdorf took her up thankfully, though in a worried tone. " We must at least find something provisional, mustn't we ? "

" Germany is a comparatively naïve country, bristling with strength," Arnheim said, as though he had to meet his lady's reproach with some apology. " It has been introduced to gun-powder and fire-water."

Tuzzi smiled over this figure of speech, which struck him as decidedly daring.

" It cannot be denied that Germany is regarded with increasing dislike in the circles that our Campaign is intended to embrace." Count Leinsdorf could not let the chance pass without slipping in this remark. " Also, alas, in the circles that it already embraces," he added cryptically.

But he was a little startled when Arnheim declared that this did not surprise him. " We Germans," Arnheim said, " are an ill-fated nation. Not only do we dwell in the heart of Europe, we also suffer as the heart itself does. . . ."

" Heart ? " His Highness asked involuntarily. He would have expected not ' heart ' but ' brain ', and would also have been more inclined to admit that.

But Arnheim stuck to ' heart '. " I dare say you remember," he said, " that not very long ago the city council of Prague placed a large order in France, although we had also made a tender, as goes without saying, and would have carried out the order more efficiently and more cheaply. It is nothing more or less than an emotional prejudice. And I must say I do entirely understand it."

Before he could go on, Stumm von Bordwehr, who was enjoy-ing himself, signified that he wished to say something, and launched forth into an explanation. " Everywhere in the world," he said, " people toil and moil, but nowhere so much as in Ger-many. Everywhere in the world nowadays they make a lot of noise, but most of all in Germany. Everywhere business has got out of touch with age-old culture, but it is worst of all in the Reich. Everywhere the flower of youth is put into barracks, of course, but the Germans have even more barracks than anyone else. And so in a certain sense it is a fraternal obligation," he concluded, " for us not to hang back too far behind Germany. I hope I shall be excused if what I say sounds a bit paradoxical, but the fact is, the intellect is full of such complications nowadays ! "

Arnheim nodded in agreement. " Perhaps America is even worse than we are," he added, " but America is at least utterly naïve, without our intellectual dichotomy. We are in every respect the nation at the centre of things, where all the motives of all the rest of the world coincide. It is we who are most urgently in need of a synthesis. And we know it. We have something like a consciousness of sin. But after admitting that frankly at the very beginning, in all fairness, I think, it must also be conceded that we suffer for the others, as it were making ourselves the prototype, the personification, of all their errors, in a certain sense being cursed or crucified, or however one may wish to express it, on behalf of the whole world. And a change of heart in Germany would undoubtedly be the most significant thing that could happen. I conjecture that in the divided and, as it seems, somewhat impassioned attitude of opposition to us of which you have just spoken there is some vague awareness of this."

Now Ulrich joined in. " You gentlemen underestimate the Germanophile feeling there is. I am reliably informed that any day now there is going to be a very strong demonstration against our Campaign, the reason being that in national circles it passes for anti-German. Sir," he said to Count Leinsdorf, " you will see the people of Vienna demonstrating in the streets. There will be an outcry against Baron Wisnieczky's appointment. It is assumed that our friends Tuzzi and Arnheim are working together under cover, while you, sir, do all you can to hamstring German influence on the Collateral Campaign."

In Count Leinsdorf's eyes there was now something reminiscent both of the calm of a frog's eyes and of the irritability of a bull's.

Slowly and with a warm and friendly expression Tuzzi lifted his gaze to Ulrich's face and kept it fixed there, with a questioning look.

Arnheim laughed heartily and stood up. He would have liked to cast the Permanent Secretary an urbanely jesting glance, in order to laugh off the absurd insinuation made regarding the two

of them ; but since he could not catch Tuzzi's eye, he turned
away to Diotima.

Tuzzi meanwhile took Ulrich by the arm and asked him where
he had got his information. Ulrich told him that it was no secret
but a widespread rumour, receiving widespread belief, and that
he had heard it at the house of friends. Tuzzi brought his face
closer, compelling Ulrich to turn slightly aside from the circle,
and with this modicum of privacy achieved he suddenly murmured
very softly : " Do you still not know why Arnheim's here ? He's
an intimate friend of Prince Mosyoutov's and *persona grata* with
the Czar. He keeps in touch with Russia and is supposed to
influence this Campaign here in a pacifist direction. All un-
officially. Private enterprise, so to speak, on the part of his
Russian Majesty. An ideological affair. There's something for
you, my friend ! " he concluded mockingly. " Leinsdorf hasn't
a notion of it ! "

Permanent Secretary Tuzzi had received this information
through his official machinery. He believed it because he considered pacifism a movement that was in keeping with the outlook a beautiful woman would have, and this explained why
Diotima was so enraptured with Arnheim and why Arnheim
spent more time in Tuzzi's house than anywhere else. Before
learning this Tuzzi had been on the brink of becoming jealous.
He considered ' spiritual ' sympathies possible only up to a
certain point, but he did not care to make use of devious methods
in order to ascertain whether this point had been passed or not ;
he had therefore been compelled to go on trusting his wife. But
if in this his sense of a model manly bearing had proved itself
stronger than merely sexual feelings, these latter feelings did
nevertheless arouse just sufficient jealousy in him to make clear
to him for the first time that a man with a profession never has
the time to keep an eye on his wife, unless he means to neglect
the work he has undertaken in the world. He did indeed tell
himself that if even an engine-driver was not allowed to take his
wife along on the footplate with him, how much less, then, a man
whose concern it was to conduct the affairs of an empire was
entitled to be jealous. And yet the high-minded ignorance in
which he thus remained did not accord well with the character
of a diplomat ; it deprived Tuzzi of some of his professional self-

confidence. So he was extremely thankful to feel himself restored to his old sense of security when everything that had been worrying him seemed to be explained away in a thoroughly harmless manner. It even looked to him like a little punishment for his wife that he should now know all about Arnheim while she still saw nothing but the human being in him, never dreaming that he was an emissary of the Czar. Tuzzi again began, with the greatest of enjoyment, to ask her for little scraps of information, requests that she acceded to half graciously and half impatiently. He had thought out a whole series of seemingly harmless questions, and from the answers he meant to draw his own conclusions. He, the husband, would have really liked to tell the ' cousin ' something about it all and was just pondering how he could do this without discrediting his wife, when Count Leinsdorf once again took command of the discussion.

Count Leinsdorf was the only person who had remained seated, and nobody had noticed anything of the struggle going on in him, faced as he was with all these mounting difficulties. Now, however, his fighting-spirit seemed to be restored. He twirled his Wallenstein mustachios and said slowly and firmly :

" Something must be done ! "

" Have you come to a decision, Count ? " they asked him.

" Nothing has occurred to me," he replied simply. " Still, something must be done." And there he sat like a man who does not mean to stir from the spot until his will has been accomplished.

Such a force radiated from this attitude of his that every one of the others felt how the futile endeavour to get hold of something that could be done jogged about inside himself or herself like a penny that is somewhere there inside the money-box, which no amount of shaking would make come out through the slit again.

" Oh, really," Arnheim said, " one mustn't let oneself be influenced by occurrences of that sort ! "

Leinsdorf did not answer.

And so once again the whole thing was gone over, with a repetition of all the proposals that had been put forward in the hope of giving the Collateral Campaign a content and a meaning.

And each time Count Leinsdorf's reply came like the swing of a pendulum that is in a different position each time but which always swings the same way : " This can't be done out of consideration for the Church That can't be done because of the free-thinkers. The Central Association of Architects has protested against this. The Finance Ministry has qualms about that." And so it went on and on, always in the same manner.

Ulrich, who took no part in this, felt rather as if the five people who were arguing here in this room had just crystallised out of some fluid obscurity that had been enwrapping his senses for months past. What had he meant by telling Diotima one must take possession of unreality ? Or, another time, that one must abolish reality ? There now she sat, with such remarks of his in her memory, and might be thinking heaven knows what about him. And what on earth had made him tell her that one should live like a figure on the page of a book ? He assumed that by this time she would have passed it all on to Arnheim.

But he also assumed that he was just as thoroughly aware as anyone else what time of day it was and knew the price of, say, an umbrella as well as the next man. If at this moment he nevertheless occupied a position midway between his own and that of the others, this was not garbed in the guise of some queerness such as might come with a muffled and absent state of consciousness ; quite on the contrary, he once again felt the flooding in upon him of that brightness which he had already experienced while he was with Bonadea. He remembered how, not so very long ago, in the autumn, when he had gone to a race-meeting with the Tuzzis, there had been an incident causing very large and suspicious losses to the punters and the peaceable crowds of race-goers had in a twinkling been transformed into a sea of people pouring into the enclosure and not only smashing up everything within reach but rifling the cash-boxes as well—until finally the police succeeded in transforming them back into an assembly of people who had come out to indulge in a harmless and customary amusement. Confronted with such happenings it was ridiculous to think in terms of metaphors and vague, blurred, borderline manifestations of something that might or might not be capable of manifesting itself in the form of life itself.

Ulrich felt himself penetrated by an awareness, still fresh and immaculate, that life was a crude and desperate condition in which it was no use thinking overmuch about tomorrow, since one had

quite enough trouble with today. How could one fail to see that
the human state was not mere mutability, a floating evanescence,
but something that yearned to achieve the most concentrated
substantiality, because every irregularity must make it afraid of
falling utterly to pieces ? Or (to go even further) how could a
sound observer fail to recognise that this compound of anxieties,
urges, and ideas that life was, which at best misused ideas in order
to justify itself, or exploited them as stimuli, nevertheless—and
precisely as that which it was—had the formative and binding
influences on ideas which was what gave them their natural motion
and limitation ? One does of course press the wine from the
grapes. But how much more beautiful than a pool of wine could
ever be is the vineyard on the hillside, with its indigestible crude
earth and its endless rows of shining stakes made of dead wood !
' In short,' he reflected, ' creation does not come about for the
sake of a theory, but——' and he was about to conclude : ' as a
result of sheer power ', when another word all unexpectedly
intervened and his thought ended like this : ' no, it arises out of
power and love, and the usual combination between these two
is wrong ! '

At this moment power and love once again did not mean to
Ulrich quite what they usually mean. All that there was in him
of a tendency towards malevolence and hardness of heart was
implied in this word ' power '; it meant the efflux of every
unbelieving, matter-of-fact, wide-awake attitude. After all,
there was a streak in him of the harsh, cold, and violent, and
obviously it had played its part even in his choice of a career ; in
other words, it was perhaps not quite without some element of
cruelty in his intentions that he had become a mathematician.
This was all as closely interwoven as the dense foliage of a tree,
hiding the trunk itself.

And if one spoke of love not merely in the ordinary sense, but,
at the sound of the word, found oneself yearning for a state that
made everything—everything down to the very atoms of the body
itself—different from the poverty-stricken state of lovelessness ;
or if one felt that one might just as easily have every quality as
none ; or if one was under the impression that the like of what
happened was only the like of it now because life—full to bursting
of conceit with its Here and Now, but in the last resort a very

vague, even a downright unreal condition !—poured itself head-long into the few dozen cake-moulds of which reality consisted, or that in all the circles in which we continually revolve there is a piece missing, and that of all the systems we have set up there is not one that possessed the secret of stillness—then all these things, however different they might look, were also connected with each other like the branches of a tree, completely mantling the trunk, concealing it.

In these two trees his life grew, divided. He could not say exactly when his life had entered into the sign of the tree with the hard, tangled ramage ; he only knew it had happened early : even his immature Napoleonic schemes had shown him to be a man who looked on life as a problem he had set himself, something it was his vocation to work out. This urge to make an onslaught on life, and so to dominate it, had always been very marked in him, however it expressed itself : whether as a rejection of the existing order or as a varied striving after a new one, or as logical or moral demands, or even merely as an insistence on keeping the body in good fighting-trim. And everything that, as time went on, he had called Essayism and the Sense of Possibility and of Fantastical, as opposed to Pedantic, Precision, the demands that history should be invented and that one should live the history of ideas instead of the history of the world, that one should clutch hard at everything that could never be quite realised in practice, so that one might ultimately reach a stage of living as if one were not a human being at all, but merely a figure in a book, a figure with all the inessential elements left out, the essential residue of it undergoing a magical integration—all these terms in which his thoughts had expressed themselves, and which were anti-realistic in their abnormal epigrammatic intensity, had one thing in common : they brought an unmistakably ruthless passion to bear upon reality.

What was more difficult to recognise, because they were more shadowy and dreamlike, were the ramifications of the other tree that was a reflected image of his life. What was at the root of it was perhaps some primal memory of a childlike relationship to the world, all trustfulness and abandonment ; and this had lived on as a haunting sense of once having beheld the whole wide earth in what later fills only the flower-pot in which morality's miserable little herbs send up what sprouts they can. The sole attempt to reach full development on this gentle shadow-side of his being had, without a doubt, been that regrettably rather absurd affair with the major's wife ; and that, again, had also been the beginning of a set-back from which there had been no recovery. Since then, though leaves and twigs were continually being blown about on the surface, the tree itself had disappeared from sight ; and only by such signs as the fluttering of the leaves could one tell that it was, after all, still there.

This inactive half of his personality showed itself most clearly, perhaps, in his involuntary conviction that the active and busy half was no more than provisionally useful—a conviction that was like a shadow cast upon the active half. In everything he set about—which meant physical passions just as much as intellectual ones—he had finally come to see himself as one held captive by preparations that would never be finished ; and in the course of the years his life had run out of the sense of necessity as a lamp runs out of oil. His development had evidently split into two roads, one lying on the surface, in the light of day, and one dark and closed to traffic ; and the condition of moral standstill that had settled down upon him, which had been oppressing him for a long time (and perhaps more than was necessary), could be explained only by the fact that he had never succeeded in joining up these two roads.

Now, remembering that the failure to achieve this union had lately been apparent to him in what he called the strained relationship between literature and reality, or between metaphor and truth, Ulrich suddenly recognised that this image was by no means merely a random inspiration sprung up in one or other of those conversations, like aimless meandering paths, that he had recently been having with the most unsuitable people. It amounted to far more than that. For as far back as human history goes these two fundamental attitudes can be distinguished : that of the metaphor and that of unequivocality. Unequivocality is the law of waking thought and action, which prevails equally in a compelling conclusion in logic and in the mind of a blackmailer driving his victim along before him, step by step, and it arises from the exigency of life, which would lead to doom if conditions could not be shaped unequivocally. Metaphor, on the other hand, is a combining of concepts such as takes place in dream ; it is the sliding logic of the soul, and what corresponds to it is the kinship of things that exists in the twilit imaginings of art and religion.   But besides this, whatever life holds in the way of ordinary liking and dislike, agreement and rejection, admiration, subordination, leadership, imitation, and all their counter-manifestations, these manifold relations man has to himself and to Nature, which are not yet purely objective and perhaps never will be—it all cannot be understood otherwise than by means of metaphor.   Without doubt what is called the higher humanism is nothing but an attempt to fuse together those two great halves of life, metaphor and truth, after the preliminary of carefully separating them.   Yet if one has separated everything in a meta-phor that might be true from what is only froth, what generally happens is that one has gained a little truth, but has destroyed the metaphor's whole value.   And so, although this separation may have been inevitable in the course of our intellectual evolution, it has had the same effect as boiling down a substance in order to thicken it, a process in the course of which the really vital forces and spirits escape in a cloud of steam.   Nowadays it is often difficult to avoid the impression that the concepts and rules of moral life are merely metaphors that have had all the goodness boiled out of them and which have the insufferably greasy kitchen-vapours of humanism billowing around them.

And if it is permissible to make a digression here, it must be the following : one consequence of this impression, which vaguely hovers over everything, has been what the present age ought, if it were honest, to call its veneration for the baser instincts.   For nowadays lying is a consequence less of weakness than of the con-viction that a man who is successful in life must be capable of telling lies.   Violence is resorted to because after long and futile talking the straightforwardness, the unequivocality, of it comes as an immense relief.   People form themselves into groups because obedience to orders enables them to do everything they have long been incapable of doing out of personal conviction, and the hos-tility that exists between these groups provides them with the wide-awake, never-resting reciprocity, the action and counter-action, of vendetta, whereas a general state of mutual love would very soon put them all to sleep.   Whether human beings are good or evil is not the point.   It is simply that they no longer know their way about between the lowlands and the heights.   And this disorientation, this loss of the connecting-link, has yet another paradoxical consequence :   the vulgar profusion of intellectual jewellery with which mistrust of the mind nowadays tricks itself out.   It is significant that a number of perfectly ordinary phenomena, which set up to betoken a striving towards humanism, now in fact betoken the absence of it :   for instance, the coupling of a ' philosophy ' with activities that cannot stand more than a little of it, such as politics ;   the universal tendency instantly to turn every view-point into a stand-point and to take every stand-point for a point of view ;   the need that fanatics of every degree feel to repeat again and again the one and only illumination that has been granted them, multiplying it all around them as in a hall of mirrors. . . . All in all, the impression arises that what must be completely excised from all human interrelations is the displaced soul that has got into them.

And in the moment when this thought struck him, Ulrich felt that if his life had any meaning at all it was precisely this :   in it the two fundamental aspects of the human condition manifested themselves in their separateness and their way of working against each other.   Obviously people like himself were already being born, but as yet they were few and far between, isolated ;   and being thus isolated himself, he could not re-unite the broken links, restore the lost orientation.   He was under no illusion as to the value of his experimental thinking.   It might well be that he never put one thought to another without logical consistency, but still, it was rather as if he were placing one ladder upon another, and in the end the topmost rung was very remote, swaying at a height far above the level of natural life.   He felt a profound dislike of this.

And perhaps it was for this reason that he suddenly looked at Tuzzi.

Tuzzi was talking.   And as though his ears had just been opened to the first sounds of morning, Ulrich heard him saying :

" I am not in a position to judge whether there are no great human and artistic achievements nowadays, as you contend.   But one thing I am justified in asserting is that foreign policy is nowhere so difficult as in this country of ours.   It seems pretty safe to predict that even in the Jubilee Year French foreign policy will be dominated by the idea of *revanche* and of colonial possessions, the British by that of their moves towards a check-mate on the chessboard of the world, always using their pawns to keep the opponent in check, as their mode of procedure has been described, and the German, finally, by what they refer to, in a somewhat ambiguous manner, as their place in the sun. But our old Empire has no needs of any kind, and this is why nobody can now know what views circumstances will by then have thrust upon us ! "

It seemed that Tuzzi was trying to put on the brakes, to utter a warning. He was evidently talking without any ironical intention. The whiff of irony came merely from the ingenuous matter-of-factness of his approach, the dry husk around the conviction that he put forward, which was that a lack of worldly needs was a very dangerous matter indeed. Ulrich felt revived by this, as though he had been chewing on a coffee-bean. Meanwhile Tuzzi's attitude of warning had stiffened further, and it was in this spirit that he concluded what he had been saying. " Who today," he asked, " can take it upon himself even to think of putting great political ideas into practice ? Such a man would have to have a streak in him of the criminal and of the speculator heading for bankruptcy. Surely you don't want that ? The function of diplomacy is to conserve."

" Conservation is what leads to war," Arnheim countered.

" That may well be so," Tuzzi conceded. " Probably the only thing one can do is to choose the best moment in which to become involved in it. Think of the story of Czar Alexander the Second. His father Nicholas was a despot, but he died a natural death. Alexander, on the other hand, was a high-minded ruler who began his reign by instantly introducing liberal reforms. The result was that Russian liberalism led to Russian radicalism, and after three unsuccessful attempts to assassinate him, Alexander fell a victim to a fourth."

Ulrich looked at Diotima. She sat very straight, looking attentive, solemn and splendidly voluptuous, as she corroborated what her husband had said.

" Yes, that is so," she said. " From what I have seen of intellectual radicalism during our endeavours I have gained the same impression : if it is given an inch, it will take an ell."

Tuzzi smiled. It seemed to him he had won a little victory over Arnheim.

Arnheim sat there, his lips, like a half-opened bud, pouting as he breathed. And Diotima, like a locked tower of flesh, gazed towards him across a deep valley.

The General polished his horn-rimmed spectacles.

Ulrich said slowly : " That is only because the endeavours of all those who feel themselves called upon to restore the meaning to life have one thing in common nowadays, namely that wherever not merely personal views, but verities, might be arrived at they despise the operation of thinking. To make up for that, wherever it is the inexhaustibility of views that counts, they decide for short-cut ideas and half-truths."

Nobody made any answer to this. And why should anyone have answered anyway ? Things said like that are, after all, mere words. The concrete thing was that they were six people sitting in a room, having an important discussion, and what they said, and also what they did not say, while this went on, and above all emotions, fancies, possibilities, was all contained in this concreteness, without these details being of equal importance to the whole ; it was all contained in it much as the obscure motions of liver and stomach are contained within a fully dressed person who is just putting his signature to an important document. And this order of precedence must not be harmed—that was what reality consisted of !

Ulrich's old friend Stumm had now finished polishing his spectacles. He put them on and looked at Ulrich.

Although Ulrich believed he had always only been toying with these various people here, now all at once he felt very forlorn among them. He remembered having felt something similar some weeks or months earlier : a little puff of Creation's breath struggling against the petrified lunar landscape into which it had been exhaled. And it seemed to him that all the decisive moments of his life had been associated with such a sensation of amazement and loneliness.

But was there a trace of anxiety in it too, this time ? Was that what was bothering him ? He could not quite define what his feeling was. Roughly, it conveyed to him that he had never yet in life made a real decision and that he would soon have to make one. But he did not think this in clear-cut terms ; he only felt it in this discomfort that had befallen him, as though something were trying to snatch him away from these people among whom he was sitting. And yet, although they were a matter of complete indifference to him, his will suddenly struggled against this with arms and legs.

Count Leinsdorf, to whom the silence that had meanwhile fallen brought back a sense of a practical politician's obligations, said in a tone of exhortation : " Well, what is to be done ? We must, after all, do something decisive, at least provisionally, in order to forestall the dangers that threaten our Campaign ! "

At this Ulrich attempted something utterly senseless.

" Sir," he said, " there is only one task for the Collateral Campaign—that it should constitute the beginning of a general spiritual stock-taking. We must do more or less what would be necessary if what was due in 1918 were the Day of Judgment and the old spirit had to be terminated and a higher one begun. What you should do is found, in His Majesty's name, a terrestrial secretariat for Precision and the Spirit. Until that is done, all other objectives remain unattainable, or at best they are sham objectives." And he added something of what had been occupying his mind during the last few minutes when he had been lost in thought.

While he was speaking it seemed to him that not only were everybody's eyes popping out of their sockets, but it was as though surprise caused the upper part of their bodies to rise up and away from the part they were sitting on. What they had obviously expected was that he would follow their host's example and produce an amusing anecdote. And when it turned out that there was no joke, there he sat among them like a small child surrounded by leaning towers, which surveyed his simple-minded game with a faintly affronted air.

Only Count Leinsdorf looked at all amiable, though somewhat astonished. " That's right enough," he remarked. " But still, it is our duty to get out of the stage of mere allusions and go on until we get hold of something True, and the fact of the matter is that here Capital and Culture have left us very thoroughly in the lurch."

Arnheim evidently thought he ought to save the great nobleman from being taken in by Ulrich's jesting.

" Our friend is haunted by a particular idea," he said, launching into exposition. " He believes that right living can be produced synthetically, just as one can produce synthetic rubber or nitrogen. But the spirit of man "—and here he turned to Ulrich with the most perfect of his gentlemanly smiles—" unfortunately has the limitation that its vital manifestations are not susceptible to cultivation in the way that experimental mice are bred in the laboratory. On the contrary, a huge grain-store only just suffices to support a few families of mice ! " He asked the others to forgive his making use of such a daring analogy. But he was well content with it, all the same, because there was something in it of that aura of large land-owning and scientific farming which he associated with Count Leinsdorf, and at the same time it was a vivid expression of the difference between ideas that were and ideas that were not accompanied by a sense of responsibility for their realisation.

But His Highness shook his head rather irritably. " I quite understand what he means," he said. " There was a time when people grew naturally into the conditions they found waiting for them, and that was a very sound way of becoming oneself. But nowadays, with all this shaking up of things, when everything is becoming detached from the soil it grew in, even where the production of soul is concerned one really ought, as it were, to replace the traditional handicrafts by the sort of intelligence that goes with the machine and the factory." This was one of those remarkable utterances to which His Highness did sometimes find himself giving voice, to his own and everybody else's surprise. It was all the more surprising now because until he began to speak he had merely been staring at Ulrich with a flabbergasted expression.

" But everything Herr von —— is talking about is of course totally impracticable ! " Arnheim emphatically declared.

" Upon my word, and why ? " Count Leinsdorf asked curtly and aggressively.

Diotima now interposed. " But, Count," she said, saying it as though she were pleading with him to do something one does not like to speak of in so many words, namely to come to his senses,

" we have already tried everything my cousin is talking about—
ages ago ! What else, surely, *are* such long and difficult discussions
as we have been having this evening ? "

" Indeed ? " His Highness retorted tetchily. " I for my part
thought from the very start all these clever men wouldn't get us
anywhere ! Psychoanalysis and relativity and all the rest of the
stuff—in the long run it's all nothing but vanity ! Every one of
them wants to rearrange the world in a special way of his own.
Let me tell you, Herr von —— may not have expressed it perfectly, but at bottom he's quite right. People are always up to
something new the moment new times begin, and nothing sensible ever comes of it ! "

The nervous strain and anxiety caused by the frustrated course
of the Collateral Campaign had come to the surface. Count
Leinsdorf, having stopped twirling his mustachios, was now fret-
fully twiddling his thumbs, without being aware of it. Perhaps
something else had also come to the surface : his dislike of
Arnheim. For, although Count Leinsdorf had been amazed
when Ulrich had begun talking about ' spirit ', he then found he
quite liked what he heard. ' All this talk about it from fellows
like this Arnheim,' he thought, ' is nothing but a lot of flim-flam.
There's no need for it. After all, what is religion there for ? '

But Arnheim was upset, too ; he was white to the lips. Up to
now it had been only to the General that Count Leinsdorf had
used the tone he had just used in speaking to him ! He was not
the sort of man to take that lying down ! Yet for all that he could
not help being impressed by the decisiveness with which His
Highness had taken Ulrich's side, and this again aroused his own
distressful feelings towards Ulrich. He was at a loss because he
had wanted to have a thorough talk with Ulrich and had not been
able to get an opportunity to do so before this clash took place
in front of everyone. And so it came about that he did not
return Count Leinsdorf's attack. Simply ignoring it, he suddenly
addressed Ulrich, and with all the tokens of being in a state of
intense agitation, mental and physical.

" And do you yourself believe in everything you have just
said ? " he asked sternly, paying no heed to the demands of ordinary civility. " Do you believe such things are practicable ? Are
you really of the opinion that one can live purely according to

'laws of analogy'? And what then would you do if His Highness were to give you a completely free hand? Do tell us, I most
earnestly beg of you!''

It was an awkward moment.

Diotima remembered, oddly enough, a story she had read in the
newspaper some days previously. A woman had been found
guilty and given a dreadful sentence for having been accessory
to her lover's murder of her aged husband, who had not 'exer-
cised marital rights' for many years and yet had refused to agree
to a separation. This affair, with its almost medical details and a
certain perverse attraction it held, had caught her attention. The
circumstances of the case were such and everything was so understandable that one did not feel any of the persons involved were
to blame, so little chance had any of them had to help themselves;
it was, on the contrary, an unnatural general state of things that
brought such conditions into existence. She could not understand why she should think of this just now. But she also found
herself thinking of how Ulrich had recently talked to her a great
deal in his 'floating and flickering' manner, and she was vexed,
because he always followed it up with some piece of effrontery.
And she herself had spoken of how in some privileged human
beings the soul might issue forth out of its insubstantiality. The
conclusion she drew from all this was that her cousin was precisely
as unsure of himself as she was of herself, and perhaps just as
passionate too. And at this moment all this was interwoven—in
her head or in her bosom, that deserted seat of Count Leinsdorf's friendship—with the story of the guilty woman, in such a
way that she simply sat there with parted lips, feeling something
frightful would probably happen if Arnheim and Ulrich were
allowed to go on like this, but, what was still worse, that it would
happen with a vengeance if they were not left to go on, if anyone
were in any way to intervene.

But while Arnheim was attacking him Ulrich had been looking
at Permanent Secretary Tuzzi.

It was only with an effort that Tuzzi prevented his delight and
curiosity from showing in his furrowed tan face. Now, it seemed,
the goings-on in his house were about to explode as a result of the
contradictions they contained. He had no sympathy for Ulrich
either, if it came to that. What the fellow said went all against

the grain with him, for he was convinced that a man's value lay in his will or in his work, and certainly not in emotions and ideas ; and as for talking such nonsense about metaphors, he found it positively indecent.

Perhaps Ulrich sensed something of this, for he remembered having once told Tuzzi that he would kill himself if the year of his 'holiday from life' were to pass entirely without having produced anything. These were not exactly the words he had used, but he had nevertheless made it painfully obvious what he meant, and he felt ashamed of himself. Now once again he got the feeling, for which he could not quite account, that some decision was close at hand. Thinking at this moment of Gerda Fischel, he recognised the danger that she might come to see him and continue their last conversation. It suddenly became clear to him that, even though he had only been toying with the whole affair, they had already reached the farthest limits of what could be said in words, and that from this point onwards there was only one step that could be taken : it meant fondly falling in with the girl's hovering wishes, intellectually ungirding oneself and laying one's sword aside, and surmounting the 'second', the 'inner ramparts'. But that was madness. He was convinced that it would remain impossible for him to go so far with Gerda, and that he had only taken up with her at all because he was on safe ground with her. He was in a peculiar state of sober, irritable exaltation, and in this state he saw Arnheim's agitated face before him and caught something of the reproach Arnheim was just flinging at him, that he was not " reality-minded " and that " forgive my saying so, such a crass Either–Or " was " all too juvenile ". But he no longer felt the slightest urge to make any retort to this. He glanced at his watch, smiled soothingly, and observed that it had grown very late and was indeed too late to carry the argument further.

With this he had for the first time regained his contact with the others. Permanent Secretary Tuzzi even stood up, and afterwards cloaked the discourtesy of the move only faintly by strolling up and down. Count Leinsdorf had calmed down meanwhile ; he would have been pleased if Ulrich had been able to 'take the Prussian down a peg or two', but since nothing of the sort happened, he was content to let it go at that. 'If one likes a person, one likes him, and there it is,' he thought. 'And the other chap can talk all the clever stuff he likes, it doesn't make any difference!' And with a daring, though of course quite unconscious, approach to Arnheim's notion of the Mystery of the Whole, he added cheerfully, as he contemplated Ulrich's expression (which was at that moment anything but particularly intelligent) : "One might almost go so far as to say that a nice, likeable person simply can't say or do anything utterly stupid."

The party rapidly broke up. The General stowed his horned-rimmed spectacles away in the pistol-pocket of his trousers, after having vainly tried to get them into the skirts of his tunic ; he had not yet found a fitting place for this civilian instrument of wisdom. " Here we have the armed peace of the intellect ! " he said to Tuzzi as he did so, full of jollity and geniality, alluding to the speed with which everyone was departing.

Only Count Leinsdorf conscientiously kept them all back for a moment longer.

" And what then have we finally agreed on ? " he asked. And as nobody had any answer to give, he added reassuringly : " Well, well, we shall see in time, we shall see ! "

117   *Rachel's fateful day.*

THE awakening of the man in him and the resolve to seduce Rachel had made Soliman as cold-blooded as the hunter is at the sight of the game or the butcher at that of the beast that he leads to the slaughter. But he did not know how to attain his object, what methods were to be used, and under what conditions they must meet to make it possible at all. In a word, the will of the man in him made him aware of all the weakness of the boy. Rachel too knew what must come, and since she had so obliviously held Ulrich's hand in hers and had gone through the adventure with Bonadea, she was quite beside herself ; that is to say, she was in a state of, as it were, great erotic distraction, which descended like a flowery rain upon everything, and upon Soliman too. However, circumstances did not favour them, but caused delays. The cook was ill and Rachel had to sacrifice her days off, and the amount of entertaining that went on kept her busy in the house. Furthermore, although Arnheim was often with Diotima, it seemed as though a decision had been taken to keep more of a check on the young people, for he seldom brought his Soliman with him, and when he did so they saw each other only for minutes and in their mistress's and master's presence, and then gazed at each other with the blank, sullen expression on their faces that they thought appropriate.

At this period they very nearly began to hate each other, because each caused the other to feel the anguish of being kept on too short a chain. Soliman, besides, succumbed to a wild urge to commit violent escapades. He planned to escape out of the hotel by night, and so that his master should not know anything about it he stole a sheet and tried, by means of cutting and twisting, to make a rope ladder out of it ; but he could not manage it, and made the ill-used sheet disappear down a light-shaft. Then he brooded for a long time in vain on how one might clamber down and then again up the outside of a building by holding on to the caryatids and window-sills, and on his errands by day he studied the buildings of this architecturally famed city with an eye to the advantages and difficulties they offered from a cat-burglar's point of view. And Rachel, having been hastily and whisperingly informed of these plans and the obstacles to them, when she switched off her light at bed-time not infrequently thought she saw the black full-moon of his face on the pavement down below or that she heard a chirping call, to which she would then timidly reply, leaning far out of her window into the empty night, until in the end she had to admit that the night was indeed empty. But she was no longer cross about these romantic disturbances. She gave herself up to them in yearning melancholy. The object of this yearning was actually Ulrich, and Soliman was cast in the role of the man whom one does not love and to whom one will nevertheless abandon oneself—a point on which Rachel was in no sort of doubt whatsoever. For the fact that she was not allowed to be with him, that for some time past they had hardly

ever spoken to each other except in a whisper, and that the displeasure of those in authority over them had descended upon
them both, had much the same effect on her as a night full of
uncertainty, uncanny happenings, and sighs has on anyone in
love : it all concentrated her smouldering fancies like a burning-
glass, the beam of which is felt less as an agreeable warmth than
as something one will not be able to stand much longer.

And Rachel, who did not waste her time with rope-ladders and
mountaineering fantasies, was the more practical of the two. The
misty image of an elopement for life soon dwindled into that of
one secret stolen night, and the night—since that too remained
unattainable—into a quarter of an hour when they might happen
to be unobserved. And after all, neither Diotima nor Count
Leinsdorf, nor for that matter Arnheim, when their ' office ' made
it imperative for them to remain sitting together after some large
and unprofitable gathering of the intelligentsia, exchanging
worried reflections about the outcome of it all (which often kept
them there for an hour longer heedless of any other need), gave
a thought to the fact that one such hour was made up of four
quarters of an hour. But Rachel had worked it all out.

Lately, because the cook, although better now, was still not
quite up to the mark and had permission to go to bed early, the
young maid had much more to do than ever before, which brought
with it the advantage that nobody could possibly know just where
she was at any particular moment, and she was, besides, spared
as much as possible of the parlour-maid aspect of her work. As
a test—more or less in the same way that a person who is too
cowardly to commit suicide goes on making sham attempts at it
until one of them happens, by mistake, to turn out successful—
she several times smuggled Soliman into the apartment, he being
provided with an excuse to prove his diligence in the event of
being discovered, and had hinted to him that it was also possible
to find the way to her bed-chamber from indoors—and not only
from outside, by swarming up the front of the house. However,
the young lovers did not get any further than sitting and yawning
together in the hall and spying out the lie of the land through the
key-hole, until one evening, when the sound of the voices in
the drawing-room had been going on and on as monotonously
as the sound of threshing, Soliman, making use of a wonderfully

romantic phrase he had picked up from some novel, declared he
could possess himself in patience no longer.

And once they were in her little room it was he, too, who bolted
the door. But then they did not dare to turn on the light, and for
a while, blind, and as though the loss of sight had also deprived
them of all their other senses, they stood there opposite each
other like statues in a park after nightfall. True, Soliman did
think of squeezing Rachel's hand or pinching her thigh to make
her shriek—for such were the methods by which he had hitherto
achieved his masculine conquests—but he had to control himself,
because they must not make any noise ; and when nevertheless
he did make a crude little attempt, the only effect of it was an
irradiation of impatience and indifference from Rachel. For
Rachel could feel the hand of destiny pressing in the small of her
back and thrusting her forward, while her nose and forehead
grew icy cold, as though she were even now drained of all her
illusions. And Soliman too began to feel quite high and dry, and
awkward to the very marrow of his bones. It was as though there
could never be an end to their standing rigidly opposite each other
there in the darkness.

Finally it was the more high-minded but also somewhat more
experienced Rachel who had to play the seducer. And in this
she was aided by the resentment she now felt in place of her
former love for Diotima ; for since she was no longer content to
have a share in her mistress's sublime raptures, but was carrying
on her own amorous affair, she had changed a great deal. She not
only told lies in order to cover up her meetings with Soliman ;
she even went so far as to tug at Diotima's hair when she was
combing it, so taking her revenge for the vigilance that kept
guard on her innocence. But what now annoyed her most was
something that in earlier days had most entranced her, namely
that she had to wear the cast-off chemises, drawers, and stockings
that Diotima gave her ; for even though she cut this underlinen
down to a third of its former size and quite remodelled it, she
still felt imprisoned in it, feeling that she was wearing the yoke
of morality next to her bare skin. Yet it was this underwear
that now gave her the ingenious idea she had so much need of in
the present situation. She had, of course, already told Soliman
about the changes she had for some time observed in her mis-

tress's underclothing, and now, in order to find a point of departure that the situation cried out for, all she had to do was to show him.

"Look," she said, in the darkness displaying to Soliman the white moon-beam frill of her little drawers, "you can see for yourself how wicked they are. And if they're carrying on like that, you can be sure too they're deceiving the master with all this about the war they're getting ready for in there !"

And when the boy in a gingerly way fingered the delicate and dangerous drawers, she added rather breathlessly :

"I bet your pants are as black as you are, Soliman. That's always the way, they say."

And Soliman vengefully, and yet gently too, dug his nails into her thigh. In order to free herself, Rachel had to make a movement towards him, and had then to do and say this and that, all of which produced no real result, until in the end she used her little sharp teeth, setting to work on Soliman's face (which was childishly pressed against hers and at every movement she made kept on getting clumsily in the way) as though it were a big apple. And then she forgot to feel shame at these efforts, and Soliman forgot to feel shame at his awkwardness, and through the darkness the aerial storm of love came raging like a gale.

It was with a thud that it set the lovers back on firm ground again, when, vanishing through the walls, it let them go. And now the darkness lay between them like a lump of coal with which the sinners had blackened themselves. They did not know what the time was and, overestimating the amount of time that had passed, they were afraid. To Soliman, Rachel's half-hearted final kiss was like a molestation. He insisted on switching the light on, and behaved like a burglar who has got his swag and is now wholly intent on getting safely away. Rachel, who had quickly and shamefacedly put her clothes to rights, looked at him with a gaze that was fathomless and aimless at once. Her towsled hair hung over her eyes. But somewhere deep behind her eyes she was again beginning to see all the vast images of her love of honour, which she had forgotten until this moment. Apart from wishing herself all possible virtues, she had also wished for a handsome, rich and romantic lover : and here now was Soliman, standing before her, not even properly dressed yet, horrifyingly ugly, and a teller of stories of which she did not believe a single word. Perhaps if there had still been darkness she would quite have liked to cradle his thick-featured, tense face in her arms a little longer before they parted from each other. But now, with the light blazing, he was her new lover and nothing more, a thousand men shrunken into one rather ludicrous little manni-kin and the one who excluded all others. As for herself, she was once more a servant-girl who had let herself be seduced and was frightened of having a baby, which would bring the whole thing to light. She was simply too intimidated by this transformation even to give a sigh.

She helped Soliman to finish dressing (for in the confusion the boy had flung off his tight little jacket with the many buttons), but it was not out of tenderness that she helped him : it was only in order that they might be downstairs again the faster. It all seemed to her far too dearly bought, and discovery would have been the last straw. Soliman, on the other hand, when they were ready, turned to her with a tremendous smile, whinnying delightedly, for he was, after all, very proud of himself. Then Rachel swiftly seized a box of matches, switched off the light, softly drew the bolt, and, as she was about to open the door, whispered to him : " You have to give me one more kiss ! " For that was the proper way. But to both of them it tasted as though they had tooth-powder on their lips.

When they arrived in the hall they were amazed to find that they were still in time : the talk they could hear on the other side of the door was still going on in just the same way. When the visitors began to leave, Soliman had disappeared ; and half an hour later Rachel was combing her mistress's hair with great care and almost with the humble devotion of former days.

" I am glad my words of admonition to you have not been spoken in vain," Diotima said approvingly, and she, who failed to gain any real satisfaction in so many matters, now, well satis-fied, benevolently patted her little maid's hand.

118 *Well then, go and kill him!*

WALTER had changed out of his office suit into a better one and was at Clarisse's dressing-table knotting his tie at the looking-glass, which in spite of its curvilinear and devious frame, all in the latest style, threw back a shallow and distorted image, the glass being cheap and probably warped.

" And they're quite right ! " he was saying irritably. " This precious Campaign is all humbug ! "

" What do they get out of going round shouting ? " Clarisse asked.

" What does anyone get out of life at all, these days ? If they march through the streets, at least they form a procession—each one senses the body of the other ! At least they're not *thinking* and not *writing*. Oh, something or other will come of it all right ! "

" And do you really think the Campaign deserves all this indignation ? "

Walter shrugged his shoulders. " Didn't you read in the paper about the resolution the German spokesmen have sent to the Prime Minister ? All about affronts and wrongs to the German population and so forth ? And the sneering resolution passed by the Czech Association ? Or the little paragraph about the Polish Deputies having left for their constituencies ? For anyone who can read between the lines that one says the most, for the Poles are the people that are always decisive in the end, and they're leaving the Government in the lurch ! The situation's acute. This is no time to irritate everyone by having a general patriotic campaign ! "

" When I was in town this morning," Clarisse told him, " I saw mounted police going by, a whole regiment of them. A woman told me they're going to hide them somewhere."

" Of course. There are troops standing by in the barracks, too."

" D'you think something'll happen ? "

" Nobody can possibly tell ! "

" And then they'll ride into the crowds ? It's frightful, really, come to think of it, being all mixed up with those great horses."

Walter had found it necessary to untie his tie and was knotting it all over again.

" Have you ever been in anything like that ? " Clarisse asked.

" When I was a student."

" Not since ? "

Walter shook his head.

" Didn't you say just now that it'll be Ulrich's fault if there's trouble ? " Clarisse asked, trying to get certainty on this point.

" No, I didn't ! " Walter protested. " The trouble with him is he doesn't care one way or the other about political events. I only said it was just like him to go and start off something of this sort in an irresponsible way. He moves in the circle that's to blame."

" I want to come to town with you," Clarisse announced.

" On no account ! It would excite you too much." Walter said this very decisively. At his office he had heard all sorts of things about what might happen at the demonstration, and he wanted to keep Clarisse away. For it would not do at all for her to be mixed up in that hysteria rising from large crowds ; Clarisse had to be treated as carefully as if she were pregnant. The word ' pregnant ', though he did not utter it, was like a lump in his throat, so unexpectedly did it occur to him, linking the brittle irritability of his wife, who refused herself to him, with the foolish warmth of approaching motherhood. ' But,' he told himself not without pride, ' there *are* such links between things, which reach beyond ordinary concepts,' and he felt some irrational pride when he suggested : " If you'd rather, I'll stay at home with you."

" No," she replied. " At least you must be there."

She wanted to be left alone. When Walter had told her about the demonstration that was to take place and had described what such a thing looked like, she had pictured the procession as a great serpent all covered with scales, each single one of them moving by itself of its own accord. She wanted to see for herself that it was so, but she did not want a long argument about it.

Walter put his arm round her. " I'll stay at home, shall I ? " he asked, in repetition of his offer.

Clarisse brushed his arm away and, taking no more notice of

him, went and got a book from the shelves along the wall. It was a volume of her Nietzsche.

But instead of leaving her now, Walter pleaded : " Let me have a look at what you've got there ! "

The afternoon was drawing to an end. All through the house there hovered a vague premonition of the coming of spring : it was like hearing bird-song, though muted by glass and brick-work. There was an illusory scent of flowers rising from the smell of varnish on the floor, from the upholstery and the polished brass handles of the doors. Walter held out his hand for the book. Clarisse clutched it tight in both hands, one finger in the place where she had opened it.

And what took place now was one of those ' frightful ' scenes in which this marriage was so rich. They were all on the same pattern. Imagine a theatre, with the stage sunk in darkness ; then the lights go on in two boxes opposite each other, and in one of them is Walter, in the other Clarisse, these two distinguished among all men and women, and between them the deep black abyss warm with invisible human beings. Now Clarisse opens her lips and speaks, and then Walter answers, and the whole audience listens in breathless silence, for never before did human talent succeed in producing such a spectacle, such a play, full of sound and fury. . .

And this was what it was like now too, with Walter holding out his hand, his arm stretched out imploringly, and Clarisse a few steps away from him, with one finger tightly wedged between the pages of the book. Opening it at random she had hit on that splendid passage where the Master speaks of the impoverishment that comes with the decay of the will and which manifests itself in all forms of life as detail running riot at the expense of the whole. ' Life forced back into the most trivial forms . . . everything else poor in vitality '—the phrase stuck fast in her memory, though of the drift of the larger context, which she had run her eye over an instant earlier before Walter had once again disturbed her, she had only a vague general sense, the gist of the meaning. And now, in spite of the unfavourable nature of the moment, she made a great discovery. For although in this passage the Master spoke of all the arts, even, indeed, of all the forms that human life assumes, the examples he used were all taken from literature ;

and since Clarisse was without any appreciation of general principles, it suddenly appeared to her that Nietzsche had not grasped the full implication of his own ideas—for they applied also to music ! And while thinking this she heard her husband's morbid playing of the piano as vividly as though he were really playing at her side, with his emotional *rallentando* and the hesitant, as it were stumbling and stuttering, way the notes came out as soon as his thoughts began drifting over towards her and—to employ another of the Master's expressions—' the secondary, the moral tendency ' overwhelmed the ' artist ' in him. Clarisse could very well recognise by the sound of it when Walter mutely desired her, and she could see the music draining away out of his face until it was only his lips that shone, and he looked as though he had cut his finger and were about to faint.

And that was what he looked like now too, nervously smiling and stretching out his hand towards her. All this was of course more than Nietzsche could have known, and yet it was like a sign that by chance she had opened the book just at a place illuminating this. Now, suddenly seeing, hearing, and understanding it all, she was struck by the lightning-flash of inspiration, and there she stood upon a high mountain called Nietzsche, which had buried Walter beneath it, but which itself only just reached as high as the soles of her feet. (The ready-for-use or ' applied ' philosophy and poetry of most people who are neither creative nor, on the other hand, unsusceptible to ideas consists in just such shimmering coalescences of another man's great thought with their own small private modification of it.)

Meanwhile Walter had stood up and was moving nearer to Clarisse. He was determined to drop the whole idea of going to the demonstration, which he had wanted to join in, and to remain here with her. He saw how, as he drew closer, she stood leaning back against the wall, all repugnance ; and this attitude, this deliberate pose of the woman shrinking away from a man, unfortunately, instead of making him feel the same abhorrence she felt, on the contrary, only aroused in him those male urges that would have been the fitting cause of her attitude in the first place. For a man must be capable of commanding and of imposing his will on a reluctant person ; and suddenly this need to prove himself a man meant just as much to Walter as the need to battle against the last scattered remnants of the superstition of his youth, which was that one must be in some way special. ' One doesn't have to be in any way special ! ' he said to himself defiantly. It seemed to him mere cowardice not to be able to get on without that illusion. ' We are all inwardly capable of excesses,' he thought disdainfully. ' We have the morbid, the horrifying, the solitary, the malevolent, in ourselves. Each of us could do something that only he could do. But that in itself doesn't mean anything ! ' He felt bitter about the delusion that one should have the task of developing what was unusual instead of reabsorbing those easily corruptible outgrowths, and, by assimilating them, injecting some new life into the blood of civilised man, which was far too much inclined to grow sluggish. This was the way he thought, and he was looking forward to the day when music and painting would no longer be anything more to him than a sublime pastime. His wishing for a child was part of his new task. The desire, which had dominated him in his youth, to be a Titan, a new Prometheus, now produced its last consequence, which was that he began, in a rather exaggerated way, to believe that one must first of all become just like everyone else. He was now ashamed of not having any children ; he would have liked to have five children, if Clarisse and his income had permitted, for he felt an urge to be the centre of a cosily glowing circle of life, and what he wished for was indeed to surpass in mediocrity that great mediocre mass of humanity that is the backbone of life, whereby he disregarded the contradiction that lay in the desire itself.

But, perhaps because he had spent too long thinking about it, or perhaps because he had slept too long before changing to go out and then at the same time beginning this discussion, now his cheeks were hot. And it was apparent that Clarisse instantly realised why he was coming closer to her book. This subtlety of their adjustment to each other's moods, in spite of the painful signs of her dislike, at once stirred him mysteriously, so that his male brutality began to waver, and once again his plain simplicity went to pieces.

" Why won't you show me what you were reading ? Please do let's talk ! " he pleaded timidly.

" One can't ' talk ' ! " Clarisse snapped.

" How overwrought you are ! " Walter exclaimed. He wanted

to get the book away from her still open at the place where she had been reading. Clarisse obstinately held it to herself. But after they had been struggling for a little while, Walter could not help wondering : ' What on earth do I want with the book anyway ? ' and he let Clarisse go.

At this point the matter would really have been closed, if in the very instant when she was released Clarisse had not pressed up against the wall even more tensely than before, as though she had to flee from some threat of violence and were trying to get backwards through a stiff and springy hedge. She was breathless and pale, and in a hoarse scream she flung at him : " What you'd like to do is reproduce yourself in a child instead of achieving something yourself ! "

This accusation came spurting out of her mouth at him like venomous fire.

And in spite of himself Walter once more gasped out his : " Do let's talk ! "

" I won't talk ! I loathe the sight of you ! " Clarisse answered, once more in full possession of her voice, and moreover using it so purposively that the effect was as if some heavy china dish had crashed to the floor midway between her and Walter.

Retreating slightly, Walter looked at her in astonishment.

Clarisse did not really mean it as unkindly as it sounded. It was merely that she was afraid of after all giving way out of softheartedness or easygoingness. For then Walter would at once bind her to himself with swaddling-bands, and that was the last thing that must be allowed to happen now, just when she wanted to reach a decision on this whole question.

The situation had become ' acute '. She could feel this word, thickly underlined, inside her head, the word that Walter had made use of in explaining to her why people were going to demonstrate in the streets. For Ulrich, who was connected with Nietzsche through the fact that he had given her Nietzsche's works as a wedding-present, was on the other side, on the side against which the ' acute ' spear-head would be directed if trouble broke out. And Nietzsche had just now given her a sign. And if in all this she saw herself standing on a ' high mountain ', what was a high mountain but a pointed mound of earth, an acute angle ? So here were quite peculiar interlockings of things, which doubtless no one else had ever been able to unravel, and even to Clarisse they did not seem entirely clear ; but for this very reason she wanted to be alone and therefore she had to drive Walter out of the house. The wild hatred that flared up in her face at this moment was not of the unmixed and serious kind, but only a physical fury in which the personality itself was but vaguely involved ; it was a pianist's *furioso* such as Walter was also capable of. And so it happened that, after he had been staring at his wife, dumbfounded, for a while, he too suddenly and as it were by delayed action grew quite pale and bared his teeth ; and in response to her saying she loathed the sight of him he called out : " Beware of genius ! You of all people—beware ! "

His outcry was even more violent than hers had been ; and he himself was struck by horror at the dark prophecy he had uttered, for it had been stronger than himself, had simply burst out of his throat. Now suddenly he saw everything black in the room around him, as though there had been an eclipse of the sun.

It had also had its effect on Clarisse. She fell silent.

An emotion as overpowering as an eclipse of the sun is certainly no simple matter ; yet however it had arisen, the unforeseen thing that had happened at the core of it was that Walter's jealousy of Ulrich had suddenly exploded. Why did he, in that very explosion, call him a genius ? What the word signified for him was more or less the same as overweeningness, which does not know that pride goeth before destruction. Walter all at once saw pictures from the past rising up before his inner eye. Ulrich coming home in uniform, the barbarian who was already having affairs with real women, while he, Walter, although he was the elder, was still writing poems about stone statues in parks. . . . Then Ulrich coming home with the latest news of the spirit of precision, of speed, of steel. . . . And for the humanist Walter this too had amounted to invasion by a barbarian horde. In relation to his younger friend Walter had always had a secret uneasy sense of being the weaker, both physically and in initiative ; but at the same time he had seen himself as embodying the spirit and the other as embodying only the brute force of the will. And what strengthened this view of his was that the relationship between them had always been this : Walter for ever being moved by the beautiful or the good, Ulrich going about shaking his head over things. Such impressions are lasting. If Walter had managed to see the passage in the book for the sight of which he had been wrestling with Clarisse, he would certainly not have interpreted it in the way Clarisse did. He would not have seen the dissolution it described, which displaced the will to life and forced it out of the totality into the realm of detail, as a rebuke to his own tendency to muse and ponder over artistic questions. On the contrary, he would have been convinced that here was an excellent description of his friend Ulrich. It began with the over-valuing of detail, such as is peculiar to the modern superstition of empiricism, and ended with a barbarian degeneration that had eaten its way to the very core of the ego, turning the whole man into what he, Walter, had called the Man Without Qualities or Qualities Without a Man, a condition that had even brought it about that Ulrich, in his megalomania, went so far as to approve of this term.

All this was what Walter meant with his vilifying cry of 'genius!' For if anyone at all had the right to call himself a solitary individual being, he thought he was that person; and yet he had given that up in order to work his way back to the natural human task, and in so doing he felt himself a whole epoch ahead of his friend. All the same, while Clarisse remained silent, making no retort to his denunciation, he was thinking: 'If she says one single word in Ulrich's favour now, I won't be able to stand it!' and he was shaken by hatred as though by Ulrich's living arm.

In his excessive excitement he felt how, if she did, he would snatch up his hat and dash out of the house. Already he could feel himself rushing along through streets without seeing them. In his imagination the houses were actually blown sideways by the wind as he went rushing past. It was only after some time that he slackened his pace, and then he looked into the faces of the people he passed. These faces, these eyes glancing companion-ably into his, gradually quieted him. And now too he began, in so far as his consciousness had remained outside this fantasy experience, to explain to Clarisse exactly what he meant. But the words shone in his eyes instead of in his mouth. How, after all, was anyone to describe the bliss of being among one's fellow-men, brothers all? Clarisse would say that he lacked individual-ity. But there was something inhuman about Clarisse's towering self-confidence, and he did not want to go on complying with the overbearing demands it made upon him ! He felt most painfully the desire to be enclosed, together with her, with her inside some order, some pattern of things, instead of drifting along in this open and unbounded delusion of love and of private anarchy. ' Underlying everything one is and does, and even at times when one feels oneself to be in opposition to others, one must feel the presence of a fundamental movement towards those others ' : that was approximately what he would have liked to tell her now. For Walter had always been lucky in his relationships with people ; even while quarrelling they would feel attracted by him, and he by them, and so the somewhat banal view that there is, inherent in the human community, an equalising force that rewards effort and efficiency and always asserts itself in the end, come what may, had become a permanent conviction in his life.

There were people—it occurred to him—who were attractive to birds ; birds came flying to them of their own accord, and these people themselves often had something bird-like in their expression. He was indeed convinced that every human being had his correspondence in an animal, one with which he was in some inexplicable way related. This was a theory he had once worked out for himself ; it was not scientific, but that did not bother him, for he believed that musical people had an intuitive aware-ness and understanding of much that lies beyond the scope of science. From his early childhood it had been established that his own creature was the fish. He had always been intensely attracted towards fishes, though there was also some horror mingled with the feeling, and at the beginning of the holidays he had always had a rare old time with them : he would spend hours and hours standing at the water's edge, angling, drawing them up out of their element and laying their corpses beside him on the grass, until suddenly the whole thing would end in a revulsion that was very close to panic. And fishes in the kitchen had been among his earliest passions. The bones from the filleted fish were put into a *Weidling*, a boat-shaped receptacle, glazed greenish-white like grass and clouds, and half-full of water, in which—for some indefinable reason connected with the laws of the kitchen-realm—the skeletons were left lying until the meal was prepared and ready to serve ; only then did they find their way to the garbage. To this receptacle the little boy was mysteriously drawn, and for hours on end he would keep on finding childish excuses for coming back to it, but when he was asked outright what he was doing there, he would be struck dumb. Today he would perhaps have been able to answer that the magic of fish lay in the fact that they did not belong to two elements, but rested entirely in one. Again he saw them before him, as he had often seen them in the deep mirror of the water, and they did not move as he himself did, upon solid ground, along a surface that was its own frontier to the empty sphere of the second element. (' At home neither here nor yonder !' Walter mused, elaborating the thought in this direction and that, ' belonging to an earth with which one shares no more than just that little space taken up by the soles of one's feet, and with all the rest of one's body rearing up into air—an element through which the unsupported body would fall, an element one has to displace in order to be there at all !') No, fishes' ground and air and drink and food, their fear of enemies, and the shadowy passing of their loves, and their grave—it all enclosed them. They moved in that by which they were moved, in a way that man experienced only in dreams, or perhaps in the yearning desire to be restored to the sheltering tenderness of the maternal womb—this latter being a belief that was just beginning to come into fashion. But why then did Walter kill the fishes, snatching them out of their water ? It caused him an unspeakable, holy delight ! And he did not want to know why—he, Walter, the enigmatic !

Yet had not Clarisse once said fish were simply the great middle class of the watery kingdom ? He shuddered at the insult. And while—in the state he had conjured up in his thoughts and in which he was thinking all this—he was hastening through the streets and looking into the faces of the people coming towards him, it had become good weather for fishing. At least, though it was not yet raining, there was a flicker of moisture falling through the air, and the pavements and the road, as he noticed all at once, were now dark brown, and indeed must have been so for some time.

Now the men who were making their way along, on the pavement and in the road, all seemed to be dressed in black, with bowler hats but without collars and ties. Walter registered this fact without astonishment. At any rate this was not the middle class. Evidently these men were coming from some factory, moving along in loosely knit groups ; and others, who had not yet finished their day's work, thrust their way hastily between them, just as he did. He began to feel very happy. Only the bare necks reminded him of something that was disturbing and even slightly sinister. And then suddenly rain came pouring out of the picture ! People scattered and ran. There was something slashed open in mid-air, a flashing of white. Fish came raining down. And over everything there floated a tremulous, tender, seemingly unattached and irrelevant cry of a single voice— someone calling to a little dog, calling it by its name.

These last transformations were so entirely independent of him that they took him by surprise. He had not been aware that his thoughts were in a dream, drifting along with incomprehensible swiftness upon a flood of images.

Glaring, he looked up, straight into the face of his young wife.

Her face was still twisted with dislike. He felt very unsure of himself. He remembered that he had been going to elaborate a reproach in detail and at length : his mouth was still open. But he did not know whether minutes had passed, or seconds, or only the thousandth part of a second. At the same time he was warmed by a trace of pride, as after an ice-cold bath the skin is set flickering with ambiguous shudders, signifying more or less : ' Just look at me, see what I can stand ! ' But in the same instant he was no less overcome by shame about this outbreak of subterranean forces. After all, he had just been about to speak of how whatever is ordered, whatever is self-controlled and is content to have its place in the larger circle of things, is spiritually far loftier than the abnormal, and now here were his convictions all lying with their roots in the air, plastered with the volcanic mud of life !

And so his most vivid emotion after coming back to his senses was actually terror. It seemed to him certain that something terrible was about to befall him. This fear was without any rational basis. It was simply that, still thinking half in images, he was seized by the idea that Clarisse and Ulrich were coming to snatch him out of the picture he was in.

He collected his thoughts, trying to shake off these waking dreams. He wanted to say something that would make it possible to continue in some rational way a discussion that had been

paralysed by his own violence ; and indeed he already had something on the tip of his tongue, but an inkling that his words would
come too late, that meanwhile something else had been said and
something else had happened, without his knowing about it, held
him back. And suddenly, catching up again with the time that
had elapsed, he heard Clarisse saying to him :

" If you want to kill Ulrich, well then, go and kill him ! You
have too much of a conscience. An artist can only make good
music if he has no conscience ! "

It was a long time before Walter could bring himself to understand this. Sometimes, after all, one grasps the meaning of
something only by oneself giving an answer to it ; and he hesitated to give an answer because he was naturally afraid of betraying
his temporary absence of mind. And in this state of uncertainty
he realised, or he let himself be convinced, that Clarisse had really
given utterance to what was the source of the alarming flight of
ideas that he had just experienced. She was right ; for if he had
been permitted any and every wish, he, Walter, would often have
had no other wish than to see Ulrich dead. Such a state of things
is not altogether rare in friendships (which generally do not
dissolve as quickly as love does) when they constitute an intense
challenge to the value of one or both of the persons involved.
And it was not meant very bloodily, for in the next moment when
he imagined Ulrich dead, his bygone youthful love for the friend
now so suddenly lost reappeared, at least partly ; and just as in
the theatre the civilised inhibition against the monstrous deed is
removed by a great artificially contrived emotion, so too it almost
seemed to him that the thought of a tragic solution also con-
ferred a beautiful distinction upon him who was allotted the role
of the victim.

He felt very exalted, although he was timid by nature and could
not bear the sight of blood. And although he sincerely wished
that Ulrich's arrogance should break down some day, he would
not have done anything to bring even this about. But thoughts,
of course, are primarily without any logic, however much one
may attribute it to them ; it is only the unimaginative resistance
put up by reality that introduces into the poem Man the awareness
of the contradictions there are. So perhaps Clarisse was right
when she asserted that an excess of civilised, ' middle-class '

conscience might be hampering to the artist. All this was going on in Walter at the same time, as he gazed at his wife irresolutely and with dismay.

" If he hampers you in your work," Clarisse went on eagerly, " then you have the right to do away with him ! " She seemed to find this stimulating and enjoyable.

Walter wanted to stretch out his hands to take hold of her, but his arms were as though pinned to his sides. Yet he did somehow seem to come closer to her.

" Nietzsche and Christ perished of their half-heartedness ! " she whispered in his ear.

That was all absurd. How did she manage to bring Christ into it ? What was that supposed to mean—that Christ perished of half-heartedness ? Such comparisons were only embarrassing. All the same, Walter still felt some indescribable incitement radiating from the movement of her lips : it was clear that his own hard-won determination to throw in his lot with the majority of mankind was constantly exposed to temptations arising out of his suppressed and nevertheless violent need to be something exceptional.

He seized hold of Clarisse, holding her as hard as all his strength permitted, and prevented her from moving. Her eyes were like two little discs suspended straight in front of his.

" I don't know how you manage to get such ideas ! " he said several times in succession. But he got no answer. And without meaning to, he must at the same time have drawn her closer to him, for Clarisse set the nails of her ten out-splayed fingers against his face, like a bird, stopping him from bringing it any nearer to hers. ' She's mad ! ' Walter realised. But he could not let her go. Her face was now of an ugliness that was beyond all comprehension. He had never in his life seen a lunatic ; but this, he thought, must be what they looked like.

And suddenly he groaned : " So you're in love with him ? "

Of course this remark was not particularly original, nor was it a subject that they had never argued about before. But now, in order to avoid coming to the conclusion that Clarisse was insane, he preferred to face the possibility that she was in love with Ulrich. This self-sacrifice was probably not quite uninfluenced by the fact that Clarisse, whose thin-lipped Early-Renaissance

beauty he had always admired, now for the first time struck him
as ugly ; and this ugliness, again, was perhaps connected with the
fact that her face was no longer tenderly veiled by love for him,
but was stripped bare by his rival's brutal love. All this produced
an abundance of complications, which hung tremulously between
his heart and eye as something of an entirely new kind that had
just as much general as private significance. But if, in uttering
the words ' So you're in love with him ? ', he himself had groaned
quite unhumanly, that was perhaps because he had already
become infected with Clarisse's madness, and this somewhat
frightened him.

Clarisse had gently freed herself. But then she came closer
to him once more of her own accord and in answer to his question
repeated several times, as though she were chanting : " I don't
want a child from you ! I don't want a child from you ! " And
in between she kissed him several times, swiftly and fleetingly.

Then she was gone.

Had she really also said : ' He wants a child from me ? ' Walter
could not remember with certainty that she had said it, but he
heard it, as it were, as a possibility.

Filled with jealousy, he stood at the piano, feeling a breath of
something warm and something cold blowing on him from either
side. Were they the currents of genius and of madness ? Or
those of indulgence and of hate ? Or those of love and of the
spirit ? He could imagine that he might leave the road clear for
Clarisse and lay his heart upon that road so that she should walk
over it and he could imagine that he might annihilate her and
Ulrich with tremendous words. He was undecided whether to
hurry off to have it out with Ulrich or to begin writing his sym-
phony, which in this moment might turn into the eternal strife
between the earth and the stars, or whether it would be a good
thing first of all to cool his excitement off a little in the naiad pool
of Wagner's forbidden music. The indefinable condition in which
he had been gradually began to dissolve into these speculations.

He opened the piano and lit a cigarette, and while his thoughts
were scattering further and further afield, his fingers on the key-
board were beginning to play the billowing, marrow-softening
music of the wizard from Saxony. And after this slow discharge
of emotion had been going on for a while, it was quite clear to

him that his wife and he had both been in a state in which they were not responsible for their actions ; but in spite of the embarrassment this caused him, he realised it would be futile, so soon afterwards, to go and look for Clarisse in order to explain this to her.

And suddenly he felt drawn to be among human beings. He clapped on his hat and went off into town in order to carry out his original intention and join in the general excitement, if he could find out where it was going on.

While he was walking he was pervaded by the sense of bearing along within him a troop of dæmonic warriors, whose captain he was and whom he was leading to join up with the main body. But by the time he had got into the tram, life was beginning to look quite ordinary. The thought that Ulrich must be on the other side, that Count Leinsdorf's mansion might be stormed, that Ulrich was perhaps now dangling from a street-lamp, was being trampled under rushing feet, or, in another version, was defended by Walter and brought, trembling, to safety by him—these were, at the most, mere fleeting shadows on the bright daylight pattern of the well-regulated journey, with the fixed price of the ticket, definite stops, and the warning tinkle of the bell, a pattern to which Walter, now breathing more calmly again, felt himself akin.

119 *A counter-mine and a seduction.*

IN these weeks it looked as though events were hastening towards some conclusion, and for Director Leo Fischel too, who in the Arnheim matter had been patiently holding out, waiting for his counter-mine to blow up under the enemy, the hour of satisfaction came. Unfortunately it was an hour when Frau Klementine happened not to be at home. So he had to be content to walk into his daughter's room, carrying in his hand a midday newspaper that was usually well informed about what was going on on the Stock Exchange. He sat down in a comfortable chair, jabbed his finger at a small news-item, and asked complacently :

" And now, my child, do you know why the deep-thinking financier tarries in our midst ? "

At home he never referred to Arnheim otherwise than in these terms, in order to show that he, as a serious-minded man of business, did not care a rap for the admiration his women-folk felt for the rich 'gas-bag'. And even if hatred does not engender clairvoyance, still, a Stock-Exchange rumour not infrequently has a core of truth, and Fischel's dislike of the man made him instantly pick up the hint thrown out in the newspaper and fill in the whole picture correctly.

" Well, do you know ? " he repeated, trying to catch his daughter's eye and hold it in the triumphant beam of his own gaze. " What he wants is to get the Galician oil-fields under the control of his own group of companies ! "

And with this Fischel got up again, grabbing his newspaper as one might grab a dog by the scruff of its neck, and left the room, because he had just thought of ringing up some people in order to make quite sure. He had the feeling that what he had just read was precisely what he had been thinking all along (from which it may be seen that the effect of Stock-Exchange news is the same as that of the higher forms of literature), and he was satisfied with Arnheim, as though, after all, nothing else could have been expected of such a sensible man, thereby completely forgetting that hitherto he had considered him to be a mere gas-bag. He was not going to bother to explain the significance of his announcement to Gerda ; every additional word would only have weakened the impact of the facts, which spoke for themselves. ' What he wants is to get the Galician oil-fields under the control of his own group of companies ! ' Feeling the weight of this plain statement still on his tongue, he retreated, merely adding in his thoughts : ' Those who can afford to play a waiting game always win in the end ! ' This was an old Stock-Exchange maxim, which, like all the verities of the Stock Exchange, supplemented the eternal verities in an extremely accurate way.

The moment he was out of the room Gerda gave way to her feelings. She would never let her father have the pleasure of seeing her disconcerted or even taken by surprise. But now she wrenched the wardrobe open and seized hat and coat. Then she hurried to the looking-glass to tidy her hair and smooth her dress. And then she stayed sitting in front of the glass, contemplating her face doubtfully. She had made up her mind to dash straight off and see Ulrich. It was a decision she had reached in the instant when it occurred to her, while her father was making his disclosure, that this news was something of which Ulrich, of all people, must be informed as quickly as possible ; for she knew enough about relations in Diotima's circle to realise how important it would be to him. And in the instant when she reached this conclusion it seemed to her that her feelings began to get under way, like the movement of a crowd that had been delaying for a long time : she had been forcing herself to pretend that she had forgotten Ulrich's invitation to visit him, but no sooner had the first sensations begun to detach themselves from the dark mass and move slowly ahead than an irresistible urge to run and shove entered into those further behind. Though she could not make up her mind, it had made itself up of its own accord without taking any notice of her.

' He doesn't love me ! ' she said to herself as she gazed into the glass, contemplating her face, which had become even sharper and more pointed in the last few days. ' And how could he possibly love me if I look like this ? ' she thought listlessly. But then she added immediately and in defiance : ' He isn't worth it ! It was all just imagination ! '

She was overcome by utter discouragement. All that had been going on recently had sapped her strength. Her relation to Ulrich seemed to her now as though for years she had with the greatest of care been complicating something that was really quite simple. And Hans, with his puerile caresses, was a strain on her nerves ; she had been reacting violently, and recently sometimes with contempt, but Hans responded with still greater violence, behaving like a boy threatening to do himself some hurt, and when she had to calm him down, she would find herself again being embraced by him and again being moved by his shadowy caresses. And with all of this her shoulders grew thin and her complexion lost its freshness.

Gerda felt that she had finished with all these torments when she opened her wardrobe to take out her hat. And the anxiety that made her linger in front of the looking-glass now ended with her quickly getting up again and rushing out, though without in the least being liberated from this anxiety.

When Ulrich looked at her as she came in, he knew everything. She had even put on a veil, such as Bonadea used to wear on her visits. She was trembling in every limb and trying to hide it by behaving in an artificially casual manner, which made an absurdly stiff impression.

" I've come to see you, Ulrich, because I have just had some very important information from my father," she said.

' Dear me, how odd ! ' Ulrich thought. ' Now she's suddenly calling me by my first name ! ' This forced display of intimacy infuriated him, and in an attempt to keep this from being notice-able, he tried to explain Gerda's exaggerated behaviour to him-self as an effort to eliminate from her visit any traces of the ominous, or indeed of any special significance at all, and to present it as a rational event that was merely somewhat belated. From all this the opposite could be concluded : the girl's intention was obviously to go the whole way.

" We've been calling each other by our first names for a long time, except that I haven't done it in words before this, because I felt we always tried to avoid facing the implications," Gerda explained. She had been rehearsing her entrance on the way and had been prepared for the astonishment that it would cause.

But Ulrich cut the whole scene short by putting his arm round her shoulder and kissing her.

Gerda gave way like a candle growing soft. Her breathing, her fingers fumbling towards him, were those of one who had lost consciousness.

Now he was invaded by the ruthlessness of the seducer, who is irresistibly attracted by the vacillation of a soul that is dragged along by its own body like a prisoner in the grip of his captors.

Through the windows a faint glimmer of wintry afternoon light penetrated into the darkening room, and in a streak of this bright-ness he stood holding the girl in his arms. The head he saw was yellow and sharply outlined against the soft pillow of the light, and an oily hue lay over the face, so that in this moment Gerda looked almost like the mere dead body of a girl. Slowly he kissed her, covering with kisses all the bare skin between the hair of her head and the neck of her dress, having as he did so to overcome a slight feeling of repugnance, until her lips touched his, coming towards them in a manner that made him think of the frail little arms that a child puts round a grown-up's neck. He thought of Bonadea's beautiful face, which when it was in the clutches of passion was reminiscent of a dove whose plumage is ruffled in the claws of a bird of prey ; and he thought of Diotima's statuesque grace and her favours that he had not enjoyed. How strange it was that instead of the beauty that these two women could and would bestow on him, what now lay beneath his gaze was Gerda's intense and distorted face, hideous in its helplessness.

But Gerda did not long remain in this waking swoon. She had meant to shut her eyes only for a fleeting moment, but while Ulrich was kissing her face it was for her like the stars standing motionless in the infinity of space and time, so that she lost all sense of the duration and limits of the experience ; but at the first slackening of his effort she woke up and got firmly on to her feet again.

These had been the first kisses of real, as opposed to merely pretended or imagined, passion that she had given, and, as she felt, received ; and the response in her body was as tremendous as though this moment alone had made a woman of her. But it is with this process very much the same as with having teeth pulled out : although immediately afterwards there is less of the body there than there was before, one nevertheless has a sense of greater completeness, because a cause of uneasiness has at last been removed. And when she reached this stage Gerda pulled herself up full of fresh resolution.

" You haven't even asked what I came to tell you, Ulrich ! " she exclaimed to her friend.

" That you're in love with me," Ulrich replied, rather dashed.

" No ! That your friend Arnheim is deceiving your cousin. He's playing the fond lover, but what he's really after is something quite different ! "

And Gerda told him of her father's discovery.

This information, in all its simplicity, made a deep impression on Ulrich. He felt he was under an obligation to warn Diotima, who was floating along on outspread pinions of the soul, heading straight for a ridiculous disappointment. For in spite of the malicious satisfaction with which he rounded out this picture for himself he could not help also feeling sorry for his beautiful cousin. But this feeling of pity was hugely out-balanced by his cordial appreciation of Papa Fischel; and although Ulrich was now on the verge of bringing great sorrow upon him, he did honestly admire Fischel's reliable, old-fashioned business man's intelligence, equipped as it was with splendid convictions; for it had triumphantly succeeded in exposing the mysteries of a new-fangled Great Mind, and in the simplest way possible.

As a result of this news Ulrich's mood had shifted a long distance away from the tender demands placed on him by Gerda's presence. He was amazed now to think that only a few days earlier he had been capable of considering the possibility of opening his heart to this girl. ' Surmounting the inner ramparts,' he thought, ' is what Hans calls this infamous notion of two love-ridden angels ! ' and in his thoughts, as though he were running his fingers over it, he enjoyed the wonderfully smooth, hard surface of the sober form that life has taken on in modern times, thanks to the sensible endeavours of Leo Fischel and those who hold the same sort of views as he.

So the only answer he gave was : " Your Papa is a wonderful man."

Gerda, who was permeated with a sense of the importance of her news, had expected something different ; she did not know what effect she had been expecting her communication to have, but it ought to have been something like the moment when all the instruments in an orchestra, wind and string, strike up in unison. The indifference with which Ulrich reacted to it again painfully reminded her that in his relation to her he had always set up to be the advocate of the average, the ordinary, and all that was sobering. For although she had tried to make herself believe that this was merely a prickly form of amorous approach, one to which, after all, she found the prototype in her own girlish heart, now, however—' when they had really begun to love each other ', as it went in the somewhat child-like formula she used in the privacy of her own mind—a desperate lucidity warned her that the man to whom she was about to give everything did not take her seriously enough. In realising this, she again lost a large part of the confidence she had gained ; but on the other hand this 'not being taken seriously enough' was wonderfully pleasant to her, doing away with all the strenuousness that was involved in keeping up the relationship with Hans. And when Ulrich praised her father, although she did not understand how he could do so, at this moment, she felt that a vague sort of order had been re-established, one that she had upset by hurting her father for Hans's sake. Yet her mild awareness of making a somewhat odd return to the bosom of the family, doing it by leaving the path of virtue, confused her to such an extent that she put up some gentle resistance to the pressure of Ulrich's arm and uttered the words :

" Let us first of all seek and find an understanding in human terms. The rest will follow of its own accord ! "

These words were a quotation from a manifesto concocted by the ' Community of Action ', and for the present moment they were all that was left of Hans Sepp and his circle.

However, Ulrich had put his arm round her shoulder again, because since he had heard the news about Arnheim he had been conscious that there was something important he had to do, but that first of all this episode must be brought to an end. All he felt about it was that it was extraordinarily tiresome to have to go through everything the situation required, which was why, after she had freed herself, he at once laid his arm round her again, this time, however, using that wordless language which makes it clear, without force, and yet more distinctly than words can do, that any further resistance is useless.

Gerda felt the masculine force radiating from this arm, felt it moving down her spine. She had lowered her head and was gazing obstinately down at her lap, as though there she held, collected as in an apron, the thoughts by the aid of which she would ' seek and find an understanding ' with Ulrich ' in human terms ' before that was allowed to happen which would then be the crowning of it all. But she felt her face becoming ever stupider and emptier, until finally it floated upwards like an empty husk, the eyes in it lying beneath the eyes of the seducer.

He bent down and covered this face with the ruthless kisses that stir the flesh. Then, as though she had no will of her own, Gerda let herself be drawn to her feet and led away.

It was about ten paces that they had to take in order to reach

Ulrich's bedroom, and the girl leaned on him as heavily as someone wounded or sick. Like an alien thing one foot moved ahead of the other, although she was not being dragged, but went of her own accord. Such an inner void, in spite of so much excitement, was something Gerda had never known before. She felt drained of blood and was icy cold. Yet when they passed a looking-glass, which seemed to show her reflection as something much too small and far away, she saw in it that her face was coppery red, with flecks of pallor.

And suddenly, as often happens in a street accident, when the eye has become supersensitive to the whole scene with all its instantaneous elements, she now took in all the details of the man's bedroom, which had closed in around her. It occurred to her at the same time that with more shrewdness and calculation she might perhaps have been able to make her entry here as Ulrich's wife. This would have made her very happy, but still, even as it occurred to her she groped for words to say that she was not seeking any advantage : she had come only to ' give herself '. Not finding the words, she told herself : ' It has to be ', and opened the collar of her dress.

Ulrich had let her go. He could not bring himself to give a lover's fond aid to her in undressing, and stood apart, flinging off his own clothes.

Gerda became conscious of the tall, straight body of the man, mighty in its equipoise of beauty and potential violence. Panic-stricken, she noticed that her own body, even though she was still standing there in her underclothes, was becoming covered with goose-flesh. Once more she groped for words to help her. How utterly wretched a figure she was, standing there ! What she would have wished to say was something that would turn Ulrich into her lover in the way she vaguely imagined, in some infinitely sweet dissolution that could be attained without doing anything of what she was on the verge of doing. It was something as wonderful as it was formless. For a moment she saw herself standing together with him in an immeasurable field of candles, which grew out of the earth, row upon row, like pansies, and at a signal all at once burst into tiny flames at their feet. But since she could not utter a single word of this, she merely felt disconcertingly plain and wretched. Her arms trembled. She was incapable of going on undressing. And her bloodless lips tight-ened in order not to break into uncanny, wordless twitchings.

Now Ulrich, who had noticed her agony and seen the danger that the whole struggle up to this point might easily turn out to have been in vain, came up to her and untied the ribbon at her shoulders.

Gerda slid into the bed like a boy.

For an instant Ulrich saw a movement that was simply that of a naked adolescent and of no more erotic appeal than the twist and twinkle of a fish. He guessed that Gerda had decided to make all haste in getting through an experience that could not be avoided any longer ; and never had it been so clear to him as in the instant when he followed her to what an extent the impassioned entry into another body is a continuation of the child's liking for secret, even vicious hiding-places. His hands found the girl's skin still rough and bristling with fear, and he himself felt taken aback instead of being drawn towards her. He disliked this body, which was already flabby and yet still immature. What he was doing seemed to him utterly senseless. He would indeed have liked nothing better than to escape out of this bed, and to stop himself from doing so he had to summon up everything he could in the way of thoughts that would help the situation. So it was that in frantic haste he set about persuading himself of all there is nowadays in the way of general reasons for acting without sin-cerity, or faith, or scruple, or satisfaction ; and in utterly aban-doning himself to this he found—not, it is true, the rapture of love—but a half-crazed rapture reminiscent of a massacre, of sex-maniacal homicide or, if there can be such a thing, sex-maniacal suicide, a state of being seized and rapt away by the dæmons of the void, who have their habitation behind all the painted scenery of life.

All at once, by some obscure association of ideas, his situation reminded him of the fight he had had one night with the ruffians in the street, and he decided that this time he would be quicker. But at this instant something horrible began to happen.

Gerda had gathered up all her inner resources, transforming them into will-power and so fighting down the shameful fear she was suffering from. It was as though she were going to her execution, and in the moment when she first felt Ulrich, in this unaccustomed nakedness, beside her and his hands touching her, her body flung this will off—flung it clean away. Somewhere deep in her breast she could still feel unutterable friendship, a tremulously affectionate wish to embrace Ulrich, to kiss his hair, to repeat with her own lips every utterance of his voice, and it seemed to her that if she were to reach his essential being she would melt away in it like a little snow in a warm hand ; but that was an Ulrich fully dressed and as usual, moving about in thé familiar rooms of her parents' house, and not this naked man whose hostility she all at once sensed, this man who did not take her sacrifice seriously, although he gave her no quarter, no breathing-space in which to think what she was doing.

And all at once Gerda realised that she was screaming. Like a tiny cloud, like a soap-bubble, a scream hung in the air, and others came after it. They were little screams, gasped out of her breast as though she were wrestling with something : a whimpering, cries of *ee-ee* rounding out and floating up into the air. Her lips were writhing and twitching, as wet as in mortal lust, and she wanted to leap up, but she could not. Her eyes would not obey her ; they were sending out signals that she had not allowed them to send. Gerda was clamouring to be let off, as a child does when it is to be punished or is being taken to the doctor and cannot go a single step further because it is torn and twisted by its own shrieks. She had drawn her hands up to her breasts and was threatening Ulrich with her nails, and her long thighs were convulsively pressed together. This rebellion of her body against herself was terrible. She had an overwhelming sense of the theatrical in all this, of being on a stage and acting it all, but of sitting at the same time, alone and desolate, in the dark auditorium, unable to prevent her destiny from being acted out before her, violently and with screams, indeed involuntarily taking part in the performance herself.

Filled with horror, Ulrich stared into the tiny pupils of the veiled eyes, out of which the gaze came strangely rigid, and watched, aghast, the queer movements in which desire and taboo, the soul and the soulless, were inexpressibly intertwined. Fleetingly his eye caught a glimpse of pale fair skin and of short black hairs that shaded into red where they grew more densely. It had gradually become clear to him that what he was confronted with

here was a fit of hysteria ; and he did not know what to do about
it. He was afraid that these frightfully distressing screams might
grow louder. He recalled that suddenly yelling at, or slapping, a
person in this condition was supposed to stop the attack. The
intangible element of the *avoidable*, of the senseless and unnecessary, that was associated with this horrible thing made him reflect
that a younger man might perhaps try to get further with Gerda
even now. ' Perhaps then one might get past it,' he thought.
' Perhaps the very worst thing to do is to give way to her now,
after the silly little goose has gone too far for once.' He did not
do anything of the sort. But such irritable thoughts went on zig-
zagging through his mind while he was automatically, ceaselessly,
whispering words of comfort to Gerda, promising that he would
not do anything to her, explaining that nothing had happened to
her, asking for her forgiveness ; and these weightless words,
words like chaff swept together in the horror of the moment,
seemed to him so ridiculous and undignified that he had at the
same time to fight off the temptation simply to grab an armful of
pillows and press them over this mouth, suffocating these shrieks
that could not be stopped.

At last, however, the fit began to wear off and the body became
quieter. The girl's eyes filled with tears, and she sat up in bed,
the little breasts drooping slackly from a body not yet again under
the control of the conscious mind. Ulrich breathed deeply in
relief and once again felt returning to him all his loathing of the
inhuman and merely physical nature of the experience that he had
had to undergo.

Now normal consciousness came back to Gerda : something in
her eyes opened, as it is with a sleeper whose eyes open a while
before consciousness returns to him, and for a second she stared
ahead of her in bewilderment. Then she became aware that she
was sitting there naked. She glanced at Ulrich, and the blood
came flooding back into her face in great waves.

Ulrich could not think of anything better than to repeat once
more everything he had whispered to her. He put his arm round
her shoulder, drew her to his chest, comfortingly, and pleaded
with her not to take what had happened too much to heart.

Gerda found herself once more in the position in which she had
been overtaken by her fit of hysteria, but now everything seemed

to her curiously pale and forlorn. The opened bed, her own bare body in the arms of a man eagerly whispering to her, and the feelings that had brought her here—she knew very well what it all amounted to, but she knew too that in the meantime something ghastly had happened, something she remembered only reluctantly and in a blurred way, and although it did not escape her that Ulrich's voice now had a more tender ring, all she concluded from this was that for him she was now an ill person, and told herself that it was he who had made her ill. But it seemed to her that nothing mattered any more, and she had no other wish than, without having to say a word, not to be there any more.

Lowering her head, she thrust Ulrich away from her, groped for her chemise and pulled it on over her head like a child, or like a person who is past caring about himself one way or the other. Ulrich helped her. He even pulled her stockings on for her, and he felt indeed as if he were getting a child dressed.

Gerda swayed when at last she stood on her feet again. Memory brought back to her the emotions with which she had left home, where she was now about to return. She could feel that she had not passed the test, and she was deeply unhappy and ashamed. She did not speak a word in answer to anything Ulrich said. Something that was quite remote from here and now came back to her : once he had said about himself, jokingly, that solitude sometimes tempted him to commit excesses. She did not bear him a grudge. Only she never again wanted to hear him say anything.

He offered to go and get a cab. She only shook her head, pulled her hat on over her ruffled hair, and went away without looking at him.

As he watched her walking away, with her veil now carried in her hand, Ulrich had the feeling that he was standing there like a schoolboy. Of course he ought not to have let her go away in that state ; but he had not been able to think of any way of stopping her. Besides, since he had had to help her, he himself was only half dressed, and this too lent a sense of the unfinished to the serious mood in which her departure left him. It was as though he must first of all be fully dressed if he was to come to a decision about what was to be done with himself.

120 *The Collateral Campaign causes uproar.*

REACHING the centre of the city, Walter realised that there was something in the air. Admittedly, people were going about their business no differently from at other times, and carriages, motor-cars and trams were driving along just as usual. and if here and there an unusual movement could be noticed, it faded out again before one could quite define what it was. Nevertheless, everything seemed to bear some little mark, as it were an arrow, and one that pointed in a definite direction, and Walter had gone only a short distance when he became aware that he himself seemed to be wearing this sign. He let himself be borne along in the direction in which it pointed, and he had the sensation that the official from the Department of Fine Arts, which he was, but also the struggling painter and musician, and indeed even Clarisse's tormented husband, were giving way to a person who was not in any of those definite conditions. The streets too, with all their bustle and their over-ornate, pompous buildings, were entering into a similar ' pristine condition ', as he called it in his thoughts ; for the impression it made on him was approximately that of a crystalline form beginning to soften under the action of some fluid and returning to an earlier condition. However conservative he was when it was a matter of rejecting innovations and anything that bore the mark of the future, where he himself was concerned he was equally ready to condemn the present, and the dissolution of the ordered pattern, which he had sensed, was positively stimulating to him. The crowds of people that he encountered made him think of his dream. They radiated an atmosphere of mobility and haste, and some communion among them, which seemed to him more primal by far than the ordinary one that is brought about by intellect, morality and a shrewd system of safeguards, turned them into a free and loosely woven community. It made him think of a huge bunch of flowers when the strings have been untied, so that it opens, yet without falling apart ; and it made him think, too, of a body from which the clothes have been removed, so that it stands there in its smiling nakedness, which has no words and no need of words. And when, quickening his pace, he soon found himself confronted with a large contingent of police standing by, even that did not strike him as a disturbing element ; on the contrary, the sight of it delighted him like that of a military camp waiting for the alarm to be given, and all the red collars, the dismounted riders, and the movement of smaller units reporting their arrival or departure, stirred his senses into a war-like mood.

Beyond this point, where a cordon was obviously about to be drawn across the street, though it had not yet been closed, Walter was immediately struck by the gloomier atmosphere ; there were almost no women about on the pavements, and the prevailing uncertainty also seemed to have swallowed up the gay uniforms of the officers who were usually to be seen idly strolling about these streets. But there were many people, like himself, making their way into the city, and the impression that their movement made was now different : it was reminiscent of chaff and litter being blown along by a strong gust of wind. And soon he saw the first groups beginning to form, held together, as it seemed, not only by curiosity but equally by indecision whether to follow the unusual attraction further or to turn round and go home.

To his questions Walter got various answers. Some to whom he spoke replied that what was going on was a great patriotic demonstration ; others said they had heard that it was a demonstration against certain patriots who were making busy-bodies of themselves. Opinions were equally divided on the question whether the prevailing agitation was agitation on the part of the German population about the Government's flabby policy of yielding to Slav demands, which was what the majority believed, or whether the agitation was in favour of the Government and a call to all Kakanians of good will to march shoulder to shoulder in protest against these continual disorders. These people were camp-followers like himself, and Walter learnt nothing that he had not already heard rumoured in his office. Yet an urge to gossip, which he could not control, made him go on and on asking. And whether the people whom he joined on his way told him that they themselves did not know what was going on or whether they regarded the whole thing as a joke, making ironical remarks about their own curiosity, still, the further he went, the more unanimous was the grave supplementary comment that it was high time for *something* to be done, even though nobody volunteered to state clearly *what*.

And the further he went in this way, the more often he noticed on the faces into which he glanced a look of something irrational and overbrimming, overflowing the bounds of reason. By now it seemed to have become a matter of general indifference what was happening at the place whither they were all being drawn. The mere fact that something unusual was going on seemed indeed to be enough to work them into a frenzy ; and although the term 'frenzy' must be understood only in a weak figurative sense, indicating a very ordinary degree of mild excitement, there was nevertheless something to be felt in it of a remote kinship with long-forgotten states of ecstasy and transfiguration, as it were a growing unconscious readiness, in all of these people, to jump out of their clothes and indeed out of their skins.

And, exchanging surmises and saying things that were not at all in character, Walter fell in with the rest, who were gradually transforming themselves from little crumbling groups of people standing about, waiting, and people vaguely walking along, into a procession moving towards the supposed scene of events and, though without definite intention, was markedly gaining in density and inner force. But all these emotions were still at a stage when they somewhat resembled rabbits scampering about near their burrows, at any instant prepared to scurry back into them, when from the front of the disordered procession, which was far ahead and out of sight, a more definite sort of excitement came rippling back towards the rear. Up there a little band of students or, at any rate, young men, who had already taken some action or other and had come, so to speak, 'straight from the battlefield', had joined up with the crowd. There was some talking and shouting that was not intelligible at this distance, distorted scraps of information and waves of inarticulate excitement ran through the crowd, and, according to their temperament and what they could make of it all, people felt indignation or fear, pugnacity or the pressure of a moral imperative, and now began to thrust forward in a mood in which they were guided by thoroughly ordinary emotions, which took on a different form in each of them but which, in spite of their dominant position in the individual's consciousness, had so little intellectual significance that they combined into one single vital energy, turning all these people into one single vast body and exerting more influence on the muscles than on the brain.

Walter, who was now in the midst of this moving throng, also became infected and was soon in an over-stimulated, empty state that was rather like an early stage of drunkenness.

Nobody really knows how such a change comes about, at a certain moment turning individuals with wills of their own into a crowd with only a single will, capable of going to the wildest extremes of good and evil, and incapable of stopping to think anything out, even if the individuals of which the crowd is made up have for the most part spent their whole lives devoting themselves to nothing so much as to moderation and level-headedness. Probably what happens is that when a crowd has no outlet for its emotions all these excitements, this energy working up to the point when it will have to be discharged, are canalised into every channel that may happen to open up. And presumably those who set the example and lead the way will always be those who are the most excitable, most sensitive and least capable of withstanding pressure, that is to say, the extremists, those who are capable of committing sudden acts of violence or rising to sudden heights of sentimental generosity ; these persons are the points of least resistance in the whole mass. But the shout that is uttered through them more than it is really uttered by them, the stone that somehow gets into their hands, the emotion into which they burst—all this opens the way on which the others, who have been generating excitement in their own midst to the point where it has become unendurable, then come surging along blindly and senselessly, and it all gives to the acts committed round about the character of mob-action, which is felt by all to be something that is half compulsion and half liberation.

What is interesting about this sort of excitement, which can be observed equally well even in the behaviour of the spectators at any sporting contest or of an audience listening to a speech, is, incidentally, not so much the psychology of its discharge as the whole problem of what causes the readiness to get into such a state at all. For if everything were as it should be where the meaning of life is concerned, then so it would be too with all that is meaningless, senseless, in life ; and this negative side would not necessarily be accompanied by symptoms of mental deficiency. This was something that Walter knew better than most people, and he had plenty of suggestions in his mind for the reform of this state of things, which all came to the surface now, so that with a stale, sick feeling he kept on struggling against the communal tide of emotion, which nevertheless entranced him.

In a moment of temporary lucidity he found himself thinking of Clarisse. ' It's a good thing she isn't here,' he thought. ' She wouldn't be able to stand up to the pressure of it.' But in that very moment a stab of grief prevented him from following this thought to its conclusion : he had suddenly remembered the dreadfully distinct impression of insanity she had made on him. ' Perhaps,' he thought, ' I'm mad myself, not to have noticed it all this time ! ' And he thought : ' I *shall* be soon if I go on living with her.' Then he thought : ' I don't believe it ! ' Then he thought : ' But it's absolutely obvious ! ' And then he thought : ' Between my hands her darling face has frozen into a grotesque mask.' But he could not think it out clearly any further, for his mind was dazzled with hopelessness and despair. All he could feel was that in spite of this grief it was incomparably finer and better to love Clarisse than to be drifting along here with the rest, and, shrinking from his own fear, he pressed deeper into the ranks of those with whom he was marching.

Meanwhile, though by another route, Ulrich had reached the Palais Leinsdorf. As he went in through the archway, he observed that there was a double guard at the entrance, and a large detachment of police standing by inside the courtyard.

His Highness welcomed him in a calm and collected manner and showed himself to be already informed on the point that he had become the target of popular displeasure.

" There is something I must withdraw," he said. " I once said to you one could be pretty sure that when a great many people were in favour of a thing, something sensible would come of it. Of course, there are exceptions to the rule."

Shortly after Ulrich's arrival the major-domo came up, bringing the latest news, which was that the demonstration was approaching the Palais. In a discreetly concerned manner the man then asked whether the gate and the shutters were to be closed.

His Highness shook his head. " Dear me, what an idea ! " he said in his easy way. " They'd only be pleased, don't you know, because it would look as if we were frightened. And besides, there are all these stout policemen down there that have been sent along to look after us ! "

Then, turning to Ulrich, he added in a tone of moral indignation :

" Very well then, let them come and smash our windows ! I've said all along these clever men wouldn't get us anywhere."

It seemed that working within him there was some deep resentment, which he concealed under an appearance of dignified calm.

Ulrich had just walked over to the window when the procession arrived. Along the edge of the street there were policemen keeping step with it, and the onlookers scattered before them like a cloud of dust stirred up by the firm tread of the marching column. Here and there, besides, there were vehicles wedged tight in the crowd, with the relentless current flowing round them in endless black waves, on which there danced, as it were, the frothing foam of the light-coloured faces. When the spear-head of the marching crowd came into sight of Count Leinsdorf's great house, it seemed as though some command made them slow down ; an immense ripple ran back along the column ; the advancing ranks closed up, jamming together ; and the picture that resulted was for a moment reminiscent of a muscle tightening before the blow is launched.

In the next instant this blow whizzed through the air. And it was a weird enough sight to behold : in the multitude of faces the mouths suddenly opened wide in one massed shout of indignation, which thus became visible before the roar itself was heard. In rhythmical succession the groups of faces snapped open in the instant they came on the scene, and since the shouting of those further away was blotted out by the louder shouting of those who had meanwhile arrived, one could, if one directed one's gaze into the distance, observe the mute spectacle repeating itself time and again.

" The jaws of the populace ! " said Count Leinsdorf, who had for a moment come up behind Ulrich. He said this with great solemnity and as though it were a standing phrase such as ' our daily bread '. " But what *is* it they're shouting ? I can't make it out, with all this din."

Ulrich said he thought they were mostly shouting ' Shame ! '

" Yes, but isn't there something else as well ? "

Ulrich did not tell him that from the mass of darkly dancing shouts of " Shame ! " there not infrequently arose a long-drawn, clear cry of " Down with Leinsdorf ! " He even thought he had several times heard calls of " Hurrah for Germany ! " interspersed with " Up Arnheim ! ", but on this point he could not be entirely certain, because the thick window-pane blurred the sounds.

Ulrich had made his way here as soon as Gerda had gone, for he felt the need to tell Count Leinsdorf, if nobody else, the news that had come to his ears and which exposed Arnheim beyond all expectation. But so far he had not been able to bring himself to say anything about it.

He looked down on the dark surge of bodies below the window, and memories of his military days made him say to himself contemptuously : ' One could sweep the whole street clear with a single company ! ' He could almost see it before his eyes : all these threatening mouths transformed into one single foaming maw, and the awful apparition then suddenly invaded by panic, growing slack and flaccid at the edges, the lips sinking slowly over the teeth. And then all at once his imagination again transformed the menacing black crowd, now into a flock of hens scattering before a dog that rushes into their midst. As these images occurred to him, it was as though everything malevolent in him had once again contracted into one hard knot ; but the old satisfaction of contemplating how man, the being that is moved by moral impulses, withdraws before man, the being that advances with insensate brutality, was, as always, a two-edged sensation.

" Anything wrong ? " Count Leinsdorf asked. Walking up and down behind Ulrich, he had in fact received the impression, from a strange movement of Ulrich's, that the latter must have cut himself on some sharp edge, although there was nothing far and wide that provided a chance to do so.

And when no answer came, he stopped, shook his head, and said :

" After all, we must not forget that it is not yet very long since His Majesty reached his generous decision to grant the people the right to take a certain part in the conduct of its own affairs. So it is understandable that people have not yet generally attained a degree of political maturity in every respect worthy of our Sovereign's magnanimous confidence. I believe I said as much at our very first committee meeting."

Listening to these words, Ulrich abandoned his intention of informing either His Highness or Diotima of Arnheim's machinations, for despite all antagonism he felt more closely related to him than to the others. He now realised that the memory of having set upon Gerda like a big dog upon a howling little one had been haunting him all the time since ; but it seemed to bother him less as soon as he thought of Arnheim's infamous behaviour towards Diotima. The episode of the screaming body that had staged a scene before two impatiently waiting souls was something that could, if one liked, be regarded even from the farcical side. And these people under the window here, at whom Ulrich was still staring down, spellbound, without taking any notice of Count Leinsdorf—they too were only staging a farce ! That was what he found so fascinating. Undoubtedly they were not out to attack anyone or tear anyone to pieces, although they looked just as if they were. They showed every sign of being very thoroughly worked up, but it all lacked that kind of seriousness which drives people on towards a line of firing rifles ; it lacked even the seriousness with which people turn out to watch the fire-brigade. ' No,' he thought, ' what they are up to is a performance much more like a ritual act, a consecrated play with affronted emotions of the profoundest kind, some half-civilised, half-savage vestige of communal actions that the individual does not need to take seriously down to the very last detail.' He envied them. ' How pleasant they are even now, at this stage, when they are trying to make themselves as unpleasant as possible ! ' he thought.

The protection against loneliness that a crowd provides came radiating up from below, and his having to stand up here without it—something that he felt for an instant as vividly as if from down in the street he were seeing his own image behind glass, set in the wall of the house—seemed to him the expression of his destiny. It seemed to him he would have had a better destiny if he had been capable now of flying into a rage or, on Count Leinsdorf's behalf, giving the alarm to the guard standing by downstairs, and, on the other hand, of feeling at one with the same people on some other occasion and being on good terms with them ; for anyone who plays cards with his fellow-men, who bargains with them, quarrels with them, and enjoys the same pleasures, is at liberty to give orders to fire on them now and then too, without its seeming to be anything out of the ordinary.   There is a certain way of being on good terms with life that permits every man to do as he likes, and does not bother about him, the only condition being that life can do as *it* likes with him : this was what Ulrich was thinking of.   And this is perhaps a rather queer rule, but it is no less reliable than a natural instinct.   It is obviously this that exhales the confidential scent of all human buoyancy and thriving-ness, and anyone who lacks this capacity for compromise, anyone who is solitary, ruthless, and deadly in earnest, unnerves the others in the same way as a caterpillar does, which, though it is not dangerous, is repellent.   At this moment he felt utterly oppressed by a profound repugnance for the unnaturalness of the solitary man and for his intellectual experiments, a feeling that can be aroused by the turbulent sight of a crowd in the grip of natural and communal emotions.

The demonstration had meanwhile been gaining in intensity. Count Leinsdorf was walking agitatedly up and down the room, now and then casting a glance through the second window.   He seemed to be in great distress, although he did not mean to show it ; his protruding eyes were like two hard little marbles standing out from among the soft furrows of his face, and sometimes, as though struggling in anguish, he stretched his arms, which he held crossed behind his back.

Suddenly Ulrich realised that he, who had been standing here at the window all the time, was being taken for the Count himself. All the eyes down below were focused on his face, and sticks were being brandished at him.   A few steps further away, where the street curved, giving the impression of vanishing off-stage, into the wings, most of the performers were already, as it were, taking off their grease-paint ; there would have been no sense in their going on making menacing gestures with no one to watch them, and in a way that seemed to come quite naturally to them when they reached that point the excitement instantly disappeared from their faces ; indeed, there were not a few among them who laughed and joked as merrily as if they were out for a picnic. And Ulrich, observing this, also laughed. But those who were just passing below the window thought this was the Count laughing at them, and their rage rose to a terrible pitch. And now Ulrich laughed all the more and without restraint.

But suddenly he broke off in disgust. While his eyes were still glancing now at the threatening faces with the open mouths and now at the jolly faces further away, and as his spirit refused to go on absorbing these impressions, a strange transformation took place in him. 'I can't go on with this life, and I can't go on rebelling against it !' was what he felt. But at the same time he felt behind him the presence of the room, with the big paintings on the wall, the long Empire desk, the stiff perpendicular lines of the bell-ropes and the curtains. And that in itself now had something of the quality of a little stage, on which he stood right in front, in the opening between the curtains, while outside, on the greater stage, the drama went past ; and these two stages had a peculiar way of uniting, without regard for the fact that he stood between them. Then the room as he knew it to be there behind his back, his impression and awareness of it, contracted and turned inside out, passing through him or flowing past him like something very soft and yielding all around him. 'What an odd spatial inversion !' Ulrich thought. The people were moving along behind him, and he had passed through them and arrived at some point of nothingness. Or perhaps they were moving along before and behind him, and he was being lapped by them like a stone lapped by the ever-changing, ever-constant ripples of a stream. It was an experience that was only half comprehensible, and what struck Ulrich most about it was the glassiness, emptiness, and tranquillity of the condition in which he found himself. 'Can one really leave one's own space, entering into a second, a hidden one ?' he wondered. For he felt just as if some chance had taken him through a secret connecting-door.

He shook these dreams off with such a violent movement of his whole body that Count Leinsdorf looked at him in amazement, and paused in his pacing up and down the room.

"What is the matter with you today?" His Highness asked. "You take it all too much to heart. I stick to what I said: we must win over the Germans by way of the non-Germans, no matter how painful it may be."

Hearing this, Ulrich found it possible at least to smile again, and looked thankfully into the Count's face, marked with those many knots and furrows. There is a special moment just before an aeroplane lands, when one feels the ground rising up again, all plastic and voluptuous, out of the map-like flatness to which it has been reduced for hours on end, and the old meaning that terrestrial things once more assume seems to grow out of the ground itself. This was what Ulrich felt now.

But, incomprehensibly, at the same moment the resolve shot through his head to commit some crime—or perhaps it was only an amorphous, transient thought, for it was not associated with any clear idea of anything. Possibly it was somehow connected with Moosbrugger, for he would have liked to help that lunatic whom fate had brought together with himself in much the same random way as two people find themselves sitting on the same seat in the park. But all that this ' crime ' really amounted to for him was the urge to shut himself out from things, or to depart from the sort of life with which one has come to terms, living among other people. What is called a ' disloyal ' or ' politically unreliable' outlook, or even mere ' misanthropy ', this inner attitude, that he seemed, for countless reasons, to have a right to and, for just as many reasons, had to put up with, was something that did not ' arise '—something for which there was no evidence or justification: it was simply there. Ulrich knew quite well that it had been with him all his life long, but it had seldom been as intense as it was now.

It is probably safe to say that in all the revolutions that have ever occurred on this earth the man of intellect has always come off worst. Revolutions begin by promising to create a new civilisation; they make a clean sweep of everything the spirit has achieved to date, as though it were enemy property; and they are overtaken by the next revolution before they can surpass the heights previously attained. So what are called epochs of civilisation are nothing but a long series of signs saying No Road, indicating enterprises that have failed. And the notion of taking up one's position outside this series was far from new to Ulrich. All that was new about it was the intensified symptoms of a decision, indeed positively of an act, that seemed to be already on the way to accomplishment. He did not make the slightest effort to provide this notion with any substance. For some minutes he was content to be permeated with the feeling that what would follow now would be different and not again merely something general and theoretical, which he was tired of by now: he would have to set about some personal scheme of action, something in which he would be involved with all his being, as a man of flesh and blood, with arms and legs. He knew that in the instant of committing this strange 'crime', which his consciousness had not yet defined, he would no longer be able to stand up squarely to the world; but it was a mystery to him why the sensation it aroused in him should be one of mingled passion and tenderness. This sensation in its turn merged with the very odd spatial experience he had had a short time earlier (and he could wake a faint echo of it still, if he wished to), when events on this side and that side of the windows had fused, inexplicably becoming one, and with it formed an obscurely exciting relationship to the world, which would perhaps have led him, if he had had more time to contemplate it, to that voluptuous joy experienced by mythical heroes who were devoured by the goddesses they wooed.

However, his musings were interrupted by Count Leinsdorf, who had meanwhile fought out his own fight.

" I must stay at my post here," His Highness began, " and face this insurrection out. I *can't* very well go away. But you, my dear fellow, really ought now to go along to your cousin as quickly as you can, lest she is frightened by what is happening and perhaps makes a statement to one of our journalists that might not be quite suitable at the present juncture. Perhaps you would tell her——" He paused once more before reaching a decision. " Yes, I think the best thing would be to tell her this: Strong remedies produce strong effects! And tell her besides: Those who set out to make life better must not shrink, in a critical situation, from resorting to the cautery or the knife ! " He pondered once again. He looked almost alarmingly resolute, and' his little beard rose up. But then it sank again, pointing vertically downwards, as, on the verge of saying something, he suddenly thought better of it. However, in the end some of his innate kindliness broke through, and he continued : " Apart from that, do make her really understand that she must not be frightened—not in the least frightened ! One never need be afraid of the wild men. The more there really is in them, the sooner they'll adjust themselves to real conditions once they're given the chance. I don't know if it has ever struck you, but the fact is there has never yet been an opposition that didn't change its tune when it took over the helm. And, you know, that isn't, as one might think, just something that goes without saying. On the contrary, it is most important. The fact is, it's the cause of what I call the hard core, the thing one can count on, the continuum, in politics ! "

121   *Talking man to man.*

WHEN Ulrich arrived at Diotima's, he was told by Rachel, who let him in, that madame was not at home, but that Herr Dr. Arnheim was in the drawing-room, waiting for her. Ulrich said he would wait too. He did not notice that at the sight of him his remorseful little ally had blushed scarlet.

There was still some unrest in the street, with people jostling this way and that, and Arnheim was standing at the window. He now came across the room to shake hands with Ulrich. The unexpected chance of this hesitantly sought-after meeting made his face light up, but he wanted to be careful and could not find the right way of beginning. Nor could Ulrich, for his part, make up his mind to launch straight into the matter of the Galician oilfields. And so after exchanging the first few words the two men, relapsing into silence, went over to the window together and stood there looking down at the stir going on there below.

After a while Arnheim said :

" I fail to understand you. Is it not a thousand times more important to come to grips with life than to write ? "

" Well, I don't write," Ulrich retorted briefly.

" How right you are ! " Arnheim said, immediately adjusting himself to this reply. " Writing, like the pearl, is a disease. Look——! " He raised two of his beautifully manicured fingers and pointed down at the street, with a movement that, for all its speed, had something of a papal blessing about it. " There the people come, singly and in packs, and from time to time something within jerks a mouth open and it shouts. Another time the same man would write. Yes, how right you are ! "

" But surely you yourself are a celebrated author ? "

" Oh, that doesn't signify ! " After this reply, which in a pleasant manner left the whole thing open, Arnheim turned to face Ulrich, confronting him as it were broadside on, and, standing chest to chest with him and spacing his words slowly, said : " May I ask you something ? "

Naturally, it was impossible to say no. But since Ulrich had instinctively retreated a shade, this rhetorical courtesy served as a noose to draw him closer again.

" I hope," Arnheim began, " that you don't bear me any ill will after our last little clash of opinion. I should like to think that you reckoned to my credit the sympathy that I feel for your views, even if, as is indeed not infrequently the case, they seem to be at variance with my own. And so may I then ask you whether you really stand by what you said about—I should like to sum it up this way—about the necessity of living with a restricted conscience where reality is concerned ? Do I express myself rightly ? "

The smile with which Ulrich responded was as much as to say : ' I don't know. I'm waiting to hear what else you have to say.'

" You spoke, didn't you, of its being necessary to leave life in a state—as it were—of equipoise, in the way metaphors are, which are inconclusively at home in two worlds at once ? Besides that, you have said a number of things to your cousin that are extraordinarily interesting. It would be sadly mortifying for me if you were to regard me as anything in the nature of a Prussian mercantile militarist, devoid of understanding of such things. But

you say for instance that it is only the indifferent aspect of ourselves from which our reality and our history arise. If I understand you right, what you mean here is that the forms and types
of events need to be renewed, and that until that happens it is in
your opinion to some extent a matter of indifference what happens
to Tom, Dick, and Harry ? "

"What I mean is," Ulrich took this up warily and reluctantly,
" that it is all reminiscent of a textile that is manufactured by the
thousands of bales and technically to a very high degree of perfection, but the patterns are old-fashioned and nobody bothers to
improve on them."

"In other words," Arnheim interposed, " I understand you
to be saying that the present-day state of the world, which is
undoubtedly unsatisfactory, is due to the fact that our leaders
believe they are under the obligation of making history—world
history !—instead of bending all human energy to the task of
pervading the sphere of power with ideas. One might even more
usefully make a comparison with a manufacturer who goes ahead
with production and only takes his bearings *from* the market
instead of regulating it. You can see that your ideas affect me very
deeply. But for that very reason you must also understand that
these ideas sometimes strike me, a man who is continually having
to make decisions that keep vast industries going, as positively
monstrous ! For instance, when you demand that we should give
up attaching any reality-value to our actions. Or when you
demand that we should abandon the ' provisionally definitive ' (as
our friend Leinsdorf so delightfully puts it) character of our
actions. For, after all, one can't really quite do without it ! "

"I demand nothing at all," Ulrich said.

"Oh, I dare say you demand more ! You demand awareness of
the experiment ! " Arnheim said this vivaciously and warmly.
"In your view the responsible leaders should come to see that
their job is not making history but drawing up reports on experiments, to provide the basis for further experiments. I am charmed
with the notion. But then what about, for instance, wars and
revolutions ? Can one reawaken the dead once the experiment has
been carried out and taken off the schedule ? "

Ulrich did after all now succumb to the charm of talking, which
lures one to go on and on in much the same way as smoking does ;

and he replied that probably everything one did ought to be tackled with all possible seriousness for the sake of getting on with it, even if one knew that fifty years after it had been done every experiment would turn out to have been futile. But this ' perforated seriousness ' was, after all, far from being anything unusual : people risked their lives often enough in sport and for nothing. Psychologically, therefore, there was nothing impossible about living experimentally. All that was missing was the determination to assume responsibility of a kind that was in a certain sense unlimited.

" This is where the decisive difference lies," he concluded. " In the old days people felt as it were deductively, starting from certain definite assumptions. That time is past. Nowadays we live without any guiding idea, but also without any method of conscious induction. We go on trying things as haphazardly as an ape does ! "

" Brilliantly put ! " Arnheim confessed readily. " But now will you allow me one last question ? Your cousin has mentioned more than once that you take great sympathetic interest in a pathologically dangerous man. I understand that, incidentally, very well. Besides, there is still no proper method of dealing with such people, and society's attitude to them is disgracefully irresponsible. But in the present circumstances, which leave no other choice but that this man should be killed though he be in an ultimate sense innocent or that he should go on killing innocent people—would you let him escape in the night before his execution if you had the power to do so ? "

" No ! " Ulrich said.

" No ? Really not ? " Arnheim asked, suddenly very animated.

" I don't know. I believe not. I might of course make excuses for myself by saying that in a world where nothing is as it should be I have no right to act according to my own convictions. But I shall simply admit that I don't know what it would be right to do."

" The man undoubtedly has to be put out of harm's way," Arnheim said thoughtfully. " And yet during the period of his attacks he is a dwelling-place of the dæmonic, which in all virile epochs has been felt to be akin to the divine. In earlier times the man would have been sent into the wilderness when his fits came upon him. Even then he might perhaps have committed murder,

but in some great vision, as when Abraham set about slaying
Isaac ! That is it ! Nowadays we don't know what to make of
such things, and there is no longer any sincerity in what we do ! "

Perhaps Arnheim had been carried away into uttering these last
words, without himself quite knowing what he meant ; the fact
that Ulrich could not summon up enough ' heart and folly ' to
give an uninhibited answer of ' yes ' to the question whether he
would rescue Moosbrugger had spurred on his own ambition.

But although Ulrich felt this turn the conversation had taken
to be almost an omen, unexpectedly reminding him of his ' resolve '
at the Palais Leinsdorf, he was irritated by the extravagance with
which Arnheim embroidered on the Moosbrugger problem ; and
these two things combined to make him ask, dryly, but intently :
" Would you set him free ? "

" No," Arnheim replied, smiling. " But I've been wanting to
make another suggestion to you." And without giving him a
chance to put up any resistance, he went on : " It's a suggestion
I've been wanting to make for a long time, in the hope that you
will then give up your mistrustful attitude to me, which does,
frankly, grieve me. I wish, indeed, to win you over to my side !
Now, have you any idea of what a great commercial enterprise
looks like seen from within ? It has two heads. One is the
management and the other is the board of governors. And above
both there is usually yet a third, the executive committee, as you
call it in this country, consisting of representatives of both and
meeting daily or almost daily. Those who sit on the board of
governors are, it goes without saying, men who have the confidence of the majority-shareholders——" Only now did he pause
to let Ulrich speak if he wished to, and it was as though he were
putting him through a test to see whether or not he had yet been
struck by anything. " As I was saying," he added after a while, as
though prompting Ulrich, " the majority-shareholders nominate
their trustees on the board of governors and the executive committee. Now, have you any clear picture of what this majority
is ? "

Ulrich had not. He possessed only a vague collective notion of
finance, made up of clerks, counters, coupons, and papers that
somehow resembled ancient documents.

Arnheim prompted him once again. " Have you ever cast your

vote in the election of a board of governors? You have never done so!", he immediately added, answering his own question. "And there is really no sense in envisaging it, since you will never own the majority of shares in a company."

He said this so definitely that Ulrich might almost have felt ashamed of lacking such an important quality; and it was indeed typical of the way Arnheim's mind worked that it moved effortlessly and in a single stride from the dæmons to the board of governors.

Smilingly, he continued: "There is one person I have not mentioned up to now, and this is in a sense the most important one. The words I used were 'majority-shareholders', which sounds merely like some unassuming plurality. Yet the fact is that it is almost always one individual who is the chief shareholder, a person unnamed and unknown to the general public, screened behind those whom he sends along in his place."

Now of course Ulrich began to have an inkling of the fact that these were things one could read about in the newspaper every day; still, Arnheim certainly had a way of making them sound mysterious. His curiosity piqued, Ulrich asked him who held the majority of shares in Lloyd's Bank.

"That is not known," Arnheim answered quietly. "Or, rather, it would be truer to say that though the initiated know, of course, it is not usual to speak of it. But now let me touch upon the core of these things. Wherever there are two such forces, on the one side the person who really wields the power, on the other the board of governors, what automatically appears is the phenomenon that every possible means of profit-making is exploited, whether it be moral and pleasant to contemplate or no. When I say 'automatically', I mean it literally, for this phenomenon is to a high degree independent of the personal element. The person who really wields the power does not directly take a hand in the carrying out of his directions, and the individual members of the management are covered by the fact that they act not on personal grounds but as functionaries. This relationship is one you find on all sides nowadays, and not by any means exclusively in the financial sphere. You can be sure that our friend Tuzzi would give the signal for war with the clearest conscience in the world, even if, as a man, he may be incapable of actually shooting an old dog.

And thousands of people will send your *protégé* Moosbrugger to his death because none of them but three need to do it with their own hands! This system of ' indirectness ', developed to the point of virtuosity, is what nowadays guarantees each individual, and society as a whole, the possession of a clear conscience. The button one presses is always white and shining, and what happens at the other end of the line concerns other people who are, again, not those who press the button. Does it strike you as abominable ? In this way we cause thousands to die or vegetate, we set moving avalanches of suffering, and do nevertheless also achieve something! I should almost go so far as to say that what is manifested here, in the form of social division of labour, is nothing but the dualism in man's conscience between the end that is approved and the means that are tolerated—it is the same thing, even if in a form that is grand and dangerous ! "

Ulrich had shrugged his shoulders in answer to Arnheim's question whether he found all this abominable. The split in the moral consciousness, of which Arnheim spoke, this most frightful of the phenomena in modern life, was something that had always existed, but it had acquired its appallingly clear conscience only in recent times, as a consequence of the universal division of labour, and in this form it also had something of the magnificent inevitability of the latter. It went against the grain with Ulrich to indulge in indignation about this. On the contrary, and as though in defiance, he had the comical and pleasant sensation that one can get from tearing along at sixty miles an hour, leaving a dust-bespattered moralist standing by the wayside, cursing.

And so when Arnheim ceased to speak, the first thing he said was :

" Every form of division of labour can be developed. The question you ought to ask me is therefore not whether it strikes me as ' abominable ' but whether I believe we can attain conditions more worthy of us, without having to turn back on the way."

" Ah, your general stock-taking ! " Arnheim took him up. " We have got the division of our activities excellently organised, but in doing so we have neglected to create institutions to look after their correlation. We are continuously destroying morality and the soul by means of the newest contrivances and believe we can keep them together with the old household remedies of religious and philosophic tradition ! I do not really like to indulge in this sort of mockery," he amended, " and in general regard wit as something very equivocal. But on the other hand I never regarded it as a mere joke when you made the suggestion to Count Leinsdorf, in the presence of all of us, that the conscience itself should be reorganised."

" It was a joke," Ulrich answered curtly. " I don't believe it's possible. I would sooner believe that it was the Devil who constructed the European world, and that God has decided to let His rival show what he can do."

" A very pretty idea ! " Arnheim said. " But why then were you annoyed with me for being disinclined to believe you ? "

Ulrich did not answer.

" What you have just said," Arnheim continued, quietly and stubbornly, " is also in contradiction to the very enterprising and energetic remarks you made some time earlier about the method by which we might approach a right way of living. Indeed, quite apart from whether I can agree with you on points of detail or not, I am in general struck by the extent to which you are a compound of active tendencies and indifference."

And when Ulrich still seemed to find it unnecessary to give any answer, Arnheim said, with the degree of civility that was necessary to counter-balance Ulrich's incivility :

" I only wanted to draw your attention to the extent to which nowadays in matters of economic decisions—on which, in any case, almost everything depends—one has also to work out the problem of one's moral responsibility oneself, and how fascinating this makes such decisions."

Even in the blend of reproof and modesty with which this was said there lay a faint undertone of the persuasive.

" Forgive me," Ulrich said. " I was thinking about what you were saying." And as though he were still sunk in thought, he added : " I wonder whether you also regard it as a form of indirectness and division of consciousness in keeping with the spirit of the times to fill a woman's soul with mystical emotions, while considering that the most sensible thing to do is to leave her body to her husband ? "

Arnheim changed colour slightly at these words, but he did not lose control of the situation.

" I am not quite sure that I know what you mean," he replied quietly. " But if you were speaking of a woman you loved, you could not say that, for the pattern of reality is always richer than those mere outlines which we call principles."

He had walked away from the window and now made a gesture inviting Ulrich to sit down with him.

" You don't give up your freedom lightly ! " he continued, in a tone of mingled appreciation and regret. " But I know that for you what I represent is an antagonistic principle rather than a personal opponent. And those who are privately the bitterest opponents of capitalism are in business not infrequently its best servants. I think I may even say that to some slight extent I myself can be reckoned among them. Should I otherwise presume to say this to you ? Uncompromising and passionately enthusiastic people, once they have seen the necessity of making a concession, usually become its most brilliant champions. And so, whatever the odds may be, I mean to carry out my intention : I suggest that you should enter into the service of my firm."

He made the suggestion in a deliberately casual way ; indeed, he seemed to wish to diminish the obvious impact, the surprise that he was of course sure of creating, by speaking rapidly and unemphatically. Without meeting Ulrich's astonished gaze, he now began, as it were, to give a list of the details that would have to be settled in the event of an acceptance, a matter, however, in which he did not wish at least at the moment to exert any personal influence. " It goes without saying that to begin with you would not have the training and qualifications," he said smoothly, " to assume a leading position, and you would in any case probably not feel inclined to do so at once. I would therefore offer you a position at my side, which we might call that of secretary-general, a position that I should like to create especially for you. I hope that you don't find the suggestion insulting, for I do not at all picture this post as carrying an alluring salary with it. I should rather put it like this—that in this work you should be able to find your way in time to earning any income that you may wish. And I am convinced that when a year has gone by you will understand me quite differently from now."

And yet, when Arnheim concluded this speech, he felt that he was agitated. At this moment he was actually surprised at having now really made such an offer to Ulrich, since the refusal of it would only put him at a disadvantage, whereas on the other hand an acceptance would not bring any pleasing prospect with it. For the notion that this man sitting opposite him here might be capable of achieving something that he himself could not achieve had vanished in the course of the conversation, and the urge to corrupt him and get him into his power seemed senseless now that it had become articulate. His having been afraid of something that he called this man's ' wit ' struck him as unnatural. He, Arnheim, was a man of great consequence. And life has an obligation to be simple and straightforward for such as he ! A man of this sort is on good terms with everything else that is great and of consequence, in so far as it is possible for him to be so ; he does not rebel romantically against everything, he does not cast doubt on everything : that would be against his nature. But on the other hand, of course, there are the beautiful and ambiguous things, and one gathers to oneself as much of them as is possible. Never before, Arnheim thought, had he felt as intensely as in this moment the solidity of western civilisation, with its wonderful network of forces and inhibitions. If Ulrich did not recognise this too, then he was nothing but an adventurer, and the fact that he had almost caused Arnheim to be tempted into thinking of—but here words, even those unspoken words at the back of the mind, failed Arnheim. He could not bring himself to formulate clearly, even to himself, the notion that he had contemplated taking Ulrich on and binding him to himself as an adopted son.

It would not have mattered very much if he had formulated it, for it was, after all, a thought like countless others that one does not need to answer for, and was probably inspired by some kind of melancholy about life such as forms a residue to every life of action, because one never finds the thing one would be content with ; and perhaps the thought had not come to him in this disputable form at all, perhaps he had only felt something that might have been expressed in this form. Nevertheless, he did not wish to remember it. It was only that he had, glaringly clear in his head, the awareness that if the years of Ulrich's life were subtracted from his own, what was left over would not amount to anything much ; and, of course, behind this there was the more shadowy, second awareness that Ulrich ought to serve him as a warning against Diotima.

He recalled often having felt his relationship to Ulrich as being somehow comparable to a subsidiary crater from which one can deduce something about the uncanny happenings in the main crater, and he was made somewhat uneasy by the fact that here the eruption had now taken place and the words had poured forth, making their way into outer life. ' What's to be done,' it flashed through Arnheim's head, ' if the fellow accepts ? '

So the moments of tension were drawn out, moments during which an Arnheim had to wait for the decision of a younger man on whom he had bestowed importance only by an act of his own imagination.

He sat there, very stiff, his lips parted in a hostile expression, thinking : ' There's sure to be some way or other of settling the whole thing, if it's really too late to get out of it now.'

While emotion and cogitation were following their course in this manner, the situation had not come to a standstill. On the contrary, question and answer had followed upon each other in a quite normal way.

" And to what qualities," Ulrich asked drily, " do I owe this offer, which can scarcely be justifiable from the business man's point of view ? "

" In this matter you are constantly mistaken," Arnheim replied. " In a position like mine one does not look for the justification, even from the business point of view, in terms of mere cash. What I might lose on you is quite immaterial compared with the profit I hope you will represent ! "

" You arouse my curiosity to the utmost," Ulrich remarked. " I have rarely been told that I represent anything profitable. In my special subject I might perhaps have become a little asset, but even there, as you know, I have turned out a disappointment."

" The fact that you possess unusual intellectual capacity," Arnheim answered (still in the tone of quiet confidence that he outwardly preserved), " is something about which you yourself are quite clear, without my having to tell you. But it is not quite unthinkable that we have keener and sounder minds already working for us. It is, however, your character, your human qualities, that for certain definite reasons I should like to have permanently at my side."

"My qualities?" Ulrich could not help smiling. "Oddly enough, you know, friends of mine call me a man without qualities. . . ."

Arnheim let a little gesture of impatience escape him, indicating more or less: ' You needn't tell me things about yourself that I know far better than you by now, anyway.' In the twitching that ran across his face, ending up in a jerk of the shoulder, his dissatisfaction asserted itself, while the words still flowed on according to plan.

Ulrich caught this expression, and he was so easily irritated by Arnheim that now, after all, he did give the discussion the hitherto avoided turn and spoke with complete candour.

They had meanwhile risen from their chairs again, and, moving a few steps away from his companion, so as to be able to observe the effect of his words all the better, he said:

"Now that you have put so many weighty questions to me there is something I should like to know myself before coming to a decision!"

And when Arnheim made a gesture of assent, he went on in a frank and matter-of-fact tone:

"I have been told that your participation in everything connected with our Campaign here—with your interest in Frau Tuzzi as well as in my humble self thrown in for good measure—is meant to play its part in your acquiring large areas of the Galician oil-fields."

Even in the failing light it was noticeable that Arnheim turned pale. He walked slowly towards Ulrich. Ulrich had the feeling he must be prepared for a sharp answer, and he deplored the fact that through his incautious straightforwardness he had given the other the chance to break off the conversation at the moment when it became too disagreeable for him to carry it further. He therefore said as affably as possible:

"Please understand me rightly, I don't wish to be offensive, but this discussion of ours could not entirely fulfil its purpose if we did not conduct it with utter frankness."

For Arnheim these few words and the time it took him to cover the short distance across the room were sufficient to allow him to regain his composure. Coming up to Ulrich he smiled, laid his hand on, indeed his arm round, Ulrich's shoulder, and said reproachfully :

" How can you let yourself be taken in by a Stock-Exchange rumour like that ? "

" I didn't hear it by way of rumour. It came to me from someone who is very well informed."

" Yes, I have heard that such things are being said. But how could you believe it ? Of course I am not here exclusively for pleasure. Unfortunately I can never manage to get right away from business. And I will not deny having had talks with various people about these oil-fields, though I must ask you to regard this confession as confidential. But all this, of course, is not what really matters ! "

" My cousin," Ulrich resumed, " has not the slightest inkling of this preoccupation of yours with oil. She has been entrusted by her husband with the task of gathering what she can about the purpose of your sojourn here, since the view prevails that you are in the confidence of the Czar. But I am quite convinced that she is not carrying out this diplomatic mission well, being as sure as she is that she is herself the sole reason for your continued stay."

" You put things extraordinarily crudely ! " Arnheim's arm shifted, so giving Ulrich's shoulder a friendly little jerk. " Subsidiary implications are perhaps interwoven with everything, and everywhere. But though I dare say you intended to speak sardonically, your frankness closely resembles that of an unmannerly schoolboy ! "

The arm around his shoulder made Ulrich unsure of himself. It was ridiculous and disagreeable to feel oneself as it were embraced ; indeed, it was positively a wretched feeling. But then, it was a long time since Ulrich had had a friend, and this, perhaps, was part of the reason why it was slightly bewildering. He would have liked to shake off this arm, and involuntarily stirred in an effort to do so. Arnheim, for his part, obviously noticed these little signs of restiveness, but did his utmost to ignore them. And so, perceiving the awkwardness of Arnheim's position, Ulrich decided it was only civil to stand still and put up with this contact, which was having an increasingly queer effect on him, like that of a heavy weight sinking into a loosely piled-up dam

and so tearing it apart. For there was indeed an outwork of
solitude that Ulrich had built up around himself, without even
meaning to ; and now life, in the pulse-beat of another man,
came pouring in through a breach. It was a silly feeling, ludicrous,
and yet at the same time faintly exciting.

He thought of Gerda. Then he remembered how even before
that Walter, the friend of his youth, had aroused in him the desire
to find himself once again agreeing with someone as wholeheartedly and unreservedly as though there were no differences in
the whole wide world other than those caused by liking and dislike. Now, when it was too late, the desire for that welled up in
him again, in silvery waves, as in the flowing of a mighty river the
ripples of water, air, and light fuse, in the distance, into one single
silveriness ; and this was so entrancing that he had to be on his
guard against yielding to it and bringing about a misunderstanding, in this ambiguous situation he was in. But as his muscles
tightened he remembered how Bonadea had said to him : ' Ulrich,
you are not a bad person, it's only that you make it difficult for
yourself to be good ! '—Bonadea, who had been so amazingly
clever that day and had also said : ' After all, in dreams you don't
think either, you experience things ! ' And he had said : ' I was
a child, as soft as the air on a moonlit night . . .' and he recollected
now that the image he had had before his eyes as he said so had
actually been a different one : it had been the tip of a burning
magnesium-flare. And in the flying sparks that tore this tip to
shreds of light he had seemed to know his own heart. But that
image was from long ago, and he had not quite dared to utter it,
and had succumbed to the other. And anyway, it had not been
in that talk with Bonadea, but something he had said to Diotima,
as he now remembered. ' Right down at their roots the diversities
there are in life lie very close together,' he felt, looking thoughtfully at the man who, for reasons that were not altogether clear,
had proposed to become his friend.

Arnheim had withdrawn his arm. Once more they stood in the
window-bay where their conversation had begun. Down in the
street the lamps were now shining peacefully, but there was still
a lingering sense of the stirring events that had taken place earlier
in the day. From time to time closely knit groups of people came
past, talking excitedly, and now and then a mouth would open and

a threat would leap out, or some wavering " Hoo-oo ! " followed by guffaws. It all somehow suggested a state of semi-consciousness. And in the quiet light rising from this still restless street, between the straight lines of the curtains falling to the floor and framing the picture of the darkened room, he saw Arnheim's figure and felt his own body standing there, one half brightly lit, one half black, this chiaroscuro lending both a passionate intensity.

Ulrich recalled the cheers for Arnheim that he had thought he heard, and it seemed to him that whether Arnheim was or was not connected with what had been going on, here now, in the Cæsarean tranquillity that he displayed, set in this picture that was the painting of an instant, as he stood gazing meditatively down into the street, he had the air of being the dominant figure in it all and, moreover, of feeling the weight of his own presence in each glance cast upon him. At his side one came to understand what self-possession, the true consciousness of self, meant. Consciousness alone cannot impose order on all the swarming and twinkling of the world, for the keener it is, the more limitless the world becomes, at least provisionally ; but the consciousness of self that is self-possession walks in like a producer entering the theatre and turns it all into an artificial unity of good fortune. Ulrich envied this man his good fortune. At this moment nothing, it seemed to him, would be easier than to commit a crime against him, for in his craving always to be the centre of a picture, to hold the centre of the stage, the man conjured up all the old tags of drama. ' Unsheathe your dagger and fulfil his destiny ! ' Ulrich heard these words ringing in his ears utterly in the tone of a bad actor's ranting, and yet involuntarily he contrived to move so that he stood half behind Arnheim. He saw the dark, broad expanse of the neck and shoulders there before him. It was especially the neck that exasperated him. His hand went through the pockets on the right side of his body, fumbling for his pocket-knife. He raised himself on tip-toe and then once more looked over Arnheim's shoulder, down into the street.

In the twilight outside people were still being swept along by an invisible tide, as grains of sand are borne by the waves of the sea. There was no doubt of it, something was bound to follow on this demonstration, and the future was sending its wave out far ahead. There was a kind of suprapersonal, creative interpenetration going on among the people, but it was, as always, extremely vague and casual. This was more or less the way that Ulrich felt what he saw, and for a short while it held his attention. But he was too sick and tired of it to be capable of analysing it coolly now.

Carefully he lowered his heels again, faintly ashamed of the little by-play in thought that had a moment earlier caused him to raise them from the floor : all that simply wasn't worth the bother. All at once he felt hugely tempted to clap Arnheim on the back and say to him : ' Thanks ! I've had enough of all this, I want to try something new. I accept your offer.'

Since, however, in reality Ulrich did not do this either, the two men let the answer to Arnheim's question go by default. Arnheim took the conversation up again at an earlier point :

" Do you ever go to the moving pictures ? You ought to ! " he said. " At its present stage of development cinematography may not look as if it had any very great future, but wait until larger commercial interests—say, electro-chemical or colour-chemical interests—become bound up with it, and in a few decades you will see a development that nothing will stop. What will set in then will be a process in which all the achievements of modern science will be brought into play to heighten effects, and whatever our writers and our æsthetic theoreticians may boast of then as to their own part in it, it will be an art based on Associated Electrical or German Dyes Incorporated. Horrible, my dear fellow ! Do you write ? No, I asked you that before, didn't I ? But why don't you write ? How sensible ! The poet and philosopher of the future will arrive via the gang-plank of journalism. Haven't you noticed that our journalists are getting better and better and our poets are getting steadily worse ? Unquestionably, this is a process in accordance with the laws of evolution. Something is on the way, and for my part I have not the slightest doubt about what it is : the age of individualism, of great personalities, is coming to an end ! " He leaned forward. " I cannot quite make out, in this light, what sort of face you pull at that ! I fire my shots almost in the dark ! " He laughed a little. " You uttered a demand for a general spiritual stock-taking. Do you believe in it yourself ? Do you really believe that life is susceptible to being regulated by the spirit, by the mind ? Of course you said so. But

I don't take you at your word, for you are of such a nature that you would embrace the Devil himself for being the one man without a peer ! "

" What's that a quotation from ? " Ulrich asked.

" From the suppressed preface to *The Robbers*."

' The suppressed one, of course ! ' Ulrich thought to himself. ' It would never be from an ordinary one.'

" Spirits that are allured by the abomination of vice, for the grandeur that looms about it," Arnheim went on quoting from his capacious memory. He felt that now he was once more in control of the situation and that Ulrich, for whatever reasons, had yielded ground. What he sensed beside him was no longer an antagonistic hardness, and it also seemed there need not be any further mention of the offer ; this had ' passed from him ' in a quite fortunate manner. But just as a wrestler knows when his opponent is slackening and then puts everything he has into finishing him off, so he felt the need to let the full weight of his offer sink in and have its effect. Therefore he continued :

" I think now you will understand me better than at first. And so I confess to you quite frankly that there are times when I feel I am alone. When people are ' new ', they think overmuch in commercial terms. But when commercial families come to the second or third generation, they lose their imagination. Then they produce nothing but impeccable administrators and army officers, and go in for castles, hunting lodges, and nobly born sons-in-law. I know these people all over the world. There are fine, intelligent people among them, but they are not capable of producing even a single idea remotely connected with that last state of being restless, independent and perhaps unhappy, which I have just illustrated by my quotation from Schiller."

" I'm sorry I can't stay and go on talking about this," Ulrich said. " Frau Tuzzi is evidently waiting at some friend's house until everything is absolutely quiet. But I must go. And so you think then that, understanding nothing of business or financial matters, I nevertheless have in me this restlessness that is such a good thing from the business point of view, in that it removes from business the excess of its own nature as business ? " He had switched on the light preparatory to taking his leave, and stood waiting for an answer.

With majestic camaraderie Arnheim once more laid his arm round Ulrich's shoulder, a gesture that now seemed to have become established, and replied :

" Forgive me if I have said rather too much, in a solitary mood. Business and finance are coming to power, and one does sometimes wonder what we are going to do with this power ! I do hope you don't take it amiss."

" Oh, quite on the contrary ! " Ulrich assured him. " I have made up my mind to think your proposal over very seriously."

He spoke rapidly, and his haste was perhaps a sign of tension.

And so Arnheim, who stayed behind, waiting for Diotima, was left somewhat disconcerted, and afraid that it would be anything but easy to find a decent way of getting Ulrich to see that the whole thing would be better dropped.

122 *The way home.*

ULRICH went home on foot. The night was fine, but dark. The houses, standing tall and compact, formed that strange confined space, open at the top, which is called *street*, and high above it, in the air, there was something going on—wind, or clouds, in greater darkness. The streets were now as empty as if the earlier unrest had left everything sunk into deep slumbers. Whenever Ulrich did encounter another pedestrian walking in the opposite direction, the ring of the other's steps came towards him for a long time all by itself, like the heralding of some grave news. In such a night as this it was possible to feel the significance of events as in a theatre. One felt that one was an apparition in this world, something that created the effect of being larger than it really was, something that rang and echoed and, when it passed across an illuminated background, had its shadow walking with it like some huge, jerking clown, now rising to his full height and at the next instant once more creeping humbly at the walker's heels.

' How happy one can be ! ' he thought.

He walked through an archway in a stone passage, some ten paces long, that ran parallel to the street, separated from it only by thick buttresses. Darkness leapt out of recesses, ambush and murder flickered in the dimly lighted cloister : a violent, ancient, and bloodthirstily solemn happiness gripped the soul. Perhaps this was too much. Ulrich suddenly imagined with how much complacency and inner ' stage-management ' Arnheim would have walked along here in his place. And at that he lost all pleasure in his shadow and the ringing of his footsteps on the pavement, and the spectral music in the walls faded out. He knew that he would not accept Arnheim's offer. But he now seemed to himself to be nothing more than some phantom wandering through the gallery of life, aghast at being unable to find the frame it should slip into ; and he was thoroughly relieved when before long his road brought him into a district that was less oppressive and less grand.

Wide streets and squares opened out obscurely before him, and the buildings were ordinary buildings, serenely spangled with storey upon storey of lighted windows, but devoid of any bewitching element. Coming out into the open, he caught the feeling of this tranquillity, and, without rightly knowing why, remembered some childhood pictures he had been looking at a short while earlier, photographs of him and his mother, who had died young, and he recalled the sense of strangeness with which he had gazed at that little boy so happily smiled upon by a beautiful woman dressed in the style of a bygone era. There was the extremely intense idea of a good, affectionate, bright little boy, which had been everyone's picture of him ; there were the hopes for him that were as yet outside his own ken ; there were vague expectations of a distinguished and brilliant future, something like outspread wings, a golden net opening out to enfold him. And although all this had been invisible in those early days, decades later it was there on the old photographs, plain and distinct for him to behold ; and from the midst of that visible invisibility, which might so easily have become reality, he saw gazing out at him his own childish face, still babyishly soft and blank, with the slightly cramped expression due to having to stand quite still. Looking at these photographs, he had felt no trace of affection for that little boy, and even if he did contemplate his beautiful mother with some pride, the main feeling the whole thing left him with was that of having escaped some frightful danger by the skin of his teeth.

Anyone who has undergone this experience, having encountered his own gaze and seen himself, mantled in some bygone instant of complacency, looking out at him from old photographs, and the whole thing so odd that it seems some sort of glue must have dried up and fallen out of the relationship, will know what Ulrich felt like. And he wondered what this glue consisted of and why with so many other people it worked all right.

He had now reached one of those green spaces, bordered with trees, that form a broken ring, indicating the line of the old city-walls, and he might have crossed it in a few strides, but the broad strip of sky, long-drawn above the trees, lured him to turn aside and follow the direction in which it seemed to point. And now the discreetly glimmering festoons of lights, withdrawn as the firmament itself, that floated along the edges of this wintry little park, were something he seemed to be continually approaching without ever drawing any nearer.

' It's a sort of intellectual foreshortening, a perspective of the mind,' he said to himself, ' that brings about this ever-recurring tranquillity in which night follows night and which, extending from one day to the next, evokes a permanent sense of life in concord with itself. For where most things are concerned, the main pre-condition of happiness is not, of course, that contra-dictions should be cleared up, but that they should be caused to disappear, as the gaps between the trees disappear when one looks down a long avenue. And just as for the eye of the beholder the visual relationships between things always shift in such a way that what arises is a picture dominated by the eye, one in which the immediate and near-at-hand appears large, but further away even the huge appears small, gaps close up, and finally the scene as a whole rounds out into a single ordered smoothness, so it is too with invisible relationships, which the brain and the emotions shift in such a way that unconsciously something comes about that causes one to feel one is master in one's own house. And this then,' Ulrich said to himself, ' is the operation that I myself do not carry out in a satisfactory manner.'

He stopped for a moment, where a large puddle blocked his path. Perhaps it was this puddle at his feet, and perhaps it was also the bare, besom-like trees on either side, that in this instant suddenly conjured up in him the sense of country road and village and aroused that monotonous condition of the soul, half-way between fulfilment and futility, which comes with living in the country. This was the sort of thing that had more than once tempted him to try a repetition of that first voyage of escape which he had made in his youth.

' It all becomes so simple ! ' he felt. ' One's emotions almost go to sleep. One's thoughts drift apart like clouds after a thunderstorm, and all at once a fine, clear sky breaks out of the soul ! Now perhaps there's a cow standing in the middle of the lane, radiantly bright, gazing into this sky, and there is an urgency about it all that makes it seem as though nothing else in the world existed ! A passing cloud may cause the same thing to happen all over the countryside : the grass turns dark, and a while later the same grass is all wet and twinkling—nothing else has happened, but still, it's a voyage as from one shore of a sea to the other. Or an old man loses his last tooth, and this trivial event is a landmark in all his neighbours' lives, one from which they can date their memories. And so too the birds sing round about the village every evening and always in the same way, when with the setting of the sun the stillness falls : but every time it happens it's something new, as though the world were not yet seven days old. In the country,' he thought, ' the gods still come to mortal men. There one is something and experiences things. But in town, where there are a thousand times as many experiences, one is no longer capable of relating them to each other. And I suppose that is how life begins to become more and more abstract, in the notorious way we know.'

But while he was thinking this, he was also aware of how this extended man's power a thousand times, and how, even if from the point of view of every detail it diluted him tenfold, as a whole it enlarged him a hundredfold. For him, Ulrich, there could be no serious question of going back on it all. . . . And what occurred to him then was one of those seemingly out-of-the-way and abstract thoughts that so often in his life took on such immediate significance, namely that the law of this life, for which one yearns, overburdened as one is and at the same time dreaming of simplicity, was none other than that of *narrative order*. This is the simple order that consists in one's being able to say : ' When that had happened, then this happened.' What puts our minds at rest is the simple sequence, the overwhelming variegation of life now represented in, as a mathematician would say, a unidimensional order : the stringing upon one thread of all that has happened in space and time, in short, that notorious ' narrative thread ' of which it then turns out the thread of life itself consists. Lucky the man who can say ' when ', ' before ' and ' after ' ! Misfortunes may have befallen him, or he may have writhed in agony : but as soon as he is capable of recounting the events in their chronological order he feels as well content as if the sun were shining straight on his diaphragm. This is the thing that the novel has artificially turned to account : the traveller may go riding along the highroad in pouring rain, or be walking through crackling snow, the temperature thirty degrees below freezing-point, and still the reader will feel a cosy glow. This is something it would be hard to understand if this everlasting epic device, by means of which even nannies soothe their little charges, this tried and tested ' intellectual foreshortening ', this ' perspective of the mind ', were not part and parcel of life itself. In their basic relation to themselves most people are narrators. They do not like the lyrical, or at best they like it only for moments at a time. And even if a little ' because ' and ' in order that ' may get knotted into the thread of life, still, they abhor all cogitation that reaches out beyond that. What they like is the orderly sequence of facts, because it has the look of a necessity, and by means of the impression that their life has a ' course ' they manage to feel somehow sheltered in the midst of chaos. And now Ulrich observed that he seemed to have lost this elementary narrative element to which private life still holds fast, although in public life everything has now become non-narrative, no longer following a ' thread ', but spreading out as an infinitely interwoven surface.

When, having come to this conclusion, he began to walk on, he did, it is true, remember that Goethe had written in an essay on art : ' Man is not a didactic being, but one that lives and acts and influences.' Respectfully, he shrugged his shoulders. ' At the most,' he thought, ' only in as far as an actor loses his awareness of the scenery and his make-up, and believes his acting is really action, is it permissible for man today to forget the uncertain background of knowledge on which all his activities depend.' But this thought of Goethe must have been faintly mixed up with the thought of Arnheim, who was always misusing Goethe by way of corroboration for what he said. The fact was that in the same moment Ulrich was disagreeably reminded of the unusual uncertainty it had caused him to feel Arnheim's arm around his shoulders.

He had meanwhile come out from under the trees to where the little park was bordered by the streets, and walked along looking for the best way home. Peering up to see the names of the streets, he almost ran full tilt into a shadowy form that detached itself from the surrounding darkness, and had to pull up short in order not to knock down the prostitute who had stepped in his way. There she stood, smiling instead of showing annoyance at his having almost charged into her, like a bull, and Ulrich suddenly felt that this professional smile created a little pool of warmth here in the night. She said something, speaking to him in those threadbare words that are intended to allure and are like the dirty dregs of all the men who have gone before. " Coming home with me, my little one ? " she said, or something of the sort. She had sloping shoulders like a child's ; some fair hair strayed out from under her hat ; and in the lamplight there was something pale, a haphazard loveliness, about her face. What was concealed under her nocturnal make-up was perhaps a young girl's freckled skin. She was much smaller than Ulrich and had to look up into his face, and yet she said ' my little one ' to him and said it once more, in her indifference finding nothing out of place in the phrase she made use of a hundred times every night.

Ulrich was touched by it. Instead of brushing her aside, he stopped and gave her the chance to repeat her offer, as though he had not caught her words. Here, all unexpectedly, he had found a friend, one entirely at his service in return for a small remuneration. She would take trouble to be agreeable to him and to avoid everything he might not like. At a sign of agreement from him she would slip her arm through his, with a gentle confidence and a faint hesitation such as arises only when old friends and intimates meet again for the first time after a separation not of their own making. And if he promised to double or treble her usual price and put the money on the table at the start, so that she did not need to think about it any more and could abandon herself to the carefree obliging state of mind that is brought about by having concluded a good piece of business, it would become apparent that pure indifference has the same merit as all pure feelings, which is that of being free of personal presumption and of functioning without the vain confusion caused by emotional demands.

Half seriously, half flippantly, these thoughts went through his mind, and he could not bring himself utterly to disappoint this little person who was waiting for him to accept her offer. He realised that he felt a certain desire to meet with her liking and approval. But, feeling somewhat unsure and clumsy, instead of simply chatting with her for a moment in the lingo of the street-corner, he fumbled in his pocket and then, having pressed into the girl's hand a note approximately equivalent to the price she would have asked, walked on. Her hand, for the one instant he had held it firmly in his, had been strangely resistant from surprise. He had spoken one single friendly word. But, leaving her behind, he was convinced that now she would join her colleagues, who were whispering nearby in the darkness, and would show them the money and finally utter some jibe, so giving vent to her feelings about what she could not rightly understand.

This fleeting encounter remained vivid in his mind for a little while, as though it had been some tender idyll. In spite of that momentary feeling of warmth and friendliness for the girl, he had no illusions about her crass poverty and debasement ; but when he pictured to himself how she would have turned her eyes up, with one of those faint, awkwardly artificial sighs that she had learned to produce at the right moment, it seemed to him—he did not know why—that there was, after all, something touching about this profoundly base and utterly untalented acting done for an agreed sum : perhaps because it was the ham-acting of the human comedy itself. And while he had been speaking to the girl, an obvious association of ideas had reminded him of Moosbrugger—Moosbrugger, the pathological play-actor, the pursuer and destroyer of prostitutes, who had walked through that disastrous night just as Ulrich was walking through this night now. When the street, the house-fronts, had ceased to sway like stage-scenery, remaining steady for a moment, he had run into the unknown being who had been waiting for him by the bridge, that night of the murder. What a wonderful anagnorisis that must have been, a shock of recognition rippling from the crown of the head to the soles of the feet ! Ulrich felt it for a moment in his own body. It bore him upwards like a wave. He lost his sense of balance, but he had no need of it : the movement itself carried him along. His heart contracted, but his imaginings, extending illimitably, soon became blurred and gradually dissolved in a sort of enervating voluptuousness. He tried to sober up. Evidently he had for so long kept to a life without inner unity that now he was even envying a madman for his delusions and belief in his role ! But, after all, Moosbrugger was fascinating not only to him but to everyone else as well, wasn't he ? In his mind he heard Arnheim's voice asking : ' Would you set him free ? ' And he heard himself answering : ' No. Probably not.'

' A thousand times no ! ' he added, yet at the same time felt, like something suddenly dazzling him, the image of an act in which the movement of reaching out, as it springs from extreme excitement, and the being moved by it both fused into one in an ineffable communion in which pleasure was indistinguishable from compulsion, sense from necessity, and the highest possible degree of activity from blissful passive receptiveness. Fleetingly he recalled the view that the unfortunate beings afflicted by such states are the embodiment of repressed urges common to all, the incarnation of everybody's mentally committed murders and violations done in fantasy. Well then, let those who believed themselves justified in doing so deal with him in their own way, let them try him and condemn him, and so re-establish the balance of their morality, after he had served his purpose and satisfied their urges by his act !

The split in him was different ; it lay precisely in the fact that he repressed nothing and so could not help seeing that what the murderer's image faced him with was something no stranger, or any less familiar, than any other image in the world, and every one of them was just like his old images of himself : half of it sense, consolidated, and half of it nonsense, dissolving, oozing out again ! A rampant metaphor of order : that was what Moosbrugger was for him ! And suddenly Ulrich said : "All that——!"

making a gesture as though thrusting something aside with the back of his hand. He had not said it only in his head, he had said it aloud, and now suddenly he pressed his lips tightly together, finishing the sentence in silence : ' All that has got to be settled and done with ! ' He did not want to know any more of what ' all that ' was in detail. ' All that ' was what had been occupying his mind, tormenting and sometimes enrapturing him too, since he had taken his ' holiday ', fettering him as a dreamer is fettered, for whom all things are possible but one, which is to rise and move. All that led to impossibilities of every kind, from the first day on, right down to the last minutes of this walk home ! And Ulrich felt that now at last he must either live for an attainable goal like anyone else, or get seriously to grips with these ' impossibilities '. And now having reached the neighbourhood where he lived, he hurried along through the last street with the queer feeling that something was in store for him at any moment. It was a feeling that lent him wings, one that seemed to be flowing towards action, and that yet was devoid of content and hence again, oddly, a sensation of freedom.

Perhaps this would have passed off as so much else had. But when he turned the corner into the street where he lived, after he had gone a few yards it seemed to him that there was light in the windows of his house, and shortly afterwards, when he reached the garden gate, he saw that in fact it was so. His old man-servant had asked for permission to spend the night with relatives somewhere in another district ; he himself had not been home since the episode with Gerda, which had occurred during daylight ; and the gardener and his wife, who lived in the basement, never entered his rooms : but there were lights on everywhere. Strangers must be in his house—burglars whom he was about to take by surprise. Ulrich was so abstracted and so entirely under the spell of this extraordinary sensation of freedom that he walked straight up to the house without stopping to think. He expected nothing definite. He saw shadows on the windows that seemed to indicate there was only one person moving about inside. But there might after all be more than one and he vaguely wondered whether he would be shot at when he entered the house. Should he himself be prepared to shoot ? In a different state of mind Ulrich would probably have gone to get a policeman or at least

have reconnoitred before deciding what to do ; but he wanted
to be left alone with his feelings and he did not even bother to
draw the pistol he was carrying, as he sometimes did since that
night when he had been knocked down by street-ruffians. He
wanted . . . he did not know what . . . let it roll on !

However, when he had pushed open the front door and entered
the house, it turned out that the burglar he had been obscurely
envisaging was merely Clarisse.

123 *The turning-point.*

WHAT had doubtless played a certain part in Ulrich's behaviour
was a conviction he had had all along that everything would somehow turn out to have quite a simple and harmless explanation
after all—that disinclination to believe the worst with which one
always goes into danger.

But then, in the hall, when all unexpectedly his old servant
appeared, he almost knocked him down. Fortunately he stopped
himself in time, and so learnt from him that a telegram had come,
which had been taken in charge by Clarisse, who was waiting
upstairs. Madam had arrived about an hour ago, just as he, the
old man, had been about to leave. Madam had refused to be put
off, and he had therefore thought it proper to stay too, forgoing
his night out for the time being. For if the master would permit
him to make the observation, the young lady had struck him as
being in a very agitated condition.

When Ulrich, having thanked him, went into his own rooms,
he found Clarisse lying on a divan, slightly turned on her side,
with her legs drawn up. Her straight slim figure, the boyish cut
of her hair, and the elongated lovely face, supported on her arm,
that gazed at him as he opened the door—it made an exceedingly
seductive picture. He told her that he had taken her for a burglar.

Clarisse's eyes flashed like rapid firing from a revolver. " Perhaps I am one ! " she retorted. " That old fox of a servant of

yours was set on not letting me stay here at any price. I told him
to go to bed, but I know very well he's been hiding somewhere
downstairs. Nice place you have here ! " She held out the telegram to him, without stirring. " I wanted to see for once what
you come home like when you think you're alone," she went on.
" Walter's gone to a concert. He won't be home till after midnight. But I didn't tell him I was coming here."

Ulrich tore the telegram open and read it, at the same time half
listening to what Clarisse was saying.

He suddenly grew very pale, and read the message a second
time, unable to believe the strange words. For some time now,
although he had neglected to answer various enquiries of his
father's about the Collateral Campaign and in the matter of the
' diminished responsibility ' feud, he had not received any
admonishing letters ; but somehow he had not given the matter
any thought. Now here, in a punctilious manner curiously com-
pounded of half-suppressed reproach and funereal solemnity, and
obviously drafted with meticulous care by his father in person—
here was this telegram informing him of his father's death.

They had had but little liking for one another. Indeed, Ulrich
had almost always found the thought of his father unbearable.
And for all that, as he read the quaintly sinister wording of the
telegram for the second time, what he thought was : ' Now I am
all alone in the world ! ' He did not mean it in the literal sense
of the words, which would have gone ill enough with the relationship that was now at an end ; it was rather that he felt himself
amazedly floating upwards, as though a mooring-rope had
snapped. It was an instantly established condition of estrange-
ment, of alien aloofness, from a world with which he had been
linked, up to this moment, through the person of his father.

" My father's died ! " he said to Clarisse, lifting the telegram
in his hand with a touch of involuntary solemnity.

" Oh, I say ! " Clarisse responded. " Congratulations ! "
And after a little meditative pause she added : " I suppose you'll
be frightfully rich now ? " She glanced round with curiosity.

" I don't think he was more than moderately well off," Ulrich
replied somewhat forbiddingly. " I've been living beyond his
means, here."

Clarisse acknowledged the rebuke with a quite small smile, a sort of little bow-and-scrape of a smile. Many of her expressive movements were hasty and, in a cramped way, exaggerated, rather like the bow made by a boy who has to give a social demonstration of how well brought up he is.

She was left alone for some moments, since Ulrich had gone out of the room, with a word of excuse, in order to give instructions connected with his going away. When she had left Walter after the violent scene they had had, she had not gone far, for outside the door of their apartment there was a seldom-used staircase leading up to the loft, and there she had sat, wrapped in a shawl, until she heard him leaving the house. She had some vague idea about the lofts for stage-machinery in theatres ; up there, then, from where the pulley-ropes ran, she sat, while Walter made his exit down the stairs. She pictured to herself how between calls the actresses sat in the rafters over the stage, wrapped in shawls, and looked down, watching ; now she too was an actress, and the play was going on down there at her feet. In all this her favourite old idea turned up again : life was a drama, and one was there to act it out. Quite definitely there was no need to understand it by the light of reason, she thought to herself. What, after all, did anyone know about it, even someone who knew more than she did ? But one had to have the right instinct for life, like a storm-petrel ! One had to spread out one's arms— and with her that meant one's words, one's kisses, one's tears— one had to spread them wide like wings ! In this notion she found some compensation for the fact that she could no longer believe in Walter's future. She looked down the steep well of the stairs, where Walter had gone a little while ago, and, spreading out her arms, kept them raised in that position as long as she could : perhaps in that way she could help him ! ' Steeply upwards and steeply downwards are opposites akin in their potency, and each goes with the other ! ' she thought. ' Jubilant diagonals through the world ' was what she called her raised arms and her gaze into the depths. She abandoned her intention of secretly going off to see the demonstration in town. What did she care about the ' herd ' ! Now the immense drama of the elect had begun !

And so Clarisse had gone to Ulrich. On the way she had now and then smiled her cunning smile, whenever it occurred to her that Walter thought her mad as soon as she let slip any sign of her greater insight into their joint condition. It gratified her to know that he was afraid of having a child by her and yet could hardly wait for it. What she herself understood by ' mad ' was something in the way of being like summer-lightning, or of being in such a heightened state of health that it frightened other people, and this was a quality that she had developed in her marriage, step by step, with the growing of her superiority and her dominating position. All the same, she knew that she was sometimes incomprehensible to other people. And so when Ulrich came back into the room, she had the feeling she must say something to him in keeping with an event that cut so deep into his life. She leapt up from the divan, paced a few times through the room and the rooms beyond, and then said : " Well, my sincere condolences, old boy ! "

Ulrich looked at her in astonishment, although he knew this tone of hers, which she produced when she was nervous. ' Sometimes then there's something so startlingly conventional about her,' he thought. ' It's like coming across a page in a book that's been bound in by mistake and really belongs to some other book.' She had not uttered her phrase with the appropriate expression, but had flung it at him over her shoulder, obliquely, and this heightened the peculiar effect of hearing not a false note but, as it were, the wrong words to the tune, quite out of place. One got the somewhat uncanny impression that she herself consisted of many such tunes with the words all wrongly attached to them. Now, when Ulrich did not answer, she stopped in front of him and said : " I must have a talk to you ! "

" Can't I give you a drink or something ? " Ulrich asked.

Clarisse raised her hand to shoulder-height and fluttered it to and fro in refusal. She collected her thoughts and began : " Walter is dead set on having a child by me. Can you understand that ? " She seemed to wait for an answer.

What could Ulrich have said in reply ?

" But I don't want to ! " she exclaimed violently.

" Well, don't go and get in a rage about it," Ulrich said. " If you don't want to, it can't happen anyway."

" But that's what's driving him to his doom ! "

" People who're always thinking they're going to die live long. You and I'll have been old and shrivelled for ages when Walter,

white-haired and the director of his record-office, will still have
that boyish face of his ! ''

Clarisse turned thoughtfully on her heel and walked away from
Ulrich. At some distance she took up another position and ' held
him with her gaze '.

" You know what an umbrella looks like when the stick's been
taken out of it ? Walter collapses when I turn away from him.
I am his stick, and he's my——" what she had been going to
say was ' umbrella ', but then something much better occurred to
her " —he's my shield, my protector," she said. " He thinks he
has to shield me. And so that he can protect me properly the
first thing he wants is to see me going round with a big belly.
Then he'll talk me into believing that a mother with any natural
feelings breast-feeds her child. Then he'll want to bring the
child up according to his own ideas. You know all that yourself.
He'll simply usurp rights and have a terrific excuse for turning
us both into philistines. But if I go on the way I have up to
now, and keep on saying no, then it's all up with him ! I'm simply
everything to him ! ''

Ulrich smiled incredulously at this sweeping assertion.

" He wants to kill you ! " Clarisse added swiftly.

" What ! I thought it was you who suggested it to him ? ''

" I want to have the child from you ! " Clarisse said.

Ulrich whistled through his teeth in surprise.

She smiled like an adolescent who has made an ill-mannered
demand.

" I shouldn't like to deceive anyone I know as well as Walter,"
Ulrich said slowly. " It's not the sort of thing I care for."

" Oho ? So you're *awfully decent*, are you ? " Clarisse seemed
to attach a significance to this that Ulrich could not understand.
She reflected, and only after a while returned to the attack :
" But if you love me, he has you in the hollow of his hand, hasn't
he ? ''

" How is that ? "

" But it's quite obvious. Only I don't quite know how to put
it. You'll find yourself compelled to be considerate to him.
We'll both be very sorry for him. Of course you can't simply go
and deceive him, so you'll try to give him something to make up
for it. Well, and that sort of thing. And the main thing : you'll

force him to bring out the best that's in him.   After all, you can't
deny that we're hidden inside ourselves like statues in blocks of
stone.   One has to chisel oneself out !   We have to force each
other to do it ! "

" All right," Ulrich said.   " But you're much too quick in
assuming that it's going to happen."

Clarisse smiled again.   " Rash, *perhaps* ! " she said.   She came
up to him and linked her arm, in a friendly way, with his, which
hung limp at his side without shifting to make room for hers.
" Don't you like me ?   Aren't you fond of me ? " she asked.   And
when Ulrich did not answer, she continued :   " But I know you
do like me.   I've noticed often enough the way you look at me
when you come to see us !   Do you remember—did I ever tell
you you're the Devil ?   That's the way it seems to me.   Understand me rightly, I'm not saying you're a poor devil—that's
someone who wants evil because he doesn't know any better.
You're a great Devil, you know what would be good but you do
the very opposite of what you'd like to do !   You think the sort
of life we all lead is abominable, and that's why you say, out of
sheer contrariness, one has to go on leading it.   And you say in
that frightfully decent way :   ' I don't deceive my friends ! ' but
you only say that because you've thought to yourselves hundreds
of times :   ' I should like to have Clarisse ! '   But because you're a
Devil, you have something of God in you too, Ulo !   Something
of a great God !   Of one who tells lies so as not to be recognised !
You want me . . ."

She had gripped both his arms, standing before him with her
face lifted to his, her body curving back like a plant that is gently
touched at the petals.

' Now in a minute her face will be drenched in that queer look,
the way it was that time ! ' Ulrich thought anxiously.   But it did
not happen.   Her face remained beautiful.   In place of her usual
narrow smile, she smiled with parted lips, an open smile that
showed a little of the teeth, as though she was about to bite.   Her
mouth took on the shape of Cupid's double-curved bow, a pattern
repeated in the line of the eyebrows and once again in the translucent cloud of her hair.

" What you have wanted for a long time," she went on, " is
to seize me between the teeth in your lying mouth and carry me

off, if only you could bring yourself to show yourself to me as you really are ! "

Ulrich freed himself gently.

She let herself drop on to the divan as though he had pushed her, and pulled him after her.

" You oughtn't to exaggerate so wildly," Ulrich said in reproof for these words.

Clarisse had let go of him. She closed her eyes and rested her head on both hands, her elbows on her knees. Her second attack had been repelled, and now she intended to convince Ulrich by means of ice-cold logic.

" You needn't be such a stickler for words," she replied. " It's only a manner of speaking if I say Devil or God. But when I'm alone at home, usually all day long, and go roaming round the neighbourhood, I often think to myself : Now if I go to the left, it's God that'll come, if I go to the right, the Devil comes. Or I've had the same feeling when I had to pick something up and could do it with my right hand or with the left. When I've shown Walter this, he's put his hands in his pockets, in downright panic ! What he delights in is flowers, or even a snail. But honestly, isn't the life we lead terribly sad ? Neither God comes nor the Devil. I've been going round like this for years now. And what *can* come, anyway ? Nothing. That's all, if art doesn't by some miracle succeed in bringing about a change ! "

At this moment there was something so gentle and sad about her that Ulrich gave way to the temptation to touch her soft hair with his hand.

" You may very well be right in the details, Clarisse," he said. " But with you I can never understand the connections, and the leaps you make in the conclusions you draw."

" They're quite simple," she answered, still sitting in the same attitude as before. " It's just that with the passing of time I've developed an idea. Listen ! " Now she straightened up and suddenly became quite vivacious again. " Didn't you yourself once say that the state we live in is full of cracks, through which, so to speak, another state, an impossible one, peers out at us ? You don't have to answer, I've known this for a long time. Naturally every human being wants his life to be in order, but nobody has it ! I play the piano or I paint. But that's just as if I were to put a screen across in front of a hole in the wall. You and Walter have ideas into the bargain, and I don't understand much about that, but there's something wrong there, too, and you said that out of laziness and habit one just doesn't look at that hole, or one lets oneself be distracted from it by bad things. Well, the way it goes on is quite plain : that hole is what we've got to get out through ! And I *can* ! I have days when I can slip out of myself. Then one stands—how shall I put it ?—peeled out of a husk in the midst of things, and the dirty rind is peeled off them too. Or one is connected by the air itself with everything there is, like a Siamese twin. It's an incredibly magnificent state to be in. Everything turns into music and colour and rhythm, and then I'm not the housewife Clarisse, the state to which I was born and brought up, but perhaps a glittering splinter that drives into some immense happiness. But after all you know all this yourself ! For that's what you meant when you said that reality carries an impossible condition within itself and that instead of giving one's experiences a turn towards oneself and regarding them as something personal and real, one must turn them outwards, like something sung or painted, and so on and so on. Oh, I could repeat the whole thing to you exactly ! " This ' and so on ' recurred like a wild refrain as Clarisse went on pouring forth torrents of talk, and almost each time she added to it the assertion : " And you have the strength to do it, but you won't. I don't know why you won't, but I shall go on battering away at you ! "

Ulrich had let her go on talking. Here and there he had shaken his head in mute disagreement, when she attributed to him something far too wildly impossible, but he could not summon up the energy to argue with her. He left his hand resting on her hair, his finger-tips could almost feel the confused pulsation of her thoughts inside the skull. He had never before seen Clarisse in such a state of sensual excitement, and it affected him rather oddly to see that even in her slim, hard body there was room for all the loosening and soft expansion of a woman's glowing passion : and in all this too there was the eternal surprise at the sudden opening up of a woman whom one has known only as shut away in herself and proof against all temptations, and it did not fail to have its effect. Although her words offended against reason, they did not repel him. For while they would come close to his inner being and then again move away from it, to the point of absurdity, this continual swift movement was like a whizzing or buzzing, and what counted was not the quality of the sound, beautiful or ugly, but the intensity of the vibration. He could feel that listening to her was making his own decisions easier for him, like some wild music, and only when at last it struck him that she herself would never find a way out of the tangle of her words, nor bring them to any end, did he shake her head a little with his outspread hand, as though to call her back and remind her of reality.

But what happened now was the opposite of what he had intended : Clarisse suddenly came to grips with him. She flung one arm round his neck and pressed her lips to his so quickly that he had no time to resist ; he was thoroughly nonplussed. With one quick movement she pulled her legs up under her and slid towards him so that she was practically kneeling on his lap, and he could feel the little ball of one breast against his shoulder. He could not grasp much of what she was saying. She was stammering something about her power to redeem and about his cowardice, and he understood her to say that he was a ' barbarian ' and that this was why she wanted to conceive the redeemer of the world by him and not by Walter. But actually her words were no more than a raving random murmur close to his ear, a hasty muttering under the breath, something more concerned with itself than with communication, and only here and there out of this rippling stream could a single word or phrase be picked up, such as ' Moosbrugger ' or ' Devil's eye '. In self-defence he had seized his little attacker by the upper part of her arms and pressed her down on to the divan, and now she struggled against him with her legs, thrust her hair into his face and tried to get her arms round his neck again.

" I shall kill you if you don't give in ! " she said in a high clear voice.

She was like a boy who in his mingled tenderness and vexation refuses to be put off, so heightening his excitement more and more. The efforts of taming her prevented him from being more than faintly affected by the current of desire in her body. Nevertheless, in the moment of putting his arm firmly round her and pressing her down Ulrich had felt it violently. It was just as if her whole body had penetrated into his sensations. He had known

her so long and had often indulged in a bit of horse-play with her,
but this was different—this close and intimate contact with a little
creature, its heart wildly bouncing, that was at once familiar and
a stranger ; and when Clarisse's movements now, fettered by his
hands, grew quieter and the relaxing of her muscles was tenderly
reflected in her eyes, that almost happened which he did not want
to happen. But in this instant he remembered Gerda, and it was
as though now once again, and even more urgently than before,
the demand stood there before him—the demand that he should
come to final terms with himself.

"No, I won't, Clarisse," he said, and let her go. "I want to
be left alone now. I have a lot to do before going away."

When Clarisse realised that he was inflexible, it was though with
harsh jerking and jolting the cog-wheels in her head shifted into
another gear. She saw Ulrich standing some paces away from her,
with a painfully twisted expression on his face, saw him talking.
Uncomprehendingly she stared at him, and while she followed the
movements of his lips she began to feel a growing revulsion. Then
she noticed that her skirt had slipped above her knees, and she
jumped up. Before she could grasp anything of what had happened she was on her feet, patting her hair and her clothes to
rights, as someone does who has been lying in the grass, and said :
"Of course you've got to pack, I won't keep you any longer ! "

Once more she smiled her usual smile, which oozed out,
mockingly, uncertainly, through a narrow slit. And so she
wished him a good journey.

"By the time you come back we shall probably have Meingast
staying with us. He's written to say he's coming. And that," she
added casually, " is what I really came to tell you."

Ulrich held her hand hesitantly.

One of her fingers rubbed playfully against his hand. She
would have given anything to know what in the world she had
been saying to him : she knew there must have been all sorts of
things, because she had been so worked up that she had forgotten
it all. She knew more or less what had happened, and she did
not mind, for her feeling was that she had been brave or self-
sacrificing and Ulrich had been timid. Her only wish was that
they should part good friends, and in such a way that he should
not be left in any doubt about it.

She said lightly : " It'll be just as well if you don't tell Walter anything about this visit of mine, and what we've been talking about is between ourselves, of course, till next time."

At the gate she held out her hand to him once again and refused to be seen any further on her way.

When Ulrich went back into the house he felt strange. He had to write some letters, to let Count Leinsdorf and Diotima know he was going away, and he had various other matters to clear up, for he could see that taking over his inheritance would keep him away for some considerable time. Then he stuffed various little personal objects and some books into the cases already packed by his servant, whom he had sent off to bed, and when he had finished he no longer had any desire to go to bed himself. He was at once worn out and over-stimulated after the eventful day he had had : and these two conditions, instead of diminishing each other, alternatingly increased, so that, tired out though he was, he felt unable to sleep.

Not really thinking, but following the oscillation of his memories, Ulrich began by admitting to himself that the impression he had already had at various times—that Clarisse was not merely an unusual person but one who was probably at bottom already mentally ill—no longer allowed of any doubt. And yet during her attack, or whatever one might call the state she had been in a short time ago, she had said a number of things that were disconcertingly like some things he himself said. This was yet another matter to which he might have devoted long and hard thinking, but all it did, oddly enough, was to remind him—and, moreover, in an unpleasant way that was at variance with his drowsy state—that he still had a great deal to do.

Of the year that he had granted himself almost half had already gone by, without his having settled any of the problems. It flashed through his mind that Gerda had urged him to write a book about it all. But he wanted to live without splitting himself into a real and a shadowy half. He recalled the moment when he had talked to Permanent Secretary Tuzzi about these things. He saw himself and Tuzzi standing in Diotima's drawing-room, and there was something dramatic about it, something stagy. He remembered having said lightly that he would probably have to write a book or kill himself. But even death, when he considered it now, and as it were at close quarters, was a solution that did not really correspond to the state of mind he was in. For when he followed the thought of it up further, imagining that now, instead of setting out on his journey, he might kill himself before morning came, it struck him that to do this, in the moment when he had received the news of his father's death, would simply mean bringing about an unfitting conjunction of events!

He was in that state of semi-sleep in which the patterns of the imagination begin to race after each other. He saw before him the barrel of a gun, and saw himself looking down into the darkness of it, saw in it a shadowy nothingness, the obscurity that blocked the depths, and felt there was a strange concord and a queer coincidence in the fact that this same image of a loaded gun had in his youth been a favourite image of his, expressive of his will, charged as this will had always been with purpose, and always trained on its target. And all at once he saw, one after the other, many such pictures as that of the pistol and that of himself standing together with Tuzzi. There was a meadow in the early morning. Then, seen from a train, there was a long, winding river-valley, filled with dense evening mists. Then, at the far end of Europe, there was a place where he had parted from a woman he had loved: the woman's image had gone, but that of the unmetalled roads and the thatched cottages was as fresh as if it had been only yesterday. The hair in the arm-pit was all that was left of another woman he had loved. Shreds of tunes occurred to him. Someone's characteristic movement. . . . The smell of flower-beds—unnoticed once while violent words were spoken over them, words born of the profound emotions in the speakers' souls—now came back to him, the scent of flowers out-living the forgotten words and people. A man on various paths, a man it was almost painful to look at: he himself . . . like a row of puppets abandoned, the springs broken long ago. . . . One would think such random images were the most transient of things in the world, but there comes a moment when the whole of life splits up into such images, and they alone stand along the road of one's life; it is as though this road led only on from them and back to them again, and as though destiny did not take its bearings from resolves and ideas, but from these mysterious, half-meaning-less pictures.

But while he was moved almost to tears by this senseless impotence in all the endeavours of which he had ever boasted, now, in this strung-up sleepless state, there unfolded—or, it ought almost to be said, there happened all around him—feeling upon feeling of a weird and marvellous kind.

In all the rooms the lights were still burning that Clarisse had turned on while she was alone, and the excess of light flowed to and fro between the walls and the things, filling the space in between with a fluid presence, something that was almost alive. And probably it was the tenderness of sensibility inherent in every painless exhaustion that altered the totality of sensation in his body ; for the body's ever-present, even though unheeded, self-awareness, which has only vague frontiers at any time, now passed over into a softer and larger condition. It was a loosening, as though a tightly knotted ribbon were coming undone. And since, after all, nothing really altered either in the walls or in the things, and no God entered the room of this man who did not believe in any gods, and since Ulrich himself by no means let the lucidity of his judgment slip from him (in so far as his fatigue did not deceive him on this point), it could only be the relation between himself and his surroundings that was subject to this transformation ; and of this relation it was again not the material aspect, nor could it be his senses and his reason, which are what soberly correspond to that : what seemed to change was an expanse of feeling, deep as water in the sub-soil, on which at other times these pillars of objective perception and thinking were based. And now the pillars were softly shifting apart or merging with each other—for this distinction too had in the same instant lost its meaning.

' It's a difference of attitude. I am becoming different and so whatever is connected with me is becoming different too,' Ulrich thought, sure that he was observing himself closely.

But it might also have been said that his solitude—a condition that existed, after all, not only within him but also around him, thus connecting both—it might have been said, and he himself felt this, that this solitude was growing ever denser or ever larger. It passed through the walls. It grew out into the town. Without actually expanding, it grew out into the world. ' What world ? ' he thought. ' There *isn't* any ! ' It seemed to him that this concept no longer had any meaning. But Ulrich had still retained so much self-scrutiny that this exaggerated expression at the same time affected him as disagreeable. He did not search for any other words. On the contrary, indeed, from this point onward he began drawing closer again to wide-awakeness, and after a few seconds he started up. Day was breaking, its grey pallor mingling with the swiftly withering brightness of the artificial light.

Ulrich jumped to his feet and stretched. Yet something remained in his body, something he could not shake off. He passed his fingers over his eyes, but his vision even now retained something of that softness, an aura of that gentle interfusion with all things. And all at once, in a way difficult to describe, which was like a draining away of strength, simply as though he were no longer capable of denying it, he realised that he was once again standing exactly where he had stood once before, many years ago. He shook his head, smiling. ' An attack of the major's wife ' was what he mockingly called this state. His reason told him there was no danger, for there was no one with whom he might have repeated such a folly. He opened a window.

The air outside was indifferent, an everyday, ordinary morning air, and in it the first sounds of the city's life striking up. While the coolness rinsed his temples, he became aware of how the European's distaste for vague dreamy emotionalism was once again filling him with its hard clarity ; and he resolved to meet this turn of events, if it must be, with all possible precision. And yet, standing there for a long time at the window and gazing out, unthinkingly, into the morning, he still had within him something of that twinkling, sliding intermutation of all the feelings there were.

He was surprised when all at once his man-servant entered in order to call him, wearing the solemn expression of someone who has got up early.

He took a bath, rapidly did a few vigorous exercises, and then drove to the railway station.